Books by the same author.

A Passing Storm

A My thanks to my editor and proof reader: Lauren Sanders
Also for the cover design: Steven Paull

Published by YouWriteOn.com, 2010

A CIP catalogue record for this title is available from the British
Library.

To *Madeleine* – Assistant Section Officer (Nora Baker) Noor Inayat Khan GC, MBE, Croix de Guerre with Gold Star.
Noor was the bravest of them all.

A Dangerous Moon

Bernard Lawson

To Matthew
with very best wishes

Leonard.

Thanks for all
your help.

Chapter 1

Newcastle 1943

Catherine picked up some messages from her desk and threw them aside when her orderly brought her a tray of tea and poured her a cup. She began to drink it listening to the tormented screams from drill sergeants on the parade ground outside her office. The orderly corporal appeared at her door and saluted. 'Excuse me Ma'am, Commander Brown would like to see you immediately.'

'Thank you Corporal Jennings,' Catherine said and continued to drink her tea.

'She stressed immediately, Ma'am.'

Catherine smiled. 'Corporal Jennings, one must never rush one's tea. I shall be along in a moment.'

When the door closed, Catherine poured herself another cup. 'She can bloody well wait.' Five minutes later, Catherine left her office.

*

Commander Brown looked at her watch. 'I said immediately. How long does it take to walk from your office to mine, Somerville?' Catherine ignored the question. She was not invited to sit. 'This,' Commander Brown spat, waving a letter in front of Catherine, 'arrived a moment ago. It says you've to be in London tomorrow at 0900. If it hadn't been handed to me by a dispatch rider I would have ripped it up.' She leaned back in her chair and glared at Catherine. 'What's this all about, Somerville?'

Catherine shrugged. 'Unless I read it I have no idea, Commander.'

'Then take it and stop shrugging like some gormless adolescent.'

Catherine's eyes ran over the London address and the few lines of type. The signature beneath was a scribble. She shook her head. 'I really have no idea what this is about, Ma'am.'

'Well I do and I don't like it one little bit, Somerville.' Her ruddy cheeks glowed. 'It's some sort of trick to grab unofficial leave, isn't it?'

'If it were I certainly wouldn't own up to it—'

'Don't you be lippy with me, Ensign. Who the hell do you think you are?'

The telephone rang. Brown snatched the receiver. 'What is it? ... What? ... Who is this?' Commander Brown sat up straight. 'Oh! I beg your pardon, Sir. Yes, yes, I did. I have it here, Sir.' Brown's lip curled as her eyes lifted towards Catherine, 'She's with me now. Would you like to speak to ... right ... yes, yes I've got that, but may I say that this will leave me short-staffed ... of course not Sir, I was merely ... yes, very good, Sir. Goodbye, Sir.' The commander replaced the receiver and exhaled. 'Your father is a general isn't he, Somerville?'

'Was that my father—'

'No, it wasn't,' Brown snapped. 'Commodore Greene ... a chum of your father is he?'

'I've no idea, Commander.'

'What does the Royal Navy want with you?' Catherine shrugged but said nothing. 'I told you not to shrug, Somerville. You've got a tongue, use it.' Brown's sigh was one of resignation. 'Your appointment has been changed to 1430.' Commander Brown became thoughtful and in her silence began to chew on a pencil. 'This is very inconvenient, Somerville. I shall have to cancel your three classes tomorrow. How can we win the war if we carry on like this?' Brown's eyes became organ stops when she caught Catherine's smile. 'Do you think this is funny, Ensign? One big joke is it? I have a job to do and so do you. The army needs wireless operators and we have to train them.'

'Of course, Commander. I'm sorry.'

Commander Brown leant back in her chair and looked at Catherine, her lips pressed together with contempt. 'Have you made a request for a transfer, Ensign Somerville?'

'No Ma'am, but on that question—'

'I don't believe you,' Brown said leaning forward. 'You know the rules, Somerville. They apply to everyone whatever their background. Every application has to be approved by me. How can I expect any discipline in this camp if my junior officers show little respect for it? With your upbringing you should know better.'

'I haven't applied for a transfer,' Catherine said, 'although I'd like a change ... do something more useful. Anyone can do what I do.'

'Wrong! I'm reluctant to say this Somerville but you are a first-class wireless operator and instructor. I can't spare you so that's that.' The lip resumed its curl. 'I want you back here immediately you're done, do you hear? Now get out.'

*

As the taxi pulled up outside a house in Montagu Mews, a young woman Catherine's age, and from her corps, appeared at the door. 'Hello Ma'am, made it then. I'm Harcourt-Williams. Would you like me to take that?' she said pointing at Catherine's gas mask case.

Catherine glimpsed a pleasant face made attractive by a smile. 'No thanks. I use it as a shoulder bag.' Catherine smiled at the young woman's expression. 'It was sunny when I left Newcastle. How long has it been raining here?'

Through a brilliant smile, the young woman said, 'All morning, Ma'am. Still, it cleans the streets don't you think?'

Susan Harcourt-Williams led Catherine into a small sitting room. It had a cluttered bookcase and two sofas facing each other. Between the sofas was a low, long table, on which stood a vase filled with freshly cut lavender. Catherine bent and took in its fragrance. She was reminded of the lavender garden in front of the lake at her home in Yorkshire and the scent it produced when the wind blew from that direction. Behind one of the sofas, close to the window, was a piano on which stood a small bust of Beethoven.

'I've booked you into the officers' club, Ma'am,' Susan said. 'Is your luggage at the station?'

'No. I shall be heading straight back.' Catherine noted the look of surprise in Susan's blue eyes. 'Why this place?'

'The professor uses it when he wants some privacy,' Susan said. 'He's a Cambridge don. Make yourself comfy, he won't be long. Cup of tea while you're waiting, Ma'am?'

'What! Oh, yes, thank you. What on earth does a Cambridge don want with me?'

Susan stopped at the door and turned. 'No idea Ma'am, but I doubt if you'll return to your unit today.'

Catherine removed her service cap and placed it on top of her gas mask case, then ran her fingers through her dark hair, subconsciously tucking a loose strand behind her ear. She fixed her eyes on a print of Dedham Lock and Mill. When she was much younger, her father asked his driver to take her to Dedham so she could see the mill while he was on some army business in nearby Colchester. That afternoon had been sunny with clear blue skies, unlike the huge cumulus clouds that filled the Constable canvasses. She took a seat and picked up a magazine, flicked through it and threw it back onto the sofa again, yawned, glanced at her watch, then around the room and back at her watch. She stopped drumming her fingers on her knees and removed the letter from her gas mask case.

The door opened. 'Here we are. I expect you could do with this after such a long journey,' Susan said placing the tray on the centre table, 'and I found some biscuits. Not very interesting, I'm afraid.'

'Do you live here?'

'I'm only here to meet and greet, then shut up shop after, Ma'am.'

'Cheltenham College?'

'Roedean, Ma'am.'

'You must know Elizabeth Wyatt.'

'Yes Ma'am. How do you know Lizzy?'

'She's my cousin.'

Their eyes met and held for a second. Susan smiled. It sent an unexpected frisson through Catherine's body. 'You're not really travelling back to Newcastle this evening, are you Ma'am?'

'Yes,' Catherine said feeling a little flushed. 'I'm duty officer tomorrow.'

'Well, if there's anything else you'd like, just call out.'

'Thank you.' Catherine followed Susan out of the room with her eyes. She looked across at the piano and met the penetrating stare of Beethoven. She closed her eyes, relaxed and heard the opening bars to his sixth Symphony as the rain beat against the window panes.

Chapter 2

The professor was tall, slim and much younger than Catherine had imagined, perhaps because her tutor at Oxford was much older. 'Ah! Hello! Filthy weather.' He could not hold her eye and his hand was soft in her firm grip. 'I see Miss Harcourt-Williams is looking after you. Ah! Biscuits, how did she manage that?' He took one, bit into it and began pouring himself some tea. 'Newcastle wasn't it?' and without waiting for Catherine's reply said, 'bit grim up north,' imitating a northern accent.

'I'm from the north.'

'Whoops, sorry.' He sat opposite Catherine, smiled and began rubbing his hands together as if out of excitement or warming them, before opening the file he had brought with him. He took another biscuit. He dunked it into his tea and held it there while he read something. When he raised the biscuit towards his mouth the sodden part fell into his cup with a plop. He was so absorbed in what he was reading he didn't seem to notice. Catherine smiled and put her hand over her mouth, giving a little cough when he looked up. 'We're just going to have a little chat,' he smiled, 'get to know what you've been up to.'

'Would you mind telling me what this is about? I have no idea why I am here.'

'Let's just say you have come to our notice and you may be useful to us.'

'By us, I presume you mean the Intelligence Services?'

He smiled but didn't answer Catherine's question. 'I haven't had time to read this so let's briefly go through it. I see you are presently serving with a detachment of the Women's Transport Service in Newcastle.' He looked up and smiled, 'The FANYs as my mother knew them in the Great War.' He then began muttering in a whisper as he turned a page of her file. '...father the Earl Somerville, a serving major general, Victoria Cross at Loos...umm, I say.' His eyes rose, his lips broadened then his head lowered again. 'Mother - served as an ambulance driver with the FANY on the Western Front, interesting, awarded a Military Medal and Croix de Guerre with bronze star.' He reached for his cigarette case. 'Impressive.' Catherine didn't comment, she had grown up with the adulation of her parents' war record. The professor removed a cigarette from a silver case and went to light it. 'Oh sorry, do you?' he said offering her one, snapping the case closed when she shook her head. He lit the cigarette and inhaled the smoke. Catherine sat further back in her seat. 'Lady Catherine−'

'It's Ensign.'

'Yes, of course.' He removed his spectacles, scratched the bridge of his nose and replaced them. He watched Catherine cover her opening mouth with her hand. 'I appreciate it was a long journey, but try to stay with me. Now, your home is Mountfields House in Yorkshire.' In a sudden revelation he said, 'Mountfields House, good lord, that's your home, well I never, one of my favourite houses along with Chatsworth, not dissimilar really.' Catherine witnessed his eyes taking him back there. 'I think it's the setting that does it. Those delightful grounds, lakes, the colours in autumn−' The professor was shaken from his saunter through her father's park when he picked up his cup, took a sip and noticed the sodden biscuit floating in his tea. 'Oh dear.'

'Shall I pour you another?'

He removed his spectacles and rubbed his eyes. 'How old were you when you went to the Sorbonne?'

'Seventeen.'

'Umm young, that was nineteen…'

'Thirty-seven.'

'The Germans entered Paris in June 1940 and you were still there then. Why was that?'

Catherine's head lowered as if she carried the shame of that day on her own narrow shoulders. Her mind went back to June 1940. She remembered how the men wept. The professor looked up at her and brushed some burning ash from his jacket. He picked at a scorch mark. 'Ensign?'

'I wanted to finish my degree.'

'Wasn't that risky?'

'I was just another face in the crowd.'

'Weren't you worried that you may be betrayed?'

'No, I wasn't. All who knew me thought I was French, a provincial girl from Amiens where I was born. At first it was a game I played, pretending to be French. I even registered as French. I suppose I was vain enough to think I could fool them, and I did. It was never questioned. No one doubted it.'

'I don't doubt it either,' he said. 'It was confirmed today that you would pass as French.'

Catherine's eyes grew. 'By whom?'

'Madame Sandre, I believe you met her on the train. We wanted to see how well you spoke French.'

The woman had joined the train at Durham and noticed Catherine reading Honoré de Balzac's, *Le Vicaire des Ardennes*. She began speaking French to Catherine, an endless conversation until the woman alighted at York. 'Why on earth should you want to know that?' she asked, but he ignored her and began writing something in his notebook. She turned to look out of the window; it was still a blur of liquid grey. This has got to be about Bletchley Park, she thought. She knew about Station X. Her cousin Elizabeth worked there, but why pass as French? It made no sense.

'What do you think of the Germans?' he suddenly asked.

Catherine was silent for a moment while she took in the significance of the question. Her eyes found Beethoven sitting on the piano. 'I feel rather sad that such an intelligent, highly industrial and cultured nation fell under the spell of a monster when they were down-at-heel. On a personal level my governess was German. I practically grew up with her son, Paul; I liked them both very much. As a young girl I imagined myself to be in love with Paul.'

The professor removed his spectacles, covered the lenses with his breath and began to wipe them with a grubby handkerchief. Catherine saw that his eyes were a dark blue when they lifted and focused on her face.

'Did you imagine being in love with Ludwig Hoffmann too?'

It seemed at that moment as if the temperature in the room dropped below zero, yet her cheeks became quite hot. 'I don't know how you—'

'You saw a great deal of him, I believe,' the professor interrupted. Catherine's eyes narrowed, as if she was trying to discover in her mind where this conversation was beginning to lead. 'Did he think you were French too or did you let him know you were English?'

'There was little point in changing my story for him.' Catherine shifted on her seat. 'Why are you interested in Ludwig Hoffmann?'

'We were aware German Intelligence was infiltrating the Sorbonne before the war. Top universities are great recruiting grounds for the intelligence services. They are full of young people with misguided ideology. We had our own people at the Sorbonne.'

Christ! He thinks I'm a spy, she thought. 'What has that got to do with me?'

The professor's eyebrows rose sending his spectacles sliding down the bridge of his nose. 'Calm down, Ensign. Just tell me about your relationship with Herr Hoffmann.'

'What's it got to do with you?'

'He's German. Aren't we at war with Germany?'

'He was a year ahead and in a different faculty. I got to know him through friends. Herr Hoffmann and I always spoke German when we met, which helped my German conversation. He graduated a year before me and returned to Germany. That's all there is to it.'

'Not quite all though, is it?'

'Oh! What have I missed out?'

'He was your lover?'

She gasped as she jumped to her feet. 'How dare you speak—'

'Please sit down Ensign. Hoffmann boasted that he was your lover.'

'Boasting is a thing men do when they don't get their own way, isn't it ... to enhance their stupid egos?'

The professor began to scribble some notes. Catherine took long deep breaths. She felt the walls of the room closing in on her. At first she liked Ludwig Hoffmann. In some ways he reminded her of Paul. Whenever they met they conversed in German, but she never gave him any encouragement to form a closer relationship, she didn't want that, although he made it obvious to her that he did. At a party after Hoffmann's graduation, she had felt unwell and left early, little knowing that her drinks had been spiked and the perpetrator had offered to see her home. She woke the following morning blinking as sunlight streamed through the open curtains of her bedroom. Her mouth was dry and her head ached. She was suddenly aware of a presence beside her and turned her head sharply towards the sleeping figure of Ludwig Hoffmann. She stepped on her clothes when she climbed from her bed. There were blood stains on the sheet where she had been sleeping. In the bathroom she examined her thighs and between her legs; her worst fears were confirmed. Tears came to Catherine's eyes. She sat on the bidet washing, trying to piece together the events of the night before, but she couldn't remember leaving the party or how she got home. She went to the bedroom punching at him, screaming at him to leave and then locked herself in her bathroom until he was gone. She never saw Ludwig Hoffmann again. He returned to Germany two days later after bragging to all their friends that he had plucked her cherry.

Catherine felt her body tremble. The professor saw it. 'Are you all right?'

'Yes, thank you.' She watched him light up another cigarette. She was convinced he thought her a German spy. 'I shall be making a formal complaint about this interrogation to my father.' He didn't answer her. 'There was no need to force me down here under false pretences.'

'You were invited down here. You're not under arrest.'

'I'm not a spy,' she snapped. He ignored her and continued to write. When he stopped he lit another cigarette while the other burned in the ashtray. 'Must you smoke so much?'

He rose from the sofa and opened a window, quickly closing it again when he was sprayed with rain. He removed his spectacles and began to dry them. 'Because your father is important we kept an eye on you in Paris ... please sit, Ensign.'

'My father was spying on me!' She almost spat the words out. 'I don't believe you!'

'Compose yourself, Ensign. Your father was not involved. It was obvious there was going to be a war and we had our eyes on Herr Hoffmann because he was involved with the German intelligence services. We simply kept a fatherly eye on you.'

'Not quite,' she whispered under her breath.

'This is not an interrogation and I'm not making any allegations, I assure you. Now why don't we have some more tea?'

It was as if Susan had been listening at the door waiting for her cue; she entered the room with her dazzling smile, carrying a tray of freshly made tea, like an actress in a second-rate play. She wasn't wearing her uniform jacket. Her slim figure was attractive although the professor showed no interest in it. She placed the tray on the table and gave Catherine a flirtatious smile which brought a little colour to the latter's cheeks. Susan took the other tray and felt Catherine's eyes follow her out of the room.

'Err, thank you Miss Harcourt-Williams,' the professor called out and then he half smiled at Catherine. 'Shall I be mum?'

The edgy atmosphere calmed. Catherine picked up her cup and saucer and walked to the window. She couldn't imagine her father would have been kept in ignorance of what was going on at the Sorbonne, particularly once war was declared. He had sent a message through the British Embassy before it closed urging her to return to England immediately and was angry with her when she refused, but later recanted when she explained the situation to an official. She had not felt threatened and wanted to finish her degree, yet the more she thought about it now, she knew her father must have had someone looking out for her. He was obsessed with her security.

The professor bit on another biscuit. 'Have you heard of the Sicherheitsdienst?'

'No.'

'It's the intelligence wing of the SS. Herr Hoffmann is now an Obersturmführer in that service. They're a bad lot, as bad as the Gestapo. Some say worse.'

'Then Herr Hoffmann has found his niche, but what has this to do with me?'

'Where did you learn to speak German?'

'My governess taught me. I told you, she was German, a Jew whose husband was wise enough to leave Germany in the mid 20s. I learnt German from the mother and practiced it with her son Paul. He was treated as one of the family. My mother was very fond of him.' Catherine watched the professor stand and move towards the window she had just left, as if they were deliberately keeping arm's length from each other. He raised the cup to his mouth, his eyes fixed outside watching the rain beat against the square panes of glass. He remained silent as if he was absorbing what she had said or waiting for her to expand upon it. 'You have to understand there was no war when I knew Ludwig Hoffmann,' Catherine continued. 'Chamberlain had waved his piece of paper saying, "Peace in our time" hadn't he? My father didn't believe it of course, but I did. Hoffmann finished his degree and returned to Germany before war was declared. I stayed on another year to finish mine.'

The professor returned to the sofa and flicked through a couple of pages of her file. 'When you returned to England you began another degree at Oxford−'

'German Literature as I expect you know.'

'German governess - German friends - German literature...'

'Oh for heaven's sake. I've read Émile Zola but that doesn't give me the urge to work down a coal mine.'

His face broke into a smile and briefly met her eye. 'I see you achieved a first; congratulations. Did you enjoy Oxford after the Sorbonne?'

'I would rather have stayed in France and fought with the partisans.'

'Do you think you would have achieved anything by doing that? A bunch of amateurs against an extremely well-trained and highly disciplined army, informers infiltrating every cell—'

'You're beginning to sound like my father.'

He jotted something on his pad, this time she didn't bother to try and read it. 'You returned to England after you graduated?'

'I was forcibly smuggled back by a couple of daddy's henchmen. He of course denied it.'

'They weren't your father's men, they were ours,' he said with a little arrogance in his voice. 'You became a risk.'

'A risk! Why? I'm not important.'

'Don't you understand you are a direct descendent of one of England's oldest families,' he said irritably. 'Your father is a serving general and recipient of the Victoria Cross, a personal friend of Winston Churchill and the king. If the Germans had any idea of this and got hold of you it would have been a propaganda coup for them.'

Catherine was shaken by the professor's forceful tone. Her shoulders sagged. 'I had a huge argument with my father over that. Poor Daddy, I had no idea.' Catherine glared at him when he smiled. 'And what is so amusing?'

'Do you know Paris well?'

Her eyes rolled to the ceiling. 'I'm bored with this.' She glanced at her watch. If she left now, she thought, she could catch the five o'clock train.

'Just a few more questions, Ensign. How well do you know Paris?'

Catherine closed her eyes and sighed. 'As well as any Parisian I suppose.'

He looked up, leaned back on the sofa and placed his hands behind his head. He had a long, thin neck which accentuated his

Adam's apple. The red, blue and brown stripes of his Winchester College silk tie had stains on it. 'Do you shoot?'

'Of course, I live in the country.'

'Not everyone in the country can afford a pair of Purdey shotguns.' His smile was full of sarcasm. 'Good shot?' He watched her shrug. 'I see you're also a skilled wireless operator.'

'I really don't know why you invited me here. You know everything about me anyway.'

Catherine watched him remove his spectacles, something that was now beginning to annoy her. He rubbed his eyes and stifled a yawn. She smiled. He was beginning to bore himself.

'I wanted to meet you,' he said replacing his spectacles, 'just to confirm a few things.' He looked her in the eye and held her gaze. 'Are you capable of killing someone in cold blood?'

Her eyes did not blink or leave his. 'Yes.'

He felt an involuntary shiver then a sudden surge of pleasure. 'What makes you so sure?'

'Because at this very moment I'd like to shoot you.'

He threw his head back when he laughed. Catherine watched him begin to write. The only sound in the room was the rain beating against the window. It was quite soothing to listen to until from the kitchen a great crash of crockery shattered the peace followed by Susan cursing. The professor looked up briefly, unsure whether he had heard the word correctly. He briefly glanced towards Catherine, smiled and returned to his writing. After his final full stop he abandoned his cigarettes for his pipe. 'I think we're done for now.'

'That's it?'

'For now, yes.'

Catherine seemed paralysed for a moment, then she stood and put on her cap unsure whether she ought to salute him or shake his ink-stained hand. She did neither. 'What was the real purpose of this interrogation?'

'I've already said it wasn't an interrogation. You'll be hearing from us,' he said without looking up.

'What do you want from me?' she snapped spinning round and facing him before she reached the door. 'I don't even know your name or what this is all about!'

'Oh, that doesn't matter at this stage. Miss Harcourt-Williams will see you out.'

Catherine tightened her lips and clenched her fists. She had been dismissed without as much as a single explanation. The rain continued to beat against the window. 'Would you at least call me a taxi? I need to get to Kings Cross.'

'Why on earth do you want to go there?'

'I've been ordered to return to Newcastle this evening.'

He looked at another sheet from the file and lifted his eyes to her. 'Commander Brown isn't it? We'll sort that out. We may need to talk to you again, quite possibly this evening, if not, tomorrow, so you'll have to stay. Enjoy a weekend in London.' He smiled and stood. 'Well Ensign, we got through this bit of it a little war-torn perhaps but unscathed, so now I have to make a telephone call. If you hang on for five minutes I'll give you a lift. I'm off to St James' Street so I'm going your way. Belgrave Square, isn't it?'

Chapter 3

By the time they crossed Oxford Street into North Audley Street, the rain had eased to a drizzle. Catherine sat in the car analysing the past hour. If it wasn't an interrogation then it was a very strange interview, she thought. At first everything was centred round Ludwig Hoffmann, then it drifted toward her language and wireless skills, the very skills needed for Bletchley Park, but why her ability to shoot? Then that question he asked in earnest, could she kill someone in cold blood? Why should he want to know a thing like that? Catherine was certain that she couldn't kill anyone let alone in cold blood, not even Ludwig Hoffmann. She had only joked that she could, but the professor seemed satisfied, even happy with her answer. Her mind searched for some connection. It began to trouble her - *shoot someone in cold blood*. She was still in deep thought as they approached Grosvenor Square.

'I'd like you to join me for dinner this evening - at the Ritz.'

These were the first words either had spoken since they left Montagu Mews. It was as if he had spent the journey summing up the courage to speak to her. Catherine's expression made him colour when she met his eyes. 'Oh Lord, I didn't mean…' He almost drove into a parked army jeep as he turned into Grosvenor Square, ignoring the soldier shaking his fist. The professor glanced at Catherine whose eyes were cold and fixed on his. 'What I meant was, I had a brief conversation with the fellow who invited you down here. He'll make this all clear to you this evening, over dinner.'

'At The Ritz?'

He shrugged and gave a lopsided smile. 'We like to keep things informal.'

'Is this anything to do with Station X?'

He winced as if he had been stung by a wasp. 'Good God! What do you know about Station–' he spluttered, 'who told you about … don't even mention that name again.'

'I thought everyone knew about it,' Catherine said playfully. She clenched her teeth to stop smiling as the car juddered to a halt.

When he faced her his cheeks were crimson. 'What do you mean everyone knows? It's meant to be highly secret.' He stared at the steering wheel then squeezed it with both his hands as if trying to throttle it. 'You really ought not to talk about that place you know. You could be locked up for it.'

He looked quite shaken. The veins in his neck had swollen, his cheeks flushed red. Catherine was amused by his discomfort. 'Many girls from my Corps work there—'

'God Almighty! The security in this country is hopeless,' he cried out to the roof of the car. After a moment's silence he opened his eyes and took a deep breath, then pressed the ignition button. The car jumped forward. 'Please don't mention that place again and regarding this evening, we're simply continuing this chat over a bite. A bit unconventional perhaps, but that's how we do things in the firm and it would save time.' He pressed the ignition and again they leapt forward.

'I should take it out of gear, if I were you.'

His upper lip rose a little like an unfriendly dog as he placed the gearstick back into neutral. From his peripheral vision he watched her moisten her lips with her tongue, which made them glisten in the sunlight that had replaced the rain. He found that quite sensual and felt sudden desire for her. He looked ahead and sighed heavily. Not a chance in hell. Her world, he knew, ran on a different meridian than his.

'Who are we meeting?' she said without facing him.

'Commodore Greene.'

'Oh yes, Commodore Greene.' She removed the letter from her gas mask case and read the signature. The scribble began to form into the name Greene. 'Why the brass?'

'He heads the department. By the way, we've sorted it out with Commander Brown.'

'I expect she found it very inconvenient.'

He glanced at her but said nothing. As they navigated their way round Hyde Park Corner and turned into Grosvenor Crescent, he said, 'Let's say eight. The Ritz is easy for you from Belgrave Square and please Ensign, do not discuss our conversation with anyone.'

The invitation had suddenly become an order, Catherine thought. 'Go round the square as if you're going back on yourself, just there... the house with the green MG outside.'

He pulled on the brake and looked round at the elegant white stucco fronted houses; the trees in the gardens in the middle of the square were in full leaf. 'I've always liked this square,' he said, 'but it's a bit too rich for my blood.' When he met her eyes his smile failed to cover his feeling of social inferiority. 'Eight o'clock, then.'

*

The maid looked surprised when she opened the door and saw Catherine. She gave a quick bob of her body. 'Lady Catherine. We weren't expecting you.'

'Hello Betty. How's your mother?'

'Much better, thank you,' Betty said taking Catherine's service cap. Catherine's eyes rose to the floor above, where music was blasting from one of the rooms. 'It's Miss Elizabeth, Lady Catherine. She has a friend with her.'

A smile spread her lips. 'Lizzy!'

'If you're in for dinner I'll let cook know, Lady Catherine.'

'I'm out this evening Betty.' She climbed to the next floor and entered the drawing room where Al Jolson was blaring out; *I'm sitting, sitting on top, top of the world.* Elizabeth, a cigarette between clenched teeth, was dancing with another member of the Women's Transport Service. The two young women stopped when they saw Catherine standing at the door. Elizabeth screamed and threw herself into her cousin's arms while the other girl walked across the room and switched off the gramophone.

'Jenny, come and meet my cousin, Catherine.'

'How do you do, Ma'am,' Jenny said shaking Catherine's hand.

'Jenny, you're a guest in our home. There's no Ma'am here, only Catherine.'

'I told you Cathy wasn't stuffy,' Elizabeth said locking her arm through Catherine's. 'Are you on leave?'

'If only.'

Jenny picked up her packet of cigarettes and matches and put them in her gas mask case. 'I have to meet my brother; he's on leave, so I'll see you later then Liz. Nice to meet you, Catherine.'

When Jenny was gone, the cousins went out together and had tea at Fortnum & Mason. After tea they returned home. Elizabeth followed Catherine up to her bedroom where the latter began to remove her uniform. 'Pour me a gin, Liz. I'll have it in the bath.'

When Elizabeth returned with the gin, Catherine was almost naked. 'So why are you in London?'

'I have to see someone this evening.'

22

'A man,' Elizabeth said with some excitement in her voice.

'Yes, but it's not what you think.' Catherine took a sip from the glass. 'Umm, I need this. Give me some Dutch courage to face this fellow this evening.'

'Can you put something on? Your tits are putting me off my gin,' Elizabeth said and threw Catherine a dressing gown. She went and looked out of the bedroom window. She saw a young woman leaning back against the railings, flirting with an officer from the Royal Navy. 'Bugger, with your languages and wireless skills they are probably recruiting you for Bletchley just as I have left there. Jenny and I have been posted to Grendon Underwood. We're to report there on Monday. That's why we have a seventy-two hour leave pass.'

'What's at Grendon Underwood?'

'It's a wireless station. That's where they decode all German wireless traffic. I shall be monitoring traffic that comes in from agents in the field. It's all terribly hush, hush.'

'You'll be monitoring German agents?'

'No dummy, ours, in France.' Elizabeth took another sip of her drink. 'Special Operations Executive, Churchill's secret little army. Saying those words will put you in the clink. They work mainly behind the lines causing trouble for Jerry and we decode the messages they transmit. Are you aware there are women from our Corps in SOE—'

'From the FANYs?'

'I've seen them training at Beaulieu. I'm surprised they haven't tried to recruit you. Please keep mum about this Cathy otherwise I'll be in trouble.'

Her stomach suddenly felt hollow as the cold hand of realization dawned. Catherine hardly heard what Elizabeth said. Now the professor's questioning was beginning to make sense to her. She was being interviewed to join SOE. Catherine looked across at her cousin. 'Talk to me while I take a bath.'

Elizabeth lit another cigarette and sat on the chair under the window, which she opened a little. She watched Catherine climb into the bath and disappear under the bubbles for a few seconds, just as she always had when they were children. Catherine emerged from the soapy water and said, 'Are you sorry to leave Bletchley?'

'Yes. There's this fellow ... George.'

Catherine met Elizabeth's eyes and smiled. 'George...'

'He's one of the civvy boffins, from Cambridge, brilliant mind, more your sort really.'

'I've had enough of them. Apart from his brilliant mind, what's he like?'

'Lovely, he's ten years older than me but that doesn't matter, he makes me laugh.' Elizabeth began to chew her bottom lip. 'He wants us to take a room. Spend a night together.'

'So he's got a dirty mind too.'

Elizabeth blew out a long thin line of cigarette smoke. 'I've never done it before. Been close to it a few times with a couple of other chaps, but chickened out when the knickers were coming down. I'm afraid of being caught out.' She threw her cigarette out of the window and stood. 'Let me wash your back.'

'I met an old school chum of yours today... Susan Harcourt-Williams.'

'Susan. Where did you meet her?'

'At an interview,' Catherine said climbing out of the bath. 'The first of two, I think ... hope.'

'I wasn't in Susan's crowd. What was she doing at your interview?'

'To fetch and carry and shut up shop. She's in the WTS.' Catherine said drying herself. Elizabeth followed her to the bedroom.

'That's odd. I thought she'd joined the navy. She was always set on it. Let me do that.' Elizabeth took the hairdryer and a brush from Catherine. 'What did you think of her?'

'She played the dumb blonde which didn't suit her.'

There was a knock at the door followed by the maid saying Jenny had returned.

'Ask her to wait in the sitting room, Betty. I'll be down in a minute,' Elizabeth said. 'Well, where's the interview?'

'The Ritz.'

'Oh! Are you sure it's an interview?'

'Yes, very.'

'We'll be round the corner from there, at the Mirabelle, dinner, dancing. Join us later.'

'Maybe. Must dash,' Catherine said, kissing Elizabeth's cheek.

*

The professor introduced Catherine to Commodore Greene at a table away from other diners. After a handshake she took her seat and when the waiter left the table Greene said, 'You have signed the Official Secrets Act Ensign, so what we discuss does not leave this table. Now, I've ordered some Champagne to go with the oysters, natives, just come in season,' Greene said. He looked up and smiled. 'You have some interesting skills that would be very useful to me. I'll explain over pudding then you can think about it over the weekend and come back to me on Monday. They do a splendid Dover sole here or would you prefer the sea bass, always a good choice?'

After dinner, Catherine did not want to go to the Mirabelle. She strolled home through Green Park towards Hyde Park Corner. Her head was buzzing with what Commodore Greene had discussed. 'I will send you to Scotland where you will be trained in very special skills by three senior NCOs from the SAS. It will be tough, very tough. After, you will be dropped into France and make your way to Paris. So, report to me at St James's Street 0930 Monday with your answer,' he said as they parted. A black car pulled up and in the blink of an eye he was gone.

She did not need the weekend to think about their conversation, she had already made up her mind. 'I'm going to Paris,' she called out to the stars above Green Park.

'Then say 'ello to Jerry for me,' a man's voice said from behind a tree. The sound of a girl's giggle followed.

Catherine swallowed. She had momentarily forgotten about them.

Chapter 4

'Good. From this moment you will be under my command,'
Commodore Greene said after Catherine agreed to his offer. 'I will
have your orderly pack your kit in Newcastle and get it shipped to
your home in London, or would you prefer it to go to Yorkshire?'

'London, Sir.'

'When you're in France, your cover here will be that you have
been posted to Canada as an assistant to the military attaché. By the
way, you're no longer an ensign you've been promoted to
lieutenant.'

Catherine offered Commodore Greene a smile. 'Thank you,
Sir.'

'You'll earn that promotion, Lieutenant. I'm going to put you
through some very tough specialist training including parachuting.
Does that worry you?'

Catherine blew out her cheeks. 'Parachuting ... gosh, er no Sir, I
shall look forward to it.'

'Good, that's the spirit. After that you'll travel to Scotland.
Nobody on the circuit knows about the men training you and they
will know nothing more than they need to know about you. As I
have said, it will be a very tough four weeks; many men have
failed a similar course. Learn quickly and for your own safety it's
vitally important not to whisper or even hint to a soul what these
fellows are teaching you, not even to your father.'

Their eyes met. Catherine saw the creases at the corner of his
dark brown eyes deepen. 'I understand, Sir.'

'As far as all the other intelligence services are concerned you
do not exist.'

'How did you find me tucked away in some dark office in
Newcastle, Sir?'

He smiled. 'Pure chance. My assistant attended a seminar; your
father was one of the speakers. She overheard two subalterns
talking during a break. One told the other he met the general's
daughter when he was briefly posted in Newcastle. He waxed
lyrical about your... er, looks and added that you have brains too.
When my assistant overheard him say that you were a wireless
expert who spoke fluent French and German, she investigated you.

The trail took her back to the Sorbonne. The rest you know by the interview with Professor Blake.'

'I was under the impression he thought me a spy.'

'Our only worry was whether Hoffmann knew that you were English.' He stood and went across and opened a window. As he looked across St James's Square and said, 'Stroke of luck you knowing Hoffmann. I'll talk about him when you return from Scotland.' He smiled and sat back in his seat. 'You have all the qualifications I require for this job Catherine, now I want to see if you have the physical and mental abilities too. It will be hard work, very hard work. These fellows are tough, unforgiving professionals. They demand the best. I have brought them in just for this one job. They're not happy about it. They would prefer to be in the field making a nuisance of themselves.'

He doesn't trust his own people, Catherine thought. 'Just me and three men, Sir,' she said.

He smiled. 'I've arranged an orderly for you. She's in Scotland preparing for your arrival as we speak. That will balance things out a bit. Well, Lieutenant. Good luck. See you when you return.'

*

Catherine was the only passenger to alight from the train on a deserted station platform at Carrbridge, the stop before Inverness. She felt a cold wind find its way down the back of her collar as she looked about for the member of her Corps whom she was expecting to meet. A slender figure dressed in khaki appeared from the bushes adjusting her skirt. The young woman's pretty face broke into a smile as she caught sight of Catherine.

'Hello again Ma'am, sorry, got caught short,' she said offering a casual salute that seemed an afterthought rather than any respect for rank.

'Harcourt-Williams. I might have guessed.'

'Me again, Ma'am. We're billeted in a god-awful place; closest pub to our camp is in Grantown, ten miles away. Have you done something to upset the brass?'

'Is this another day away from your clerical work... Susan isn't it?'

Susan smiled. 'Yes, Ma'am. Four weeks this time, Ma'am. I'm here to make your stay more comfortable; darn your socks, wash your back, that sort of thing.' Susan picked up Catherine's suitcase and when they reached the jeep, threw it in the back. I hope you

27

packed some woolly knickers. It's bloody freezing up here. The camp's about twenty miles away. I see you've been promoted, congratulations,' Susan said then proceeded to complain about conditions in camp.

'Tell me about the men.'

'As blokes or soldiers...'

'I'm only interested in them as soldiers.'

Their eyes met. Susan smiled. 'They're a tough-looking lot,' she said crunching into a higher gear. 'Holloway, that's the squadron sergeant-major, he's in charge. I'm not under his orders. I have to report to you. He told me to stick to my own duties when I asked him what gives; typical, you'll get nothing out of him. As for the other two...'

'What about the other two?'

'Panhanagan and Peters... well, Peters looks a nasty piece of work, always looking at my tits and bum and he makes no bones about it, and then there's Panhanagan, he's a bit tasty. Of course he'll go for you. You're very beautiful, you know.'

Catherine caught Susan's flirtatious glance. 'Officers do not fraternise with sergeants, Susan. He'll know that, so you're welcome to him.'

Susan smiled. She smiled a lot. 'If I'm going to be stuck here isn't it best I know why?'

'No, you just do what you have been asked to do.'

'I say, that sounded like a slap on the wrist. I've been told this is all very hush hush so there must be a good reason for being in this god-forsaken place?' She caught Catherine's look of disapproval. 'Whoops, sorry.'

Catherine glanced at Susan. The 'oh gosh,' and 'I say,' didn't trip naturally from her lips, her body language suggested a sharper mind than that. Catherine threw her another glance as Susan turned to her. She flashed Catherine an easy, happy smile as if they were a couple of chums out on an adventure. Catherine smiled too.

'Almost there. I'll get a brew on for us before bed. That's what the men call tea and scoff is food. It's a whole new language and it gets rather colourful. I hope you haven't got sensitive ears. My vocabulary is simply bursting with new words. My mother would simply die if she knew what they meant.'

*

28

When the jeep pulled up outside the hut, Catherine stared at it. She met Susan's eyes which lit up and she shrugged her shoulders in the spirit of a seasoned girl guide. Once inside Catherine could see a great deal of effort had been made to make them comfortable. 'Our room is this side of the mess-room and theirs is the other.'

'What about the washing facilities?'

'There's one shower and four basins. We share those. Holloway has devised times for their use. The lav is a bit primitive and a thirty yard dash from here, a bugger if it rains and it rains a lot. The Engineers come and empty it once a day so it doesn't pong,' Susan said, smiling at the expression on Catherine's face.

*

Catherine slept surprisingly well on the soft springy bed, and in the morning Susan woke her at seven with a cup of tea. 'Morning, Ma'am, those three lunatics are out on a run. I'll grab the shower while you're having your tea.' Then she walked across to her bed, removed her pyjamas, wrapped a towel around herself and went to the shower. Catherine felt embarrassed by this. She had never shared a room before and had only been naked in front of her cousin Elizabeth.

When she was also showered and dressed, she followed Susan into the mess-room to meet the men for the first time. None of them were wearing any badges of rank. One of the men glanced up at Catherine, and instead of standing as was expected when an officer entered the room, he stared at her and nudged his colleague. Given Susan's description of him it was Peters. She guessed the handsome face who glanced up at her was Panhanagan. The third man cooking breakfast had to be Holloway.

'Squadron Sergeant-Major Holloway,' Catherine said turning to him. 'I'm Lieutenant Somerville, reporting to you for duty.'

Peters sounded like a pig when he snorted and began to roll a cigarette. Panhanagan's lip rose at the sound of her upper-class voice, which didn't go unnoticed by Catherine. His face lowered back to his book.

'Morning Ma'am,' Holloway replied without facing her. 'Welcome to Holloway Prison. Because it's your first day you had a lie in. Susan, go and take a hike for ten minutes. You can have yours when I've spoken to Miss Somerville.'

Susan pulled a face. 'I don't take my orders from you, Squadron Sergeant-Major.'

'Do as the squadron sergeant-major says, Susan.'

Susan tossed her head when she caught Holloway's eye, then sneered at the smiling Peters as she went outside to smoke a cigarette.

'Thank you, Ma'am. I understand you've done your jumps.' Catherine nodded. 'Good, that alone puts you above most of the men in this man's army. Now we are going to turn you into a proper soldier. As from tomorrow, reveille will be at six. You'll start with stretching exercises and then have a five mile run to work up an appetite for breakfast. We take turns taking you out; the other two clean up the mess-room and cook breakfast. As an officer you're excused all that.'

'I'll take my turn like the rest of you.'

Peters imitated a pig again. Panhanagan was lost in his book.

'No you won't Ma'am you'll be out on the run. Now—'

'What about Susan?'

Holloway looked into her eyes as if he wasn't used to being interrupted. 'She'll help, if that's all right with you, Ma'am.' Catherine nodded. 'Now take a pew and drink your brew,' Holloway said handing her a mug of tea. Catherine accepted it and winced at its sweetness. 'Breakfast coming up, Ma'am.'

'I don't eat breakfast, Squadron-Sergeant Major.'

'A couple of things you will learn around here Ma'am...' Holloway said as he placed in front of her a plate filled with eggs, bacon, sausages, mushrooms, tomatoes and fried bread, '...is you'll start the day with a good scoff inside you and honey in your tea, lots of it. You'll need the energy. Now, tuck in, Ma'am. We've had ours.'

'I couldn't eat a quarter of that.'

'You might not today Ma'am, but you will tomorrow.' Peters took a sausage when Holloway turned his back and winked at Catherine. Her eyes shone with approval. Panhanagan threw his book aside and looked into the air. She glanced at its title, *Seven Pillars of Wisdom by T.E.Lawrence*. Panhanagan's face fell within her vision. His eyes lifted to hers. Something inside her stirred. She quickly averted her eyes and bit delicately into a piece of sausage.

'Right, down to business,' Holloway continued. 'I'll talk as you eat, Ma'am. First we don't stand on ceremony here. I'm Jim. I'm going to teach you how to stay alive on the run; that means catching and eating anything that moves. I understand you already have wireless skills. What's your key speed?'

'Thirty.'

Holloway stopped what he was doing and looked across at her. 'Well, I can't match that. If you can send Morse at that speed we'll skip it and stick to other things, getting lost in the woods and setting it up without any nosey parker spotting it. This ugly sod is Ted; he'll teach you detection and evasion. He's been doing it all his life, mainly from the police. You'll need to know if any one or more people are following you, and also, you must learn to follow someone undetected yourself. Finally, that's Panhanagan. We don't know his first name, he keeps it quiet. It's probably some Nancy boy's name. He's the assassin. He'll be teaching you firearms and unarmed combat. Learn quickly otherwise you'll hurt; the ground's hard out there. He'll also teach you how to kill with a knife. It's not a pleasant thing for a young lady to learn, but you'll have a good instructor. I've seen Panhanagan at work.'

Catherine looked across at Panhanagan and detected the quiver of a smile. She would have expected the assassin to be Ted, he looked the type. She chewed on some more sausage and glanced back at Panhanagan who was now buried in his book again. It seemed to Catherine that he wanted to be anywhere but where he was. When he turned a page his eyes rose to hers again. Catherine guessed he was sizing her up, deciding whether she could kill a man in cold blood as the professor had asked. His look of contempt suggested she couldn't. She decided she wasn't going to like him.

'After Panhanagan has had you for four weeks Ma'am, you'll know how to drop a man so he's dead before his body hits the ground. By the lack of interest from Panhanagan he doesn't think you can hack it. You've got four weeks to prove him wrong.'

Catherine met Panhanagan's eyes. 'I won't cry if I break my nails, Sergeant.'

Another snort as Ted stuffed into his mouth the bacon Catherine had left. Panhanagan remained unmoved. She suddenly turned to him irritated by his eyes boring into her. 'I will prove you wrong, Sergeant Panhanagan.'

Panhanagan looked to the ceiling. He was unhappy about being in Scotland. He wanted to get back to France and blow up a few more railway lines, kill more Germans and have sex with more French women. Training some two-bit female toff to use a weapon

31

was an insult to his professionalism. He had voiced this in no uncertain terms to his squadron commander, but to no avail. He decided he would give her a hard time then spoke for the first time. 'This is all a bloody waste of time.'

'Knock it off, Panhanagan. The army has gone to a lot of trouble setting this place up for just one person, so they must think Miss Somerville worth it; in my book that makes our job important and we'll get on with it for the four weeks we're out here.'

'If she lasts that long.'

'All right Panhanagan, cut the crap,' Holloway snapped. 'Any questions, Ma'am?'

Catherine liked Holloway. 'If we are to be so informal then I'm Catherine.'

'We never call officers by their first name, Ma'am.'

'Ma'am makes me sound like a matron.'

Ted and Panhanagan looked at each other and grinned.

'Matron or not you're an officer,' Holloway said. 'After breakfast Ma'am, you'll change out of your uniform and into combats. Did Susan give you the kit we brought for you?' Catherine shook her head. 'Dozy cow. Jim, did you give Susan Miss Somerville's kit?'

'Forgot.'

'Twat! I'll make sure you have it when you finish your breakfast Ma'am. Now, it's taken us years to achieve what you have to learn in thirty days, so there'll not be much leisure time. Did you bring any civvies, Ma'am?' Catherine nodded. 'Good. If we're on schedule with your training, we'll all go to Inverness as a group on Saturday evening and have some scoff and a pint or two. Sunday morning is leisure time; lunch at 1300, work begins at 1400. How's all that sound, Ma'am?'

'Excellent, Jim.'

Holloway looked up at Catherine and smiled. 'Susan, come and have your scoff,' he called out and laid the plate on the table. 'OK Ma'am, I think we're going to get along just fine. Panhanagan, wash the dishes.'

Catherine knew that was Holloway's way of putting Panhanagan in his place.

*

In the first week Panhanagan gave her the hardest time. On her morning run, his pace was deliberately faster. He was so lean and fit he hardly broke a sweat, while she fought for breath in silence so he couldn't hear her lungs bursting, but he knew by her rolling head she was struggling. Some mornings he would put a large pack on his back and still outpace her. Catherine guessed it was done to intimidate her, but she ran on, and on, ignoring his silent mocking of her. After a shower and breakfast, she spent two hours on small arms training. Panhanagan faced her while she pointed an unloaded Walther PPK pistol at him; first at his left eye and then right foot, then his right eye then left foot, to provide her with some control over direction and elevation of firing. She would have to repeat the exercise with a loaded magazine and finally with a silencer attached to the weapon. Once she had completed the exercise, Panhanagan made her strip the weapon then assemble it until it became second nature to her, then clean it even though it hadn't been fired.

'That weapon has to be a part of you, like the fingers on your hand. Until then you do not discharge a single round from it,' Panhanagan said in his usual dismissive manner.

After a week she had still not fired a shot. The sheer mundane repetition of it made her want to scream. She was convinced it was another of Panhanagan's games in trying to break her. It was only when she did begin to use live rounds on his 'pop up' targets, which he controlled by string, that Catherine realised the value of the previous exercises. After a tea break, Panhanagan taught her unarmed combat and how to swiftly dispatch a man with a knife. She knew he took perverse pleasure in rendering her helpless in his vice-like grip, while she wriggled like a fish on the end of a line.

One morning at the end of his session, just before lunch, Panhanagan told her to stand up straight and face him. He raised his arm and fired two quick shots at her. They cracked past her ear leaving her ashen-faced and shaking. 'You idiot!' she screamed. 'Why did you do that?'

'From now on I'll be doing that every morning,' he said casually. 'Next time keep your eyes open otherwise you won't see who's shooting at you.'

Catherine was still shaking after Panhanagan left her to make his way to the mess-room. When she joined them at the table Panhanagan avoided her eyes and began flirting with Susan. Jim Holloway noticed the tension and smiled. 'Did Panhanagan take a pop at you, Ma'am?'

She slammed her knife on the table and glared at Holloway. 'He almost shot my head off.'

Holloway offered a sympathetic smile. 'We all go through that, Ma'am. Panhanagan was letting you know what it's like to receive incoming, someone firing at you. If ever it does happen in the field, you won't curl up and freeze. Better a couple of rounds from a Walther PPK to begin with. It will be the Bren gun next, now that is scary.'

Holloway and Peters laughed. Catherine's eyes moved towards Panhanagan who shrugged his shoulders. She left the table and went outside. Susan joined her.

'Do you have to flirt with that idiot, Susan?'

'I'm not,' Susan said lighting a cigarette. 'He's coming on to me because he knows he can't have you. Don't let him goad you, Ma'am. It's not me he wants. I've seen the way he reaches out to you with his eyes. Can't you feel it?'

'I don't want him. I don't like him and I've had enough of him.' Catherine removed her hand from Susan's grip. 'Stop calling me Ma'am, Susan. When we're alone I'm Catherine. I need a friend out here.'

'Don't let Panhanagan see he's getting to you.'

Back inside the hut, Holloway winked at Catherine when she sat back at the table. Peters lowered his eyes, and Panhanagan stared her straight in the face and smiled. Catherine felt Susan's knee under the table hit hers.

*

After lunch, Ted drove her to Inverness. He took her to a café, and he followed her to the table and ordered two teas. 'Tell me everything you saw in this café when you walked in,' Ted asked. Catherine looked thoughtful. 'All right then, how many people are in here? No, don't look around.' Catherine shook her head. 'You have a hell of a lot to learn,' Ted whispered, 'and being observant is one of them. Concentrate, Ma'am. It will save your life. Never sit with your back to the door. See who is in the room without looking. It takes a lot of concentration to look around you without moving your eyes, and remember the things you see. Form a picture in your head; stick it all in your memory bank, recognize the changes.' He looked her in the eye and smiled. 'The trick is to spot your man without him knowing it, then you lose him. Stay alert, Miss. Don't daydream. Daydreamers die.'

Chapter 5

The metamorphosis of Catherine was completed with ruthless efficiency in the fourth week. She now looked upon Peters and H quite differently from day one in Scotland, and had a great deal of respect for them both. Holloway was, as always, a protective older brother, Peters no longer stripped her naked with his eyes and, as much as she disliked Panhanagan's attitude and contempt for her, he was a professional. It showed in everything he did.

Panhanagan was still the most difficult to get close to, yet ironically, he was the only one of the three with whom she had had any physical contact, mostly being thrown to the ground or grabbed from behind with a knife at her throat. He worked her like a sadistic slave-driver until she had no breath left in her body, but she would not give up and took the blows like any man in his regiment. She proved herself to be tough, both physically and mentally. Panhanagan admired her for it and would tell the other two in the darkness of their bedroom at night, but he would never tell Catherine.

On the final day of the course, he watched her firing shot after shot. Her hand was steady and her eye was good. She instinctively aimed for the killing zone and fired two shots without hesitation. As far as he was concerned, she was ready to do what she was being prepared to do.

Catherine cleared her weapon and made it safe. She was aware that Panhanagan was watching her. She had warmed a little towards Panhanagan the machine, but she did not like Panhanagan the man, he was cold and deliberately unfriendly. When she finished cleaning her weapon he took it from her, checked it and stored it in the weapons box. He said nothing about her shooting the perfect score, no encouragement or praise, it wasn't his style.

'One last thing,' Panhanagan said without facing her. 'Stand over there in front of the sandbags.'

Catherine knew what was coming and braced herself for it. Panhanagan walked thirty paces and let off a whole magazine from a Bren gun at her, shouting between short bursts for her to keep her head up, to face him and keep her eyes open. When the firing pin clunked and the shooting stopped, Catherine's heart still raced.

'Someone will be trying to kill you, remember that. More often than not he'll be excited and will snatch at the trigger. He will not have had your training. You won't be nervous because you know what it feels like to have live rounds cracking past your ear. You will be calm; just aim your weapon at him and put two rounds into him. Kill him Ma'am; make sure he's dead before you turn your back on him. Now I'm done with you.'

'You don't like me very much, do you Panhanagan?'

'I'm not here to be your friend, Ma'am.'

'No, but you could have at least tried to be friendly.'

'I had a job to do, now I've done it. You'll know how well the first time you're in trouble. When we leave here tomorrow I shall be having a week's leave before I return to a proper job and we'll never meet again, which suits me just fine.'

'I shall be glad to see the back of you too, Panhanagan.'

'Oh yea, then why have you been flashing those fine eyes at me for the past month?'

'You arrogant, conceited pig,' she cried. 'You'd be the last man I would ever try to encourage.'

His usual contemptuous smile irritated her, and when he turned his back on her she moved quickly towards him, but she was too slow and was thrown to the ground. He dived on top of her, grabbing her wrists and forcing them above her head. She struggled, but could not budge him. His body pressed hard into hers.

'Let me go, Sergeant. You're hurting me.'

'You're in this position because you lost your rag. Now you can try to free yourself.'

'I can't move.

'Then you're dead and all because those big blue eyes failed to melt my heart. You might remember not all men will fancy you as much as you fancy yourself.' He felt her trying to wriggle free. 'There you go again, wasting energy, losing it instead of keeping your head.'

'You've proved your point Panhanagan, now let me go.'

'In a tight situation Ma'am and you're in a tight situation, always keep your head and remain calm. What the fuck have I been teaching you for the past four weeks?' Panhanagan looked into her contracted pupils. She was breathing heavily, her teeth gritted behind her tight lips. When she relaxed and stopped struggling he let go of her. He rose and offered Catherine a hand to pull her up, which she took, kicking him hard between his legs when she was on her feet. He yelped and bent double to ease the pain. She hit him hard on the back of the head sending him crashing to the ground.

He looked up at her wincing with pain. 'At least you've learnt something.'

'I hate you, Panhanagan. You're a pig. Lower than a pig, a snake.'

When she turned to leave, he grabbed her ankle and she was pulled to the ground again, crying out as her body hit solid earth. His grip made her cry louder. 'Now your whole family is looking down at the box as it's lowered into the ground because again you turned your back.' His mouth was so close to hers she could feel his warm breath. She turned her head away from his lips, convinced that he was going to kiss her. She wriggled to free herself, but only managed to put herself in a worse position. Now Panhanagan was between her widespread legs, she could feel his genitals pressed into hers. 'Enjoying this Ma'am? Is this what you really want?'

'I'd rather die.'

'You probably will, but it won't be a man's cock that will kill you.' He swiftly climbed to his feet and looked down at her drawing her knees together into a more dignified position. 'Wherever they're sending you, you won't last five minutes.'

'You're a heartless bastard, Panhanagan.'

'Who gives a shit? I'm still alive.'

'No you're not. You only think you are.' Catherine avoided his grinning features. 'Just piss off Panhanagan and leave me alone.'

'That's not very nice language from a posh girl like you. I bet your mum wouldn't like to hear you speak like that.'

She watched Panhanagan disappear towards the hut. She felt exhausted and leant against a tree. 'You're quite right, Panhanagan,' she whispered, 'she wouldn't.'

*

Catherine reached the hut five minutes later and went straight to her room. Susan was asleep on her bed. She decided to leave her; it was the last day, so Susan could have a break from walking around Inverness with her. The men were clearing some of the kit from the camp. Catherine changed out of her combats and, with a towel wrapped round her, went for a shower. She returned to her room and dried herself. As she was stepping into a clean pair of knickers she caught Susan's reflection in the mirror watching her.

'Susan, please don't look at me like that. It makes me feel uncomfortable.'

'What will your boyfriend say about all those bruises?'

'Why should you presume a boyfriend would see me naked?'

She sat up and shrugged. 'Do you have one?'

'No, I don't.'

'So you're not getting your greens?'

'What makes you think I want that?'

'Doesn't everyone? Honestly Catherine, you're over twenty-one. You are allowed to have sex. It's not just for men you know. Women enjoy it too. I certainly do.'

'I really have no wish to know.'

'You read about it though. Emma Bovary and her lover... what's his name?'

'Rodolphe Boulanger.'

'Yes, him. They were at it like rabbits.'

'She ended up poisoning herself.'

'All right then, Anna Karenina and her bloke?'

'Count Vronsky. She ended up throwing herself under a train.'

They looked at each other and laughed. 'Can I be honest with you Catherine, woman to woman, no rank involved?'

'Of course.'

'I've been watching you. You haven't once fluttered your eyelashes or flirted with any of the men. Not even to get your own way. You seem to take delight in being pushed to the limit with whatever you're doing. The harder it gets the more you seem to enjoy it. They've turned you into one of them.'

'What do you mean?'

'You are a beautiful woman, but they've turned you into a bloke.'

Catherine began to giggle and couldn't stop. She went over to Susan and put her arms round her neck and kissed her cheek. 'Honestly Susan, you are funny.'

Susan squeezed Catherine to her. 'I shall miss you,' she said and kissed Catherine's cheek and then her lips. Catherine pulled back, surprised by it and stepped away from her. Susan smiled into

Catherine's eyes. 'Sorry, I get carried away. Too affectionate that's me.'

'Peters is taking me into town so no need for you to come. It will give you time to pack.'

'Thank God for that.'

'Susan… you and Panhanagan…'

'There is no me and Panhanagan.'

'Oh! I thought you'd taken a fancy to him, that's all. You've been flirting with each other since I arrived here.'

Susan smiled and went to her, fastening a button Catherine had missed. 'You're so naïve, Catherine. You see everything around you but not what's in front of you.'

'I really wish I wasn't going into Inverness. I'm absolutely shattered. See you later.'

*

After two hours of walking around the city, she went into a pre-arranged café to make notes on where and when she had spotted the men following her and where she had lost them. Holloway suddenly appeared with Peters. Catherine looked up smiling. They had a cup of tea, discussed the exercise and that was it, her four weeks training was now over. In the morning she would be away from this place and home on leave for seventy-two hours. 'Thank you gentlemen,' Catherine said with a beaming smile. 'I have no idea what sort of monster you have turned me into, but one thing is for sure, I shall never be the person I was before I arrived here.'

'It's not quite over yet, Ma'am. See you back at the camp.'

'What? How do I get...?' They were gone before she had a chance to finish her sentence. Catherine sat open-mouthed. 'Bastards.'

Catherine had no money for a taxi and only one vehicle passed on her way out of Inverness, which drove straight past her when she stuck out her thumb. Hours later, and completely exhausted, Catherine fell into her bedroom. Susan jumped out of bed and went to her. 'Oh you poor love, you look done in. Jesus, you're soaked. Hurry and get out of those wet things.'

Catherine's whole body ached as she collapsed onto her bed. It had rained then poured. She hated the SAS; they were cruel sadistic bastards. Catherine struggled to remove her clothes while Susan fetched a towel and began to dry her wet, cold body.

'Lie on the bed Catherine, on your tummy. I'll rub some oil into your calves and back. You won't get cramp or feel stiff in the morning. It's my own concoction, cinnamon oil, clove oil and menthol oil. It pongs a bit but it's a nice pong and will relax your muscles.'

Catherine did as Susan asked and laid face down on the bed. She felt the towel spread over her as if it were a blanket and heard Susan say she would be back in a moment. Her eyes opened when she felt soft, soothing hands slide along her oily skin, the palm of a hand lightly pressing into the flesh and loosening the stiff muscles up her back and over her shoulders. After what seemed an age, the hands left her. She felt the trickle of warm oil on the flesh of her bottom, followed by Susan's hands pressing into the rounded cheeks then down inside her thighs to her calf muscles. 'Ouch, they ache like hell. I was wearing the wrong shoes.'

'You're awake then?'

'Just.'

'You'll sleep well enough after I've finished with you.' The words fell from Susan's mouth in a hypnotic whisper. 'Now just relax.'

The weight of Susan's hands lightened to a soft butterfly touch. A soft voice told her to roll over onto her back. Catherine turned over and she felt warm oil trickle over her breasts which Susan began to massage. Catherine's eyes opened. 'No, don't do that.'

'Relax,' Susan whispered. 'You're too tense.'

Catherine closed her eyes, too tired to argue. After a few minutes Catherine felt Susan's lips, soft and sensual on hers, fingers moving between her legs, caressing, moving into her. Her thighs instinctively widened with instant arousal. A sigh escaped Catherine's lips. She wanted the release she knew Susan would give her and massaged Susan's tongue with hers when it entered her mouth.

Chapter 6

Only Holloway was around when Catherine walked into the mess-room at seven. She was dressed for the first time since she arrived in her full service uniform. 'Morning Jim, have you seen Susan?'

'She's left. Panhanagan took her to the station at six.'

Catherine was instantly relieved that she would not have to face her, embarrassed at what had happened in the early hours. It was the first thing on her mind when she woke. At first she thought it had all been a dream, hoped it had been a dream, until the smell of Susan's massage oil reached her nostrils. 'She should have woken me.'

'You were done in, Ma'am.'

'And Ted...'

'Securing the kit. The Engineers will be here shortly to pick everything up. After that, not a soul in the world will know that we have ever been here.' He poured a mug of tea and gave it to her. 'Have a brew. I'll make you an egg and bacon banjo if you'd like one.'

'Yes, thank you.'

'Coming up, Ma'am.'

Handing the sandwich to her, Holloway sat opposite Catherine and took a sip of tea from his mug. It had *The Governor – Holloway Prison* painted on it. Holloway's craggy features creased. 'I bet you thought I was a right bastard making you walk back in the rain in those shoes you were wearing. You thought it was all over so you relaxed. In our business you can never relax. It was your final test and I wanted to see if you could hack it. You could. I'm proud of you, Miss.'

Miss. It was the nearest she would get to an endearment from Holloway. 'I cursed you every step of the way back.' She smiled, this time showing her teeth. 'Well, it's over now.'

'No Miss, now it begins. I've no idea what they have in mind for you, but I have a hunch.'

'Am I ready for it?'

'Ted thinks you're a natural and so do I. Buggered if anyone will ever follow you without being spotted.'

'And Panhanagan,' she said in an uncertain voice, 'what does he think?'

'Do you care? Listen Miss, I know there's been some friction between you two, but he's a good bloke. He doesn't like to show his feelings. It's not in his nature. He lost his whole family in the Blitz. He regards the army as his family now and takes it very seriously, that's why he's good at what he does. He doesn't like amateurs.' Holloway finished his tea, wiped his mouth on his sleeve and shrugged at Catherine's disapproving look. 'When he first met you he probably thought that you were some posh bird out on a jolly, now he has the greatest respect for you, which isn't gained lightly, believe me.'

Catherine didn't know why, but gaining Panhanagan's respect made her feel happy. 'He hasn't said anything to me.'

Peters walked into the hut and winked at Catherine. 'Panhanagan's still not back.'

Holloway looked at his watch. 'Right, we'll get on with this without him then.' He turned to Catherine. 'Ted will run you to the station. Are you packed and ready to leave?'

'Susan has done that. She must have done it while I slept, bless her.'

'Right, I have a small presentation to make, sorry Panhanagan isn't here, but we'd like you to accept this,' he said handing her an SAS beret complete with winged dagger badge. 'These are never given away lightly, but you've earned it.'

Catherine smiled, removed her service cap and replaced it with the beret. 'How do I look?'

'There isn't a better looking trooper in the regiment, Miss.' Holloway smiled. 'Well, if I don't see you again…' He stood and saluted her. Catherine blushed, it was the first time he had done so.

'Why are you being so formal now?' she said and went to him. She embraced him and kissed his cheek. 'Look after yourself James Holloway. Hope you don't get lumbered with any more women.'

'Doubt it. I'm back with my unit next week, Ma'am.' Formality returned.

'What about me?' said Ted holding out his arms.

As they were leaving, Panhanagan arrived back in the other jeep. Holloway appeared and went to him, then waved as she left the camp. Panhanagan didn't even bother to look up. Pins and needles shot through her body and pricked her eyes. Catherine didn't know why, but she felt hurt that he deliberately ignored her. She looked over her shoulder at him and caught him turn round too.

*

The family's chauffeur was waiting for her at York station. As the car pulled up in the driveway of Mountfields House, there was a staff car with three stars on it and a WTS driver standing by the passenger door. She saw Catherine get out of the car and saluted her. 'Afternoon, Ma'am.'

'Is General Somerville arriving or leaving?'

'He's leaving, Ma'am.'

She ran towards the great front doors of the house, which opened as if by magic. 'Hello, Robins. Where's Daddy?'

'His Lordship is in the drawing room with her ladyship and two guests, my lady.'

She ran down the hall and turned right into another, then stopped before some closed double doors to regain her composure before entering.

'Catherine, darling!' said her smiling mother. 'Your father waited for you.'

Catherine saw a short, fit-looking major general with a thin military moustache and a taller brigadier with ruddy cheeks and tortoiseshell spectacles. Her father stood beside them leaning on his cane. 'Gentlemen,' he said, 'this is our daughter, Catherine.'

'Lady Catherine,' the two men said in unison.

She acknowledged them with a smile then turned to her father, almost throwing herself into his arms, as she did when a child. She kissed his lips. 'You've been promoted, Daddy.'

'And so have you, I see and is this any way for a young subaltern to treat a lieutenant general?' The two men with him chuckled. General Somerville held Catherine tightly to him while the two officers with him turned, almost in embarrassment at this show of affection.

'You have a weekend pass and I have to work. We'll catch up when we both have more time. Right gentlemen, we must make a move.' He limped on his lame leg, his arm across Catherine's shoulder and chatted to her while the three others followed. 'Show these gentlemen to the car darling; I'll be with you in a moment,' he said to his wife. When they were out of earshot Lord Somerville turned to Catherine. 'Would you like a job on my staff?'

'And be the boss's daughter ... no thank you, Daddy.'

James Somerville took his daughter by the shoulders and looked into her eyes. 'Catherine, I lost all my friends in the last war, I don't want to lose my daughter in this one.'

'What are you saying?'

'I had to go up to Newcastle, so I paid you a surprise visit only you were not there. It gave the camp commander a heart attack me turning up like that. Some WTS commander said you had been posted out and no one knew where. All mysterious and hush, hush, she said. I hope you're not biting off something more than you can chew, Catherine.'

'Please don't worry about me, Daddy. I'm all right ... promise.'

James Somerville reached the car and climbed into the back, manoeuvring his stiff leg into a more comfortable position. 'Look after your mother. When you're down in London we'll have dinner and continue our chat.'

Catherine caught her father's eye before the driver closed the door behind him. She knew by the look on his face that he would start digging when he was back in London, and wondered if Commodore Greene anticipated that too. She called out goodbye and waved at the car as it drove away.

'Catherine,' her mother said when the car had disappeared, 'how are you, darling?'

Chapter **7**

Saturday morning, Lady Somerville decided to go into Harrogate to shop for a new coat in preparation for the coming winter. As the car drove past The Crown Hotel, Catherine caught a glimpse of the back of a soldier wearing a sand coloured beret entering the building. She spun round on her seat, but he was gone. The chauffeur stopped the car in James Street outside the entrance to Hoopers department store and jumped out to open the door on Lady Somerville's side. Half an hour later they left Hoopers without buying anything. 'I'll wait until I go to London. Let's go and have some lunch, darling.'

'Shall we go to The Crown?'

'I thought Bettys.'

'I don't like the manager there. He's always undressing me.'

'Then you ought to cover yourself a little more,' Lady Somerville said glancing at her daughter's cleavage.

Catherine's eyes rose like the sun from the east and took her mother's arm. 'I like this dress and it's good to be out of uniform for once.' They walked the few yards to Bettys and were given a reserved table by the window. The manager offered them the special of the day, game soup, 'game shot on your own estate, my lady.'

'Isn't it a little warm for soup?'

'It's delicious and selling well. It always does, my lady.'

They both decided on the 'special' and watched the manager rush off flicking his fingers to his staff to pay more attention to their customers, which allowed him to devote all his time to his two important guests.

'I don't like him much either,' Lady Somerville said. 'He's such a sycophant.' Her eyes softened and she ran the back of her fingers down the soft skin of her arm. 'You're looking more like your Aunt Hannah every year that passes.'

'Temperamentally, I'm very much like you.'

Elizabeth Somerville looked happy. 'The joy you gave me when you were born.' She raised Catherine's hand to her lips and kissed her fingers. 'Where did you get that bruise on your arm, Catherine?'

Catherine felt Panhanagan's weight on it. 'Oh, I knocked against something. It's nothing.'

'I really wish you had covered yourself a little more. It's a little vulgar to show so much.'

'Honestly Mummy anyone would think I was naked. I want to look like a woman, not one of the blokes.'

'What an extraordinary thing to say.'

'Yes, it was rather. I was quoting someone, someone I once knew.'

'You always look very smart and very feminine. Now you look very healthy darling. Your cheeks are glowing, your eyes sparkling. Are you in love?'

'No Mummy, I'm not.'

'Do you have a man in your life? You never discuss them.'

'There's no one. All the friends I had at Oxford have disappeared, some are dead, some prisoners. It's best not to get involved.'

Catherine's mother gave her an understanding, sympathetic smile. The soup arrived with crusty bread. 'I saw you running round the lake at six this morning. At one time I could never get you out of bed.'

Catherine shrugged. 'I used to read in bed when I woke, now I get up and run.'

Lady Somerville tapped her daughter's hand. 'Have your soup, darling.'

After the food she had endured in the past four weeks the soup tasted delicious. It was then she thought she saw the SAS beret in the crowd across the road between St Peter's church and the war memorial. She almost choked when she saw that it was Panhanagan.

'Be careful with that darling, it's hot.'

Although there were several men in uniform walking about, his beret was such a distinctive colour she recognised it immediately. Catherine watched Panhanagan disappear down Parliament Street. She stretched her neck to see where he was heading. He stopped, looked at his watch and returned to the war memorial, then looked at his watch again. His face broke into a smile at an approaching figure of a young woman. The sun caught a glint of gold on the ring finger of her left hand when she placed it on his shoulder to kiss him. Catherine caught her mother's inquisitive eye. 'Thought I saw someone I know.'

'I imagine you know several people in this town.'

Catherine moved positions at the table to get a better look at where the two of them were heading. The manager almost tripped, rushing to her assistance. 'Is that chair uncomfortable, Lady Catherine?'

'No, it's fine. Thank you.'

'How's your soup, Countess?'

'Delicious, thank you.' When he left, Lady Somerville studied her daughter who was still gazing towards the two figures, now in animated conversation. A smile crept to Catherine's lips when she saw him mouth a curse as the young woman hurried away.

'What's amusing you, darling?'

'Amusing me?'

'Is it the sergeant quarrelling with his young lady, perhaps?'

Catherine wiped her mouth with her napkin to hide her flushing face. 'S-Sergeant?'

'The one now causing you to stammer and blush. You have the same coloured beret as he. One of the maids found it in your room and gave it to me thinking it belonged to your father. I've never heard of the Special Air Service.'

'Special Air Service?'

'Really Catherine, you have an irritating habit of repeating what is said to you when you have something to hide. The Special Air Service. I've never heard of such a unit.'

'I'm not an expert in regiments of the British Army. Ask Daddy.'

'Then why stretch your neck to follow a sergeant from that regiment, change your seat to secure a better view of him, and smile when the young lady left in a huff?'

Catherine blushed; her mother was so tediously observant. Ted Peters would have loved her. 'I can look at a fellow, can't I? Anyway, I was given that beret as a keepsake.'

Lady Somerville drank another spoon of soup. 'Be honest with me, Catherine. I saw the look of recognition in your eyes. You know him, don't you?'

'No, well yes, but only a little. He's a sergeant. Officers don't mix with sergeants.'

'Don't be such a snob, darling.'

Catherine saw Panhanagan looking around him as if undecided whether to pursue the woman or to cross the road to Bettys. Her heart raced when he entered the restaurant and asked the manager for a table. Lady Somerville caught the manager's eye.

Panhanagan grimaced when the short, balding dandy left him in mid-sentence and rushed towards a couple of women sitting by the window. Panhanagan imagined them to be important by the manager's actions. One of the women had her back to him, but the other with her, who looked in her forties, was strikingly beautiful. He caught her eye. Around him, the room was full of wizened matriarchs and their skinny offspring. He decided to leave. The matriarchs stuffed cream cakes into their mouths - their daughter's eyes followed him to the door.

'Ask that sergeant to join us,' the Countess said to the manager. 'Quickly, he's leaving.'

'Mummy! No!'

The manager, red and flustered, caught Panhanagan. 'Sergeant, please follow me. You've been invited to dine with the Countess by the window.'

So, the beauty is a countess - could be interesting, Panhanagan thought.

'Sergeant, do take a seat. Thank you for joining us. I believe you know my daughter.'

Less observant people would have missed the look in Panhanagan's eyes when he recognised Catherine. She glared at him with clenched teeth. 'What are you doing in Harrogate—'

'Catherine!'

Catherine's eyes jumped towards her mother then back to Panhanagan. 'I'm sorry, Sergeant,' she said. 'Please, join us.'

Catherine's greeting left Panhanagan in no doubt that joining them was not her idea. His smile, now more confident, irritated her which drove her eyes up towards the ceiling rose. The manager hovered behind Catherine, pad and pen in hand, his lips stretched in a smile, his eyes on Catherine's breasts. As she leaned forward he could see a patch of light brown on her white flesh. Panhanagan's eyes dwelt there too. Her lips tightened when she met his smiling features.

'I recommend the game pie, Sergeant,' Lady Somerville said observing the tension between her daughter and Panhanagan.

The manager's eyes rolled towards Panhanagan who nodded. 'And for you, Lady Catherine?'

'Nothing for me, thank you.' Catherine felt hot as Panhanagan's lips moved.

'Catherine, you really ought to have something to eat. Soup isn't enough. Surely that run this morning has given you an appetite.'

This spread Panhanagan's lips further. 'Lady Catherine isn't a great eater, but she loves to run and take long walks.'

Catherine boiled inside. Her voice remained calm when she said, 'The soup was enough, thank you Mummy.'

'Bring Lady Catherine a salad and one for me, and the game pie for the sergeant,' the Countess said to the manager. 'So, Sergeant Panhanagan, where did you meet my daughter?'

Panhanagan saw Catherine's eyes open like the doors of a furnace as he caught the heat of her gaze. 'We were on a course together, Ma'am.'

'What course was that?'

'Communications, Mummy.'

'I'm sure Sergeant Panhanagan can speak for himself, darling.' Lady Somerville exaggerated her eye movement towards the name of the regiment sewn on his uniform, 'Special Air Service. I confess I've never heard of such a regiment. Is it new?'

'Yes, Ma'am.'

'What sort of work does the Special Air Service do?'

'It's just a branch of infantry, Ma'am – a fancy name to fool Jerry.'

'The design of the cap badge is very interesting, a dagger with wings. How's the pie?'

'Very good, Ma'am.'

'Excellent. An interesting badge, Sergeant. The dagger suggests death and the wings flight. Does this mean you fly to your objective and drop in by parachute to kill your enemy?'

'Mummy, do let Sergeant Panhanagan eat his meal. He's hardly touched it listening to you.' Catherine caught the expression on her mother's face and knew this wouldn't be an end to her questions. After Panhanagan had finished his meal, she said, 'Why you are in Harrogate?'

'I was meant to join a friend but he−'

'She...'

He coughed, 'She cried off, emergency.' He caught Catherine's eye. 'I thought I might as well stay the night. Look around, enjoy the sights.'

'So you're a tourist. We have lots of those round here, don't we Mummy?'

'Where are you staying, Sergeant?' Lady Somerville asked.

'Haven't found anywhere yet, Ma'am.'

'No cosy honeymoon suite booked in advance, Panhanagan?'

'Don't whisper in company, darling. It's rude.'

When the coffee was served, Lady Somerville said, 'You'd be most welcome to stay with us, Sergeant Panhanagan. I have a meeting to chair after dinner, so I'm sure Catherine will enjoy having company. You can swap notes on communications.'

'I'm sure Sergeant Panhanagan can find better company in a pub and accommodation in a bed and breakfast if he really tried.'

'Catherine, I have invited Sergeant Panhanagan to stay with us. I'll not have our warriors walk the streets when we can offer a bed.'

Panhanagan was delighted to see Catherine colour. When he accepted the offer, Catherine kicked him under the table, certain he did so for no other reason than to vex her. She had the opportunity to express this when her mother excused herself to say hello to an elderly woman she knew. 'Why don't you just bugger off, Panhanagan? I thought I'd seen the last of you.'

'You asked me to sit.'

'I was being polite, for my mother's sake.'

His eyes dropped to her breasts. 'Nice dress, *Lady* Catherine.'

'I'm an officer and you address me as such, Sergeant. Just because your tart dumped you, there's no need to take advantage of my mother's kindness and spoil *my* leave.'

Panhanagan watched her eyes narrow. 'Your mother's returning.'

'I've just seen old Mrs Blake, darling. You won't remember her. She was one of your grandfather's parlour maids. Married late in life and did rather well.' Catherine turned and politely returned the old woman's greeting. 'Do you have any luggage, Sergeant?'

'Just a bag the manager took, Ma'am.'

The manager stood at the door bowing from the waist like a Japanese meeting his emperor, then waved as the car drew away.

'I wish I didn't find that man so repugnant,' Lady Somerville said then offered Panhanagan a dazzling smile. 'I detect a slight Norfolk accent in your speech, Sergeant Panhanagan.'

'Yes, Ma'am. I was raised on the north Norfolk coast.'

'I once had the honour of being invited to Sandringham with my husband. The Princess Elizabeth was so kind. She took us to a bird sanctuary somewhere along that coast. She's fond of birds.'

'So is Sergeant Panhanagan.'

Panhanagan ignored Catherine's remark and said, 'That's at Holme-next-the-Sea, lovely sand beach that stretches for miles. My family moved from there to London just before the war.'

'I love the quiet, barren beauty of that coastline.'

Remembering his childhood days, Panhanagan's eyes glazed, 'Nothing remarkable happens there other than the migration of thousands of wild geese between autumn and spring.'

Catherine saw a rare, gentle light brighten his expression. His voice had tenderness in it she had never heard before. So, she thought, Panhanagan likes married women, migrating birds and sandy beaches.

When they arrived at Mountfields, a man appeared from one of the two gatehouses and opened the large black gates with their golden spears glinting in the sun. They travelled along a straight road cutting through gardens that led to a bridge spanning a river. In the distance he saw the sumptuous yellow stone of Mountfields House and caught his breath. It reminded him of Chatsworth House in Derbyshire where he had once spent the day with his mother when he was a boy. Lady Somerville glanced at Panhanagan and said, 'I remember when I saw the house for the first time too. I was terrified. My poor father would have turned in his grave.'

'He's never been here then.'

'He was killed on the Somme.' She felt Catherine's hand take hers and squeeze it.

'I lost my maternal grandfather at Verdun.'

'Verdun?' Lady Somerville said surprised. 'What was he doing at Verdun?'

'He was in the French army. My late mother was from Aquitaine.'

Catherine looked at him as the car pulled up outside the house. 'So you speak French?'

'And I can count too.'

Chapter **8**

From her bedroom window, Catherine watched Panhanagan fishing. There was a soft knock at her door. Lady Somerville entered the room and joined Catherine at the window. In silence they watched Panhanagan fishing by the lake. 'Was he your lover?'

'No, he wasn't! I can't stand the man.'

'Then why are you standing watching him?'

Catherine shrugged. 'I have no idea why.'

'Tell me about him, this handsome young man who was allegedly on a communications course with my daughter, who just happens to be a wireless expert. Unless, of course, you were running it.'

'I'd rather not discuss it, or him.'

Lady Somerville took Catherine's hand. 'I spoke to Daddy. He's worried you're going to do something stupid. You know what I'm talking about, don't you? Oh, he's caught one. Look–'

'When did you speak with Daddy?'

'I telephoned him a moment ago. I wanted to know about the Special Air Service. You were obviously not going to say anything. Your father said they're quite mad. They go round blowing things up behind enemy lines. In North Africa they created carnage for the Luftwaffe. I knew that winged dagger meant something.' Catherine stood silently watching Panhanagan reel in the fish, net it, unhook it, stroke it and then gently return it to the water. The gentleness of his action belied the ruthless killer she knew him to be. She felt her mother's hand rest on her shoulder.

'I've never interfered in your life, Catherine,' Elizabeth Somerville said, as she left the window and sat on the edge of the bed, 'but this time I wish to say something. I know they send French-speaking women from our Corps into France as wireless operators, couriers and to blow up things, railways and suchlike. Elizabeth told Aunt Hannah and naturally Hannah told me. It doesn't take much to work out that you're a perfect candidate for that job, and what's more, a job I know you would jump at doing.'

'Elizabeth really ought to keep quiet about such things. That's top secret information she's dishing out.'

'So you don't deny it.'

'Please, Mummy...'

'I found this on the staircase. You must have dropped it,' she said handing Catherine her parachute wings, 'Shouldn't they be sewn on your uniform or are they a keepsake too?'

'Mummy, you know I'm saying nothing so it's pointless pursuing it. You and Daddy did your thing in the Great War and I shall do my duty in this war. I'm going for a walk. Want to come?'

'No, it looks as if it might rain and I have to chair a meeting shortly. We'll walk tomorrow,' she said rising from the edge of the bed. 'I see your Sergeant Panhanagan has disappeared.'

'He's not *my* Sergeant Panhanagan.'

*

Catherine was close to the hunting lodge on the other side of the lake when it began to rain. She ran for cover, but by the time she reached the hunting lodge she was already soaked. Inside the lodge she shivered, her wet dress clung to her body. A few minutes later Panhanagan burst into the room. Catherine closed her eyes in exasperation. 'Are you following me, Panhanagan?'

'I'll leave if you wish.'

'No,' she sighed. 'I wouldn't send a dog out in this.'

'So you have some streaks of your mother's kindness in you.' Catherine ignored him. She wrapped her arms round her body. Panhanagan grinned. 'Cold?'

'No.'

She had watched Panhanagan closely over dinner, occasionally finding her mother's eyes and smile. She knew her mother had made a great effort to make Panhanagan feel at ease, and the two of them chatted in French for some time before Catherine joined in the conversation. When Lady Somerville left the table she whispered in Catherine's ear that she liked him. 'He's very charming.' Her mother hadn't seen him with a knife in his hand.

Panhanagan looked at the initials PF and CS carved into the shape of a heart on the wall. 'Who's PF?' he asked Catherine.

'A fellow named Paul. He kissed me just where he scratched the initials. It was my first kiss. I was fourteen. Paul was two years older. Nothing else happened. Nothing would have happened. As young as he was he was a gentleman,' she said when she caught a glint in Panhanagan's eye. 'We were children.'

'So what happened to Romeo?'

'He returned to Germany with his father after his mother died.'

'And now lover boy is shooting at us.'

Catherine didn't want to think about that. She only offered a silent prayer that he was safe. They became silent again, listening to the drumming of rain against the lead roof. Both avoided the other's eyes. 'Posh place you've got. Better than our hut. Now I know what the working classes are fighting to preserve.'

'If you've got nothing to say, Panhanagan, then it's best to keep quiet.' Again they listened to the rain. 'My mother has guessed what I'm up to, so if she speaks with you I'd like you to remember the Official Secrets Act.'

'I don't know what you're up to, but I could hazard a guess. I've been in France helping out resistance groups ... bunch of wankers. Met a courier from your Corps. It's a bloody dodgy job—'

'Should you be telling me this?'

'I think you're being groomed for something more than passing messages on to a load of tossers. I think you're going to have to put someone's lights out. Could you do that?'

'I don't know, but thanks to you Panhanagan, I'm certainly capable of doing so.'

'Having flesh and blood in your sights is quite different from shooting at a wooden target.' He remembered the last man he killed. His commando knife with its long straight blade went under his victim's chin and up into the skull. The man was dead before he quietly lowered him to the ground. 'Using a knife is worse. You can feel the life leaving the body.'

Catherine went to the window and looked out without answering. The rain was relentless. She wanted to get back to the house. Her wet dress clung to her, which attracted Panhanagan's eyes and began to irritate her. 'You like killing don't you, Panhanagan? I expect it's because you have no love in you. You're dead inside.'

'Why are you being so aggressive?'

'I dislike you. The sooner you're gone the better.'

Panhanagan's eyes rose to hers as he approached her. 'I've had it up to here with you,' he said placing his hand to his chin. 'Who the hell do you think you are, Lieutenant, Lady bloody Muck? Do you think I'm with you now because I fancy you?'

'You couldn't keep your grubby hands off me in Scotland and now it's your eyes—'

'You're not my type, you conceited cow.'

54

'Because I'm single, I suppose. That woman in Harrogate, did her husband return unexpectedly−'

'Bollocks!'

'Must you swear, or are you so used to the company of whores?' Catherine said calmly. 'Are they your type, dearie?'

'I know your type, Lady Snooty. ' Panhanagan said, backing against the wall. 'It wasn't me who had my eyes on you, was it? Oh no, our Susan couldn't take her eyes off you, could she? And there you both were, shacked up together all nice and cosy.'

Catherine felt her cheeks glow. 'What are you suggesting?'

'Holloway and Peters were asleep. I couldn't sleep, so I went to the mess-room to make some tea, but I was disturbed by you two getting cosy with each other.' He walked closer towards her and smiled. 'Oh yes! Oh God!' he said. 'If Susan hadn't have put her hand over your mouth you would have squealed like a pig. It almost turned me on.'

She struck out at him. He had anticipated it and grabbed her, pinning her against the wall. He gripped her arms and forced a knee between her legs to prevent her from kicking out at him.

'Get your filthy hands off me, Sergeant.'

He tightened his grip, knowing how dangerous she could be if he loosened it. 'I've never had a bit of posh,' he said. He began moving his knee slowly between her legs and watched the anger well up in her eyes. 'No one will know,' he whispered in her ear, 'you might even like to have something hard inside you, instead of Susan's little flickering tongue.'

She spat into his face. 'You're disgusting.'

He grinned and licked her spittle from his lips. 'When did you last have a good fuck, Lieutenant?' He secured both her hands in one of his above her head and took a breast and squeezed it. 'Good tits, firm−'

'I'll have you arrested for this!'

'You've flashed these at me all day Miss Snooty, so now I'm testing the goods.' He went to kiss her, still pressing his knee firmly between her legs. She resisted, twisting her head left and right then their lips met. She pressed her lips together, while he tried to prise them open with his tongue. Catherine eventually pulled one arm free and hit him under the bridge of his nose with the palm of her hand. He yelped and let her go, holding his nose.

She pushed him clear of her. 'You'll never have me Panhanagan, never! Get out! Just get out of here and get out of my life!'

Blood poured from his nose. He inspected it on his hand. 'What you need is a fucking good seeing to. It might relax that tight arse of yours.'

'Well it won't be you, Panhanagan. I have more taste than that.' She kicked him between his legs and when he doubled up, wheezing in pain, she kicked him in the shins sending him crashing to the ground. 'Be gone before I get up tomorrow, Sergeant. I'll give your apologies to my mother.'

'Fuck you. She's a million times the woman you'll ever be, you bitch.' He watched Catherine leave the building, slamming the door behind her. 'Yes, fuck off you fucking lesbian bitch.' He sniffed and spat blood from his mouth. 'Fuck. That hurt!'

Chapter **9**

Commodore Greene sat in his office reading Holloway's report regarding Catherine's training. His office was located on the second floor in one of the elegant buildings on St James's Square, SW1. The polished brass plate on the door read, Trafalgar Exports (UK) Ltd. Other than Greene's PA and Winston Churchill himself, nobody knew what went on behind Trafalgar Exports (UK) Ltd's closed doors. The only commodity Commodore Greene had ever exported was a particular kind of intelligence officer into France.

He lowered the Holloway report and remembered how he began his career in the intelligence services when he served on Churchill's staff during the Great War. Winston was First Sea Lord. '*Quis custodiet ipsos custodes*' Churchill once said to him through a cloud of cigar smoke. 'Who will guard the guards themselves, eh Greene? Who will guard the guards themselves?'

Now it was another war and Winston was Head Boy. He had asked Greene to keep an eye on SOE. 'If there are any rotten apples, get rid of them.'

Greene knew that no matter how often a barrel was checked for bruised apples, one may be missed and turn rotten. One rotten apple can destroy the whole barrel if not discovered quickly. Greene had a barrel of apples he wanted Catherine to check and suspected that one of them was rotten.

He was shaken from his thoughts by a knock on his door. 'Ah! Catherine, take a seat,' he said smiling. She arrived wearing civilian clothes, in keeping with Trafalgar Exports (UK) Ltd. 'You look well. The highland air has put colour in your cheeks. I'm just reading Holloway's report now. He was impressed with you; all three say you responded very well to the training. Well done. Right, you'll go to France with the next moon, that's a week today. I would prefer it to be sooner, but there's a lot to get through before you go. I've got some photographs of some SOE agents I want you to study and memorize. They've gone missing. I want you to find them, or at least find out what's happened to them. With the documents are their codenames and last known address. There is also a man I think has gone rotten, Henri Blucourt, our air movement officer. He seems to be leading a charmed life, while those around him disappear. Find out what you can and deal with it.'

'You mean, kill him, Sir?'

'That's exactly what I mean. My assistant will brief you later. You know her, of course. She's Sub-Lieutenant–'

'Harcourt-Williams,' Catherine said feeling her cheeks heat a little.

Greene smiled and his expression changed to one of a priest; his fingertips pressed together, his eyes raised to the heavens. They fell back onto Catherine. 'I'll brief you the day you leave. This is a very important mission, Catherine. I'm relying on you. Meanwhile Susan will get everything you need ready for you.' He smiled and shrugged. 'She's my niece. I like to keep things in the family. She has sorted out codenames and backgrounds for your cover. You must learn them until it is second nature to you. Listen to Susan; she's good at what she does. Right, you're now a field officer for the Secret Intelligence Service known as G branch, MI6. No one but Susan and I know about you, not even the rest of my department.'

'What about Holloway, Peters and Panhanagan? They know me as much as Susan does.'

'They only know you may be connected to the intelligence service. Anyway, they disappeared in a Halifax across the Channel last night. I expect they are already a thorn in Jerry's side. So off you go. You'll find Susan at this address waiting for you.'

Susan was dressed in the blue uniform of the Royal Navy with the rank of sub-lieutenant on her sleeves. Catherine brushed past her avoiding her eyes.

'Cathy…' Susan said chasing after her.

Catherine stopped dead and spun around. 'Don't you *ever* call me Cathy; only my cousin Elizabeth calls me that.'

'I'm sorry.' Her hand went out to touch Catherine's arm, but Catherine moved from her before she made contact. 'Catherine, let's go for a drink. Talk this through.'

'Why, Susan? Why the deception, the games?'

'Intelligence is all about deception. That's the game you're playing now. I had to discover if you talked. Greene wanted to know if he could trust you to keep your mouth shut. I did all I could to make you blab, but you wouldn't. You must understand it was my job.'

'And that night...' Catherine said, moving so close to Susan's face each could feel the heat of the other's breath. 'Was that a test, another of your games?'

'Come on Catherine. You bloody well enjoyed it and you know it.'

'You're disgusting.'

Susan took hold of Catherine's wrist. 'You're a big girl, Catherine. Don't play the innocent.'

Catherine gripped Susan's hand and removed it from hers. 'Thank you for the orgasm. Can we now drop it and get on with whatever you're planning this week?'

For the next few days they worked hard on the cover stories, and the disguises Catherine had to wear for two of them. She memorized all the details regarding the agents she was going to try and find, or at least discover if they were captive or murdered by the Gestapo.

Catherine was impressed with Susan's professionalism now she was playing herself, a Cambridge graduate in mathematics and a sub-lieutenant in the Royal Navy. They went out and had dinner. When they returned to Catherine's house in Belgrave Square, they had more drinks. In the morning Catherine woke and met Susan's eyes from the pillow beside her.

'Morning... don't be alarmed, nothing happened. You passed out.'

'Passed out...'

'We were drunk. I didn't want to sleep alone so I just climbed into bed with you.' Susan winced at Catherine's expression. 'For heaven's sake, you're still dressed.'

They both were. Catherine smiled. 'So you didn't try anything on?'

'Of course I did, but you didn't want to play. You fancy Panhanagan. I could feel the chemistry sizzling between you both in Scotland even though you and I... you know...'

'Panhanagan's the last man on earth I want. Happily he's playing soldiers again, so I shall never see that conceited, overbearing, arrogant... and I shall not lose a minute's sleep over it.'

'Umm, the lady doth protest too much, methinks.'

*

59

After breakfast Susan said, 'You'll need a good wireless operator this end Catherine. She will have to work from St James's Square. I thought your cousin Elizabeth...'

'As long as she has no idea who Nora is.'

Nora was Catherine's call sign. The traffic she would send would be set to a special frequency, which only Nora's wireless operator would receive. Susan nodded. 'I'll have her transferred. She'll be bored I expect. Could she handle the hours of isolation?'

'I think so. Elizabeth is good at her job.'

'I'll keep her company when I can. That will help.' When she caught Catherine's expression Susan pulled a face. 'I don't sleep with just anyone. Elizabeth doesn't do it for me.' Susan pulled out a file. From the file she removed a photograph. It was a picture of Ludwig Hoffmann in the uniform of the SS. 'We'd like you to meet him again. Try to get into 84 Avenue Foch. Do you think you could do that?'

Catherine's eyes burned into the picture. 'Why?'

'There are files in there that would be very useful to us. It won't be easy of course, and you may never manage it, but there would be a glimmer of hope through Hoffmann.'

'You mean Greene wants me to whore for England.'

'Of course not.' Susan smiled. 'You know Hoffmann. He'll suspect nothing.'

'I hate that man for what he did to me.'

'Can we have dinner tonight?'

Catherine met Susan's eyes and shook her head. 'No, I've things to do.' She leaned towards Susan and kissed her lightly on the cheek. 'Thanks for all you've done.'

Chapter **10**

It was Friday 12th and the November moon was full. Catherine had orders to be ready to leave at 1500. Shortly after lunch, a black car pulled up outside the house in Belgrave Square. Elizabeth, who had arrived that morning, watched the driver emerge from the vehicle and stand by the rear door ready to open it for Catherine. She watched the WTS driver straighten her belt and pull her tunic down so it fitted her without creases, then adjust her peaked cap. The driver looked across to the gardens where an elderly lady was closing the gate, struggling with her two dogs. One began to bark at the driver who turned her head and ignored it. Elizabeth called out, 'Your car's here.'

Catherine gave Elizabeth her house keys. 'I shan't need these. You'd better look after them.'

'You'll need them when you return. I might not be home.'

'One of the staff will be here. I don't want to lose them.'

Elizabeth placed them on the table and turned to inspect her cousin. 'Why have you chosen your old French clothes to wear?'

'I like them.'

'They still fit you.' She smiled and ran her hand down Catherine's sleeve as if she were smoothing out a crease. 'I'm going to miss you.'

Catherine took hold of Elizabeth and squeezed her to her body. 'Look after yourself when I'm away. Don't see me out. I'll say goodbye here.'

'Have a good trip, Cathy. Don't come back with any Canadians. You'll break a lot of Englishmen's hearts. Write to me.' They kissed each other and Catherine was suddenly gone. From the sitting room window, Elizabeth saw her appear in the square. The WTS driver saluted Catherine, then took her suitcase and placed it into the boot of the car. Elizabeth waited to catch Catherine's eye, but she didn't look up; perhaps she was in tears too. Elizabeth wiped her eyes as she watched the car turn down Grosvenor Crescent, then it was gone. She walked from the window and saw a note by the telephone. *Darling Lizzy, I will miss you terribly. You have been my best friend since we were tots and I will always love you. Not only are your mother and my father twins, I feel we share the same heart and soul too. Please visit Mummy while I'm away, and love with hugs to Aunt Hannah and Uncle Edward. Lots of kisses and big, big hugs for you.*

A flush of pleasure coloured her face as she read these words. 'How odd,' Elizabeth whispered, wiping away a tear that began to swell in her eye, 'why should Cathy suddenly become so sentimental?'

*

Catherine let herself into the office and laid her key on the desk with a wireless set sitting on it. She stared at it, knowing Elizabeth would be listening to the dits and dahs of an anonymous Joe in France. Greene walked in with Susan. Both were wearing uniform. He tapped the wireless as if the head of a faithful Labrador. Catherine watched him and wondered if he thought it was going to produce the answer to some serious questions.

'Ready?' he said with a jovial expression, as if they were about to venture out on a picnic. 'Off we go then.'

*

As the car turned onto the A1 for Tempsford in Bedfordshire, Greene said, 'SOE's Madeleine has been taken, I'm certain of it. Her wireless suddenly went quiet, and then it returned three days later. The operator this end says it doesn't feel like Madeleine's touch on the keyboard. It's quite obvious German Intelligence is sending it. I'm now also certain one of our people has turned. SOE agents are flying out there into the hands of the Germans. Our trump card is that no one knows about you. Now you understand why I've kept you under wraps. I want you to discover what has happened to these agents. If the leak is in France, find it and deal with it.'

For most of the journey, Commodore Greene was asleep. When they were close to Tempsford, Susan deliberately applied the brakes a little to shake Greene awake. He spluttered and looked about him. 'Almost there, Sir' she said. 'About ten minutes.'

'Good Lord, already! Sorry Catherine... must have dozed off. How are you feeling?'

'Fine Sir,' she said with a confident smile, but she was feeling nauseous. Panhanagan was right when he said that nerves always hit you before an operation. How she wished she had that bastard with her now.

The car made its way to a small house in the shadows of a large barn. The door to the house opened as they approached it, revealing a small, middle-aged woman whose Oxbridge accent welcomed them to her home. 'I'm Rowena,' she said. 'I'm preparing some dinner; steak and kidney pie. Half an hour suit you?'

'Thanks Rowena,' Susan said, ushering Catherine through another door. 'That will give me time to sort things out.'

'You're going to parachute into the Loir-et-Cher district,' Greene said to Catherine when they were through into the sitting room. 'The Maquis who usually meet our visitors don't know you're coming, so there won't be a welcoming committee. You're on your own once you jump from that aircraft. As far as the pilot knows, it's a routine flight to drop off some supplies further along the route. He knows he has a passenger who will not be with him when he returns, but that's all. He won't even know where you will be leaving him until he reads his orders five minutes before you jump. I'll see you in the dining room shortly.'

Susan approached Catherine and said, 'Take this dressing gown. Undress; take everything off. I need to check all your clothes.'

'I've checked them.'

'I'm double-checking. It's for your own safety. There may be something you've missed. A laundry mark, anything.' When Susan had finished inspecting the clothing, she went through all the clothes in the suitcase – even the suitcase itself. She then handed Catherine a Walther PPK handgun, silencer and two boxes of ammunition. 'Panhanagan wrote saying that you were very handy with this.'

'It's a good weapon,' Catherine replied.

Susan watched Catherine check the weapon and magazine, and put it in her shoulder bag with the silencer. The ammunition was placed in the suitcase. Susan met Catherine's eyes. 'I know you have worked on this, but just one last time. Your wireless call sign is Nora. These are the fake identification papers, ration books etc, for your three identities. Use them wisely, Catherine. After graduation you worked at a lycée in Lyon, married Dominique Régnier, no children, now moved back to Paris to find a better job. If the Germans check you out you will be safe. Our people have made it look as if you, or should I say Madame Catherine Régnier, worked there.' Then Catherine was handed a gold ring. 'Put this on.'

Catherine tried on the ring. It fitted. 'And my husband?'

'You met and married him in Lyon.'

'And where is he now?'

'That's down to you. You left him. Like most men, he was unreliable,' Susan smiled, 'so you are footloose and fancy-free again. All the toiletries I've packed were brought back from Paris last week by another agent, so they're safe.'

'You've thought of everything.'

'I hope so. Your face is the only real problem. It's one that stands out in a crowd and that's not good in this line of work. People will remember it, better to look grey, invisible. Do something less glamorous with your hair... hide it under a hat, a plain dark hat, and wear the spectacles I've given you. The lenses are plain glass. I've put them in your case.' Finally, Susan handed Catherine an overcoat; navy blue, unfashionable and inexpensive. 'Take this with you rather than the one you have. You can turn it inside out, so in effect you have two coats. The one you're wearing is too expensive. Again, it will draw attention to you. Remember, you're a schoolteacher not an aristocrat.' Their eyes met. 'Never forget that Madame Régnier. While you're in France, Lady Catherine Somerville no longer exists. How does it feel to be one of us?' Susan smiled. 'There's just one more thing...'

The capsule was light brown in colour; small, insignificant looking. 'I don't want it,' Catherine said, giving it back to Susan. 'Thanks anyway.'

'Best take it with you. Think of it as another possible weapon if you're in a tight spot.' Catherine nodded, replaced the pill in the little box and put it into her pocket. 'These,' Susan said handing her two more, 'are sleeping pills with a difference. They will knock someone out in seconds and keep them out for at least seven hours. Again, very useful in a tight spot and they dissolve in liquid. They're a different colour from the cyanide, so you won't get them mixed up. I've packed a pair of shoes that has a false heel, so you can hide the pills in there. Any questions?'

'Are you sure Elizabeth doesn't suspect anything?'

'Yes, I am. Do you now regret agreeing to her being your wireless operator this end?'

'No, she's good. I just don't want her to know it's me sending. She will worry herself to death.'

'She'll think the field agent Nora is simply a Joe, who taps out Morse at the other end of the line.' Susan gave Catherine an affectionate smile. 'Right, steak and kidney pie...'

*

'All done?' Greene said as the two young women entered the sitting room. Catherine nodded.
'I've had your wireless transmitter checked out. Now let's go and eat something.'

An hour later, Susan drove them out to the far end of the airfield and the three of them left the car. 'You'll be in my thoughts day and night, Madame Régnier,' Commodore Greene said. 'Good luck and please don't take any unnecessary risks. Just come home in one piece.'

An RAF sergeant travelling as crew fixed on Catherine's parachute. She climbed the steps to her seat and the sergeant passed the two suitcases up to her, then attached them to a rope once he was aboard. Catherine looked down at Susan and Commodore Greene as the engines fired into life. Both gave her a naval salute as the door was closed, then they watched the aircraft take off and disappear into a clear moonlit sky.

'Right Susan, let's get home.'

'Uncle Charles...'

'Yes.'

'Oh, nothing... I'm sure we've covered everything.'

Chapter **11**

Obersturmbannführer Erich von Model stood at the large window in his office at 84 Avenue Foch in Paris, the headquarters of the Sicherheitsdienst. He gazed along the length of the avenue. The leaves had fallen in heaps on the ground and were already turning dark brown. Paris was now into winter. He caught his reflection in the window, smiled and adjusted his tie and the Knight's Cross at his throat. Model was a handsome man in his early thirties whose head may have been a mould for any bust depicting the Greek god, Apollo. Although he considered himself as Hermes, the god that liked to trick people, for that was his role as a counter-intelligence officer. When he was a boy his mother paraded him around the great Prussian homes, just as Leopold paraded young Wolfgang throughout the drawing rooms of European royalty, but unlike Mozart, Model was an aristocrat. He considered those in the Nazi party uncouth, proletarian thugs; an opinion he kept very much to himself. Yet it suited him to be one of the Party's members. He disliked the French for killing off their aristocracy and the Russians for killing off theirs, but he was very fond of the English for their social order, something he admired. He liked England. He had been educated at Harrow, and while there, he was often invited by school friends to many of England's great houses. Model was a gentleman, but crude, something he liked to think he got from his English boarding school days, where bodily functions and parts amused the boys so much. The English are a nation that likes to play games; but they seem happy to come second, it just isn't cricket and all that.

Spying was a game. He never considered the English played it well. He had broken the SOE network in Holland when he was attached to the Abwehr, and was immediately promoted to head the Sicherheitsdienst in Paris. His success in Holland had almost been repeated in France.

Model complimented himself that Paris was free from British Special Operations Executive agents. He and his assistant Ludwig Hoffmann questioned all captured agents. It was so easy to arrest these poor souls, Model knew. They were betrayed by informers or double agents, even by their own carelessness at SOE headquarters in London.

'Amateurs,' he whispered to his reflection. 'Incompetent fools.' A knock on his door interrupted his thoughts. 'Come.'

His young assistant entered the room. Model smiled amiably. Ludwig Hoffmann was intelligent, he knew. He had been sensible enough to marry a general's daughter, which kept him away from the fighting, but Hoffmann had delusions of grandeur, something Model didn't like from the middle order of society. Hoffmann was keen and his French was very good, but he was not a Prussian. He much preferred working with fellow Prussians.

'Ah, Ludwig,' he said in a friendly tone. 'Why are you looking so glum on this fine morning?'

'Our tracking station has picked up another wireless signal in Paris, Herr Obersturmbannführer.'

Model looked to the ceiling. 'These British will never learn,' he sighed, 'lambs to the slaughter. Did they get a bearing on it?'

'It was too quick, Herr Obersturmbannführer. Probably a message to confirm an arrival.'

'Would you care for some tea?'

'No thank you, Herr Obersturmbannführer. Perhaps London is suspicious about the traffic we are sending and has sent someone to investigate. I can have the Gestapo keep an eye on all known SOE safe houses and if someone does call, we'll have him.'

'No, no Ludwig, these people work in teams. Keep an eye on the houses; if you see him, don't arrest him; have him followed. See where the chase leads us.' Model placed his cup and saucer on his desk, and touched the rim of the cup with his fingertip. 'Meissen. I had it delivered yesterday.' He glanced up at Hoffmann. 'Have you spoken to Siegfried?'

Hoffmann walked towards one of the great windows and looked down into the avenue, where only moments ago Model had stood surveying the same scene. There was hardly a soul around. 'Siegfried says that there has been no Lysander traffic for weeks, Herr Obersturmbannführer. Our informers in the Maquis have not reported any parachutists either.' He ran a finger round the back of his shirt collar. 'Of course, our man could be a woman. We know the British are now using women as wireless operators, because of Madeleine. This one may have slipped in unannounced, or has been here all the time; a sleeper, or perhaps come up from the south.'

Model nodded thoughtfully. 'It's possible.' He laid the palms of his hands, with their perfectly manicured fingernails, upon his desk and stretched his fingers as if to inspect them. 'One thing is certain, this wireless operator will call London again and when he, or she does, we'll close in.' He looked up and smiled. 'Good, see to it. Oh, Ludwig, speaking of Madeleine, I'm still waiting for your report on her.'

Hoffmann's eyes were suddenly unable to meet his superior's. 'I'm sorry Herr Obersturmbannführer, I have completed it, but it hasn't been typed yet.'

Model's lips tightened. 'How long must Berlin wait for these reports? Are you trying to make me look as incompetent as those Gestapo idiots next door?'

'We're snowed under with paperwork, Herr Obersturmbannführer. Anna-Marie returned to Germany last week; compassionate leave, remember, her parents, that last raid on Hamburg—'

'Why hasn't she been replaced?'

'We've been told to make do with the staff we have.'

'You mean I'm now on a budget like some peasant family after Christmas? Have you tried 82 next door or 86? They must have a spare typist.'

'They haven't, Herr Obersturmbannführer. We could always employ a French typist.'

'Are you mad?'

'She'll handle nothing sensitive, just help clear the backlog. Corporal Hock can do the rest.'

'There must be other German girls in Paris. What about the Abwehr at Boulevard Raspail? They must have a woman they can spare. Surely Steiner can kick one of them from his bed and send her over here.'

'You are aware how they try to obstruct your work, Herr Obersturmbannführer, since you so brilliantly showed them how it should be done in Holland.'

'You don't have to kiss my arse, Ludwig. Just find a typist.'

'I'll try them, but if not we really will have to try to find a local girl. Hock will never manage to finish it before you go to Berlin, Herr Obersturmbannführer.' Hoffmann glanced hopefully at Model. 'I'll vet her personally.'

Still pleased with the compliment he received from his junior, Model chuckled and wagged a finger at Hoffmann. 'I bet you will Ludwig. The general's daughter is not enough for you now you've swollen her belly for the Fatherland, eh? I should be careful not to be caught cheating on her, otherwise her father will have you transferred to the Russian Front,' he chuckled again. 'Right, I must go for a meeting with those idiots at number 82. See to it then and make sure she's pretty. I don't want to look at some hairy French sow plucking at her moustache all day. I'll see you in the morning.'

*

Ludwig Hoffmann buttoned up his greatcoat and left 84 Avenue Foch to join his friends at his favourite café along the Champs Elysées. After another cognac he began to laugh at a story told by one of his comrades. All three looked up at an attractive young woman who passed them. Because Hoffmann was the only one of them who spoke good French, he was encouraged by his friends to call her back to join them for a drink.

'No,' he said, 'that is not how a German gentleman should behave. How would you like your sister being bellowed at by a Frenchman if they had invaded Berlin?'

'A fine lecture Ludwig, meanwhile we've lost her. You need a lesson in the fine art of relaxation from that queen von Model, don't you think, Hans? So many beautiful women in Paris and I have not had one of them yet, only whores.'

'And that is all you will ever get, Dieter,' Hoffmann replied. 'They despise us. Have you noticed the way the French look at any woman seen with a German soldier?'

'There lies your problem, Ludwig. You should look at the girl and not the person watching her,' Hans laughed. 'I have a beautiful mistress and you could have one too. Here, take a look at her picture. Look at that face, those eyes, her lips, those wonderful breasts.'

Hoffmann leaned across to take a closer look at the photograph. 'Very nice. How did an ugly sod like you manage that on your limited French?'

'Simple, I first learned it in Latvia. My God there's some beautiful women in Latvia−'

'Just get on with it Hans.'

'Patience dear friend. I spotted Gabrielle dining with her husband in the Café de Lyon and thought, very nice too, so I had

69

my orderly follow them home to see where they lived. The following day I had her husband arrested on a bogus charge. When his lovely spouse came to my office and begged me to release him, I said I would personally investigate the charge and let her know the outcome in a few days if she returned. When she returned I gave her the bad news that there was evidence to prove he was involved in resistance activities. Of course she looked surprised and very nervous when I told her men have been shot for less. She begged me to release him. One thing led to another. After two hours of bliss I told her that her husband will remain free for as long as I enjoy our meetings. Now she is beginning to enjoy them too. These French... ooh la la!'

Dieter laughed. Ludwig shook his head. 'That is no way for an officer of the Reich to act.'

'Don't be such a hypocrite. You've cheated on your wife ever since you've been here,' Hans said, signalling to the waiter to bring more drinks.

As Dieter began a story about a girl from Arras, Hoffmann raised his eyes towards a young woman who walked past the café. He hardly gave her a second glance. There was nothing remarkable about her to draw his whole attention, but he briefly caught a glimpse of her features, aware only that they contained a pair of round, horn-rimmed spectacles, a protruding lip and straw-coloured hair under a woollen black hat. Following her were two other women. He turned his attention to the prettier of the two, admiring the way the coat she was wearing clung to her trim figure. It showed the gentle sway of her hips as she made her way along the Champs Elysées. Desire ran though his body like an electric current. It had been two weeks since his last woman, a nervous nineteen year old from the suburbs. He was shaken out of his thoughts by the raucous laughter from his two friends.

*

Catherine had spotted Hoffmann in the café by the window with two other SD officers. He did not give her a second glance as she passed. Her disguise had worked. She had been keeping an eye on him since she arrived in Paris. It was easy because he was a man of habit and, now he was back in the city, he returned to the places he once enjoyed as a student. Her meeting with him could wait, she thought. She had other things to complete before she would reacquaint herself with Ludwig Hoffmann.

70

Catherine knocked at the door of the fourth address she had memorised from Commodore Greene's list. The woman who opened it was short and keen-eyed. Her eyes seem to take in everything of Catherine's features as if she wanted to remember the face. Catherine left the house feeling uneasy and guessed her identity with this particular disguise was now limited. She left the Clichy district and made her way by metro to Gaîté where she alighted and cut through the cemetery to Boulevard Raspail. It was a road she knew well. She reached the Boulevard du Montparnasse, crossed the road where the café De La Rotonde was situated, and stopped at Rodin's statue of Honoré de Balzac.

'Bonjour Honoré,' she whispered, just as she had done every morning for three years from the first floor flat directly behind where she now stood. She turned and looked up at the window. Behind it was the sitting room where she had spent many evenings with friends putting the world to rights. Behind the second window was the bedroom in which she was raped by Hoffmann. His features entered her mind; the ready smile, the Aryan charm and her fingers encircled the handle of her PPK in her coat pocket. She continued along the Boulevard Raspail until she reached the Rue Huysmans intersection. There she stopped to look around her. Further along the boulevard was the flat she wanted to visit.

The animal instincts within her sensed danger; she could feel her skin prickle and her stomach feel hollow as her eyes searched the street. So it was with great caution that she crossed the road. 'Form a picture in your head,' Peters had said. 'Put everything in its place.'

Boulevard Raspail is a dual carriageway with a centre section for pedestrians, and is lined with trees. She descended the stairs to a public lavatory past a man urinating in a urinal. He turned and exposed himself to her. She ignored him and locked herself in one of the cubicles that stank of piss. She checked her PPK, screwed on the silencer and removed the safety catch. On leaving the cubicle, the man was still there masturbating. His movements quickened at the sight of Catherine. Again she ignored him. Don't lose your concentration, she said to herself. She walked half way up the stairs and looked through the railings for anyone standing around or sitting in a parked car. She felt a hand move up her dress. She turned and hit the man so hard he crashed down the stairs and lay unmoving at the bottom. 'Christ,' she whispered. Her instincts told her to leave the place quickly.

As she left the lavatory's entrance, a car arrived from nowhere with a screech and braked heavily alongside her. She almost vomited with fear, certain she had been caught. Her hand automatically gripped the handle of the PPK, but she released it when the two men who had jumped from the car pushed her aside and disappeared into the building she was about to visit. A soldier stood outside guarding the entrance, with a submachine gun across his chest. He shouted in German at Catherine to move on, then '*allez allez*' with a dismissive gesture of his hand.

Catherine backed away. Minutes later she saw the same two men appear, dragging another from the building. A woman with them was screaming, pleading the man's innocence. One of the Germans hit her hard, sending her crashing to the ground. The car sped off to the first intersection where it turned and doubled back in the direction of the Boulevard Saint-Germain. When they had gone, Catherine went to see if the woman was all right. Once she had secured the woman's confidence, she questioned her about her neighbour and was told the Gestapo had arrested him a month ago. Now there was only the wireless operator Madeleine left to find.

When Catherine arrived at the Rue de Sèvres intersection with Boulevard Raspail, the car she had just witnessed driving away was parked outside the Hotel Lutetia. She approached an old woman who was resting against a building opposite and asked if the hotel had been requisitioned by the Germans.

The old woman's red eyes lifted to the bespectacled young woman before her. 'You're not from this part of the city are you?'

'No.'

'It's all changed. The Abwehr has that building.' She glanced about her as if looking for eavesdroppers. 'Anyone taken into there never leaves it alive.' The old woman crossed herself and gave Catherine another long look. Her eyes seem to wander into the distance, as if she were remembering the street in better times. Catherine turned her head in the direction the old woman was looking. She also remembered the Boulevard Raspail in better times.

Catherine took the Sèvres-Babylone Metro to Madeleine, conscious of the station's name and the agent she wished to find and made her way along Rue Tronchet, towards Boulevard

Haussmann. A child ahead of her threw a toy out of the pram which the mother didn't see. Catherine picked it up then looked into the pram at the baby. 'She's very sweet, Madame. How old is she?'

'Almost a year.' The child threw the toy from the pram again and as both women bent to pick it up, it gave Catherine the opportunity to get a better look at the man who she was sure was following her. He too had stopped and was casually looking into a shop window behind her. She had seen him before somewhere. The light brown coat and hat looked familiar.

She crossed the road into Boulevard Haussmann with the young mother and said goodbye to her before making her way further along the road. She stopped and looked in a shop window at a display of women's fashion. The man in the light brown coat walked past her. It was then she caught the reflection of another man across the road she felt she had also seen earlier. He was crouched over his shoe tying a lace. She used the window to search for other motionless men, then casually stepped inside the shop and went to one of the counters. Catherine took a woollen cardigan and placed it against her body, inspecting it in the mirror. The man in the light brown coat was also in the shop, looking through some women's silk scarves. Although their eyes did not meet, she saw him glance towards her. She now knew for certain she was being followed by at least two if not three others.

She took a dress from the rack and began to put Ted Peters' lessons into practice. In the changing room she sat to think through her movements. In her mind she retraced her steps back to the Boulevard Raspail. 'Think, think, think,' she whispered to herself. She had not seen anyone of their description close to the building she was visiting. They had obviously been inside one of the flats watching out for her, which meant they had expected her to be there. Then she remembered where she had seen them both, standing together thirty feet away as she spoke to the old woman, one lighting the other's cigarette. There were definitely only two of them. As Ted Peters had said, "once you know how many are following you, then you can begin to lose them."

She checked her Walther PPK and placed it back into the deep pocket of her coat, then left the changing room.

'How much is this?' she asked the sales assistant, then replaced the dress back on the rack saying it was too expensive.

Catherine left the shop. She considered the men were following her to see where she would lead them, otherwise they would have attempted to arrest her long ago. She eventually lost them in the crowded Gare St-Lazare, when she had disappeared into the women's lavatory. Inside one of the cubicles, she turned her coat inside out from grey to navy blue, removed her blonde wig, spectacles and the cotton wool in her cheeks and top lip. She then stuffed them all in a bag that she had folded up in her pocket and then left the lavatory looking a different woman. She passed the man in the light brown coat, who glanced up at her in a way any man would look at an attractive woman. Catherine doubled back alighting at the Opéra, where she walked into the busy street towards the Place de la Concorde.

In a café close to the Champs Elysées, she ordered a coffee and a cognac to settle her nerves. Her whole body began to shake and her hands trembled. The woman she had seen the previous day had obviously alerted the Gestapo, which confirmed the agent that had lived in her building had also been betrayed and captured. She would deal with her later.

Catherine's romantic idea of helping France rid itself of the Nazi tyranny vanished from her mind like a dream in waking. She could trust no one. She finished her coffee, convinced it was no longer safe to pursue her search for Madeleine. Now she would make a move on Hoffmann. He may have the answer.

Chapter **12**

The sound of Model's boots hammered across the polished wooden floor as the door slammed behind him. 'Those incompetent idiots from the Gestapo lost that woman,' he bellowed at Hoffmann. 'She gave them the slip at Gare St-Lazare. If it hadn't been for those heavy-handed Abwehr clots arresting that man in Boulevard Raspail, we would have caught her knocking on the door.'

'But she didn't and may not have done, Herr Obersturmbannführer. She may have been an innocent bystander.'

'She matched the description our informant gave us.'

'Madame Blanc was found dead this morning, Herr Obersturmbannführer. Shot in the heart and head. All the signs of a professional job...'

'What!' Model sat and put his face in his hands. It had been a stressful evening at home with the boy. Such a dear boy... why did he like Biarritz so much? Such a ghastly place... 'Any ideas?'

Hoffmann shrugged. He looked towards Model who caught his eye.

'What?'

'I instructed the Gestapo not to arrest that woman, on your advice, but to follow her.' When Model's eyes lifted, Hoffmann said, 'you said it would be better to follow and discover–'

'Shut up, Hoffmann. Strategies change according to the situation. Anyway, we had enough evidence. A woman fitting her description has been seen calling on other properties once lived in by SOE agents. That's no coincidence. They should have arrested her.'

'Surely it's a job for the French police. They can find her and arrest her for murder. We'll then have a legitimate reason for demanding her release into our custody.'

'This is our legitimacy,' Model said pointing to his SD badge. 'What can those French goons do? The Gestapo had her and lost her.'

'Perhaps they thought she would lead them to the wireless set.'

'They should let us do the thinking, Hoffmann.'

'But they have a point, Herr Obersturmbannführer.'

Model's lip curled as he eyed his young colleague. 'We no longer have her, that's the point, Obersturmführer.' He sat down and looked up at his assistant. 'A bird in the hand, Hoffmann is better than thinking of one on your cock. Now our bird has flown.'

'She may not be the wireless operator, a courier perhaps.'

'Stop quibbling, one will give us to the other!' Model's voice rang round the room. He poured himself some water and took a few sips of it, with a pill to calm the ache in his head. 'Are we anywhere near to locating this wireless? Has she been sending recently?'

Hoffmann's eyes avoided Model when he answered. 'The last location detected was somewhere in... in the 16th district, Herr Obersturmbannführer.'

'On our own doorstep!' Model's voice was deafening. He leaned towards Hoffmann and said through gritted teeth, 'In the Bois de Boulogne I expect. I imagine she had trouble stepping over all the fornicating soldiers of our glorious Reich, just to set the damn aerial up.'

'I've put tracking stations in the three areas she is sending from, Herr Obersturmbannführer. We'll soon have her.'

'She's making fools of us, Hoffmann.' Model looked at his watch. 'I'm away tomorrow. Give this your priority.'

'Of course, Herr Obersturmbannführer.'

Model walked to the door and stopped at Corporal Hock's desk. 'Have you found a replacement typist yet, Obersturmführer?'

'No, Herr Obersturmbannführer, but headquarters has confirmed we can use a French woman if she speaks German and is thoroughly vetted.'

'I've already given you permission to do that, Hoffmann. There was no need to alert headquarters of our shortcomings. Why am I surrounded by incompetent fools? Just get on and find a bloody typist. I want to see her arse planted firmly on that empty chair in this office when I return.'

'I'll give it priority.'

'No you won't, Obersturmführer. You'll give that woman the Gestapo lost priority. Get Corporal Hock to find a bloody typist.'

After Model left, Hoffmann returned to Corporal Hock's office and looked at the great pile of paperwork in the in-tray, and more piled on another desk. He lit a cigarette and walked over to the window where Avenue Foch was patterned in the shadow from moving clouds. He watched a young woman crossing the road pushing a pram. Holding onto her coat was an older child. Hoffmann drew on his cigarette listening to the tapping of Hock's typewriter, the ding of the bell and the slide of the carriage return after each line of type. The mother had now stopped and was slapping the small child's leg, like a man on a cart whipping his horse to make it walk faster. Helga's face came to his mind. Soon she would give birth to their first child then she would join him in Paris. 'Helga,' he whispered and shook his head. He knew he had made a mistake with Helga and must now pay the consequences of it. She was a reasonably attractive woman, certainly no beauty like her sister and not so much fun. Helga had a docile personality. At parties she would cling to him, offering little conversation to their group, yet jealous of other women who clung to his words or laughed at his stories. When he first met her, he was impressed that her father was a general, so he paid her some attention. He was a little drunk and slept with her that night. He tried to avoid her after that. Hoffmann closed his eyes when he remembered Helga coming to see him two months later with the news that she was pregnant. He sighed. For him it had been a one night stand, it was her sister Julia he wanted.

'Are you any nearer to finding Anna-Marie's replacement, Corporal Hock?' Hoffmann asked without turning to face him.

Hock sprang to his feet. 'No, Herr Obersturmführer. The French don't want to work here.'

Hoffmann, whose calm nature was rarely rattled, frowned. 'Then your leave will be cancelled so you can clear the backlog. I want it finished before Obersturmbannführer von Model returns from his leave.'

Hock's face dropped. He had planned on going home to Germany to see his mother. 'Yes, Herr Obersturmführer.'

Hoffmann turned to Hock and motioned him to sit. Hock was a thin young man with a large Adam's apple, fair hair and a crooked nose, upon which sat a pair of metal-framed glasses; a runt suited to be nothing but a clerk.

Encouraged by the sudden sunlight lighting up Avenue Foch, Hoffmann decided to stroll over to the Saint-Germain-des-Prés district in the 6th arrondissement, where the Abwehr had their offices in the Hotel Lutetia. They may have a girl they could spare for a couple of weeks until he found a permanent replacement.

Hoffmann left the office and took in a breath of fresh air. On a fine day, as it was now turning out to be, it was a pleasant walk from his office. He strolled across the Pont d'Iéna and past the Eiffel Tower, where the whores pranced around like second-rate fashion models, knowing that off duty soldiers came searching for a moment of *amour*. Hoffmann liked the south bank of Paris; the universities near the Jardin du Luxembourg reminded him of the time he was a student. He remembered Catherine, the beautiful French girl from Amiens and wondered what had become of her. He felt some guilt about the way he had deflowered her, but what did it matter? Her beauty had driven him to distraction and he could think of nothing else but having her. He was about to leave Paris and would never see her again, so what did it matter if he played the game by foul means. He remembered her smile. Now some other man will be enjoying her, not the sleeping beauty he had, but aroused and actively involved in her bed.

'*Tu es ravissante ma chérie,*' he said and was greeted with smiles from a Parisian whore who thought the words were meant for her.

Chapter 13

Catherine was without her disguise when she left the flat in the Rue de Mont-Louis. She made her way past the Cimetière du Père Lachaise a few streets away. She cycled past the cemetery with her wireless set strapped to the rack of her bicycle. She avoided the busy Boulevard de Charonne and made her way towards the Bois de Vincennes, a great wooded area south-east of the city. There she could lose herself in the woods to set up her wireless and send an urgent message to London. She passed a group of German soldiers, wrapped in their greatcoats, drinking outside one of the pavement cafés. They all looked up and whistled as she passed. After being followed from the Boulevard Raspail she knew she had to be careful in that part of Paris, for the Gestapo must have now circulated the picture of the bespectacled blonde; yet now as herself, she was attracting unwanted attention from German soldiers, as Susan predicted she would.

The message she sent to London was important, but dangerously long. The response she received was short ... *Expect a mongoose to call*. She acknowledged, packed away the aerial and placed the suitcase with the wireless set back on the rack of her bicycle. She then set off for the safe house back in the Rue de Mont-Louis.

She left the wood and cycled towards Avenue Daumesnil, passing a goods van driven by a German soldier racing towards the direction of the wood. Behind the van was a German army lorry full of troops. Catherine realised the van was a disguised wireless tracking vehicle. They had obviously been in the area and picked up her signal. Further along the road a barrier was quickly being erected. A German soldier with a Schmeisser submachine gun raised his hand for her to stop.

'Hello Corporal,' Catherine said in German, 'what are you up to?' Her eyes brightened with a flirtatious smile.

At first the soldier was taken aback by hearing his native tongue. 'It's only temporary.' He glanced at the suitcase strapped to her bicycle. 'Going away?'

'Returning.' Her smile broadened. 'Back to work tomorrow,' she said with a shrug.

He glanced over his shoulder at the group of soldiers behind him. 'Well, get on your way before my sergeant comes over and starts throwing his weight about. Auf Wiedersehen,' he said with a wink. She returned his smile and began to casually pedal away, her eyes fixed on the road ahead.

Back at the flat, Catherine stored away the wireless and had a bath. After, she decided to go for a walk round the Cimetière du Père Lachaise before it was closed to visitors for the night. When she arrived there, memories poured back into her mind. Ludwig Hoffmann was one of her group searching out the great names of art, music and literature now buried in various divisions of the cemetery: Oscar Wilde, Honoré de Balzac, Molière, Bizet, Chopin and Amedeo Modigliani. Hoffmann and she had been seeing each other over a few months for their German conversation outings and this visit to the cemetery was meant to be one of them. He had attempted to kiss her beside Marcel Proust's grave. It was the first time he had made any sexual move towards her. She had expected it because his eyes and flirtatious chatter had long given away what was on his mind. Hoffmann was not happy when she refused his advances. She explained to him that she did not want that kind of relationship with him. Like most men spurned, he sulked. Later he tried again against the great Monument Aux Morts. He said that he had growing feelings for her. Catherine knew exactly what was growing and again she refused, protesting this was a sacred place, and no place to do what he had in mind. She was saved from further advances by one of the girls dragging her away to see the last resting place of Honoré de Balzac, whose *Le Vicaire des Ardennes* was on their reading list. Later he apologized, saying he was overwhelmed by the scent of her whenever she was close to him. Catherine was not flattered by his words and knew his apology was more likely to be a tactical withdrawal before attempting another assault, which later proved to be right. Although she controlled her features, her forehead became bright pink and her eyes opened very wide. She unclenched her fists and took a deep breath. He had taken his revenge on her in the most villainous way.

After an hour walking round the cemetery she returned to the hotel where she was staying and read for a while. Later in her bed, she laid thinking of the message she had received, *expect a mongoose.* 'A mongoose,' she whispered to the moonlit ceiling. 'Now what's that all about?'

The following day, Catherine moved the radio back to another flat, in Rue de la Faisanderie. It was a hundred yards from Avenue Foch where she could keep an eye on number 84. Susan had told her that Hoffmann and Model were the main interrogators there, so Hoffmann may have interrogated Madeleine if she had been captured and held there. It was now time to make her move and place her head into the lion's mouth.

*

Catherine watched Hoffmann standing at the gate to the building, adjusting his cap. He returned the salute from two soldiers passing him. She watched him cross the road without looking, as if traffic would make way for him. As he made his way toward the Victor Hugo Metro station, Catherine was invisibly following him. The Avenue Raymond Poincaré was busy with people, so it was easy to blend in with the crowd. By the time they reached the Palais de Chaillot where Gustave Eiffel's creation dominated the landscape across the Seine, Catherine was beginning to wonder where he was heading, when she had the distinct feeling she too was being followed. She abandoned Hoffmann and slipped down the École Militaire Metro, boarded a train to Concorde, furtively examining all around her, and then changed trains for Gare de Lyon. There she could mingle in with the throng of people. Then she returned to the 6th arrondissement and the third of the safe houses near the Jardin du Luxembourg. Catherine found a convenient place to observe without being seen. She could see no one suspicious or recognise anyone she had glimpsed before, but the feeling that she had of being followed felt very real and would not leave her.

*

At seven in the morning, Hoffmann washed and shaved. His failure to borrow a typist from the Abwehr, when he went to see them the previous day, annoyed him. He wiped the residual soap from his face and studied his work. Model was getting increasingly worked up about the paperwork, although Hoffmann knew it was piling up and reports needed to be ready for Berlin. When he was dressed, he lit a cigarette and walked from his quarters, out into his office, to the window that looked across the Avenue Foch. The street was deserted, other than guards outside various buildings commandeered by the Third Reich. All he seemed to do these days was stare out from his gilded cage and, as elegant as the Avenue Foch was, he wanted to escape and see a little of the Paris he knew. He had a sudden urge to go to the Place de Clichy for coffee, something his group from the Sorbonne often did.

When Hock arrived for work, Hoffmann left the office. Although there was a chill in the air, the sun shone. He sat outside at a café table drinking coffee and smoking a cigarette. It was difficult to believe that his fellow countrymen were dying in their thousands at Salerno, Taranto and in the Ukraine, yet here in Paris the birds sang and one could watch the women stroll past while enjoying a cigarette. It was the perfect place to spend the war. He ordered a cognac and studied the central monument of the square, as he used to with Catherine when they came here and practiced her German. He could hear her voice in his head explaining what the statue in the centre of the square stood for. As he drew on his cigarette, it occurred to him this was the second time in as many days that he had thought of her. Perhaps, he considered, it was because he was now seeing parts of Paris he once shared with her. After drinking the cognac he paid his bill and was about to leave when his eye caught a young woman across the square. His body stiffened when he recognised Catherine, as if thinking of her magically made her appear. Mesmerized, he watched her searching in her handbag for something.

He quickly made his way across the road towards the café opposite. 'Catherine!' he gasped. 'I can't believe it's you.'

Catherine saw a grinning, almost comical face in front of her. She had played it beautifully. He didn't suspect a thing.

'I was only thinking of you seconds ago, literally seconds ago,' he laughed, his voice had risen an octave, 'and yesterday on my way to Boulevard Raspail. This is incredible.'

So that's where he was off to, she thought, to see his Abwehr chums at the Hotel Lutetia. She pushed past him, her step quickening when he called after her. She turned the corner and stopped. She faced eyes that were alive with joy at seeing her. The smile was just as charming Catherine thought, set in the handsome, intelligent face she once knew.

'It's me...' he said removing his hat, 'Ludwig.'

'I know who you are. What do you want?' she said in German.

'What do I want?' he gasped. 'What do I want?' His voice rose a little then quietened, his eyes darted about him. 'You don't even look surprised to see me.'

'I *wasn't* surprised to see you *Herr Obersturmführer*, I see you every day in every German soldier in France, and you know perfectly well why I want to escape from you, so go away. Just leave me alone,' and she pushed past him again. Catherine strode rapidly along Rue de Palme and was stopped by Hoffmann outside a small hotel that had an equally small café next door to it. 'Take your hands off me!'

To anyone passing they appeared to be a couple of Teutonic lovers reduced to quarrelling in a shop doorway. 'Catherine, calm down. Let's have a drink.'

'Do you really expect me to drink alcohol with you?' Her eyes bore into his. 'You had what you wanted from me, now just leave me alone.'

'Please Catherine, just one drink, let me explain. You wouldn't listen at the time. Just hear me out. Have one drink with me, for old time's sake.'

'Before you barbarians invaded our country, those times do you mean?'

'A coffee then, ten minutes of your time and I will leave you alone, I promise, Catherine.'

She stood breathing deeply. Any drama school in the world would enrol her after this. After a moment's silence, her eyes turned to his. 'Ten minutes and only coffee...'

*

Ten minutes became an hour.

'I was in Amiens,' Hoffmann said, 'so I called at your house. Sylvie, you see, I remember her name... she told me you had moved away.' When he saw the expression on Catherine's face he said, 'I was discreet. I went in the evening and wore civilian clothes,' he lied. 'She invited me in and we had a drink and a chat, just like old times.'

'Yet they are not like old times, so don't let's fool each other and what's more, you had no right to go there. I'm surprised you even remembered the address.'

'I found it in the university records. Once I was close to the cathedral I remembered where the house was. Anyway, it all came back to me.' His features tightened. 'I went because I wanted to see you again. I still feel something for you, Catherine,' he said placing his hand on his heart. 'I've always felt it.'

'If you loved me,' she said softly, 'you wouldn't have raped me then boasted to all my friends that I gave myself freely.'

'It wasn't rape, Catherine. We were both drunk. You cannot remember what happened. I think you felt ashamed–'

'I never saw you again, Ludwig. You disappeared without a word, like some rogue in the middle of the night. You may have left me with a child. Do you know what we do to women with German children? I don't think you even cared if you had made me pregnant.' When she looked into his eyes they still showed no guilt. 'Anyway, I'm married now.'

'Married...' He suddenly looked crestfallen.

'I may have to return to Lyon next week.'

'No! I mean, why?'

'I have a husband there, that's why. I came here to find work and there are no vacancies, even for a graduate of the Sorbonne.'

'What does your husband do?'

'What do you care what he does?' she said sharply. 'It's me we're talking about, not my husband.' There was silence between them. He laid his hand on hers. 'Don't,' she said. 'If you really want to know, he teaches at the lycée.'

'A teacher! *You* and a schoolteacher. My God! I cannot believe it. With your beauty you could have had anyone.'

'I didn't want anyone, I wanted Dominique. We met at the lycée. He was kind to me.'

'Kind! You marry a teacher because he was kind to you. I was kind to you. I always helped you. I cared for you. I loved you.'

'You raped me.'

Neither said anything for a full minute. Both sat controlling their breathing. After a short silence Catherine looked at him. 'Surely you must realize a girl of twenty-three is likely to be married. What about you, Ludwig, are you married?'

Hoffmann knew Helga wouldn't be in Paris for another two months at least, maybe three, which would give him the time to try his luck again with Catherine. 'No, I'm not married,' he lied. 'When do you intend to return to your schoolteacher?'

'I have enough money to stay another week.'

'Why isn't he with you?'

'He will join me if I secure a teaching post.'

84

He caught her eyes on the pistol holder on his waist belt. He smiled, 'are you afraid of guns?'

'Yes, is it loaded?'

'Of course.' He removed it from his holster and showed it to Catherine. 'Beautiful, isn't it... A Walther KK. German of course. Here, Catherine. Hold it.'

'No.'

'I'm showing you how much I trust you. Take it. Shoot me with it. Show me how much you hate me,' he laughed, unknowing that in her deep coat pocket she carried the same weapon. 'So you won't shoot me. Good, you have forgiven me. So stay in Paris. I will give you some money,' he said, 'even work for a couple of months if you want it, so at least you'll be earning while looking for a teaching post.'

'Doing what?'

'Typing, you will be working in an elegant building along Avenue Foch and be paid well.'

Catherine could hardly contain her excitement. She looked into his eyes and shook her head. 'Thank you, but I'm a teacher not a typist.'

'But you can type. I've seen you type.'

She shrugged. 'I'm rusty.'

He felt hope. His eyes brightened and he began to postulate on the importance of the position he was offering. He offered her a salary figure, which Catherine knew was more than a typist would normally earn, 'and you will receive special privileges for working for the Reich.'

'You mean I will eat while others starve?'

He smiled. 'I don't think it has come to that. Where are you staying?'

'I'm not telling you that.'

'I could find out.'

'So now you wish to spy on me.'

'No, of course not, just think about it. If you would like the job, come to 84 Avenue Foch tomorrow at ten. Give it a try, Catherine. If you don't like it then leave. I will understand.'

'I'll think about it.'

'Please Catherine, take the job. Come tomorrow and have dinner with me in the evening. I will try to make it up to you for my drunken behaviour. I was a student, irresponsible. Please, forgive me.'

When Catherine arrived back at the hotel, she went straight to the bathroom and ran a bath. His company made her feel dirty. She lay in the hot water going through the latter part of their conversation, looking for any weaknesses in her story. Catherine smiled; he was so intent on sleeping with her he didn't suspect a thing.

Chapter 14

After her bath, she glanced at the clock. She had made arrangements for her next transmission to be at 1800, which, she thought, would allow Elizabeth a night out if she wanted it. She took her wireless set with her to the Jardin du Luxembourg and, in the deep grey shadows, set it up. During her transmission, a German soldier appeared from the other side of a monument. He was fastening the buttons to the front of his uniform trousers, with him was a woman. Catherine realised she had interrupted an intimate moment. With her earphones on she hadn't heard a thing and cursed herself for not checking the area more thoroughly.

'What are you doing?' the soldier said in German. He collapsed and lay lifeless on the ground with two shots in him. Catherine removed the headphones and looked at the woman. She shrank away with outstretched arms, begging in French that she was only earning some money to feed her children. The silencer on Catherine's PPK gave two muffled sounds. She fell close to the German soldier's body. Catherine laid her weapon beside her, completed the message and waited for a response. Panhanagan had been wrong; it was easy to kill in cold blood. Now she had killed four; the pervert in the lavatories, two Frenchwomen and a German soldier. The soldier might bring problems with reprisals. After packing away the aerial into the suitcase she moved to the two lifeless bodies. Looking around her she saw no movement; it was silent apart from a light wind blowing through the last leaves of the deciduous trees. Catherine pulled the woman's knickers down, so they hung off one of her ankles and undid the buttons on the soldier's trousers, then she hurriedly left the park.

Strolling down the road towards the Boulevard Raspail, she said *bon soir* in response to the friendly greeting from two passing policemen. When she looked back at them over her shoulder, they returned her smile and gave her a salute.

Back at her hotel, she cleaned her weapon and replaced the four rounds of ammunition she had discharged, something Panhanagan had drilled into her to do. When she caught sight of herself in the mirror she asked 'What's happening to you?'

*

At nine-thirty the next morning, Catherine left the hotel for Avenue Foch. Hoffmann was waiting for her at the front gate to number eighty-four, confident she would come. He looked pleased with himself. 'I knew you would come. See, I waited for you.'

She drew back from him when he went to kiss her. 'Ludwig,' she whispered. 'Please don't do that. I'm a married woman.'

'Catherine,' he said speaking German, 'I was trying to be friendly, nothing more.' Hoffmann led her into the building and up a flight of marble stairs; his boots echoing round the hall. 'Two good friends of mine you will soon meet work on this floor. I'm on the fourth floor.' As they entered the room a corporal clerk jumped to attention.

'When is Obersturmbannführer von Model back, Corporal?'

'Next Monday, Herr Obersturmführer.'

'This is Madame Régnier. She's agreed to help turn that mountain of typing,' Hoffman said, pointing at the pile of files on Hock's desk, 'into a molehill. Madame Régnier's German is excellent Corporal, so you'll have no problems communicating with her.'

Corporal Hock returned Catherine's smile, then he followed her with his eyes as she was ushered into Model's office. It was a large, sumptuous room, too grand for an SS counter-intelligence officer. Suspended from a high ceiling hung a magnificent chandelier, its crystal glass glittering like pinpricks of light in the great dark dome at night. Huge windows lit up the room during the day, their tapestry furnishings matching the seats and sofas. The polished parquet eventually led to a large desk, placed at the furthest point from the door, giving its occupier an air of majesty. Impressive paintings in gilt frames adorned the walls. They showed colourful Parisian dandies and their ladies in velvet and silk, rosy cheeks and ivory breasts, not yet the victims of Robespierre, another *dictateur sanguinaire*, like Hitler, whose portrait hung on the wall behind the desk. Hitler's hand was on his hip in a haughty pose, his demeanour one of arrogance, his menacing eyes reaching across the room towards Catherine. She glanced round the room with a disinterested air, unlike Hoffmann who was swallowed up by its magnificence.

Catherine wondered if she ought to be impressed and muttered some words to please him. 'Very nice,' she said in German.

'With your grasp of German,' he said, 'is that all you can say? Catherine, it's magnificent.' He was full of reptilian charm. 'Hock doesn't speak French, so we can talk without him earwigging. I'm in another room next door to this office, not so grand, but still magnificent. My private quarters are through there.' Their eyes met. Back in Hock's office Hoffmann said in German, 'Corporal Hock will let you know what you have to do.' Catherine looked across the room and caught Hock's shy smile. 'I'm sorry Catherine, I can't stay. I have an unexpected meeting next door, so I will leave you in the capable hands of Corporal Hock.'

'You'll be sorting out paperwork mostly. As you can see, there's a lot of it,' Hock said.

'What do you do?' she asked Hoffmann in French.

'I use my language skills, mainly questioning troublemakers working for the British, those that make life difficult for the law-abiding French.'

'Is your English good?'

He smiled. 'Remember the English film we went to see?'

'The Thirty-Nine Steps.'

'You have a wonderful memory, Catherine. I did not have to read the subtitles, while you complained and were irritated by them because you couldn't concentrate on the story, so you refused to go and see another English speaking film with me. Do you remember that?' Catherine avoided his eyes when they penetrated hers. 'Model, my boss, speaks English as if he were a native of that country; four years at Harrow and all those years living in English aristocratic homes, shooting, fishing. They stick together these aristocrats. He likes to come and talk with the prisoners about England, as if it were his home rather than Germany. Model is a snob and a queer like the English aristocrats.'

'Do you know any English aristocrats?'

'No, I don't.'

'Then how can you judge the English so readily? Just because a German aristocrat is homosexual, that doesn't mean English aristocrats are too. You should know better than to make a generalization like that.'

'Ah, my sweet Catherine... still the argumentative student, I see.'

'Ludwig, I'll work here on one condition.'

'And what is it?'

'Answer me this, I've been told you beat confessions out of women. Is that true?'

There was irritation in his voice when he said, 'I have never beaten any woman. I am not the Gestapo. Not all Germans are bad, Catherine. We are the people of Beethoven, Goethe...'

'Aren't the Gestapo also the people of Beethoven, Goethe?'

'Please do not compare me to those thugs.'

Catherine was taken aback by his sudden anger. 'You still have the SS emblem on your lapel. The French regard them as thugs too.'

His voice lowered and the smile returned. 'Well, I'm not and you're under my protection. You will never hear any screams from prisoners in this building. I can assure you.'

She smiled in a flirtatious way. 'Prisoners... do you have dungeons here?'

He laughed. 'Quite the opposite; they occupy the top floor, very comfortable accommodation. I'll show you. Here, through my quarters.'

Catherine followed Hoffmann through his quarters to a small frail-looking wooden staircase to the top floor. The fifth floor consisted of seven former servant's rooms; small, poorly lit and now converted into cells. 'See, no blood on the walls or floor. No chains. Comfortable seats, soft beds, blankets, pillows, books to read, a bathroom and two lavatories.'

'Yet no prisoners...'

'The last has only just left. We only interview them here, keep them for a few days, a week, sometimes longer, until we are satisfied with the information they give us. When they leave here they go to prison like any other criminal, to keep them from making further mischief.'

'Should you be telling me this?'

'It's not a state secret. Occupation of a country brings fear, fear of the unknown. France has laws for its citizens as we do in Germany. It's no different in war. Have you seen how our soldiers behave in Paris?'

'Yes, on the whole I have found them very polite.'

What Hoffmann had told her sounded so innocent. Catherine began to wonder if the charm was a mask to hide the monster he was or may be. She felt that she hardly knew him, the man who had once been a friend. As they walked through his quarters, on

90

their way back to the office, he stopped her and pressed her against the wall. He ran his lips over her neck. She closed her eyes. 'Ludwig, please don't otherwise I shall leave.'

'I want you. I've dreamed of you being in my arms again and now you are.' His hand went to her breast. She made no attempt to remove it. 'I can feel your heartbeat. It's pumping with passion.'

'For my husband.'

'In the biblical sense I'm your husband.' His hands moved over her breasts, down the curves of her hips, then clasped the cheeks of her bottom. When his hand moved to the front, between her legs, she gripped his wrist. He was amazed by the power of her grip.

'That hurts.'

'Then stop.'

He let go of her, held his wrist and stretched his fingers. 'For one so slim and fragile you have a great deal of strength, Catherine.' He straightened his uniform and adjusted his tie. 'I have to go. Don't forget our dinner date tonight.'

She looked into his eyes with a hint of a smile. 'As long as you remember that I'm a married woman, Ludwig.'

'Corporal Hock,' Hoffmann said emerging from his office. 'Please make Frau Régnier comfortable and show her what needs to be done.'

Catherine met Hock's eyes. Hoffmann noticed the cartilage move in Hock's throat, an uncontrolled movement from a young man with no experience of women and ill at ease in the presence of a beautiful one. Hoffmann looked at Hock with contempt, knowing he would be dreaming of having her, a dream as far from reality as travelling to the moon. He turned to Catherine and told her he was sorry to desert her so soon. 'Duty calls,' and added that he hoped that he would be through by luncheon.

When Hoffmann left, Corporal Hock swallowed again and blushed. 'Your German is very good, Frau Régnier.'

Her eyes rose to his. The colour in his cheeks deepened. Catherine sensed she could make use of this young man's obvious infatuation for her. 'Thank you,' she said. 'You're very kind.'

'You put me to shame. I hardly speak a word of French. I learnt some English at school, but I cannot speak it well,' he said. 'Do you speak any English?'

'Not a word.'

He hadn't the confidence to hold her eyes and spoke to her shoes. 'The typing is mostly mundane reports, nothing sensitive; only I deal with that.'

When Hock's eyes rose she offered him a flirtatious smile, which turned his cheeks red again. 'You must have an important job.'

'Oh, I just type things.'

'Yes, but important things.'

'I suppose they are,' he said growing half an inch.

'I'm sorry you have been lumbered with me. Obersturmführer Hoffmann told me he was going to be here to show me what to do.'

'He had to go next door to see the Gestapo. A German soldier was murdered in the Jardin du Luxembourg last night.'

'Was it the Maquis?'

'We don't think so. That is, Obersturmführer Hoffmann doesn't think so. He thinks it's either a crime of passion, as you French say, or a British—' He stopped himself saying agent. He realised this was sensitive information and although Hoffmann had employed Catherine himself, he didn't know how far to trust her. Hock laughed and said, 'I heard the woman found dead with the soldier had her, you know,' he said gesturing with his hands, 'her Schlüpfer, down round her ankles.'

'Then surely it was a crime of passion.'

'The Gestapo say it has all the signs of a professional killer. A shot in the heart, one in the head. The killer was no amateur.'

Killer! The word hit Catherine for the first time. She was no different than Panhanagan. She lowered her eyes, like a schoolgirl flirting with a Prefect. 'You're well informed. I suppose, being a corporal, you need to know these things.'

Hock crimsoned when Catherine caught his eyes on her breasts. 'You sit here and I sit over there.' He went to his desk, took a pile of papers from it and gave them to Catherine. 'Start with these, see how you get on. I hope you can read these notes. I made them in a hurry. Just copy them out.'

'I'm a little rusty.'

'You'll soon get the hang of it.'

*

At lunchtime, Corporal Hock received a message to say that Hoffmann would not be back until four. Catherine had been at it non-stop and had already completed a considerable amount of work. Hock could suddenly see his leave to Germany restored. He asked her if she would like to join him at the café along Rue la Sueur for lunch. She shrugged and said she had nothing else planned. The café was one that few Germans went to. Because she was speaking German to Hock, she did not receive the accusing eyes from other women in the room or the gestures of hate from the men.

'So where's your husband if you don't mind me asking, Frau Régnier?'

'In Lyon,' Catherine replied taking a sip of coffee.

'Don't you miss him?'

She looked Hock in the eyes and said, 'Can you keep a confidence?'

Hock leaned forward. 'Yes, of course.'

'Please don't tell the Obersturmführer this, but I'm divorcing my husband. I've moved to Paris to get away from him.' Light came into Hock's eyes. She had shared an intimate secret with him; she trusted him and not Hoffmann. He was like a puppy staring at a bone in its master's hand. Catherine saw his reaction and gave him a shy smile. 'Do you have a sweetheart?'

He swallowed. 'Not at the moment. I'm too busy here to, you know, to meet anyone.'

*

After the third day of Catherine's employment, Hoffmann was happy with the amount of work she had completed, which would justify her appointment when Model returned. What didn't please Hoffmann was his extra workload during Model's absence and therefore he spent little time with Catherine during the day and at night she skilfully avoided him. The only pleasure of her company was dinner the first day of her employment. After, he escorted her back to her cheap hotel. 'Let me see your room.'

'I'll show it to you, but don't get any ideas.' Once he was in the room, he took hold of her and attempted to kiss her. 'I'm not going to sleep with you, Ludwig.'

'Then why have you let me come up here?'

She shrugged. 'I was testing you. I thought I could trust you.'

He let her go. 'You can, but it is very difficult for me. You know how much I want you.'

She couldn't look into his eyes. 'Had you been patient with me before, I might have given myself to you. I am quite passionate when aroused. There was no need to have raped me.'

'I didn't rape you. You consented. You just don't remember because you had drunk too much.' Hoffmann put a hand to her breast and squeezed it. 'I think you just choose to forget.'

'Stop it, Ludwig. If you behave yourself you might get a second chance, but not tonight, I'm tired.'

She let him kiss her goodnight. After he left, Catherine went straight to the bathroom and brushed her teeth. Then she ran a bath and scrubbed herself from head to toe. That night she slept badly.

*

Corporal Hock began feeling less nervous of Catherine and when he made a clumsy attempt to date her, she smiled politely and said it would be difficult because Obersturmführer Hoffmann had warned her that her presence in the office should remain strictly professional.

Hock's shoulders dropped. 'I know why. I've seen the way he looks at you.'

'And he has seen the way *you* look at me. You must be careful, Wilhelm.'

His face lit up when she used his name. 'I received a message that when Model returns to Paris, Hoffmann has to leave and attend one of Himmler's conferences, so we won't have him on our backs for a bit.' *And I won't have him trying to get me on mine,* Catherine thought with relief. 'Model has to continually slip away to meetings, or to visit his boyfriend in Rue de Goujon, where he has set him up in a flat which he confiscated from some Jews. He has no idea that I know that. I know a lot more than they think,' which confirmed Catherine's initial feelings of getting closer to Hock, particularly now she'd learned that Hoffmann had to leave for Berlin. 'With Hoffmann out of the way, perhaps you and I...'

She gave him a coy smile. 'Perhaps...'

When Catherine finished work, she said goodbye to Hock outside the building and made her way to Rue de Mont-Louis, the safe house close to the Père Lachaise cemetery. She began to feel uneasy, again sensing she was being followed. She went through her normal safety checks; stopping to look in windows, turning back on herself, and getting on a metro then changing at the next stop. She finished the last part of her journey on the bus, walked past the flat and lingered around some shops looking in a few windows. When she felt satisfied that it was safe to do so, she made her way back to the flat.

Catherine was dressed in a dressing gown, drying her hair after a shower, when she saw an envelope slide under the front door. With her Walther PPK in her hand, she approached the door and looked down at *Mongoose* written on the envelope. It was the contact Greene had warned her to expect. She went through all of the pre-arranged safety checks, tapped twice on her side of the door and the reply came. When she opened the door, she caught her breath.

'Panhanagan!'

Chapter **15**

'Happy to see me,' Panhanagan said in French as he entered the flat. He glanced down at the weapon in her hand and told her to put the safety catch back on.

'Was it you following me?'

'Put the kettle on. I'm busting for a cuppa.'

'Why have they sent you?'

'Because you need a baby-sitter and I'm the only mug who speaks the lingo.'

They walked into the kitchen and she pointed at the table. 'There's the kettle.'

'I thought you toffs knew how to treat a guest.'

'Is that how you see yourself?' Catherine watched Panhanagan fill the kettle and light the gas. 'I didn't spot you, you know.'

'You gave me the run-around. Peters taught you well.'

'You weren't on the bus.'

'I gave up when you climbed onto it. It was academic anyway because I knew where you were going. I know where you're staying and all the three safe houses you have. I've been watching you for almost a week. Thought it time to say hello.'

'Then why didn't you make contact sooner?'

'I wanted to know if anyone else was following you. So who's the runt you're walking out with?'

Catherine smiled at Panhanagan's description of Hock. 'That's Corporal Hock. I shall be working on him for the information I need. He shouldn't be difficult to handle. So, why are you here, Panhanagan?'

'After your fun with the Gestapo following you, it was considered by our betters... or at least *my* betters,' he said glancing at her, 'that you are too important to be left to fend for yourself, so like it or not, here I am, Lady Somerville. Actually, I prefer plain old Nora.'

Catherine smiled at his attempt at a posh accent. 'Lady Somerville is how one refers to my mother. I'm Lady Catherine.' Catherine's smile stretched her lips. She was no longer alone and surprisingly, after the initial shock of seeing him, she was pleased Panhanagan was there. 'Where have you been staying?'

'In any of the safe houses you vacate. It's probably best you move out of that grubby little hotel and stay with me. That way I can keep a closer eye on you.'

'I bet,' Catherine said. 'Cast your mind back to that kick in the balls. Your room will be the one there,' she said pointing, 'with the single bed. Mine's next door. It has a lock on the door, which I intend to use at night and I sleep with my Walther PPK.'

'You still fancy yourself then?'

Catherine smiled at his response. 'Are you hungry?'

'Yes.'

'I know a little place tucked away. The treat's on His Majesty's Government.'

'Our first date–'

'And there'll be no kiss goodnight, Panhanagan.' She went and got her coat from the peg in the hall and called out, 'I meant to tell you at Mountfields, but we got distracted. Your French accent is very good.'

Panhanagan removed his weapon from his jacket and hung the jacket over a chair. 'When you send your next signal you have to report I've made contact.'

'Who gave you your codename?'

'Sub Lieutenant Susan bloody Harcourt-Williams. That one had us all fooled.'

'She certainly did,' Catherine replied, a little uncomfortably.

'She sends her love by the way...'

It wasn't what he said that annoyed Catherine, but the way he looked at her after he had spoken the words. Her eyes burned into his. 'It doesn't take you long, does it Panhanagan? If we are to get along here you had better watch your mouth.'

He shrugged. 'Whatever. When are you due to call in?'

'Tomorrow and now you can put your coat back on. The restaurant's ten minutes from here.'

*

The following day, Catherine collected some of her clothes from the hotel after work and took them to the flat in the 20th arrondissement, where she and Panhanagan had now taken up residence. She continued to make an appearance at the hotel, leave then return in the morning before work when the night porter had finished his shift, to give the appearance that she had stayed the night. It was tedious, but necessary for her security.

After work Catherine left for the safe house at Rue de la Faisanderie where Panhanagan had taken the wireless set during the day. She needed to send a message to London, aware that the wireless direction vans were close by. She calculated that she could get her message out before they had a chance to pick up any signal. Catherine closed the curtains, went to the bedroom and coded up a message. She kept it short by sending in three parts at ten minute intervals, which would give the Germans no time to find a bearing. Hearing the rapid dit-dit-dah of the reply made her feel happy. It was Elizabeth's voice she could hear not the electronic sound coming through her headphones.

Catherine decoded the message and put the wireless set away, she turned off the lights and looked out of the bedroom for Panhanagan's signal that she was safe to leave. Then Panhanagan followed her to the hotel. She made a point of being seen by the staff and went to her room. She lay on the bed for half an hour wondering how she could manipulate Hock. Catherine knew she needed to speed things up and decided to make her move on him the following day. She left the hotel and made her way to the safe house across Paris, in the 20th district. A key turned in the door five minutes later.

After they had eaten, and returned from a short walk, Catherine said, 'I'm off to bed. Model is back tomorrow and I have to meet him at nine.' She woke at six-thirty. After a shower, she dressed and added a little perfume.

When she walked into the kitchen, Panhanagan was cleaning his weapon; applying light oil to all the moving parts then pulling an oily cloth through the barrel. He looked up. She was wearing a black dress which clung to her body. It buttoned up at the back and was low in the front, her cleavage partly covered by a white beaded necklace. She had, until today, been wearing flat shoes. Now she wore high heels. Her eyes glowed after a good night's sleep. 'What do you think? Is it over the top?'

'I'm sure it will achieve what you want it to.'

She glanced at him. When he arrived at her flat she was determined to be friendly with him, but Panhanagan was indifferent to her. His weapon seemed more important. She left the room and within a few minutes returned wearing her coat. 'Corporal Hock is the weak link in that office. Because of him, I know they have three wireless direction finding vans on standby in the areas I send from, this being one of them. I've risked sending messages broken into threes as Holloway suggested, but even that is becoming dangerous. I'll have to move around more and keep the messages even shorter.'

'What makes you think Hock will give you any information?'

'He wants to get into my knickers. You men are all alike.' Panhanagan said nothing. He was now polishing rounds of ammunition. 'I'll let Hock think he has a chance. He is already becoming bolder.' Panhanagan still said nothing. 'There's little point following me to Avenue Foch. I have a pass and you know where I shall be.' She left her PPK on the table.

'When did you last clean that?'

'Is that all that ever interests you, Panhanagan? Haven't you got anything better to do?'

'Apart from following you around Paris, no...'

'Well, I'm off.' Catherine waited for a response. 'No *good luck* or anything?' She stood looking at him, but he didn't look up. The door slammed behind her. Panhanagan went to the window and watched her turn the corner. He slipped his weapon into his concealed holster and decided he would shadow her anyway. As he had said, what else had he to do other than clean his weapon and play nursemaid to some toff? His face broke into a smile. 'But you're a tough little toff, Lady Catherine Davina Roberta Somerville.'

*

Model finished writing, then leaned back in his chair and looked up at Hoffmann. 'Has she had security clearance?'

'I knew her as a student when we were at the Sorbonne, Herr Obersturmbannführer. She's very bright, speaks perfect German, dislikes the Maquis, calls them troublemakers−'

'That's not what I asked.'

'I checked her out myself, Herr Obersturmbannführer,' Hoffmann lied. 'I can vouch for her.'

Model inspected his fingernails then looked up and smiled. 'Are you fucking her?'

Hoffmann blushed. He always found Model's crude language embarrassingly tedious. It made him sound like a Bavarian drayman rather than a Prussian aristocrat. 'Madame Régnier does not interest me, Herr Obersturmbannführer. You asked for a good-looking typist, well this one is beautiful.'

'I'll be the judge of that when I see her, Obersturmführer.' He rose from his chair, walked to the window and looked down the avenue as if searching for her. 'I can appreciate a woman's beauty for what it is, like the Greek sculptor Praxiteles with his Aphrodite, endowing her image with grace and gentleness. And how do you judge a woman's beauty, Hoffmann? By the way she affects your cock.'

Hoffmann felt his cheeks burn more. 'I love my wife, Herr Obersturmbannführer. I'm not interested in other women, no matter how beautiful they may be.'

'Oh yes, Helga, the general's daughter. Very good career move, Hoffmann.' Model turned his eyes from the window towards his assistant. 'I have to say however, I'm impressed with the work this woman has done. Well done, Ludwig. She's coming to see me at nine, you say?'

'Yes, Herr Obersturmbannführer.'

Elated, Hoffmann returned to his office and grabbed his greatcoat. He rushed downstairs and out into the street to wait for Catherine. He prayed she would be on time, because Model was a stickler for punctuality. The sky was grey and there was no sun, only a gust of wind blowing brown leaves down the central reservation. Hoffmann's heart raced when he caught sight of her. God, she's beautiful, he thought. Model's Aphrodite is stone, but Catherine is flesh and blood and yes you old queer, he thought, she does affect my cock. Hoffmann saw Catherine smile when their eyes met, which made him feel weak with desire for her.

*

'Ah! Madame Régnier,' Model stood and gave a courteous bow. 'Enchanted... Thank you Ludwig, we'll speak later.'

After Hoffmann left the room Model gestured Catherine to sit. Model's eyes roamed round her face. Hoffmann was right about her beauty, he thought as he sat looking at her from across his huge desk. His expression was as blank as an unused sheet of typing paper. He continued to look her in the eye without saying anything. It was a mind game he liked to play. Model enjoyed watching the nerves begin to crack, but this young woman did not want to play. She sat returning his gaze; as if an artist's model, unflinching, patiently waiting for the final brushstroke.

When Model spoke, he spoke in German, 'You're not afraid of me, Frau Régnier.'

'Should I be, Herr Obersturmbannführer?'

'Not if you're who you say you are.'

100

'I have nothing to hide, Herr Obersturmbannführer.'

Catherine watched a smile creep across his face. 'Be in no doubt about it, Frau Régnier. If you have I shall find it out.' His eyes were cold. 'You're overdressed for work, Madame,' he said speaking French. 'Dress down in future. I'm sure your beauty will not diminish with less revealing clothes.'

'I'm sorry, Herr Obersturmbannführer. I wanted to make an impression.'

'You have. It tells me you wish to seduce my men and take information out of this office.'

Catherine smiled into the unsmiling face before her. 'A woman's vanity does not make her a Marti Hari, Herr Obersturmbannführer,' she said.

'How well do you know Obersturmführer Hoffmann, Madame?'

'We knew each other at the Sorbonne. I haven't seen him since he graduated. Then, by chance, I bumped into him at the Place de Clichy.'

'I do not believe in chance, Madame. I think things are arranged to happen. You planned to make Hoffmann's acquaintance again, to get into this building and spy for British Intelligence'

Catherine laughed. 'Really, Herr Obersturmbannführer, I cannot think you really believe that. The position wasn't advertised. It was Herr Hoffmann who invited me to work here. I really didn't want to. I'm happy to leave if you wish me to.'

'I will decide when you leave, Madame. Close to Hoffmann are you, Madame Régnier?'

'What are you insinuating, Herr Obersturmbannführer?'

'I'm sure you know what I mean, Madame.'

'I'm a married woman. Herr Obersturmbannführer.'

'So was your Madame Bovary.' Their eyes met. 'Tell me about your family,' he said reverting to German. 'Who are your people, what do they do? How does your father earn his crust of bread?'

Model listened to what she was saying. If she was nervous of him it didn't show. In his experience, people feared him. They knew the power he had over them, of life and death. This woman was bursting with confidence as if she hadn't a care in the world, or she was oblivious to his power. She seemed very comfortable in the presence of authority, as if she were used to it, and he observed in her an inbred dignity that is acquired by a woman only through long acquaintance with the higher strata of society. She just did not seem to fit into the bourgeois background she was painting for herself. His family were Prussian Aristocracy; he recognised good breeding and she would fit comfortably in the drawing room of any high-born Prussian family. Model could see her beauty was a magnet for men's eyes, and when her eyes lifted to his, her lips moved in such a subtle manner, it was pure seduction. This woman was dangerous. He would have to keep a very close eye on her. Hock would be putty in her hands.

Suddenly he spoke in English. 'How long have you been spying for the British?'

Catherine held her composure. She had anticipated him breaking into English. She shook her head and in German said, 'I don't understand you, Herr Obersturmbannführer.'

'You do not speak English, Madame Régnier?' he said in French. 'A student of literature and you do not speak English?'

'German and French literature, Herr Obersturmbannführer. English is a clumsy language. Not that of Goethe, Molière... '

'Indeed. But Shakespeare, Milton...' he said in English. Her eyes did not narrow, or her eyelids flutter. 'Let me compliment you on your German, Frau Régnier,' he said in German to which he added a charming smile.

Model's tongue wriggled and slid like a snake from one language to another. This snake is clever, Catherine thought and dangerous. She would have to be very careful not to be lulled into thinking it was ever asleep, because it would strike and bite the moment she relaxed. Catherine sensed Model will have her followed, to discover exactly where she went and who she met. Luckily she was now protected from snakes by a mongoose. She looked at Model and smiled.

Model's eyes widened. People were supposed to fear him, not smile at him. He had the power of life and death, he was a god; one trembled not smiled, she should not feel so relaxed. Model stood. Catherine remained seated. He walked to the window, looked out, then returned to his desk. He was certain that Hoffmann had not checked her out. This woman's eyes had robbed Hoffmann of any sense. He instinctively did not trust her to be who she was making out to be. He decided he would get Corporal Hock to carry out a thorough check on her background and have one of his French informers follow her. Meanwhile she could stay. At least she was doing the work.

Model straightened. 'I'm afraid it's mostly mundane work Madame, as you have discovered. It will allow my corporal to do more important tasks. Obersturmführer Hoffmann tells me you are a professor at a Lycée by profession. If you do well, I'm sure we can help you, in one way or another, to find a post more suited to your teaching skills.'

'There are no vacancies for teaching and I will not take another man's bread from his table.'

'Ah! Someone with principles, a conscience, that is rare in France these days.'

'War makes people selfish. They are frightened, Herr Obersturmbannführer.'

'And you're not frightened?'

'There is no reason to be.'

He stood. The interview was over. Yes, Madame, he thought, you are a beautiful woman and I shall spoil that cock-happy Hoffmann's plan of getting you into his bed, if he hasn't done so already. He would send Hoffmann away to Berlin for one of Himmler's boring conferences.

'It was a pleasure to meet you, Madame,' he said with a slight bow. 'Continue to work hard. Don't disappoint me. You have a pass; an ID card and papers will be drawn up for you before you leave this evening. This allows you many privileges. It also exempts you from the curfew. We look after the people who help us, Madame,' he said, 'but severely punish those who betray our trust.' He looked her in the eye. 'I hope I have made myself clear, Madame Régnier.'

'Yes, Herr Obersturmbannführer.'

'I don't want to see that pretty little nose of yours anywhere except in front of your typewriter.' He picked up the telephone and dialled an extension number. 'Corporal, ask Obersturmführer Hoffmann to come to my office.'

103

Chapter 16

Catherine was happy that Hoffmann was leaving that afternoon; happier still when she saw his irritation when he left Model's office. Now she was inside the building, Hoffmann was no longer any use to her.

'Good night, Frau Régnier,' Model called out then told Hock in a whisper, he would not be in the following day and not to let her go anywhere near the filing cabinets.

There were eight filing cabinets in a small room which was locked. Catherine found it strange that Model was fastidious about security, yet one key fitted all eight filing cabinets, and that key was in Hock's pocket, along with the key that opened the door to the filing cabinet room. She smiled. The following day she would be alone with him occupying the whole of the floor.

*

Catherine left the hotel the following morning wearing clothes more suitable for the office, a skirt, tailored jacket and a white blouse, with only a silk chemise under it. She looked at her reflection in the mirror to see how far she needed to bend before revealing her breasts to where her nipples could be seen. She was going to give Hock a treat; whet his appetite and loosen his tongue. It wouldn't be difficult for her. Hock was a plain-looking fellow in his early twenties without, she was certain, much experience with women. She imagined Hock found his moment of *amour* down Pigalle like most German soldiers based in Paris. He would be easy to manipulate, particularly as he struggled with his breathing when he met her eye.

*

Hock immediately commented on how businesslike she looked when she entered the room. Catherine played the girly game and coquettishly said how handsome he always looked in his uniform and she laughed with him and flicked her hair. All morning they worked, but Catherine could sense Hock's unease. He seemed determined to finish the pile of papers on his desk before lunch, yet he ripped page after page from the typewriter, throwing ruined paper into the basket. They passed few words and because he had to see an officer on the second floor, she would not have the opportunity to turn on her charm over luncheon. Her plan of seduction was not working out. When she returned earlier than normal to the office after lunch, she was surprised to see that the door was unlocked and Hock wasn't there.

Hock was a floor below, listening to a friend bragging about some tart he was seeing from the suburbs. This was the price he had to pay for the loan of some money, which Hock needed if Catherine agreed to go out with him that evening. During the morning he had wanted to invite her out, but each time he was about to ask, his courage failed him. While his friend rambled on about the size of the girl's breasts, Hock went into a dream about Catherine's breasts. She seemed to like him; certainly she was friendly with him. She even touched him on the shoulder when she leant across him, which sent a frisson driving though his body and when she bent to pick up a pencil she had dropped, his heartbeat trebled when he looked down her blouse.

Without any knowledge of French he had little hope of forming a friendship with a decent French girl, so his female company had always been restricted to an occasional quickie against a wall when he could afford it. She always treated him with contempt, breathing garlic in his face as he mechanically rode her; no love, no feelings, no soft words, and when it was over she'd push him away and return to whatever bar she had enticed him from.

Catherine Régnier was classy. He had never known a woman like her. Model had told Hock to check her out thoroughly and keep an eye on her, report anything suspicious to him personally and not to Hoffmann. Stuck up Prussian poof, Hock thought. He wasn't a spy and nor was she, just a young woman trying to make her way in life after leaving her husband. Through his dreamy haze Hock felt his friend's hand on him.

'Wilhelm, wake up. You haven't been listening to a word I've been saying—'

'Friedrich,' Hock said, 'you should see the new typist we have; classy, the most fantastic tits. You can see them when she bends down.' Hock smiled at the sudden goggle-eyed interest from his friend. Someone was listening to him for once. Wilhelm Hock had something to say and others wanted to hear it, which also put a sudden stop to the bragging about the suburban scrubber.

'Is she there now?'

'She'll be back at two. Go up and wait for her,' he said giving Friedrich the office door key, 'say you're looking for a file and try to get her to bend down... it will be worth it.'

'Did you see her nipples?'

'Yes.'

'Mein Gott im Himmel,' he said clenching his fists and flushing like an excited schoolboy. 'Two o'clock you say.'

'She's always punctual. I've got to wait and collect a file from Untersturmführer Kessler. Don't leave her alone before I return.'

While Hock was on the floor below, Catherine left the office door ajar so she could hear the heavy footsteps of his boots on the marble staircase when he returned. She went to the room where the filing cabinets were and found the door unlocked. With both Model and Hoffmann away Hock was either careless or couldn't care less. She pulled at one of the drawers and it opened. At first she was too surprised to do anything other than gasp. The letter J began the list. She then tried the bottom drawer. Ls. The heavy footsteps climbing the stairs prevented her from looking in the next filing cabinet, but the top drawer opened and she had enough time to see the letter M. By the time the footsteps reached the door she was at her desk, putting a new sheet of typing paper into her machine. It was not Hock who entered the office but another soldier whose eyes immediately met hers. He ran his fingers through his fair hair, his Adam's apple jumping in his throat. 'What are you doing in here unsupervised, Fräulein?'

'It's Frau. What business is it of yours, Corporal?'

Friedrich looked taken aback by her tone. He smiled weakly and said, 'I was looking for Corporal Hock?'

'I've no idea where he is. I've just returned from lunch. Now if you don't mind, I need to get on.' There was no reply. Catherine looked up at Friedrich, who seemed to be nailed to the ground; only his bright blue eyes moved and then his lips, as they stretched into an inane grin, which froze on his face.

Friedrich tried on his charm. 'It's good to see such a pretty face in here for once, Fraulein... er... Frau.'

'Thank you Corporal. You're very handsome yourself.'
He flushed a little and stretched his neck. 'I need a file for Untersturmführer Kessler.'

'I have no access to the filing cabinets.'

'This file would be in the bottom drawer of Corporal Hock's desk.'

'I'm sorry I cannot go through Corporal Hock's desk.'

'I'll tell him I ordered you to look for it.'

'You'll have to return later. I'm not going through Corporal Hock's desk.'

Friedrich's face reddened. This game wasn't going as planned. 'Untersturmführer Kessler needs that file now. He doesn't like to be kept waiting and I don't want to get into trouble.' He fidgeted then smiled again. 'Please, I'd really appreciate it.'

Catherine guessed Hock had set this up so she decided to play along with it. Her stark features softened. 'All right Corporal, I wouldn't want to get you into trouble. What name is it?'

'W-W-Weismann,' he stuttered as she bent to open the drawer.

She looked up at his flushed features. His eyes were lost down her blouse. 'There is no Weismann here, Corporal, Corporal...'

'Oh!' he said. 'Perhaps Untersturmführer Kessler already has it. I'll check,' he said swallowing. 'Th-thanks for your help. Say hello to Wilhelm ... er, Corporal Hock for me'

'Who shall I say called?'

'Friedrich, h-he knows me.'

'Sorry I couldn't help,' she said and smiled sweetly. Catherine quickly went back to the filing cabinet as Friedrich's hurried steps were making a noisy descent down the marble stairs.

*

'Fuck me,' Friedrich said fanning his face with his hand. 'Would I love to suck on those tits?'

In his excitement to hear what Friedrich thought of Catherine, Hock had forgotten that Friedrich should have stayed with her. 'You saw them?'

'Yes,' he said indicating the size of them with an extended finger from his thumb. 'You could go blind just thinking about her.'

'She'll star in your next wank,' Hock said with a snort and was happy because he made Friedrich laugh too. Hock suddenly felt like one of the lads. He could hold his head high when they next went out and drank beer together.

'If she asks, the file was Weismann... Kessler asked for it.'

'Weismann, right.'

'I didn't need the key,' Friedrich said handing it back to Hock, 'she was already in the office.'

'Christ!' Hock coloured. He had forgotten to lock everything up. 'You were meant to stay with her. What was she doing?'

'At her desk working. She certainly didn't want to go to your desk when I asked for the file,' he said. 'I almost had to force her to look.'

Hock was pleased to hear that. Model can go to blazes with his check on her, he thought, smiling at getting one over on the poof. 'What did I tell you? Not bad, eh?'

'She's gorgeous. I told her. She said I was handsome,' Friedrich said.

'You bloody stay away from her.'

'Touchy. Are you going to try it on?'

Hock shrugged. 'I might.'

'Fat chance. A night's free drinks say you don't get there. What would she want with you, when there's Hoffmann up there?'

Hock fidgeted. He knew Friedrich was right. 'Hoffmann's away. I've got a week before he returns to stick it into her. I bet she's a goer when she's warmed up. You know what these Frenchwomen are like.'

'French! I thought she was German.'

'She's French. Getting divorced, probably gagging for it.'

'Must go. Come and join us for a beer tonight, Wilhelm.'

Friedrich had never invited him out before. 'Thanks but we may be going out tonight. I'll let you know.'

When Hock returned to the office, Catherine was at her desk typing. 'That, Frau Régnier, is what Obersturmbannführer Erich von Model likes to see, industry. It's what made the Fatherland great.'

'Someone called Friedrich called to see you about a file Untersturmführer Kessler wanted. I'm sorry Wilhelm,' she said with doe eyes, 'I had to go to your desk. I didn't want to. He ordered me to. Anyway, it wasn't there.'

He breathed on his spectacles and cleaned them. 'Weismann, I'd already taken it down.'

Catherine could feel his eyes were on her and that he was burning to say something, but he didn't seem to have the courage and began to type. She would help him out a little. Some papers slid from her desk and fluttered to the floor. His eyes followed her down as she bent to pick them up. 'I'm all fingers and thumbs today. Nerves I expect.'

'What have you to be nervous about?'

'Model.'

'Don't worry about that poof. He's not interested in you. He has his little boy at home.'

'I didn't mean he was interested in me... as a woman. I don't think he trusts me.'

'He doesn't trust anyone. He was going to have you followed, but called it off because he wanted the fellow to do something else. He asked me to do a security check on you, but I'm not going to.'

'You'll get into trouble if you don't, Wilhelm.'

'Who cares? He can't shoot me for not doing it.'

'Surely it's your duty to do so. I would have done one on you.'

Wilhelm laughed. 'I trust you and that's what counts, otherwise you would now be occupying one of the rooms above.'

'I've seen them. Hoffmann showed me upstairs...'

'He shouldn't have done that.'

'He tried to kiss me,' she said. Her eyes fell to the floor when Hock looked across at her. 'He said if I didn't give in to him, he could make life very unpleasant for me.'

'He's always taking women in there,' he said pointing at the locked door of Hoffmann's quarters. 'I'm sorry. I didn't want to shock you.' Hock swallowed. I hope I don't make you nervous?'

'No, Wilhelm,' she said lowering her eyes again. 'You're nice, kind and clever. I like you.'

'Clever?'

'Catching spies, it can't be easy.' She saw his chest physically expand.

'I'm just a clerk. I only do the paperwork. It's Hoffmann and Model who question them. Although if I could speak English I'm sure I could trap these spies into a confession,' he quickly added. 'I think Hoffmann has got his eyes on you.'

'I'm not interested in him.' She reached out and touched Hock's arm. He tensed and blushed. 'Promise you won't say anything to him. I'm only telling you because, as I said, I like you.' When she saw him smile, she said. 'I almost fainted up there, imagining what they must have gone through; trapped... no chance of escape, facing a firing squad.'

Hock swallowed. She was standing so close to him he could feel the heat of her body. 'A woman almost did escape, twice. First from the bathroom window and then from the cell window out onto the roof,' he said with a weak laugh. 'These women are tough, been trained to be. In fairness to Hoffmann and Model, they don't treat prisoners badly. The one who almost escaped was very sweet. I spoke to her once when I went to her cell with Model. You would never believe she was a spy. British swine, sending women to do their dirty work.'

'What happened to her?' she said her body brushing against him.

'I don't know.' His chest heaved. 'She... she was taken away when she refused not to attempt another escape.'

'To another prison?'

'I expect so.'

Catherine quickly stepped away from him when she heard a knock on the door and a soldier from the floor below entered the room. He was smiling. 'Corporal Hock I need a file,' he said, his eyes darting towards Catherine.

'All the files you need are already downstairs. Now clear off and tell Corporal Hesson not to send anyone else up here unless he goes through the proper channels.' The soldier's lip curled and the door slammed behind him. 'Sorry about that,' he said flushing.

Her eyelids fluttered like the wings of a butterfly. 'You showed so much authority, Wilhelm.'

'That's why I'm a corporal.'

'Why did you choose to become a clerk? Are you a pacifist?'

'I've always been a clerk. I got this job with the SD because I was in the Hitler Youth. They like that.' He then removed a black comb from his pocket and placed an inch of it under his nose imitating Hitler's moustache. 'So you're a member of the Hitler Jugend, my boy... good, very good.' He removed the comb, stood to attention and said in a high pitch voice, 'Danke, mein Führer.'

Catherine laughed, and ran her hand through her hair, twirling the end round her finger. 'You're so amusing, Wilhelm.'

His eyes shone. None of the girls in the bar ever thought he was amusing. They were common, only good for a quickie against the wall in the street outside, even though the smell of garlic reeking from their breath was like facing a gas attack. He was certain the women did that deliberately to stop their clients kissing them.

Catherine's breath didn't smell of garlic and her lips looked so soft. 'I could be shot for doing that.'

She moved a little closer to him. 'I won't tell the Führer if I see him, Wilhelm.'

'Thank you, Frau Régnier.' His top lip quivered. 'Guess what. Model's in a meeting with the Gestapo first thing tomorrow, so he won't be here all morning.'

'Why the meeting?'

'There's a British wireless operator on the loose in Paris. She's been giving the Gestapo the run around, but now they know her codename is Nora. These wireless operators never last long. We always get them in the end, or someone informs on them.'

'What's a wireless operator?'

'They send messages to their base in England by Morse code. We always catch them at it. The first time we hear the signal the listening posts have a rough idea which area it comes from, so we place a wireless tracking van in that area. Then the next time they send the signal, their location is pinpointed to a particular street, maybe two and the van moves closer, usually with a second van close by. Finally, the two vans can pinpoint the very house where the agent is. Then wham, got him. These operators send at regular times, so our wireless tracking vans are ready for them; easy really, although Nora has broken the mould. She is too quick and her messages too short for us to get a fix on her.'

'That's fascinating, Wilhelm.'

'If we don't catch them that way our informers let us know. The British trust your fellow countrymen too much. In the case of the last agent we caught, it was a jealous woman who informed on her. Nora doesn't keep to a regular timetable, which makes it more difficult and she's fast on the keyboard. Do you remember the German soldier murdered in the Jardin du Luxembourg, the one with the woman...'

'Yes.'

'Model is certain it was Nora who shot them both. You see, a signal was picked up in that area at about the time the two were shot. Model thinks that Nora was caught in the act of transmitting. The Gestapo are certain of it too and now they have a description of a woman, who may be Nora - plain, blonde, chubby features, wears horn-rimmed glasses, usually under a black woollen hat. The Gestapo had her once but she gave them the slip. Model's hopping mad about that.' He looked towards her with a sudden serious expression. 'Please don't tell your friends any of this. I'll get into serious trouble if you do.'

'I haven't got any friends in Paris, Wilhelm,' she said in a low voice. She moved even closer to him. 'And I certainly wouldn't want to get you into trouble.'

Her perfume smelt divine. In an impetuous moment he pulled Catherine to him and kissed her. He felt her tongue flicker in his mouth. His hand went straight to her breast. 'You're not wearing a bra,' he said. He had so much saliva in his mouth he struggled to swallow. He removed his hand from her breast and combed it through his hair with his fingers. 'I'm sorry, but you have wonderful breasts. I couldn't help myself.'

'I liked you doing that. It's been a long time since I've had a man touch my body.'

'May I see them?'

'What here?'

'In the filing cabinet room.'

She followed him into the room, removed her blouse and lowered the straps of her chemise. His eyes grew. He went to her and sucked on a nipple. Catherine gently pushed at his head, replaced her chemise and then her blouse, keeping her eyes fixed to his. 'Did you like that?'

'Yes... now I'm happy to die,' he said.

Catherine smiled. 'I can understand you saying that after making love to me, but not for seeing a little of my body.'

'You would let me make love to you?'

She shrugged. 'You're a very nice person and women have their needs too.'

'Mein Gott im Himmel!'

With that thought in his head, she hoped he would loosen his tongue and be more forgetful with his keys.

'Do you fancy going out tonight?' he said.

'Why not? I haven't been out for ages.'

He looked at her with large eyes and a half open mouth. 'Let me show you something. It's over here. When we captured the last agent, we found the wireless set and this code book; an absolute gold mine. Normally the agent tries to break the crystals before we manage to burst into the room. This wireless set was discovered intact. Model couldn't believe it. He reckons that it was almost as if the British wanted us to find it. Have a look,' Hock said handing Catherine a code book.

She opened it. It was a code book based on poems. She flicked through the pages as if disinterested and shrugged. 'It means nothing to me.'

'Because it's in code.'

'Have you broken it?'

'Not me but our cryptologist has.'

'That's clever. Who did it belong to?'

'An agent called Madeleine.'

Catherine went cold. So she was here. Her file wasn't in the filing cabinet. Her eyes found a leather suitcase on a table in the corner that contained the wireless set. The suitcase was identical to hers. She hadn't noticed it before. What were her people thinking? It might as well have a badge in English on it saying what it was. Panhanagan would have to buy a different suitcase tomorrow.

'Concealed in this suitcase is Madeleine's wireless set.' Hock said opening it, revealing the transmitter.

Catherine placed a hand on Hock's shoulder when she came closer to look at it. There was a sudden tension of his muscles. 'Madeleine is a French name,' Catherine said. 'Is she French?'

'British ... Madeleine was her codename. Her real name is Nora something or other. I remember the name because it's the codename for the agent the Gestapo are now looking for.'

Catherine knew an agent would never reveal her real name to the Germans, so how did they know that?

It was as if Hock was reading Catherine's mind when he said, 'We know her real name because all the mail she sends home by one of their returning Lysanders is read by Model before it leaves.'

Catherine's body chilled when he revealed that because that was exactly how agents' mail was brought back to England. It confirmed Greene's suspicions of a double agent this side of the channel. The Germans had complete control over SOE operations in Paris.

'Wilhelm,' she laughed, smacking him playfully, 'you're making all this up.'

'Really, I'm not lying to you. We even send messages back to the British on that wireless. Model likes to think of it as his trophy. The stupid British still think it's their agent Madeleine sending. They have no idea she has been taken.'

The telephone suddenly rang. Wilhelm went out into the main office and sprung to attention when he heard Hoffmann's voice. Catherine twisted one of the crystals until she heard it crack rendering the set useless. She closed the suitcase and joined Wilhelm out in the main office.

'That was Obersturmführer Hoffmann. He wanted to speak to you. I told him you were with Model. He didn't seem happy about that. I'm to apologise to Frau Régnier and hope she is managing all right. Are you managing all right, Frau Régnier?'

'Yes, thank you, Corporal Hock.' Again they laughed.

'Now, where were we?' he said putting his arms around her and squeezing her bottom.

She removed his hands. 'You were telling me a story, but I don't believe you. It sounds too far-fetched, Wilhelm. I can't believe the British are so silly to be fooled by your tricks.'

'Oh yes they are. I could tell you a lot more than that, but I daren't. It's too risky.'

'In case I'm a spy.' She began to giggle, which made him laugh too.

'Maybe I can tell you a few more stories tonight when we're more comfortable.'

'Wilhelm, I hope you're not married. I don't want to get mixed up with a–'

'I'm not married. I'd like to be... to someone like you.'

'Maybe I'll be your wife tonight,' she whispered in his ear and felt Hock shake when he heard the words.

The telephone rang. Hock answered it. 'I've got to take a file downstairs. I won't be long,' and with all caution for security gone, he disappeared from the room.

Catherine searched through the pile of files Hock had been carrying to the filing cabinet and found Madeleine's file. Her eyes quickly scanned the pages. *Wouldn't talk. Dangerous. Left Paris November 26th. Sent to Karlsruhe.* There was a receipt attached to the file for 100,000 francs. As she read on, Catherine could feel the veins in her neck swell as her blood began to boil. Before she returned the file at the sound of heavy footsteps, she removed a photograph of Madeleine and put it in her pocket. When Hock entered the office she was at her desk. He looked at Catherine's face, her eyes shone with the tears she could not hold back.

'What's the matter, Catherine?'

Chapter 17

Panhanagan walked a dog along Avenue Foch. It had been tethered to a lamppost outside a café in Avenue Victor Hugo before he removed it, its master drinking inside, talking to the barman. After a few pats on the head, the dog seemed very happy to leave and go with him. Nobody takes notice of a man with a walking stick taking some exercise with a dog. Panhanagan saw Catherine appear at the window of number 84. There was a German soldier standing beside her. Both were looking out of the window. The German soldier appeared to be standing uncomfortably close to her.

Both he and Catherine knew they needed to leave Paris and soon. He had seen the wireless direction finding vans increasing in numbers in the districts of the three safe houses and now it would be dangerous, if not impossible, to send messages from any of them. The German fist was tightening its grip. Catherine and he would have to risk taking the wireless further afield before getting out of the city.

Minutes later, he saw them appear at the front door of the building. 'So that twerp thinks he is going to be seduced by the bewitching femme fatale because of his jaw line, the shape of his nose, the wit spilling from his tongue,' Panhanagan said under his breath. He felt the weight of jealousy crush his lungs and, at that moment, he loathed the man. His hand gripped the handle of his PPK deep inside his pocket. 'Give me one excuse, you tall streak of piss.'

From across the road, Panhanagan watched them walk along the Rue des Belles Feuilles, in the direction of Avenue Victor Hugo, where he had stolen the dog. He began to feel uneasy. It was time that he and the mutt parted company. Now Catherine was arm in arm with the corporal. Panhanagan waited for them to turn the corner; he then released the animal from its lead and threw it away in a shop doorway. The dog began to follow him and would not leave when Panhanagan motioned it away. Instead, it wagged its tail and began to jump up and bark at Panhanagan in a playful manner. Panhanagan was horrified at the thought of being betrayed by a scruffy dog. He had no choice other than to break the dog's neck or abandon following Catherine, because they were approaching the café where the dog's owner had been drinking. He looked down at the animal's happy, panting face. 'You stupid bloody mutt...'

Sergeant Panhanagan had been defeated by a Parisian mongrel whose tail wagged with pleasure as it followed him down the road in the opposite direction from Catherine.

*

Catherine and Hock entered the café as an old man and woman were leaving. The old woman looked her in the eye and spat out the word, '*Salope!*'

'What did she just say?' Hock asked.

'Nothing.'

'She insulted you, didn't she?'

'No.'

'I can guess what she said. I've heard that word before, always directed at women with German soldiers.' His face was full of indignation. 'I should like to beat her for insulting you.'

'And there lies the problem, Wilhelm. France is a beaten nation. It is difficult for the older generation to accept it. It's the second time you have invaded their country in twenty years.'

'*Their* country,' he said, 'isn't it your country too?'

'I was referring to the elderly.'

He took her hand. 'Isn't France for the young, too?'

'We can accept it more, I think.'

Catherine smiled at him but cursed herself. She had relaxed for a moment and made her first mistake. Model would have questioned her until she broke for saying that. While she drank her coffee, her mind was split between listening to Hock giving her his life's history, and trying to work out in her head what she was going to do to squeeze more information out of him. If there was a double agent then she needed to know that night who, so she could kill him and leave Paris before Hoffmann returned on Monday. They had already missed the December full moon. The next for a Lysander to collect them would be January 10th. She knew Panhanagan would prefer to go south and join up with the Maquis. From there, they could escape via Spain. Hock finished his coffee and suggested they move on to another bar.

'Why don't we have something to eat here? It doesn't look expensive.' She smiled at him in a way he could not refuse her. 'And I insist on buying some nice wine.'

Hock's mind ached with indecision. He wanted to be alone with her yet he also wanted to show her off to his friends, let them see the woman he was later going to sleep with. It would also show the tarts in his local that he could attract a decent girl. He no longer needed them breathing garlic in his face while he banged them against the wall.

'Wilhelm, you're not listening.'

'I was. We'll stay here, but maybe go for a drink later. Meanwhile, what can I get you?'

The last thing Catherine wanted was an unclear head. 'Oh! A glass of wine, I think. Would you like me to order or would you like to practice your French?'

'You do it. I like to hear you speak French.'

Catherine asked the waiter to put two thirds of water into her glass and top it up with white wine, then put a large shot of vodka into a glass of beer.

Their eyes met.

'Oui Madame,' he said, with a scarcely perceptible smile, as he turned for the bar.

'Sometimes I forget you're French.' He tried to hold her eye. 'Where did you learn German? You speak it so well.'

She shrugged. 'School, the Sorbonne, German friends.'

'You went to the Sorbonne?'

'That's where I met Obersturmführer Hoffmann.'

'So you already knew him. I didn't realize that.' Hock looked disappointed. 'You know he's married. I bet he didn't tell you that.'

'I guessed he was, by the mark left on his finger where he has removed his ring.'

'You're observant. I've noticed that about you. You've got a good memory too.'

'How can you say that? You don't know me.'

He leaned forward and whispered, 'I know you have wonderful breasts,' and blushed at being so bold. He coloured more when he asked, 'How many men have seen them?'

'Really Wilhelm, you speak your mind. Am I safe with you? Tell me why you think I'm observant. No one has ever said that about me before.'

'I've watched you. Your eyes seem interested in everything around you.'

'Then I'm not that observant, otherwise I would have noticed you looking.'

He sighed when he said, 'I love looking at you.'

God, she thought, he is such a drip. The waiter brought the beer over and placed it in front of Wilhelm who picked it up and drank some. He licked his lips and nodded. 'Good.' The waiter winked at Catherine and left to take up his station, then glanced towards the corporal drinking and wondered what scheme that little beauty had up her sleeve. Catherine called the waiter back and ordered two plats du jour and the house wine. She also ordered another beer. The waiter looked into her eyes. She nodded. He smiled. Wilhelm seemed to wake from his sudden trance when she touched his hand, 'I ordered for us. I'm sure you'll like it.'

'Did you and Hoffmann ever go out when you were at the Sorbonne?'

'Only as part of a group. Remember, Hoffmann, was a foreigner. We tried to make him feel welcome. That's what it's like at a university.'

'Did he ever try it on?'

'Every man tries it on, Wilhelm. It's what men do. A woman can accept or refuse him, that's our choice.' Catherine would like to have stood on the table and screamed, 'that bastard Hoffmann raped me,' instead she was becoming irritated by Hock's sudden change of mood. She needed him to relax, but he suddenly seemed tense and showed signs of jealousy. She took his hand again and smiled. 'Wilhelm, he has never seen me or touched me as you have.'

*

They had just finished their meal when a group of young, noisy German soldiers entered the café. One knew Hock and approached him, which encouraged the others to do the same. Hock grew in his seat, pleased that at last one of his colleagues had caught him out with Catherine.

'Christ Corporal. Where did you pick up this *plat du jour*?' one asked.

118

'I'd certainly lick that plate clean,' said his friend.

They all laughed, which annoyed Hock. 'This young lady speaks German, so watch your mouth,' he stammered. He never envisaged this. They were supposed to stand and stare in awe at her and in envy and admiration of him, not to behave like louts. 'Come on Catherine, let's get out of here.' He paid the bill and, amid parting jeers, left the café. 'Don't judge all of us by them in there, Catherine.'

'I know better than to do that,' she said taking his arm. 'I have the keys to a flat close by. It belongs to a friend. I look after it when she's out of Paris. We can go there.'

They went to the flat at Rue de la Faisanderie. She knew Panhanagan wouldn't be there. She smiled to herself when she remembered how ridiculous he looked with that dog. 'Make yourself comfortable Wilhelm,' she said going furtively through her security precautions.

'I feel a little drunk,' he said. 'I shouldn't have drunk so much beer before the wine.'

'Relax. Take your jacket off,' she called out from the hall. 'Go and lie down on the bed. I'll make some coffee.'

In the kitchen, she felt his presence behind her and turned. 'I thought you were tired.'

'I don't want to lie down,' he said. 'Not alone. Let me kiss you.' She avoided that by pressing her cheek to his lips. He began squeezing a breast. She felt a rush of his breath in her ear. 'Oh God,' he stammered and forced his lips to hers. His hand moved between her legs.

'Not so fast, Wilhelm,' she whispered moving his groping fingers away from her. 'I need to go somewhere first.'

Catherine went to the bathroom and sat on the edge of the bath. She loathed herself for playing the whore. All she wanted to do was offer the carrot, but not let him eat it. She removed one of the sleeping pills from the heel of her shoe and rejoined Hock in the sitting room. He was standing looking through the window into the street.

'Wilhelm, close the curtains,' she said. 'I don't want people to see us.'

When he saw her pouring some wine he said, 'No, I've had enough. It's you I want.' Standing behind her he moved his hand inside her blouse. 'I want to do it with you now.'

'Wilhelm, what's the rush?'

'You said you'd be a wife to me tonight.'

'I know, but now I'm nervous. I don't want you to make me pregnant.'

'I love you.'

'Wilhelm...' She gripped his hand before it reached between her legs, 'just calm down a minute.'

He pulled away from her and began sulking. 'That hurt.' His words sounded slurred. She had given him too much alcohol and now she was concerned that he may pass out before she got any information from him. She joined him on the sofa and stroked his head. 'Don't be like that, Wilhelm. We were getting along just fine. It's just...'

His eyes met hers. 'For days I've been looking at you. You have no idea the effect you have on me. I'm so worked up I could burst.'

'Poor Wilhelm.'

He shrugged her away. 'I could be arrested for telling you things I shouldn't, but you're not prepared to do anything for me.'

'Why do you tell me things then?'

'Because I want to prove to you that I love and trust you−'

'You don't trust me, Wilhelm. You proved it today'

'How?'

'You really don't remember?'

His face screwed up. 'Remember what?'

'When we were talking about posting letters to England−'

'God! That again. Why are you so interested in that?'

'I'm not!' she snapped and moved away from him. 'You made out it was so important. You're all talk. You say you love me, but all you really want is to fuck me−'

'No! Don't speak like that.' He went to her and put his arms around her. She made a play at rejecting him, but when he pulled her tighter to his body she put her head on his shoulder. He kissed the hair on her head. 'Why are we arguing?'

'You're only being nice to me because you want sex.'

'Stop it, Catherine. I told you, it's not like that.' He lifted her chin and kissed her lips. 'I do trust you and to prove it I'll tell you whatever you want to know... promise.'

She pushed him away. 'I'm not interested. Take me home.'

He took hold of the glass of wine she had poured and took a gulp. Then he proceeded to tell her all she wanted to know about the infiltration of SOE and *Siegfried*, the double agent. 'He's French... SOE... Special Operations Excecutive, troublemakers. We know every poor bastard that flies into France. Even those who drop in by parachute are not safe.

The blood in Catherine's body almost frooze. When he finished speaking she shrugged. 'So we fell out over that.'

'What do you mean, *that*? I could be shot for telling you *that*.' He moved towards her and ran his hands round the contours of her bottom. 'Now do you believe I trust you?' he said. 'The evidence is all in the second filing cabinet in the cabinet room.'

'What do I care?' Now she needed to get out.

'All right then. I could tell you something that would really impress you and make us a great deal of money.'

'Is this going to be another of your stories?'

He put his hand between her legs, this time she did not try to stop him. He began to feel her through the material of her dress. She felt she ought to close her eyes and moan a little.

'Before Model was given command of the Sicherheitsdienst in Paris,' Hock whispered, 'he worked for the Abwehr. I was his clerk. Once I had to type out a list of Abwehr's agents in England,' he said, his voice becoming husky with desire. 'I have a copy of that list in my desk.'

Catherine placed her arms round his neck. 'Isn't that risky?'

'No. The bottom drawer has a false bottom. Model and Hoffmann never go through drawers. It's my insurance in case I'm ever captured. Imagine how much the British would pay for that information. It could set us up after the war. We could get married and buy our own house.' He looked into her eyes and swallowed. 'I want you now.'

'You'd be prepared to betray your agents just to be with me.'

'I'd do anything. We could disappear to Switzerland. No one would find us.' His hand now began to pull at her knickers. 'Come on Catherine, I want you.'

'Do you have any protection with you?'

His face collapsed. 'No... I–'

'Wilhelm,' she cried. 'I can't without protection.'

'I can pull out.'

'No! I'm not chancing that.'

'Christ... I'm all worked up now.'

'All right, if I do it with you, promise you'll pull out?' she said slipping the pill into his wine.

His breathing quickened 'I will I promise. I've done that before. It'll be safe.'

'All right, Wilhelm ... as long as you swear to me you'll be careful.' She watched his pathetic triumphant expression. 'Finish your wine, while I go and undress.'

'Undress here,' he said taking a mouthful of wine. 'I want to watch you.'

Before Catherine had unbuttoned three buttons on her blouse he collapsed against the table sending plates and cutlery crashing to the ground with him. She took the keys from his trouser pocket and left the room.

*

Panhanagan was still up when she returned to the flat in the 20th district. He made a theatrical display of looking at his watch when she threw her coat across a chair. She went to the kitchen and put the kettle on. Panhanagan rose and hung the coat up on a peg. 'So we're reduced to corporals now,' he said.

'And you to walking dogs.'

Panhanagan grinned. 'Bloody mutt. It was more trouble than it was worth.'

Catherine looked into his handsome features and smiled. 'You looked ridiculous,' which made Panhanagan grin again. What a contrast he was to Hock she thought. 'I have to send a message.'

'Too risky. There are wireless direction vans in the area. I saw one sitting outside a shop along Rue de la Roquette disguised as a grocer's van. They know you're somewhere around here.'

'I've got some very important information to give Greene.'

'How much did that cost you?'

Catherine glared at him. 'Just stick to looking after my back, Panhanagan.'

He walked past her with his eyes fixed firmly on hers and said, 'It's almost midnight. There's no way that cute little wireless operator in your girlfriend's office will be there. You're not thinking straight.'

She ignored his snipe about Susan, but he was right, it would have to wait until her planned morning schedule. She wanted to go to the office. Luckily it was a Saturday, so Model wouldn't be there and Hock should still be asleep. The call would have to wait.

'That cute little radio operator,' she said at last, 'is my cousin, Panhanagan. I'm going to have a bath.'

'To wash your sins away?'

The slap on his cheek was hard and it stung. The bathroom door slammed behind her, leaving Panhanagan standing rubbing his cheek. 'That fucking woman...'

*

Panhanagan went out for a walk. He was away from the action and bored. Occasionally they went out to dinner together which made up for the day's tedium, but that was becoming infrequent now Catherine had her teeth into something; something she never discussed with him. Sometimes, when her eyes lifted to his, he imagined there was a flicker of interest in him. She never looked at him the way he once caught Susan looking at her, it had been sheer lust and he remembered that night when he heard them both together. No woman had treated him the way Catherine had done. He had been kicked, slapped, punched and abused. When he was asked to go to Paris and shadow her, his first instinct was to tell Commander Greene to go hang himself, but he agreed because he felt duty-bound to do so. If anyone had to protect her, then it had to be him. He didn't expect gratitude, but the slap on the face he received woke him up to the fact that he was no more to her than a sergeant doing his job, and to stay clear of her. Then again, he provoked her into slapping him. He was jealous that she gave her attention to others while he was taking all the risks to protect her. He didn't believe she would sleep with Hock, she seemed to prefer women in her bed, but the thought that she might, just to get the information she wanted, tore his insides to shreds. He was now finding it increasingly difficult to live with her; sleeping in the room next door to her, being so close yet unable to touch her. As soon as he tried to get close to her she would back away. Half the time he wondered if she even knew of his existence, she belonged to a different club from him, one which did not allow sergeants to join. Panhanagan sighed as he approached the block of flats. He looked up at the window where she would be sleeping. It was better he knew, to put her out of his mind, do his job and then get out as soon as possible.

*

Catherine was asleep on the sofa in the sitting room with an open book in her hand, as if she had been waiting up for him. He

123

put a blanket over her, removed her PPK from her lap and went to bed himself. He woke at six to the smell of coffee. There was a tap on his door. 'Would you like a sandwich with your coffee?'

Panhanagan climbed out of bed and said, 'Thanks,' then quickly jumped back into bed again and covered himself with a sheet as she walked into the room.

Catherine smiled. 'I've got a brother, Panhanagan. I expect he's made the same way as you.'

'You've obviously never seen him first thing in the morning.'

'You put the blanket over me last night,' she said. Her eyes took in his muscular body as he sat up in his bed. 'I was waiting for you, to apologize. Where did you go?'

'For a walk. You're full of beans this morning. Quite a change from last night.'

'I'm not going to apologize for slapping you last night. You deserved it. Anyway, we'll soon be going home and I shall be rid of you.'

'That's nice.'

She threw him a shirt and asked him to put it on. 'I can't talk to you when you're half naked.'

'I'm fully naked.' He glanced at her and smiled. 'Does that turn you on?'

'No, Panhanagan. It doesn't turn me on, as you quaintly put it.' She sat on a chair and said, 'I have a job to do today and I will need your backup.'

His eyes brightened. 'Anything interesting?'

'In your vernacular Panhanagan, I'm going to put someone's lights out.'

What a cold-hearted bitch, he thought and grinned like a schoolboy about to go out on an adventure. 'Would you like me to do it?'

'Don't you think I can?'

Panhanagan couldn't answer. His mouth was full of bread and meat. Instead he nodded. When he could speak he said, 'I've told you, it's not easy to kill someone in cold blood.'

'Yes it is.' Their eyes met. 'I'm ashamed to say it was very easy. I killed an informant then a soldier and his tart who stumbled across me sending in the Jardin du Luxembourg, and some pervert in the public lavatory along the Boulevard Raspail. You might do well to remember that, Panhanagan.'

He looked pleased, as if his apprentice had passed her final test. 'Sorry about last night. What I said... I was out of order.'

'I didn't sleep with Hock. He disgusts me.' Catherine felt it mattered to her that he knew that. 'Everything I do here disgusts me. France is beginning to disgust me. You're the only one I can trust. I might even begin to like you if you cut out the crap, as Holloway once said to you. Anyway, it was successful last night. I got everything I needed to know from him and I've got his keys to the filing cabinets, so the first thing to do is to go and do a bit of snooping. Then we'll sort out the other thing,' she said and left the room.

When Panhanagan was washed and dressed he joined her in the kitchen. She was drinking coffee. 'The flat in the 16th arrondissement is no longer safe,' she told him. 'I drugged Hock once I had the information I wanted. We'll have to rely on the flat in the 6th arrondissement as an alternative to this for now. Two should be enough for the time we have left.'

Panhanagan went to the drawer and handed her the PPK. 'It has a full magazine. I've given it a good clean. The working parts move a treat.' He then handed her the silencer. 'What about sending your message from the Bois de Vincennes?'

'It's too close. I know a place north of here. We'll go there by bicycle. It'll be safer.'

Panhanagan checked the safety catch on his weapon and put it in his coat pocket. 'Ready when you are,' he said casually, as if they were about to go out on a picnic.

Chapter **18**

Elizabeth Wyatt put on her headphones and the Morse echoed in her ear. 'Susan!' she called out in an excited voice, 'Nora!'

'Decode it as soon as possible. CG is expecting some news on this call.'

When Elizabeth had decoded the message and handed it to Commodore Greene, he felt the eyes of both women locked on him. Elizabeth knew what it said, while Susan waited anxiously.

'Nora's done it,' he said and handed the message to Susan. She glanced over the words. *Prosper network finished. All shot or prisoners including Madeleine. Wireless definitely used by Germans. Now destroyed. SOE has double agent in Paris. Identity known to me. I shall deal with him.*

'You were right about that Sir,' Susan said to Greene.

'Prosper told those damned fools he was suspicious and SOE did nothing. Take this message Elizabeth and send it as soon as you have coded it. *Well done. Do what you have to then get out.*'

Greene was elated. Susan followed him to his office. 'I don't know how she managed it and so soon,' he said, 'but she's obviously taking great risks. I fear it may well become a little sticky from now on.'

'Yes, Sir.'

Greene leaned back in his chair and closed his eyes. Susan left his office, closing the door quietly behind her. 'We'll go out and celebrate tonight, Liz,' Susan said. 'I'm buying you dinner.'

Elizabeth's face was full of concern when she met Susan's smiling features. 'Susan, will you be honest with me? I promise on a sacred oath that I will not say anything.'

'What?'

'Is Nora my cousin?'

'Good Lord! What makes you think that?'

Elizabeth placed her hand across her left breast. 'For a start, this tells me. There are so many coincidences surrounding Cathy's disappearance to Canada, but the thing that has really nagged at me was a note she wrote before she left home. She said that she loved me.'

'That's natural isn't it?'

'I know she loves me as I love her. We take that for granted. Neither of us has to say it, so why did she?' Then close to tears, Elizabeth said, 'She said it in case she didn't return.'

Susan placed an arm across Elizabeth's shoulder. 'That doesn't mean she's Nora. Good heavens... there might be a thousand reasons why she wrote that note.'

'I asked her before she left if she was a member of SOE and she said she wasn't, but my gut tells me Nora is Catherine and I want you to tell me the truth.'

'Well, you'll be relieved to know Catherine isn't in SOE. I swear on everything sacred to me. Nora is French. That's all I can tell you. It's classified information. You said she didn't like flying. Perhaps she wrote the note because she was a little afraid of that.'

'Maybe I'm being paranoid. I have to say Nora is pretty hot on the keyboard. I've only known one other wireless operator who could match that speed and that's Cathy.'

Susan leaned back in her seat and stretched out her arms. 'Where would you like to go tonight?'

*

Catherine went to the office at 84 Avenue Foch, but the guard would not allow her into the building.

'You cannot work unsupervised. You haven't that clearance and you can't take any papers out either, Frau Régnier. It's the rules... you should know that.'

'It's a key to my flat. I forgot it and had to stay with my boyfriend last night.'

'Lucky fellow,' the guard said. 'All right, fourth floor you say, but I shall have to come with you,' and he returned her smile.

When the guard wasn't looking, Catherine slipped Hock's keys into the drawer of his desk. Panhanagan had the imprint of the key to the filing cabinet and would get a copy made later.

*

Sunday morning Catherine went round to the lodgings of Henri Bécourt, the man Hock had confirmed as the double agent, but like most of the German's stool pigeons and agents the Germans employed, he made a habit of moving his residence for security reasons. She returned to where Panhanagan was watching and explained she would have to go back to the office on Monday and try to discover where he was living.

127

'I don't like it,' he said. 'There's a time to get out and now's the time.'

Catherine knew that was true. She didn't like it either. She didn't care about facing Hock. She could deal with him, but Hoffmann would be back from Berlin and Model was always a danger, particularly when he discovered the broken wireless set.

*

Catherine arrived at the office and smiled at Hock when she walked into the room. His eyes fixed on hers. 'Why did you leave me the other night?'

'You passed out. I wasn't going to hang around until you woke.'

'Model is hopping mad,' he whispered. 'He's with Hoffmann now. He was asking after you.'

'What's the problem?' She moved from him when he went to touch her. 'Not here, Wilhelm.'

'I've lost my keys. Did you take them from me?'

'Why should I want them? Look in your top drawer.' She sat at her desk and took the dust cover off her typewriter. 'You've obviously forgotten you put them there because you had other things on your mind.'

He looked puzzled and when he retrieved them, a look of relief filled his eyes. 'I said you were observant.' Now looking a lot more relaxed, he said, 'Can I see you tonight? There's a certain promise you made and now I've got...' He looked over his shoulder and whispered in her ear, '...protection.'

'I've started my period.'

He blushed; women's bodily functions were disgusting to him. 'Jesus Catherine, I've been thinking about it all weekend.'

'Why's Model unhappy?'

'Sod Model.'

'Wilhelm, a woman can please a man in other ways. Now, why is Model–'

'The wireless operator I told you about, Nora, she's been sending again, this time in a completely different location as if she knows our movements,' he whispered. 'She's giving everyone the run around. There's also that wireless set I showed you. You didn't touch it did you?'

'You know I didn't.'

'It's finished, kaputt! They wanted to use it downstairs, but can't; one of the crystals is broken and they have no replacements.'

They both turned towards Model's raised voice. Hock's eyes seemed to plead with Catherine. 'He's probably just found out. For God's sake don't say I showed it to you.'

In his office Model faced Hoffmann. 'Are you telling me with all our resources spent looking for Nora we still cannot locate her?'

'She seems to be one step ahead of us.'

'And why is that?' Model was breathing in deeply to calm himself. 'This woman is getting under my skin!' He suddenly began banging his fist on the desk. 'If I end up on the Russian Front you'll be coming with me.'

'I've already instructed that any young woman carrying a suitcase is to be stopped and searched and I've circulated Nora's description to all military police and Gestapo.'

He handed Model a print of a young woman with spectacles and a woollen hat. Model guffawed. 'Any fool can put spectacles on and a hat to cover her hair. Remove the two and what have we got? Not this woman.' He sat behind his desk and looked up at Hoffmann. Suddenly calmed, he said, 'Have you considered what this agent is sending to London? What's she after Obersturmführer? SOE in Paris is finished. Siegfried has no idea when or how she came into France, that's if he's telling the truth and if he is, then they have bypassed him, so why would they do that?'

'They obviously no longer trust him.'

'Correct. They no longer trust him. Then why is she here? What's her mission, because she is certainly sending a lot of traffic back to London?'

'An assassination, Herr Obersturmbannführer.'

Model looked up at Hoffmann and shook his head. 'He is SOE. They can just order him back to England. If he refused to return then yes, I can see the possibility of sending someone out.'

'I've kept lookouts on previous known SOE safe houses, but so far drawn a blank. She hasn't been seen since the Gestapo lost her.'

Model's orderly entered the room with some coffee. Model ushered him away with a flick of his fingers. 'If London is suspicious Obersturmführer, why are they still responding to traffic coming from Madeleine's wireless? They must suspect–' He stopped when he saw the expression on Hoffmann's face. 'What?'

'We can no longer do that. The wireless set is damaged–'

'Damaged?'

'Useless.'

Model rose from his chair and walked across the room to the window overlooking the Avenue Foch. 'What happened to it, Obersturmführer?'

'One of the crystals is broken. We have no spares.'

'An accident?'

Hoffmann shrugged. 'The floor below, perhaps.'

Model poured some coffee and in a rare gesture of hospitality, poured Hoffmann a cup too. A cynical smile crept across his lips. 'What about the *femme fatale*?'

Hoffmann shook his head. 'She wouldn't know of its existence, Herr Obersturmbannführer.'

'Whenever I mention that woman the blood from your brain goes straight to your cock, Hoffmann. I asked Corporal Hock to check out Madame Régnier. He said he has. I don't believe him. I've seen him drooling over her. What's wrong with you all? You're like a dog with two dicks. I have a gut instinct about that young lady and I trust my gut. Look into it, Obersturmführer.'

'I can vouch for her—'

'Just get the Gestapo to investigate her. Meanwhile, take her to the top floor and lock her up.'

'But why, Herr Obersturmbannführer?'

Model's features suddenly appeared white and strained. 'Are you questioning my orders, Obersturmführer?'

'No, Herr Obersturmbannführer. I'll do it at once.'

*

Catherine was at her desk when Hoffmann walked into her office with two guards. He spoke in French. 'You've to come with me, Catherine.'

Corporal Hock, who had already sprung to attention said, 'Is there a problem, Herr Obersturmführer?'

'I'll speak to you later, Corporal.'

Catherine shrugged her shoulders as she glanced at Hock who watched her follow Hoffmann towards his quarters accompanied by the two guards. Hock, could feel his skin prickle with nerves. If she talked, he knew he would be shot.

'What's going on, Ludwig?' she said when they were on the top floor.

'Don't worry. Model is throwing a fit because of a problem we have. You won't be up here for long.' He looked into her eyes looking for any signs of concern or guilt, and saw only confusion.

'Ludwig,' she said, her fingers resting on his arm. 'Why am I being locked up?'

'You've done nothing wrong. Model has ordered the Gestapo to check you out. It's nothing to worry about, routine. You'll be released when they've cleared you.' Hoffmann chuckled. 'He thinks you're a *femme fatale*.' When he saw that neither guard was watching he leaned forward and went to kiss her lips.

She pulled away from him. 'Don't.'

'I know you're angry. I'll have you out of here in no time. Unfortunately, I doubt if Model will let you continue working here, then I'm sure you wouldn't want to anyway. I'll find you another job.' He stood, went to the window and looked out. 'Is there anything going on between you and Corporal Hock?' Catherine remained silent. 'Model thinks he's fucking you.'

'Charming.'

He turned and faced her. 'Has he had you, Catherine?'

She shrugged. 'I wouldn't know.'

'What do you mean, you wouldn't know?'

'Don't Germans usually fuck their women when they're unconscious?'

He leaned close enough for Catherine to feel the heat of his breath. 'I'm asking you about Hock. He's been boasting about it.'

'Just as you did after you raped me. It seems to be a German trait.'

'God Almighty. I've tried to make up for it. I got you this job, didn't I?'

'Only so you could fuck me again. Save it for your wife.'

Hoffmann grimaced and gritted his teeth. A sinister expression replaced the mask of charm. 'Hock was supposed to check you out and didn't and so was I, but I didn't, because I was trying to help you. Now I will do my duty. Give me your bag.'

Catherine looked up at him. 'Why?'

'I have to search it. I'm sorry Catherine, orders.'

She pushed her shoulder bag across the table towards him. He removed several items; female junk he liked to call it, along with a few notes and coins, a bus carnet, a set of house keys. 'These?'

'Lyon.'

He nodded and continued. A café receipt, which he looked at and smiled, 'So you still go there.' He picked out a lipstick, although he had never seen her wear lipstick. He opened it and pulled it apart then put it back together again. There were also two sanitary towels. She lowered her eyes. He replaced them in the handbag and told one of the guards to face the front. Finally, there was a pencil and notepad with nothing written on it, and a clean pair of knickers. His eyes fell down to the silk garment then back to her.

'In case of an accident.'

He nodded then inspected the label.

'They are not from Fortnum & Mason if that's what you think.'

He smiled. 'Englishwomen buy preserves from Fortnum & Mason, not their underwear.' He put everything back into her bag. 'Anytime you need to go to the bathroom let the guard know.' He turned to the guard and repeated it in German. The guard sprang to attention.

'Would you take your jacket off please, Catherine?'

'What now?'

'I have to do this.'

'You're no different from the rest of them,' she said, pulling her jacket off and throwing it at him. 'Nazi pig.'

Hoffmann smiled. He felt each pocket and threw it over a chair. She stood when he asked and closed her eyes as he ran his hands over her back, her waist, her bottom, her legs, up across her stomach and round her breasts where he met the scorn from her blue eyes. 'Satisfied or do I have to undress now?'

'If you really must know I got no satisfaction from doing that, Catherine.'

'Why don't you just get out?'

'I'm a soldier and have to follow orders.' He walked to the door and turned. 'If there is anything you want.'

'My freedom.'

'Two days Catherine, sooner if the Gestapo move themselves. Oh, I'll make sure you get a supply of those, you know, from the pharmacy.'

Then he was gone and the key turned in the door with a sickening clunk. She heard Hoffmann give orders to a guard and the other followed him out. There was a dull thud as the remaining guard rested his rifle against the wall then the scrape of a chair.

Catherine went to the window and looked out across Avenue Foch for Panhanagan. She knew she would not be able to signal to him until after dark. From the height of the top floor she had a good view of the avenue, but the great naked branches of the trees along the centre section prevented her seeing clearly what was directly across the road from her building.

'Come on, where are you, Panhanagan?' she whispered. 'Show yourself.' He didn't.

At lunchtime she was brought a tray with some food and a hot drink by one of the guards who had earlier escorted her up to the cells. She smiled at him and thanked him in German for the food. He also gave her a package, 'from the Obersturmführer,' he said. When she began speaking to him, asking where he was from, he turned looking embarrassed and said, 'I'm not to speak with you, Frau.'

'On whose orders?'

'Obersturmführer Hoffmann, Frau. I'm sorry.'

Catherine sat on the bed and searched her mind for any weaknesses in her cover story. She knew the cheap hotel close to the Gard du Nord would be searched thoroughly. In her satchel was a copy of her genuine birth certificate, some school reports from schools she never actually attended, and genuine letters addressed to her at the Amiens address; one inviting her for an interview at the Sorbonne, a letter of acceptance from the Sorbonne and a copy of her degree. They were all in the same name as that on her birth certificate. There was a photograph of her husband and a copy of their marriage certificate; all the papers were as good as originals. Susan had covered her background so neatly it would be difficult and time-consuming to unravel the truth. The hotel, as far as the French police and the Gestapo were concerned, was her home in Paris. She had paid three months of British taxpayer's money in advance and bought cheap clothes and a few toiletries to make it look as if she was living there permanently. Room service was not included, so her bed was not made up or the room cleaned by a maid, which suited her. She had taken showers, left the bath unclean and a towel lying on the bathroom floor. There were unwashed garments on the floor. It was a room that looked lived in.

Her wireless set was now hidden in the flat in Rue de Mont Louis, close to the cemetery, where she and Panhanagan lived and where he may now have to lie low. She looked out of the window left and right, nothing. Their missing security check would soon tell Panhanagan that all was not well. She always showed herself at the window on the hour. Two hours had passed and he would not have seen her. Panhanagan, she knew, would now be like a tigress on the prowl concerned for her young.

Catherine's coffee was almost cold. She winced at the taste of it and threw it across the room. The food she left. Her stomach was too knotted to hold it down. She thought of the green lawns of Mountfields far away in Yorkshire and of her mother riding her horse round the estate, unknowing the danger her daughter was in. She lay on the hard bed and closed her wet eyes. A vision of her parents came to her which gave her strength, as praying to God gives a Christian strength.

*

Corporal Hock stood like a bronze statue before Model not daring to move an eyelash, as Model continued to read through some papers. Model's face was long and deep in concentration. Hock tried to judge his mood. He knew of the dark side to Model's character and had no wish to witness it now.

'Did you check her out thoroughly, Hock?' Model said without looking up.

'Yes, Herr Obersturmbannführer.'

'So you can give me her life story. Who her parents are, where she's from, no stone left unturned.'

'Yes, Herr Obersturmbannführer.' He could. Catherine had told him everything over dinner, which as it turned out, was providential. 'Ask me anything, Herr Obersturmbannführer.'

Model's eyes rose. 'Don't presume to tell me what to do, Corporal.'

'Sorry, Herr Obersturmbannführer.' Hock reached another inch towards the ceiling.

'Did she ever go near that wireless set, Corporal?'

'Never Herr Obersturmbannführer, I always made sure that room was locked.'

Model rose from his chair, walked to the huge window and looked out. He saw Panhanagan leaning against a tree reading. 'Idle man,' he whispered aloud. 'Do you see that man there Hock? That's the French for you, sloths. He looks fit enough for any job, but what does he do, he idles his day away, while the Reich needs men to work in their factories. Guard!' he bellowed.

A guard entered the room and jumped to attention. 'Yes, Herr Obersturmbannführer.'

'See that idle man over there… there man,' he said pointing, 'against the tree reading.'

'Yes, Herr Obersturmbannführer.'

'Tell him to clear off and find a job.'

The guard's face fell into confusion. 'Tell him what, Herr Obersturmbannführer?'

Model closed his eyes. 'I'm surrounded by imbeciles.' His lover's image filled his mind. They had argued that morning. Why did he have to leave? St Tropez of all places; a ghastly town full of the bourgeois. Such a pretty boy. Then he saw Panhanagan move and noticed his limp and the walking stick in his hand. 'Go away,' he said to the guard. 'Get out.'

When the guard disappeared, Model's face was a mask of melancholy. He turned to Hock. 'Would you leave such an exquisite city like Paris for St Tropez just because of a little morning frost, Corporal? It's so easy to keep warm; a little cashmere, so light, rich, luxuriant. One can buy it in abundance in Paris.'

Hock's lip curled in contempt. So that's it, his nancy boy has left him. He suddenly felt a swell of confidence in the presence of this half man, this... sodomite. At least I, Wilhelm Gunter Hock, am a man; I have kissed women's lips, Catherine's lips, sucked and tasted her breasts, touched the very womanhood of her and when she is released, I will prove my manhood and have her completely. 'No, Herr Obersturmbannführer,' he said in a firm, confident voice, 'It's far too hot. St Tropez hasn't the culture of Paris; the palaces, the museums, the parks, the history−'

'All right Corporal, I don't want a lecture.' There was silence between them for a minute. Hock's sudden confidence shrunk in Model's shadow as he walked past him without a glance, as if he wasn't worth the effort of casting his eyes Hock's way. 'Could Madame Régnier have read any files from the cabinets?'

She hasn't said anything. Thank God, I'm safe. Hock swallowed. No longer on the summit of Mount Olympus, Hock's feet felt heavy on the parquet flooring of Model's office, his godlike body suddenly mortal, his eyes not daring to make contact. He was bronze again, erect, irrelevant. 'No, Herr Obersturmbannführer,' he said. 'She was never out of my sight.'

'With tits like those I expect she wasn't. I've seen the way you ogle her Hock, encouraged, I might add by the revealing clothes she likes to wear.' He took a seat and looked up at his corporal. 'I'm asking you this simply out of curiosity because I cannot believe it to be true. Are you fucking her?'

A nervous splutter of a schoolboy's laugh choked from Hock's throat at the coarseness of Model's question, but oh how he would love to answer that he was. 'No, Herr Obersturmbannführer. I, I'm not very successful with the opposite sex. Whores are my level, Herr Obersturmbannführer.'

Model laughed and slapped his knee. 'That's what I like about you, Hock. You are an ill-bred proletarian peasant and know it. Good man. I like that.'

Model looked at the young man's gaunt features; his unusually large ears and Adam's apple, the lenses of his wire spectacles blurred by steam from a sweating brow. Hock had nothing to offer women. He could be taken as the offspring of a feral pig, whereas Madame Régnier, Model thought in reverence, could be the daughter of Zeus and Dione. He certainly found it difficult to believe she would cavort with a minion such as Hock. But women were schemers. If Madame Régnier was after anything, a man such as Hock could be moulded and shaped into anything she wished.

'What to do with that French harlot, eh, Hock? I think I'll have another conversation with the Régnier woman; see what you two have been up to.' He looked up at his corporal, still rigidly standing to attention. 'Go Hock. Go, go. Get out of my sight,' flicking his fingers as if swatting a fly away.'Yes, Herr Obersturmbannführer. Thank you Herr Obersturmbannführer.'

Hoffmann stood when Model entered his office. 'Obersturmführer, I wish to speak with Madame Régnier.'

'Has she been cleared by the Gestapo?'

'Not yet, Hoffmann. Keep your cock in your trousers.'

The guard jumped up from his chair and unlocked the door when the two officers appeared. The second guard opened the cell door. Catherine was lying on her bed asleep. 'Well she certainly looks relaxed and unconcerned, Herr Obersturmbannführer.'

'That's the very reason I do not trust her. Wake her and take her to the interview room. I'm not sitting by her bloody bed like a hospital visitor.'

When Catherine was seated in the interview room, facing an empty chair with a table between the two, she heard Model outside the room address Hoffmann in English. The interview room door was open, deliberately, she knew, so she could hear every word spoken. 'Have the evidence typed out and let me have it. If she denies it or lies to me she will be shot. I'll give her one chance only; lock her up if she tells the truth, the firing squad if she lies.' Both men entered the room and looked towards Catherine. Model's smile was full of charm. 'Have some tea brought up, Obersturmführer.' Hoffmann met Catherine's eyes before he left. Model continued to speak English. 'You understood every word of that, didn't you? Well, I meant what I said.'

Model was bluffing and she knew it. While he was speaking to her in English, she read in her mind, Voltaire's *Candide*, a book she had studied. It kept her mind alert in the French language. It was a skill she picked up at the Sorbonne whenever English was spoken. She blotted her own language out of her head and filled her mind with French. Model seemed very relaxed, but Catherine could see he was looking into her eyes for any reaction to what he was saying. She turned from him.

'Look at me when I speak to you.'

'I'm sorry Herr Obersturmbannführer, if you wish me to understand then please use a language I understand.'

'Oh, I think you understand perfectly well, Madame,' he replied in English. 'Tea will be here shortly. I do enjoy a cup about this time. In the last war my father would hear the English guns stop firing and he would say to his men, "you can relax men, it is eleven o'clock. The English are having their tea." It's true I swear.' He chuckled. 'Elevenses, charming idea, Madame... or shall I say Madam, in keeping with your language.' Catherine's eyes rose to the ceiling. *Concentrate, concentrate.* When she lowered her eyes and met his, Model smiled. 'You have such pretty eyes Madam, and that mouth...' he whispered almost seductively as he ran his fingertip lightly across her lips. Catherine did not blink or move away from him. 'Men desire you, I can see that. Your hair, thick, lustrous, dark brown so naturally wavy, but I can imagine blonde would suit you just as well and even wearing spectacles would not diminish your beauty, Madam.' His eyes never shifted from hers. 'I know and you know I know.' His smile broadened, his eyes lowered to her breasts, whose rise and fall remained steady. 'A quirk of nature has rewarded you with such beauty, while she has been so cruel to others. How do you use your beauty, Madam? Perhaps you use it to tempt men into betraying their country or to seduce moronic boys with permanent erections into giving you secrets, for what? A taste of honey from your hive, perhaps. Ah, dear, dear, when will man ever learn?' He spoke every word with the accent of the old Harrovian, the same school as her father and brother. His voice suddenly became more sinister. 'You may fool Hoffmann with your captivating eyes, or that common little turd Hock with those wonderful breasts, but you do not fool me Madam. You see, I know who you are.' Her eyes rose to the ceiling again. He brought them back with a touch on her arm with his fingers. 'I have every respect for the English Madam, no, I shall call you Catherine... particularly English aristocracy; they have the capacity for survival... unlike the French.' He smiled. 'I recognized it in you from the beginning; your fine features, your manners and the way you sit. Who taught you that? Was it your nanny, your governess or your mother? I watched the way you held your knife and fork when you dined in our mess with the cock-happy Hoffmann... your table manners are exemplary. When I was at Harrow, I met the sisters of my chums; wonderful gels with creamy complexions, pretty noses slightly raised, and eyes that never dwelt upon the great unwashed. You, Madam, play an opposite game; a young lady of high birth, yet you pretend to come from that vulgar French bourgeois stock. Now why would you do that, Madame Régnier?' Catherine sat still, her eyes fixed to his, her expression unchanged. 'You're a female version of that wonderful yet absurd chump, Sir Percy Blakeney. I read *The Scarlet Pimpernel* while a guest of the Duke of Devonshire. Chatsworth...' he sighed, 'such a beautiful house, and those wonderful gardens... I expect you've been a guest there yourself.' She had. 'That's where I met Baroness Orczy. The old dear was getting on a bit then.' He gave a throaty chuckle. 'The baroness gave me a signed copy of her book. "*They seek him here, they seek him there*." Such fun,' he chuckled again. 'The Frenchies couldn't find that chump, but I've found you.' There was a knock on the door. 'What is it?'

'Tea, Herr Obersturmbannführer.'

'Ah, tea! Does Lady Blakeney wish for a cup?' he said speaking English again. He dismissed the guard with his customary flick of the fingers and began to pour the tea. 'Meissen,' he said. 'You would know about that, wouldn't you? You probably have lots of it in your magnificent home. Where do you live I wonder? Derbyshire perhaps or Yorkshire, Kent, Hampshire, Wiltshire; there are so many wonderful houses scattered around the Kingdom.' He pushed a cup of tea towards her. 'Your tea, Lady Blakeney, no, I'm forgetting. The family name following the title suggests the lady married into the family, does it not? No, no that wouldn't do, you were born into aristocracy. Your father would be a duke or an earl perhaps therefore the Christian name follows the title. I am right, am I not? Lady Catherine? I'll call you that. It really does suit you, you know.'

Catherine looked into his blue eyes which were full of amusement. This game he was playing was becoming chillingly real. 'Please speak German, or French; either, I don't really care just allow me to understand what you are saying.'

'You know what I am saying, Lady Catherine. I grant you have excellent German and French, but I'll wager your English is quite exquisite too; rounded vowels, crisp sentences perfect articulation. Our class has always been good with language. My father was a diplomat in England. We lived in Belgravia in the south west of London. I expect you know it, Eaton Square, Belgrave Square, such delightful London homes. I loved England; I have to tell you that. Good friends with Lord Worthington, you know him too, of course. Wonderful trout stream, good birds, elegant house. Wonderful chaps the British; so bright yet equally stupid. Your chap in London has prepared you well for what he wishes you to do,' he paused and drank some tea, inviting Catherine with a gesture of his hand to do likewise. 'Your wireless skills are commendable; very quick, good fingers, excellent technique and you may be able to lose anyone following you, I congratulate you, but they were Gestapo which takes the edge off your victory a little.' He smiled apologetically and shrugged his shoulders. 'Of course you were chosen for whatever you have been sent here to do not only because of those skills, but because of your faultless French and German, and because you know that cock-happy twit Hoffmann. How are things progressing there? Have you had him between your milky-white thighs yet, Lady Catherine?' He stared into her eyes. 'I worked you out from the very beginning...'

Catherine detected anger in the rising volume of his voice. She watched him walk to the window, open it a little and look through the metal bars. He turned to her with his chilling smile. 'We can check your papers. I know they will be very good. The British know how to forge good documents. They have such a wonderful criminal class now they have stopping shipping them off to the colonies, but there is bound to be an error somewhere, there usually is. We can check the French background you have given us; it's probably watertight, but if we keep chipping away eventually it will spring a leak.' He rose to his full height and stretched further on the toes of his highly polished boots, looking very pleased with himself. 'The area in which the British have let you down is in you yourself, Lady Catherine. Body language you see. You cannot hide who you really are.' He suddenly saw Panhanagan reading his book as he had done earlier. He snapped his fingers, 'Come here.' He looked at her motionless body and beckoned her over with his hand. She rose and went to him. 'Do you know that man across the street?' he said pointing at Panhanagan. She looked at Panhanagan with blank eyes, but inside she was never happier to see him. Model repeated himself in German.

'I've never seen him before,' Catherine said in German.

'Go and sit down,' he said abandoning English. He joined her. 'You're tough. I can see why SOE... no, I don't think you're SOE, we would have known about you,' which confirmed Hock was right, Model had penetrated the organization. 'It's a mistake to say you cannot speak English. Educated people speak English.' He lifted her chin with his fingers and looked into her eyes. Then he ran the back of his fingers very delicately over the surface of her cheek, down her chin and then her throat. 'Yes, you're very aware of what your beauty can do to a man, aren't you, Frau Régnier?' His fingers ran lightly over the curve of her breasts. 'I imagine you just click your fingers and men will fall to their knees in front of you. Well, as I said, you can make a fool of Hoffmann and that worm Hock, but not me... Frau Régnier.' He stood and left the room slamming the door behind him. The guard took Catherine back to her cell and immediately engaged the lock. She closed her eyes and took a deep breath, slowly, silently, expelling it through her open mouth. She began to shake, and for some minutes Catherine lost control of her body.

Chapter 19

Panhanagan knew there was a problem. He had moved from the base of the tree to the shadows of Avenue Foch. He recognized Model as he left the building. Model had been staring down at him while he was pretending to read a book. The other officer with Model, whom Catherine had known at the Sorbonne, had not been around for the past week. Both stood at the curb close to a black Mercedes with a private soldier standing to attention by an open door at the rear of the car. They spoke for five minutes, saluted each other and the dapper fellow climbed into the car which then drove away. The younger one stood for a moment, as if deciding whether to return inside the building, but two other officers approached him, linked arms and took him away towards the Champs-Élysées. All three looked happy. Where was Catherine?

It was very cold and now it began to rain. Panhanagan had an uneasy feeling in the pit of his stomach. He sheltered in the shadows until six and when all the lights on the fourth floor were out he became very concerned. It was then he noticed something new. A single light on the fifth floor, the floor Catherine described as the one with the cells, which until now had always been in darkness. He noticed the light flickering occasionally, as if it had a faulty fitting and took little notice of it, but now, observing it more closely the flickering light began to mean something to him. The room now had his full attention. He waited for the next pause and watched the lights begin to flick again. Dash-dot, N. Dash-dash-dash, O. Dot-dash-dot, R. Dot-dash, A...NORA. Jesus Christ!' He moved across the road. The guards, normally outside the building, had moved inside because of the rain. He searched for some pebbles and began throw them up at the lighted window, frustrated because they were not heavy enough to carry the distance to the fifth floor. He searched again for heavier stones. On the fourth attempt he hit the glass at an angle, which brought a face to the window.

Catherine could just make out Panhanagan at the front railings of the building. She threw something tied in a white handkerchief so he could follow its flight in the poor light, and heard its clatter on the road behind him. It was her lipstick. Inside the case there

141

was no lipstick but a note which read: *They suspect me - as yet they have no evidence. I am going to make an attempt to escape. If I don't make it, wait at the safe house for three days then leave Paris. Get back to your unit.*

'If you go down my Lady, we both go down,' Panhanagan whispered through gritted teeth. He moved further away from the building to allow her a better view. With his small torch he flashed out a message acknowledging that he would hang around. When her face disappeared from the window he decided that he would give her an hour. If she wasn't out by then he would attempt to gain entry into the building rather than leave her in there all night. There wouldn't be many people in there at this time. He counted the rounds of ammunition he had. He could take out as many as fourteen. He dug into his pocket, removed an apple and bit into it.

*

Catherine knew what she had to do and decided now was the time to move. She called out to the guard that she wanted to take a bath. The guard replied she couldn't leave her cell. Catherine didn't recognise the voice which was youthful, almost juvenile. The guards had obviously changed duty when she had taken a quick nap earlier. She went to the door and banged it with her fist. 'I'm entitled to a bath.'

'It's not up to me, Fräulein. I have no authority.'

'Not Fräulein... Frau Régnier. Go and speak to Obersturmführer Hoffmann.'

'He's left, Frau Régnier. The only people left on the fourth floor are the two other guards.'

'Why the fourth floor? Don't you have a guardroom up here?'

'At night we stay in the annex room off Obersturmführer Hoffmann's private quarters. It's more comfortable and has put-up beds.'

She remembered the layout; down the steps from the cells and though a door into Hoffmann's quarters, through another door into the annex at the back of the building. There was a second door that led into the office where she and Hock worked.

'I really need to have a bath. Please...'

'You're not allowed to leave your cell. I shouldn't even be talking to you.'

Her voice lowered. 'Why won't you speak with me? It passes the time.'

'Obersturmbannführer von Model said you would trick me and you mustn't leave the cell.'

'Trick you,' she laughed. 'I'm just a girl. I couldn't hurt a fly. One little bath.' There was no reply. 'If there is no one here then what does it matter? I shan't say anything to get you into trouble... I'll let you watch.' Silence, then a few moments later she heard footsteps and the key in the door turn, but the door remained closed. She turned the handle and pushed the door. It opened to reveal a nervous-looking youth pointing his rifle at her. His eyes widened and the cartilage jumped in his throat when he saw her. He looked sixteen, wearing an ill-fitting uniform and a helmet that seemed far too big for his head. 'You'll have to be quick.'

'Where's the other guard?'

'There are two of them downstairs. We change shifts in an hour.'

'So you're locked in here alone with me for an hour. What's your name?'

'Heinrich.' He lowered his eyes to her breasts. He had only ever seen pictures of a naked woman.

She smiled, which made him blush. She could see she excited him. 'How old are you Heinrich?' she said removing her clothes.

'Eighteen... almost,' he replied swallowing.

When she was naked, she picked up her clothes and put them on the bed under the youth's watchful gaze. When she took a step closer to him he instinctively raised his rifle. Catherine stopped and raised her hands. 'I surrender.' His eyes dropped to the dark triangle of hair between her legs then back to her breasts. 'You can touch if you want to. I don't mind.' His body and tongue were momentarily paralysed, then, as if wakened from a dream, he leaned his rifle against the wall, removed his helmet and ran his sweaty palm through his fair hair. Catherine could see the growing excitement in his eyes. She held out her arms to welcome him to her body and once he reached her she drew his bayonet from the scabbard with the speed of a striking viper and thrust it up under his chin into his brain. His knees caved in under him, the hot blood spurted over her face, neck and breasts. He was dead before she lowered him to the floor. From his pocket she took the keys, then moved quickly to the bathroom and washed under the shower. After she was dressed, she avoided the blood that was spreading rapidly across the floor, the smell reminding her of the abattoir on one of her father's farms. Down in Hoffmann's quarters, she listened at the door and could hear the low crackling sound of singing from a wireless. A voice said something and another replied. They were discussing fishing and the best places to fish out of Paris. There was a chinking sound of a spoon against china then a scraping of a chair. She heard one of the voices say he would ask Heinrich if he would like some coffee. Before the guard reached the stairs in Hoffmann's room, there was a sound of a crack, inaudible to the guard listening to the wireless. The body became dead weight in Catherine's arms. She took the weight against hers before lowering it quietly to the Turkish rug. Now the sound of Edith Piaf singing *Mon Coeur Est Au Coin d'Une Rue* came from the other room. The door was ajar. Catherine could see the guard was a powerfully-built man. He was leaning back in his chair with his feet up on the desk humming to the tune while flicking through a magazine. She took a deep breath then moved quickly into the room like a lioness going in for the kill. The guard looked up and, in his panic to move, fell backward onto the floor with a crash. Catherine hit his jaw so hard with the heel of her shoe it knocked him backwards. Her knees fell onto his chest and she snapped his neck with a crack.

There was no turning back now. She went to Hock's desk and removed all the papers from the bottom drawer, ran a paper knife round the edge of the base, lifted it and found what she wanted. Reading through the sheets of paper, she quickly realized it was a pot of gold for MI5. In the top drawer Hock kept a spare key to the filing room. She used the key she had made to the filing cabinets that was on the bunch Hoffmann had held earlier. Catherine knew exactly in which filing cabinet to look and found Henri Bécourt's file under the heading, *Siegfried*, a name she had been given by Hock. She made a mental note of his new address, left everything as it was, other than three dead soldiers spanning the two floors, and she left the office. As she descended the stairs, an officer she recognized two floors below hers, appeared from a room.

'Hello, Obersturmbannführer Model got you working late today?'

Catherine returned his smile and nodded. The guard at the front door saluted the officer and Catherine walked out of the building with him. She waved the officer goodnight and crossed the road. Panhanagan suddenly appeared from the shadows. 'How–'

'I'll explain later.'

*

Walking into the safe house was like entering a church for sanctuary. There was a sense of relief and the feeling of security when the door closed behind them. They were both soaked. Panhanagan could see in Catherine's eyes she was upset so he didn't try to squeeze any information out of her. That could wait. She went straight to the bathroom and ran a bath. A half hour later Panhanagan, who had already changed out of his wet clothes, watched her emerge and go to her room. He went and tapped on her door. 'Would you like some coffee?' There was no answer. He knocked again before entering. She was lying on her bed naked. 'Get out,' she snapped and heard him apologize from the other side of the door.

He was sitting at the kitchen table when she walked into the room. 'I'm sorry about that,' he said and got up to pour her some coffee. When he handed it to her she avoided his eyes. He saw that hers were red and swollen.

'No, I'm sorry. I sometimes forget I'm living with a man.' She attempted a smile. 'I'm not used to it.' She began to drink her coffee and noticed Panhanagan giving her an enquiring look. 'I killed a boy,' she said, knowing he was waiting for her to explain her escape. 'He wasn't yet eighteen. He looked younger... his poor mother.' Then she proceeded to tell him of her other two victims.

A sinister smile crept to Panhanagan's lips. 'Fantastic.'

'You're sick, Panhanagan.'

He shrugged without any emotion. 'Under the chin you say. At least it's quick. He wouldn't have known anything,' then he filled his mouth with bread.

'You're a heartless bastard. It's just a bloody game to you, isn't it?'

He grinned. 'I'll make you something to eat.'

'I have no appetite.' she said and went to leave the room. 'Panhanagan...'

'Yes.'

'Thank you for being there. I didn't feel alone and I know you're mad enough to have attempted to come in after me.' Her eyes were warm and her smile tender. She touched his arm, 'Good night,' and kissed his cheek.

Her touch made him tremor. He had held her in his arms, pressed himself against her body, touched her where he had no right to touch her and he had kissed her, but that single touch sent desire for her rushing through his body. He closed his eyes and took a deep breath. Living as a monk with a beautiful woman was having its toll on him.

She had left her bedroom door ajar. He went to it, closed it and whispered, 'Good night.'

*

When Panhanagan woke he smelt coffee, and heard the sound of eggs being whisked in a bowl. Catherine heard him yawn at the door of the kitchen. 'Hope you have an appetite.'

'You'll make someone a great wife one day.'

She looked at him with bright eyes. She had now accepted Panhanagan's presence as something that could not be helped, like an act of God. 'Would you like me to be your wife, Panhanagan?'

'No, you're lousy in bed.'

She laughed. 'Is that all marriage means to you? You'd want for nothing.'

'You mean I'd be a kept man.'

'You'd hate that, wouldn't you?' she said, then stared at him intently. 'I'm a monster. You've turned me into a monster, Panhanagan.' She served him the omelette and sat opposite him. 'I don't think you even like me.'

He shook his head. 'I don't, but the omelette's good.'

Her smile didn't reach her eyes. 'I've been awful to you, yet you're risking everything for me. I realized in that cell that I've been so selfish and I apologize to you for it. May we start again... be friends?'

His eyes found hers. 'I don't make friends with officers.'

She gave him a playful slap. 'I can see through you, Panhanagan. You're all talk.'

'Why are you being nice to me?'

Catherine shrugged. 'You make me feel safe. I have much to thank you for.' Then the mood changed when she said, 'I'm going to kill someone today. No, execute her. I have judged her unworthy to live, so I am going to execute her.'

'Is it worth the risk?' Panhanagan watched her nod. 'Stay here, let me do it. After last night the whole German army will be on the lookout for you. Stay under cover until the dust settles.'

146

'This is something I must do - want to do, for a member of my corps. Then after, we are going for the traitor Siegfried. You finish your breakfast and I'll get myself ready.' She disappeared. He was cleaning her weapon when she walked back into the room. She was almost unrecognisable to him. Catherine wore the spectacles but not a wig. Her natural hair could just be seen between a bright red beret and the red scarf wrapped round her neck. Her features were puffed out with cotton wool. She wore a coat filled with padding that took the shape out of her body and made her look overweight. 'What do you think?'

'Brilliant, but that beret will be seen a mile away.

'That is what people will remember - a bright red beret and nothing else.'

Chapter 20

After a heavy drinking session with Dieter and Hans, Hoffmann stayed the night with them and was late back the following morning. His head ached and he hoped that Model would be away from the office with his usual excuse that he was at a meeting. As he entered the building he knew there was a problem, but the scale of it hit him when he arrived on the fourth floor and saw the chaos. Corporal Hock's features were sickly grey when Hoffmann asked what was going on.

'Hoffmann!' Model shouted from across the room, 'where the hell have you been?'

'I'm sorry, Herr Obersturmbannführer... I,' Hoffmann couldn't finish. He stared at the huge corpse on the floor. The room was full of Gestapo and military police.

'Not a pretty sight, is it Hoffmann? Look at the size of that man. Six feet two inches tall and 210 pounds, yet a young slip of a girl broke his neck.' Hoffmann followed Model into his office, catching the accusing eyes of those he passed. When the door slammed closed Model turned to him, his cheeks rouge with rage. 'I ought to have you shot you cock-happy mongrel.' Model moved uncomfortably close and said between clenched teeth, 'She made a bloody fool of you Hoffmann... and that little maggot, Hock.'

Hoffmann swallowed and looked into Model's questioning eyes. 'Don't tell me she's escaped,' he said pathetically.

'Very well Hoffmann, I shan't tell you. Go and see for yourself and be careful of the pool of blood that will greet you.'

'But how? She was locked in her room and there were three armed guards.'

'How, he asks? How do you think, you idiot? She used that face and body to lure that boy into her room and instead of him thrusting his dick into her she thrust the idiot's own bayonet up into what his mother would describe as his brain. The mess is sickening. The other two had their necks broken, just like that,' he said with the click of his finger and thumb. When Model saw the expression on Hoffmann's face he continued in a sarcastic tone. 'She's a nice little school teacher from Amiens, Herr Obersturmbannführer. I knew her at the Sorbonne. I've checked her out. Butter wouldn't melt in her hot little cunt, Herr Obersturmbannführer.' Model wiped the spittle from his lips with his silk handkerchief. 'You're finished here, Hoffmann. Even that bloody father-in-law won't be able to save you on this one.' Model went to the door and opened it. 'HOCK!' he screamed. 'Could you thrust a bayonet up into someone's brain or snap a neck as if it were a dried twig, Obersturmführer?' Where did she learn to do that? Not with extracurricular activities at the bloody Sorbonne, I know. HOCK!' he called out again.

Corporal Hock entered the office and stood rigid. 'Yes, Herr Obersturmbannführer.'

'What have you told that woman?'

'Nothing, Herr Obersturmbannführer.' Hock could feel the heat of Model's eyes. 'Truly, Herr Obersturmbannführer.'

'Are there any files missing. What could she have read?'

'Absolutely nothing, Herr Obersturmbannführer. The filing cabinets are still locked.'

Model looked at Hock with contempt then crossed the room to a sheepish looking Hoffmann. 'You were duped, Hoffmann. She had you wrapped round her little finger.' Both men watched as the three bodies covered with blankets were taken from the room on stretchers. 'Three armed soldiers dead and you still think she's a typist?' he bellowed at a flushing Hoffmann. 'Do you really think you bumped into her by chance, Obersturmführer? "Oh, good heavens, it's you Ludwig," she says flicking her hair. "Oh, Catherine, what a lovely surprise," he says rubbing his balls. You stupid, bloody idiot. British Intelligence knew about you two and set it up.'

'It *was* a chance meeting, Herr Obersturmbannführer. She never saw me. It was I who noticed her from across the square,' Hoffmann said. 'Why would British Intelligence risk putting an agent in here?'

Model shook his head. 'An office full of files on British agents and you ask a question LIKE THAT.' He took a deep breath and threw his arms into the air. 'IMBECILE! Even Corporal Hock would know the answer to that.'

Hock knew exactly what Catherine wanted. He had already checked his drawer and his list of Abwehr agents was gone, and he couldn't report it without incriminating himself.

Model turned to Hock. 'I'm going to ask you two questions Corporal,' he said, 'and I want truthful answers otherwise I will stretch you up by your balls and let the crows have your cock. Did you check her out, and have you ever discussed with her anything other than routine paperwork?'

'I didn't make the security check, Herr Obersturmbannführer, I'm sorry. I was overworked. I meant to do it, but she just got on with her work and didn't seem a threat.' Hock watched Hoffmann close his eyes and shake his head, 'as for discussing anything with her, no, mein Herr, never, absolutely nothing.'

A sergeant entered the room, saluted and handed a file to Model. Model glanced through it. 'Idiots,' he said and threw the file on his desk. 'The results of the security check from the Gestapo clear her.' He shrugged. 'If she had waited a few more hours I would have released her and we would never have known about her.' Hoffmann felt sudden relief. Model shook his head. 'The fact remains you both disobeyed an order. Leave us, Hock. Get upstairs and clear up that mess,' Model said meeting Hock's nervous eyes. 'I'll deal with you later.'

'Maybe she had help.'

'Who could get into this building?'

'I can't believe she alone killed the guards, particularly in that manner. After all, Herr Obersturmbannführer, the size of that man... she just couldn't have done that.'

Model went and sat at his desk and put his head into his hands. He sat like it for a full minute while Hoffmann stood to attention. It was Hoffmann who broke the silence. 'Perhaps we ought to send our people to Amiens, Herr Obersturmbannführer. It's possible she'll make a run for it there.'

Now calmed, Model drew back from his chair and began to pace the floor with his head bent and hands clasped behind his back. Without looking up he said, 'That report has saved your arse, Hoffmann. Think yourself lucky.' He stopped and grimaced at a tooth lying on the floor next to his desk. Model stared at it. 'You may be right. She can't be on her own. She has to have help. Get the Gestapo in Amiens to go to that address she lived at, arrest anyone there and throw them into Amiens prison, then check out Hock. I don't trust him. He probably talked in return for a fuck.' He looked into Hoffmann's eyes and saw him grimace. Model smiled. 'Can you imagine them together Hoffmann, that little

150

maggot penetrating that juicy piece of fruit? Depositing a little of himself in her piggy bank.' Model revelled in Hoffmann's silent anger. As he walked to the door Model turned to Hoffmann and said, 'Go through the files and check to see if anything is missing.'

Hoffmann's shoulders dropped. 'Yes, Herr Obersturmbannführer.'

When Model was gone Hoffmann went directly upstairs to the cells. Hock sprang to attention. Hoffman's expression was one of tight lips and clenched fists. There was so much blood on the floor Hoffmann considered the victim must have been drained of it.

'I'll ask you just once; did you fuck her, Hock?'

Hock snorted nervously. 'N-no, Herr Obersturmführer.'

Hoffmann drew his pistol from its holster, cocked it and placed it to Hock's head. 'On your knees, Hock, otherwise your blood will join that poor little bastard's. Did you fuck Catherine Régnier?'

'No. I swear I didn't.'

'You were seen out with her. You boasted to Corporal Kohler that you gave her a right seeing to. "She banged like a shithouse door," you told him. I'll give you bang like a shithouse door you long streak of piss.'

Hock was now on his knees. 'I was just boasting Herr Obersturmführer. I never touched her.'

'I ought to shoot you like the dog you are, you skinny piece of shit.' Hoffmann felt the congealed blood under his feet and moved away from it. How could she do this? He thought. What has become of her? 'What information did you give her to get into her bed, Hock?'

'I'm telling the truth, Herr Obersturmführer. I told her nothing. Yes, we went out for dinner, but nothing happened. She was lonely, bored and unhappy; she's divorcing her husband so I asked her out. We did nothing. Can you imagine a girl like her taking a fancy to me?'

'No Hock I can't, but if she was after information then you'd be putty in her hands.' Hoffmann made his pistol safe and replaced it in its holster. 'If I discover that you laid just one of your grubby, nose-picking fingers on Madame Régnier, I won't tie you up by your balls, I'll cut them off. Do you understand, Hock?'

'I've d-done nothing, Herr Obersturmführer.'

'I know this woman, Hock. I was the first man inside her body. There isn't a square millimetre of that soft skin I haven't touched or tasted. I can still smell the scent between her legs. I can still taste her in my mouth. It won't go away, Hock. There's nothing about her I don't know, yet I would willingly pull the trigger on her when we catch her.' He breathed in deeply through his nose and slowly expelled his breath through his mouth. 'Madame Régnier has a sharp mind. She has a fantastic memory, so if she saw anything she will remember it. So think, Hock, think. Did you ever leave her alone? Did she ever see anything?'

'I remember dropping some papers when I was filing them. She helped pick them up.'

'What papers? Show me.'

They went downstairs to the filing cabinet. Hock removed a file and gave it to Hoffmann who took it to his office and went through every paper. Standing to attention before Hoffmann, Corporal Hock was asked to show him which papers she had picked up. Hock looked at the papers spread across Hoffmann's desk. He selected three and handed them to Hoffmann. 'I think they were the papers. I can't be sure, Herr Obersturmführer. She wouldn't have had time to remember all this. A name, perhaps if she saw it and it meant anything to her, but–'

'Shut up, Hock. If you underestimate this woman you do so at your peril. Now go. You make me sick.' Hoffmann studied the papers that Hock had given him. They were not the papers Catherine saw, it was the information he had given her. When Model returned to his office, Hoffmann went to him. 'She's after *Siegfried*, Herr Obersturmbannführer.'

'I don't believe it. They wouldn't risk an agent when they could just recall him. There has to be more.' Model pulled out Catherine's recruitment file from his desk. 'This is Frau Régnier, the picture taken of her for her pass, yes?'

'Yes, Herr Obersturmbannführer.'

Model went to the drawer of his desk and removed a sheet of paper. 'This is a sketch of the women the Gestapo lost, yes?' Hoffmann nodded. Model then drew spectacles on the photograph of Catherine and then a hat covering her hair. 'Do you see?'

'Nora is blonde and fatter in the face.'

'Padding and a blonde wig...'

'And we've not had any wireless traffic for the past two days.'

Obersturmbannführer Kühn, the head of the Gestapo, entered Model's office. He was tapping his hand with a pair of leather gloves, smiling. 'Ah, my dear Erich, I hear we had a British spy working in your office. You did well to suspect and imprison her, but she escaped and she's now on the loose. Well, don't worry; my boys will catch her for you.' His eyes found Hoffmann. 'A mere girl snapped two necks and thrust a bayonet into the skull of another. Incredible, with skills like that she was wasted at your typewriter; she should have worked for me.' He chuckled and threw another scornful look at Hoffmann.

'I shouldn't crow, Jürgen. Your boys lost the woman they followed and your office has just completed a security check on her giving her clearance.'

'They what?'

Model delighted in Kühn's discomfort. He loathed the man, a common upstart. 'We think she's Nora.'

'Impossible. My men have seen both these women.'

'Take a look at this picture, Jürgen. Imagine the face padded out with cotton wool.'

Kühn nodded. 'Such a lovely face.' He turned to Hoffmann, a smile spreading across his huge round face. 'How I would have loved to park my car in that little garage!'

'It might be a tight squeeze, eh Jürgen?' Both men laughed.

Hoffmann's eyes rose to the ceiling. Kühn was no different from Model, even though one was an aristocratic poof and the other a crude, Bavarian pig farmer, who rose through the ranks by torture and murder.

'And what's wrong with you, Obersturmführer Hoffmann?' Kühn said. 'Why are you looking so glum? Don't tell me she failed to put any mustard on your Saxon sausage.'

'Saxon sausage,' Model laughed and glanced up at the clock on the wall. 'Why don't we discuss our business over luncheon, Jürgen? I've discovered a very nice place in Montmartre.'

Kühn stopped at the door and turned to Hoffmann. 'I'm going to let my men fuck her when I catch her Hoffmann, and you can sit and watch. Then, when I have all the information I need from her, I will kill her myself.'

'That's our department, Jürgen,' Model said. 'I will question her then your men can have her, and yes, Hoffmann can watch.'

'We must drink to that, Erich.' Obersturmbannführer Kühn laughed. 'I'll pay for lunch.'

153

Chapter 21

Panhanagan shadowed Catherine across the city to Rue de la Guerre and watched her knock on the door of number 21. A stout woman came to the door. He watched them both enter the house. He melted into a shop doorway and continued to survey the area.

'I'm Obersturmbannführer von Model's personal assistant, Madame. My name is Greta Hindermann.'

'Model... is there anything wrong?'

'Just paperwork. You omitted to sign the receipt for a hundred-thousand francs. We need you to do that to keep our papers in order.'

'I didn't see you at his office.'

'I'm newly appointed.'

'Your French is very good. Would you like some coffee?'

'No thank you. That's for you,' Catherine said handing her an envelope.

The woman opened the envelope, removing a single photograph. It was the picture of Madeleine she had removed from the file. Catherine saw a confused look in the woman's eyes. 'Why are you showing—'

'Shut up,' Catherine snapped, screwing a silencer onto her PPK.

Renée Barrie gasped in alarm and backed away when she saw the weapon. 'What are you doing?'

'You're despicable,' Catherine said scornfully. 'This woman risked her life for France, to help set scum like you free from Nazi tyranny and you betrayed her for money, for greed—'

'Please, I have an elderly mother who depends on me—'

The first shot hit her in the heart. Her knees collapsed. Catherine fired the second shot into the head of the prostrate body, just above the ear, then she wrote one word on the back of the photograph: *Liberté*, and left it on the table for the French police to find. Only a few people were on the street. Catherine pulled the net curtains aside and looked to see if it was clear, then she left the house.

'What was that all about?' Panhanagan asked.

'I've just saved the hangman a job.' Her impassive features looked serene; she might have just taken communion. 'Now for the traitor Bécourt,' she said. 'We'll have to catch a metro and change at the Odéon for Avenue Émile Zola.'

'Are you sure you want to do this?'

'This is one of the reasons I'm here, Panhanagan.'

'I'd still like to see you get out of this in one piece.'

She looked into his eyes and smiled. 'Is the tough Sergeant Panhanagan becoming soft?' She removed the spectacles she was wearing and cleaned them.

'You should be careful with those. I can see there's no prescription in the lenses.'

*

When Model arrived at Renée Barrie's house with Hoffmann and a Gestapo officer it was full of French police. He looked at Renée Barrie's twisted body on the floor. 'Is this how you found her?'

'Yes, Herr Obersturmbannführer. We also found this on the table.'

Model turned the photograph over and read the word *Liberté*. 'Well, Madame Régnier,' he whispered to himself, 'it seems you did go into the files after all. The question is what other names did you pluck from them?'

'She's been dead for less than an hour, Herr Obersturmbannführer. A neighbour called in after she saw a woman leave the house.'

'Description?'

'Stout, red beret, red scarf, grey coat, spectacles, perhaps dark hair, but the beret and scarf covered most of it. That's about it.'

'Stout, that's not Madame Régnier, Herr Obersturmbannführer,' Hoffmann said.

Model gave Hoffmann a withering look then said to a Gestapo officer, 'Circulate that description immediately and put extra men on all metros and railway stations. We've been lucky. This woman could have been lying there for days before she was discovered.'

'One in the head and one in the heart; professional job, Herr Obersturmbannführer,' the Gestapo officer said.

'Madame Régnier likes to break necks and stick bayonets into young boys, but my gut tells me she is a good shot too,' Model said and turned to Hoffmann. 'You may be right about *Siegfried*. Does he have a couple of bodyguards with him?'

'Yes, Herr Obersturmbannführer.'

Model then turned to the Gestapo officer and said, 'When your people catch this woman with the red beret, I want her alive, so don't be heavy handed with her. She'll lead us to Nora.'

*

Shielded by Panhanagan in a doorway, Catherine removed the cotton wool padding from her mouth and cheeks and replaced the coat with one Panhanagan had brought with him in a shopping bag. She changed the red beret for a navy blue one which matched her coat. When she walked past a bin in the street, she dropped the bag of clothes into it.

There were German soldiers and Gestapo at the exit of the metro. 'Papers,' said a guard half heartedly, already bored with this new duty. Catherine offered him her identity papers which said she was Mademoiselle Marie Romand, a hairdresser from Lille. The soldier gave a cursory glance at the papers then glanced up at Catherine, gave her a cheeky smile and waved her on. The Gestapo officer behind him examined her more closely, but was distracted by his colleague calling him to take a look at some papers. Panhanagan walked past unchallenged. At twenty feet distance from each other, they made their way to the address Catherine had read from the file. She was aware the property was probably being watched, but had the ace card up her sleeve; her deadly silent shadow. When she knocked on the door a woman answered. Panhanagan observed the area from a safe distance and waited while the two women spoke. Catherine made her way towards the corner of the street which turned into Rue de la Croix Nivert. From the doorway of a building Panhanagan spotted two men begin to follow Catherine from both sides of the road. Panhanagan held back to see if there was a third. There wasn't. He screwed the silencer onto his PPK. His heart began to beat with excitement. At last, he thought, I can squeeze this bloody trigger. He settled behind them knowing Catherine had spotted one or both because she stopped and looked into a shop window to adjust her beret, a signal to Panhanagan that she was aware of their presence. She walked calmly to the Café Rose and took a seat inside. One of the two men followed her in and sat at a table opening his newspaper, the other stayed outside.

In the corner with two other men was her target, Henri Bécourt. Outside the café she saw the second Gestapo man move across the road, but she could not see Panhanagan. Under the table she fixed

156

the silencer on her weapon and, as the waiter unwittingly distracted the man who had followed her into the café by asking him for his order, Catherine rose, walked across to the Gestapo officer and, from behind the waiter, shot him twice. Before the two men with Bécourt registered what had happened, she killed them both. Henri Bécourt looked through frightened eyes at her. 'Who are you?'

'Your executioner...'

She pointed the weapon at his heart and pulled the trigger - clunk. The magazine was empty. Bécourt reacted surprisingly quickly, jumping to his feet and clutching her arm, but he was thrown onto his back, knocking cutlery and plates to the floor. Customers began to panic when they realized what was happening. Catherine grabbed a fork and thrust it down into Henri Bécourt's eye, which brought louder cries from the women in the café.

Panhanagan rushed into the café, his face concealed by a scarf, like a bank robber in cowboy films, his eyes quickly taking in the scene. He saw the fork sticking in a victim's eye and put two rounds into the head, not trusting the fork to have done its job.

'Where's the other one?' Catherine asked.

'Dead.'

'Get out, get out through the back,' the café owner cried, fear in his eyes for possible reprisals. They followed him out to the back of the building where a black car was parked. He handed her the keys. 'It belongs to one of those you shot. Good luck. Remember I helped you. *Vive la France!*'

Panhanagan shot him through the flesh of his arm. 'That will save your life when the Gestapo arrives, Monsieur.'

Minutes later, they were driving south towards their safe house close to the Cimetière du Père Lachaise. 'Why did that fellow have a fork sticking in his eye?' Panhanagan said, changing gear.

'I ran out of ammunition.'

'What did I teach you about counting rounds fired?' he cried. 'Christ, that's basic stuff.'

'He's dead, isn't he?'

'He certainly is now.' A smile crept across Panhanagan's lips at the memory of the fork half buried in Bécourt's eye. 'I bet he didn't see that coming. A fucking fork... fantastic.'

'Do you have to use that language, Panhanagan?' And, for the first time ever, Catherine heard Panhanagan burst into laughter which brought a smile to her face.

They dumped the car in Rue Civiale close to the Belleville Metro and caught a metro down to Phillipe Auguste station. Later, in the cemetery, Catherine sent a message to London saying her mission was completed. She heard Panhanagan call to her in a loud whisper. 'We've company. It's too late to save the wireless. Destroy it.' Then he positioned himself behind a large monument with his weapon in his hand. Catherine took her weapon from her bag and began to destroy the crystals. This, she knew, was a desperate measure and not taken lightly for she had now lost all links with London. She would decode the returned message later.

Catherine did not hear the two shots Panhanagan fired or see the two soldiers drop when they were almost on top of him. He took the Schmeisser submachine gun from one of the bodies and hung it over his shoulder then picked the other up, checked the magazine and cocked it. He went to Catherine. 'Get out. I'll hold off these clowns.' She hesitated and he pushed at her. 'Go, I'll follow you.' She looked into his eyes, a smile trying to stretch her lips, then turned and followed a route out of the cemetery she knew would be safe.

As she reached the wall she heard automatic gunfire. She checked the spare magazine in her shoulder bag while she waited at the base of the wall for Panhanagan. The German soldiers sounded nervous; they were shouting orders at each other. The light was poor and there was confusion. An authoritative voice called out for them to shut up, but the shouting and gunfire continued. Catherine felt comforted by the fact they hadn't a clue where Panhanagan was.

'Come on Panhanagan,' she whispered through gritted teeth. They had already planned for this eventuality. She was to sit tight for three minutes and then go. It would certainly be lunacy to go back now. The cemetery was large with lots of cover and a soldier as well trained as Panhanagan would make the most of it, she knew. More shouting broke the brief silence, then a short burst of automatic fire, then more shouting. Three minutes was up. She scaled the wall and lowered herself onto Rue de Rondeaux on the opposite side of the cemetery to the safe house in Rue de Mont-Louis, which meant a long, exposed walk round the cemetery wall. As Catherine made her way down the road, she saw two soldiers guarding the closed gates to the side of the cemetery, opposite Avenue du Père Lachaise.

158

'Halt!' One called as she neared them.

She looked at her watch. 'What's the problem? It's not curfew yet,' she said in French. Catherine sensed the soldiers might have been warned that the person they were looking for spoke German - neither replied. It suddenly occurred to her that the gunfire had stopped, but the German soldiers inside the cemetery were still shouting instructions to each other behind the tall brick wall. Panhanagan must have escaped. The two soldiers looked at Catherine hard trying to remember their officer's description of her. 'It's not her,' she heard one say to the other. He winked at Catherine and jerked his head in the direction she was walking. Catherine offered him a bright smile.

She was twenty yards away from the two guards as a Mercedes car passed her. It shuddered to a halt a little in front of her. A soldier got out holding a weapon which he lifted towards her. 'Halt!' he shouted and, without any hesitation, she fired two rounds and turned to run down Rue Emile Landrin as the soldier dropped. She disappeared into a block of flats as a woman left the front entrance with her dog, which began pulling on his lead barking furiously at the closing door. On the third floor, close to the stairs, a man was unlocking his front door. Catherine pushed at him and followed him in. He turned white with shock and whiter still when he saw the weapon in her hand.

Breathing heavily, Catherine looked out of the window and felt some relief that she faced the road and could see what was happening outside. There were four soldiers running up the street. Two were carrying rifles, who she recognised as the guards at the gate, the third was an officer with a pistol in his hand and the fourth carried a Schmeisser submachine gun. She replaced the two rounds she had fired into the PPK's magazine, cocked the weapon and released the safety catch. It was done with such expertise the Frenchman watching her swallowed. He had been in the army and by the way this woman handled the weapon he was aware that she knew how to use it.

'Please Madame, leave my home. They will shoot me if they catch you.'

Catherine had forgotten about the man cowering in the corner. She looked across at him. He looked petrified, which annoyed her. She glared at him with contempt. 'Be a man.'

'I have a wife, a child.'

Catherine's eyes moved round the room. 'What's through there?'

'Bedrooms, kitchen and bathroom...' He went to the window. 'They're coming back, Madame.'

She joined him at the window and saw the officer looking up at the higher floors. She pulled the man away from the window. 'Is there a fire escape at the back?'

'Yes, through the kitchen.'

She went to look and tried the door, but it was locked. The key was not in the lock. When she returned to the sitting room the front door to the flat was open and the man was gone. She rushed to the window and saw him appear in the street, pointing up at the floor on which his flat was situated. One of the soldiers remained at the front of the building, while the officer, pistol in hand, a soldier with the Schmeisser submachine gun and a rifleman entered the building. Her breathing increased when she heard the heavy boots echoing up the stairs. She closed her eyes, breathed in deeply through her nose and expelled it slowly through her mouth. With the door ajar, she crouched down behind the sofa eight feet away so she would see them enter before they saw her. The soldier with the Schmeisser burst into the room, the rifleman following. A snatched, unaimed burst of automatic fire zipped past Catherine. She shot him twice, then fired two more rounds. The rifleman collapsed over his comrade. Catherine rested the PPK on the arm of the sofa and aimed it at the door. She knew the officer was there, but he had no idea she was aware of his presence. Seconds passed; Catherine's hands remained steady. Then the officer burst into the room, his pistol firing indiscriminately. He fell dead beside the other two. Her hand began to shake as she changed the magazine of her PPK. There was still the soldier at the front guarding the house. She fixed on the silencer and took a few more deep breaths.

Now the sound of gunfire had stopped, the soldier outside the building moved onto the street looking up at the window as if he expected one of his colleagues to appear. He slung his rifle over his shoulder, confident he would not need to use it. The Frenchman with him was lighting a cigarette. He looked up when he saw the soldier beside him fall to the ground without understanding why.

'No,' he gasped when he saw an extended arm pointing in his direction. 'Please...'

*

160

'You took your time,' was all Panhanagan said when she returned to the safe house.

Catherine expected little more from him, but she could see the relief of her presence in his eyes. 'I'm glad to see you're in one piece, Panhanagan. I was worried for you,' she said as she pushed past him.

Panhanagan took her arm. 'Wait.' He looked at her coat. It was ripped at the shoulder. There was a bloodstain. 'What happened?'

'You'll be pleased to know I kept my eyes open. I need a bath.'

Another bath, Panhanagan thought. It was almost a religious act rather than one of personal hygiene. He picked up the coat from the floor and inspected the tear. 'Let me look at that wound.'

'It's nothing.'

'It's bleeding, that's enough.'

Catherine removed her jacket then she began to unbutton her blouse while Panhanagan went to the cupboard and collected the first aid kit. When he returned to her she was sitting on the edge of the bath. All she had on above her waist was a camisole. Panhanagan looked at the wound. 'Iodine... this will sting a bit.' It did. Panhanagan placed a plaster over the wound. 'If you were a Yank, they'd give you a Purple Heart for that. In our little army you get nothing, only a scar to remind you that it might have been worse.'

Panhanagan left Catherine to her bath and went to the sitting room. He sat and shook his head. How wrong he was to misjudge that woman so easily, he thought. A little toff, a spoilt brat, a waste of time, he had told Holloway and Peters. Both had disagreed with him. He picked up her weapon from the table where she had placed it. He removed the magazine; it was empty. He felt in her coat pocket and found the other; that too was empty. She had fired off twelve rounds and, knowing what a good shot she was, that was at least six dead. He began to strip her weapon and clean it. When he had completed the job he placed it back on the table. He heard the bathroom door open and then her bedroom door close behind her. Ten minutes passed and she still did not show herself. He went to her room and knocked lightly on her door.

'Come in. I'm decent.'

She was sitting on the edge of the bed with only a large white towel wrapped round her. 'I'm sorry,' he said. 'I didn't realize you had to fight your way back.'

161

'I killed a civilian.'

'What happened?'

'He gave my position away.'

'Little shit got what he deserved. How many soldiers?'

'Five.'

He suppressed a smile. Six, he had been right. 'That tear in your coat was close, another half inch...'

'I'm tired.' When she stood, she put her arms around his neck and laid her head on his shoulder.

'Then rest, put your feet up. I'll make you something to eat.'

'I'm tired of this. I just want to leave and go home.'

He gave her an affectionate squeeze and kissed the top of her head. 'We'll soon be there.'

Her arms tightened a little around his neck as she hung onto him. 'Don't leave... I was frightened. I wanted you there beside me. You give me strength, Panhanagan.' She dug her fingertips into him a little as he pressed his lips on her head again. She looked up into his eyes. Hers looked like spilt ink as her irises grew.

'You are so beautiful,' he whispered. Panhanagan lowered his lips to hers and kissed her. She felt his tongue and massaged it with hers, pulling him tighter to her. When their lips unlocked, their eyes met and held.

'Yes...' she whispered. The white towel that covered her body fell to the floor like a heap of snow. She watched his eyes touch her breasts, her belly the dark hair between her legs.

In one quick swoop he picked her up and laid her on her bed. He began to tear the clothes from his body, his flesh growing rigid with desire for her. It was the first time she had seen this physical state in a man and was excited by it. Catherine lifted her arms towards him welcoming him to her when he moved onto the bed. They kissed, sucking and biting each other's lips. 'Now...' she whispered, 'love me, Panhanagan.' She instinctively raised her knees and spread her thighs for him, her eyes fixed on his. A deep groan left her mouth when he pushed, and for a brief moment, she lost sight of his face. She clung onto his body as a shipwrecked sailor clings desparately to driftwood on a rough sea.

After, they both lay unmoving, listening to the labour of each other's lungs. When he was no longer physically able to stay inside her body, Panhanagan rolled from her onto his back. She moved on her side and faced him, staring into his features. His eyes were closed, his breathing now normal. For some minutes she just looked at him. He did not to seem to want to talk. Perhaps lovers didn't after they had made love, so she silently lay in the solitude of her contentment.

'I know you're looking at me,' he suddenly said, his eyes still closed. Panhanagan turned and looked into her face. Her cheeks were hot and red; a smile crept to her lips.

'I was,' she whispered. 'I thought you were sleeping.' She moved and rested her head on his chest, unable to suppress another smile. So that was the act of love between a man and woman, she thought and began to run her fingertips over his chest, his stiff nipples. Now she had been given licence to touch his body without embarrassment, shame or apology. She had taken possession of it and it was as much hers now as his. 'I don't know why we haven't done that before,' she whispered. 'I've wanted to.' She ran her fingers over his face. 'I gave you the opportunity to do so the other night, but you just came and closed my door. Had you walked into my room I wouldn't have objected.'

'I wasn't going to risk another kick in the balls. It's not the sort of foreplay that gets men excited.'

She laughed. She was happy and moved to look into his eyes, kissing each in turn, then his nose and his lips. 'You're my first.' When his eyes widened, she said, 'There's no blood. Another had that. I was drugged−'

'You don't have to explain, Catherine.'

'I do. He took what you should have had. In my head you're my first. That matters to me...'

'Why?'

'Because I love you... there, I've said it.' She looked into his face for a reaction. 'I love you,' she whispered again.

He cradled her in his arms. 'I knew you did, even when you were being a bitch.'

She slapped him playfully calling him conceited, then buried herself back in his arms. She loved the feeling of his protective embrace and, with her head on his chest, she could hear his heart beating. The fear of only an hour ago had left her in one almighty release. Is that what having sex with a man one loves does to one, she wondered? She winced at a sudden sting of the wound.

'Does that hurt?'

'It stings a little. I'm sure it will be fine tomorrow.' She pressed her lips on his chest and could taste the salt from his body and smell his masculine scent.

He looked at the blue flesh that had spread beyond the edges of the plaster. 'You're going to have a fair old bruise. He bent and kissed it.

'Will you teach me things? You know, what to do, how to please you... to be a good lover for you.'

Panhanagan shifted as if he was preparing himself for sleep. 'We'll have our first lesson in the morning.'

She brazenly reached between his legs and felt his flesh stir. 'How long does it take for this thing to get a second wind?' She smiled as it grew in her hand. 'Umm, so the sergeant likes this.' When he rolled above her, she kissed him. 'This time Panhanagan,' she whispered biting his earlobe, 'don't be so rough with me.'

*

Catherine woke during the early hours of the morning with her head on Panhanagan's shoulder and an arm draped over his body. She carefully moved from him and went to the kitchen for some water. Her mind was alive with the thought of escaping Paris. She knew they could stay in the flat for a few months if they were careful. Nobody knew about Panhanagan; he could go out and get the supplies or they could make their way towards Amiens, cycling there at night.

As she pondered on these thoughts, she remembered the coded message from London and went to her coat. After decoding it, she looked up and saw Panhanagan standing by the door.

'Can't you sleep?' he said.

'We've got four days to make the rendezvous for a Lysander. To be certain of meeting it, we need to make a move.'

'Too risky,' Panhanagan said filling a kettle. 'I think we would be better off staying here and make our own way back later when things quieten down.'

When Catherine moved her chair back and stood up, Panhanagan put his arms round her waist. 'I cannot let you take any more risks. After last night there'll certainly be reprisals so the French will be against you too. Any one of those bastards will give you up.'

'We could make a move for Spain.'

'Let's get some sleep. We'll talk about it in the morning.'

164

Model banged his desk with his fist so hard he winced with the pain from it. He looked up at Hoffmann who suppressed a grin. 'My career is in tatters... tatters! We'll both end up facing a bloody firing squad if we don't arrest this witch soon. She's running amok. First the Barrie woman, then four Gestapo officers, as for Siegfried, she wasn't content with sticking a fork in his eye, she shot him twice in the head as well, callous bitch. It was sickening to see it. How many soldiers were killed in that cemetery?'

'Including those outside the cemetery, thirteen in all, plus four wounded, one seriously... and a civilian.'

'I don't care about the bloody civilian.'

'Plus, of course, the three soldiers in our office the evening before.'

'Good God who are we dealing with here, the brigade of Guards or some deranged lunatic?'

'This proves she can't be alone, Herr Obersturmbannführer.'

'Didn't anyone in the café get her description?'

'Nothing to say it was definitely her. One witness said it happened so quickly the situation was confusing. People threw themselves to the ground, buried their heads in their arms—'

'What on earth was she doing in the cemetery?'

'Sending a message. By chance one of our wireless direction vans was parked close by with an officer and twenty soldiers.'

'So it must have been Nora. That Régnier bitch is Nora and you let her into our offices.'

'You approved her appointment, Herr Obersturmbannführer.' Hoffmann felt the sudden heat of Model's eyes. 'The surviving soldiers from the cemetery said the gunman was no amateur. No one actually saw who was shooting at them. Those that did are dead.'

'Well, I say Nora and that witch Régnier is the same person. God, I thought the bayonet thrust up into that boy's brain was bad enough, but a fork in Siegfried's eye...' He strode across the room and took a cigarette from the box on his desk. 'Who would have believed that young woman capable of such savagery?'

'I think she's now completed what she came to do, Herr Obersturmbannführer.'

'You're probably right. Now she has to get out. Christ, I almost admire the witch.'

'I've instructed all known Lysander landing areas to be watched–'

'She won't need a Lysander. She'll fly out on her broomstick.'

Hoffmann snorted like a schoolboy. 'Very funny, Herr Obersturmbannführer.'

'Have you set up road blocks?'

'Yes, surrounding Paris, and Madame Régnier's picture has been circulated. Her face will be seen on posters in every town and city. She'll never escape Paris, let alone France.'

Model nodded. 'Good... of course I shall have to answer for the resources used over this.' He paced the room and shook his head. 'It's unbelievable. If you sat beside her at dinner you'd never believe that sweet little English aristocrat was the devil. I shall never be able to look her in the eye again for fear she will stick something into it.'

'She's French, Herr Obersturmbannführer. The Gestapo confirmed it.'

'I don't believe it for a moment, Hoffmann. We cannot trace a single relative, not one. If I wanted to I could trace every little bastard you've left around Europe, but she's left nothing. Even a mongrel has a history. I grant you she may have been born here and her French is excellent, but that doesn't make her French. British Intelligence has done a good job creating this woman. I underestimated them.'

'But I knew her two years before the invasion of France. Her French nationality was never questioned. What makes you so certain she's English?'

'Class, Hoffmann. Something you wouldn't understand,' Model said and his eyes challenged Hoffmann to disagree. 'I know the English aristocracy,' he continued. 'I've lived with viscounts, shot with earls, dined with dukes...'

And slept with baronets, Hoffmann thought as Model began to pace the room again.

'You can put a Rolls-Royce engine into a lorry Hoffmann and it will still look like a lorry until you switch on the ignition and hear that glorious purr. Class Hoffmann; you can disguise it but you can't hide it.'

Hoffmann was spared more metaphors with the appearance of the bulky Obersturmbannführer Kühn who greeted Model with a nod. Hoffmann eyed the two men. Despite their different in class, they were as bad and as crude as each other.

Model had similar thoughts when he met Kühn's eyes. The man was uncouth, a ruthless murdering bully; common as muck and far too ambitious. 'Good morning, Jürgen,' Model said with a charming smile. 'Our gunman, it seems, was Nora.'

Kühn grunted. 'How do you know that? Not one person in the café could identify her or give a description. I'm even told the Wehrmacht didn't see who was shooting at them in the cemetery. The only witnesses in the Rue Emile Landrin are dead. If no one saw anyone then how do you know it was the bitch in the cemetery and in the Frenchman's flat?'

'Because we found her wireless set. She destroyed it of course.'

'This woman is not working alone,' Kühn said. 'I don't like being made a fool of by some little tart. I just cannot believe she alone was responsible for so many deaths. One slip of a girl against how many, and she escaped yet again?' He lit a cigarette, threw the match at the ashtray on Model's desk and missed. He made no attempt to remove it.

Model looked at Kühn with contempt and made a theatrical display of dropping smouldering wood into an ashtray. 'I think we can be certain that it was Nora in the cemetery and that Madame Régnier and Nora is the same person.'

Kühn looked across at Model. 'The abandoned wireless doesn't prove those two women are the same person, but if you're right...' Kühn spat out a flake of tobacco; it too landed on Model's desk. Model stared at it as if were a rotting corpse, then he returned his gaze to Kühn, '...if you're right, then she's the bitch who killed four of my men at that café.' His lip curled. 'God, she'll be sorry she was ever born if I get my hands on her. I have already had thirty civilians shot and will shoot thirty more if I get no information about this woman.' His neck and face became scarlet as his voice rose. 'Someone must know her. She calmly walks into a café and guns down my men as if it's an American gangster film then calmly walks out again and disappears into thin air in one of my cars.'

167

'The owner got shot trying to stop them escaping. We've arrested his waiter, but he says he was lucky not to be shot too,' Model said, watching Kühn flick ash onto the polished floor. 'Let me get you an ashtray, Jürgen. You are turning my office into a billiard room.'

'Is she SOE?'

'No. British Intelligence. London has sent her independent of the normal channels,' Hoffmann said.

'What's their game then, Erich?' Kühn said, scratching one of his chins.

'Obviously Bécourt was on her hit list. As for the Barrie woman, she was nothing; a revenge killing for betraying Madeleine... I admire that. Shows a touch of decency, don't you think?' Model caught Kühn's expression and gathered he didn't agree.

'Destroying that wireless was either an act of desperation or she has made her last contact with London and is now getting out.'

Kühn looked across at Model and nodded. He pondered on that observation for a moment. 'She'll make a break for it.'

'I really can't imagine she would have taken such risks just to assassinate Siegfried, Herr Obersturmbannführer. He was no longer much use to us now we've cleaned up Paris. The British would have known that.'

'But you haven't cleaned up Paris Obersturmführer Hoffmann,' Kühn said. 'You have a madwoman on the loose out there.'

'Siegfried didn't know about her. They bypassed him so they must have suspected him. Killing him was a message to us.'

'So enlighten us Hoffmann, what was the message?' Model asked. 'I presume she mentioned it when you were fucking her.'

Hoffmann clenched his teeth in his silence.

Kühn chuckled. He enjoyed it when the poof was crude. 'So where do you think she's heading, Erich?'

Corporal Hock sprang to attention when the three officers entered the room. They ignored him as a beggar is ignored in the street and walked to the map of Paris, which was pinned to a board and beside it, another map of France.

'She was last spotted here,' Model said, pointing to the spot with the tip of his SS dagger, presented to him by the Führer himself, 'and nothing has been seen of her since.'

168

The three men poured over the map, trying to make sense of an impossible situation. 'Where was she staying?' Kühn asked.

'At the Hotel Cambrai. It's a cheap hotel near the Gard du Nord. She's no longer there, of course. Your men checked it out.'

'I remember. Her room was a mess apparently. Clothes scattered everywhere, toiletries opened and not put away, and she had left her personal documents in a satchel. Those, by the way, confirmed her story.'

'Forgeries?'

'They were genuine Are you suggesting my men are incapable of a thorough examination? Everything was checked. She was seen coming and going by the concierge, consistent with her hours of work. She kept herself to herself and had one visitor...' Kühn's eyes moved towards Hoffmann.

Model gave Hoffmann with a withering look. 'Corporal Hock, get me Hotel Cambrai on the phone and hurry up about it.'

The telephone rang. Model snatched up the receiver and said, 'Obersturmbannführer von Model of the Sicherheitsdienst, are you the receptionist? Good ... Madame Régnier, when did you last see her? ... Not for several days ... She paid three months in advance you say ... Did she ever have anyone stay with her or visit her? ... Is that right?' Model glanced at Hoffmann, who avoided his eyes. 'When was this? Thank you,' Model replaced the receiver. 'I'll speak to you later, Hoffmann.'

Kühn chuckled like a schoolboy and wagged his podgy finger at Hoffmann. 'So we have found her accomplice. Is that where you wet your willy, Hoffmann?' Kühn picked up the telephone receiver, still chuckling. 'Get some men down to the Hotel Cambrai in the 10th arrondissement and search Madame Régnier's room again, thoroughly. I want everything in it bagged and brought back. Oh... and see if you can find a pair of German army issue underpants ... what? No, just get on with it.' Kühn was about to share some more filth when all three officers turned at the sound of Corporal Hock's voice.

'Madame Régnier said that she sometimes stays with a friend in the 16th arrondissement, Herr Obersturmbannführer.'

'Where in the 16th arrondissement?' Kühn growled.

'Rue de la Faisanderie, Herr Obersturmbannführer.'

'That's just across the road,' Kühn said. 'Why didn't you say anything about this before?'

'I didn't think it important, Herr Obersturmbannführer.'

Model's eyes widened. 'We've been getting wireless signals right under our noses and you keep that to yourself. Is this where that bitch fucked you in return for information?'

Hock looked horrified. 'No, Herr Obersturmbannführer. I-I never went to this flat.'

'You give some story about her seeing information from dropped papers,' Model continued, spittle bubbling at the side of his mouth, 'and expect us to believe that?'

Kühn's shoulders shook. 'Now you're fucked again Corporal,' and he laughed, holding his belly. When Kühn stopped laughing he said, 'You boasted to some of my men next door that you had given her one.' Kühn said. 'I expect *one* is all a runt like you could manage.' He turned and faced a shrinking Corporal Hock. 'I'm going to nail your balls to the bedpost if I find one trace of evidence that you were ever in that flat.' Kühn's menacing tone made Hock shiver.

'Hock is under my command, Jürgen,' Model said with a charming smile. 'He will answer to me... later.'

'One button, one thread or a single spunk stain on a sheet suggesting you were in that flat...' He glanced at Model, then at the map. 'So Erich,' he said congenially. 'Do you think she's still in Paris?'

'Yes I do, lying low like a rat somewhere, but she will have to show herself sooner or later.' Model turned to Hoffmann. 'Did our people pick up anything from her last transmission, Obersturmführer Hoffmann?'

'Signals still haven't broken her code, Herr Obersturmbannführer, but they think part of the message was a map reference.'

'We need that map reference. Give it top priority, Obersturmführer.'

'They'll never escape Paris,' Kühn said, his piggy eyes alert in his jowly face. 'I'll slam every door shut on them. An educated guess, Erich...where will they meet that plane?'

Model shrugged. 'There's the map of France, take your pick.'

'Is that all you can say?' Kühn said, staring at the map.

'Obersturmführer Hoffmann has deployed troops at all known Lysander landing areas, but Nora could be picked up anywhere.' He shook his head. 'And to think I once joked about the Scarlet Pimpernel.'

'Scarlet Pimpernel?' Kühn said, scratching his arse. 'What the hell's the Scarlet Pimpernel?'

Model shook his head. 'It doesn't matter Jürgen.'

'It's a novel by Baroness Orczy,' Hoffmann said to Kühn, 'set during the reign of terror–'

Hoffmann stopped speaking when he saw the lips of both Model and Kühn curl as they looked across at him.

Chapter 23

Over a month had passed since the gun battle in and around the Cimetière du Père Lachaise. Panhanagan went out during the day to buy provisions. Catherine only left the safety of the flat at night when she would stroll along the quiet, lonely streets and fill her lungs with the chilly frosted air, holding onto Panhanagan as lovers do, stopping to kiss if someone approached, not just to hide her face, but because they were in love.

Christmas and New Year had passed and they were almost into February. Neither had wished the other a happy New Year for they knew they were still in grave danger. *Happy* was not a word they associated with their situation, but in many ways they were happy, locked in the flat where they spoke of their past, but never made plans for the future.

Panhanagan gently left the bed they now shared and lightly pressed his lips on her cheek. It was warm like a child's. She stirred and in her sleep reached out for him in the vacant place beside her. He stood looking at her and delicately removed some hair from her lips then he pulled the blanket higher to cover her naked body. In the kitchen he drank some water. He was restless and could not relax. He went to the sitting room and stood at the window staring out at the moon, whose pale blue light illuminated the roofs and streets along Rue de Mont-Louis. The streets below were deserted and wet with snowflakes now beginning to fall. Even the German patrols after the shootings were no longer seen at night.

Later that morning they were going to make their way south towards Spain. They had made their decision and the weather was not going to stop them leaving now. Panhanagan calculated that Model would have guessed they were holed up somewhere and would appear again in the spring like animals from hibernation. Now was the perfect time to move because in this weather it would not be unusual to see people walk the streets or ride their bicycles with a scarf wrapped round their face for warmth, leaving only their eyes visible.

Catherine's mission was over, but his wasn't. He was charged to see her back to England safe and sound. As he contemplated this, he sensed her presence behind him, before he felt her arms encircle him, her lips on the back of his neck, then the weight of her forehead rest on his shoulder.

'Why are you in here?'

Panhanagan turned, took her face in his hands and kissed her lips. 'I just want to get going. All we have to do is get out of Paris and then we're on our way.'

'That won't be so difficult. They haven't enough men to watch it all.'

'You may be right. Last time I was out I noticed the roadblocks were gone, but then they don't need so many. Your face is plastered all round the city. A tasty reward has been offered for any information that leads to your arrest. One telephone call to say where you can be found will earn someone a very nice 500,000 francs.'

'I'm worth that much?'

'Think of the man who betrayed you just for being in his flat and the woman who betrayed Madeleine. I'm half French yet I wouldn't trust the buggers if they were the only people left on the planet. They're frightened. They want to get out of this mess alive like everyone else.'

'I'll become a blonde again. I still have the wig Susan gave me. Only the Sicherheitsdienst and the Gestapo know about her, so I won't be having the natives of Paris gawping at me. That cuts the odds a bit.'

'Do you still have her papers?'

She nodded. 'I love you,' she whispered.

He took hold of Catherine and kissed her on her forehead, then on her nose, before she pulled his face down to her lips.

*

At six, Catherine began to prepare a breakfast that would last them until evening. Panhanagan could already see a change in her. She had become her old lively self. He went and looked around the area for signs of any German patrols. A half hour later, they left the flat under a sky that had taken on the look of muddy water since Panhanagan had been out. They casually cycled, zigzagging their way through the streets north of the Bois de Vincennes, avoiding the Avenues and Boulevards by staying on the smaller, narrower streets as much as possible. Catherine led with Panhanagan behind her at a safe distance, but close enough to be of assistance should a problem arise. With her blonde hair only just visible between her scarf and beret and spectacles peering out between both, there was nothing remarkable about Catherine to attract any attention. The road block inspections were never on the minor roads, instead, on many street corners there were only pairs of soldiers stamping their feet and blowing into their hands, their rifles slung over their shoulders. They were not vigilant or even very interested. They preferred to eye passing women rather than look for one particular woman.

Catherine set a steady pace, yet it was cautious enough to change direction at a moment's notice without causing suspicion. When they crossed the Boulevard de Strasbourg, they dropped down towards the district of Champigny-sur-Marne where they rested for fifteen minutes in the Parc de Détente et de Loisirs du Tremblay.

Children were playing and mothers were chatting. There wasn't a German soldier in sight. No one gave either of them a second glance. They were no different from any other Parisians enjoying a day out. Panhanagan went and sat with Catherine. He took her hand and squeezed it. 'We're doing well,' he said. Catherine's eyes found his and he saw in them her smile, although her mouth was covered by her scarf. They watched a young woman walk by, pushing a pram, with two very young children holding onto their mother's coat. Catherine's eyes followed them along the path. How uncomplicated life was for some. She turned to Panhanagan and touched his cheek with her gloved hand. 'We'd better make a move.'

'Still Noiseau?

She nodded. 'We can put up there for the night. If there is any trouble, the Forêt Domaniale de Notre-Dame is close by. We could lose anyone in there.'

*

An old man, whose eyes were red with age and skin had the pallor of death, appeared at the sound of the bell chiming as the front door opened. Panhanagan glanced around the lobby and saw that the only way to the rooms upstairs was past the reception desk. Behind the desk was a small room where the old man sat and read when he was not busy.

'Do you have a room for the night?'

The old man looked up at the unshaven man before him. 'Papers?'

Panhanagan handed him his papers and the old man went through the ceremony of checking them and filling in forms. Catherine would have to sneak in and join him later, because she could not risk registering as Mademoiselle Berling from Arras. The Gestapo would soon be onto her.

'The police come in at nine to take away the registration cards,' he said, pushing one across to Panhanagan as if reading his mind. 'Hope you've nothing to hide, Monsieur. I don't want trouble with the police.' His red eyes met Panhanagan's frigid blue eyes. 'Money in advance.'

'Do you serve dinner here?'

'My granddaughter cooks. She's good too. People come from all around to taste her food.' The old man's eyes narrowed. 'Particularly German officers. They're good spenders. We finish serving at nine-thirty.'

'I'd like a table for two. I'm expecting a guest.'

'A woman, I suppose.' The old man nodded to himself, he had seen it all before. 'Don't forget you've paid for a single. I shall keep my eyes open, Monsieur.'

Panhanagan was given a key and he went to the first floor, where the room was located. It was small, but had a double bed. He opened the window and saw he was at the back of the hotel, away from the road. He kept the window open and draped a towel over the windowsill so Catherine would know which room he was in. When he descended the stairs, the old man was back in his small room behind the reception desk, reading a book with the aid of a magnifying glass. Panhanagan glanced up at the bell on the door. The slightest movement of the door would activate the spring and announce anyone entering or leaving the building. 'Is there anywhere I can put my bicycle for the night?' Panhanagan asked, leaning across the reception counter.

The old man looked up from his book and screwed up his face. 'What was that?'

Panhanagan repeated the question and was told to put it in the yard at the back.

Catherine smiled like a small boy out on an adventure. 'It won't be a problem to climb a few feet up the drainpipe.' And up she went, climbing unseen in the poor light into Panhanagan's room. When he joined her she was drying herself. 'What time's dinner?'

He looked at his watch and went to her. The towel slipped to the ground. 'Not for an hour.'

*

Panhanagan followed Catherine to the table. She had a handkerchief and hand covering half her face, as if she was blowing her nose. When they sat, Panhanagan had his back to the wall and could see everything. Catherine faced him with her back to all the other diners. The waitress came and apologized about the position of the table. She was young and pretty and full of smiles. 'It's not the best table in the room, but at least it's private,' she said. 'Would you like any wine?'

'Water,' Panhanagan said. Noticing the interest the waitress was taking in Catherine. 'Do you think she recognized you?' He said when the waitress had left them.

'What is she doing now?'

'Taking another order.'

Panhanagan finished the rabbit stew and wiped his plate clean with his bread. Catherine looked on disapprovingly, but said nothing. He shrugged and smiled. 'I was hungry,' he said, as if he could read her mind.

Catherine returned his smile, but sensed something was wrong when Panhanagan's eyes moved sharply from hers. Four German officers had entered the small restaurant and nodded politely at their fellow diners. They sat at a large reserved table across the room from Catherine and Panhanagan.

'Don't look around,' Panhanagan said taking Catherine's wrist. 'We've got a problem,' Panhanagan said slipping the bedroom key across the table. 'Go and get our suitcases. Leave through the bedroom window. I'll see you outside. Go now.'

Catherine didn't argue. She walked quickly to the door, and as she reached it, heard one of the Germans shout, 'HALT!'

Panhanagan rose from his seat and shot the two Germans with pistols in their hand then shot the other two as they fumbled for their weapons. The noise of the shots caused confusion then panic amongst the diners. Panhanagan grabbed hold of the waitress who stiffened, her eyes bulging in their sockets. 'I ought to fucking shoot you, you stupid cow.' He moved quickly to the door and left the restaurant, stepping over people lying on the ground.

Chapter 24

'Good morning, Herr Obersturmbannführer. Have you heard about the four Wehrmacht officers murdered out at Noiseau?'

'Yes. It's a matter for the military police.'

'A woman was involved. Young, good looking...'

'A young woman...' Model placed his briefcase on the table, in a sudden thoughtful mood. 'I think we'll involve ourselves. I can suddenly smell Madame Death.' Model shook his head. 'What's wrong with that woman? Why can't she just go to a restaurant and drink tea instead of causing mayhem?'

Both men walked to the large map on the wall. 'Madame Régnier was last seen here, in the area of the Cimetière du Père Lachaise,' Hoffmann said. 'We now know she has a male accomplice from the shootings in the café. A witness confirmed that, but we still haven't a decent description of him.'

'If they were holed up then he must have gone out to buy provisions. Did the Gestapo question the shopkeepers in that area?'

'No, Herr Obersturmbannführer.'

'They should have done,' he said curtly. 'You see to it. Let's try and get a better description of the accomplice.'

Model ran his finger along the map of Paris from the Cimetière du Père Lachaise to Noiseau. He then stepped across to the large map of France and, with one hand tucked under his arm and the other holding his chin, he stood staring at it. 'Not even a rat could have got through the wall we put up after those shootings now they feel it's safe to move.'

'But why give their position away? If they are the killers and they've reached Noiseau, they have a clear run for Switzerland.'

Model nodded. 'Or Spain.'

'Spain is much further away, Herr Obersturmbannführer. It's a greater risk.'

'You may be right, but my gut says Spain. I think we should get over there now. Find out what exactly led up to those murders. As you say, why give your position away... unless, she was recognized and they had to shoot their way out of that restaurant.'

'There can be no other explanation, Herr Obersturmbannführer.'

'Four good men dead because of that bitch,' Model said shaking his head. 'She's the devil. I'm surprised you didn't catch the pox when you stuck it into her, and by the way Hoffmann, Kühn says there is a Monsieur Régnier working at the lycée, but he is in his late fifties. Her cover is beginning to crumble. What is it about her that makes men do such stupid things?'

'Stupid things, Herr Obersturmbannführer?'

'Corporal Hock has been lying to me. Kühn tells me Hock was seen, or at least a German soldier fitting his description was seen entering the flats at Rue de la Faisanderie, with a woman fitting Madame Régnier's description.' Model glanced towards Hoffmann and delighted at seeing the force of jealousy drain the blood from his cheeks. 'I mean, Hock is not an attractive man, so it wasn't his good looks that drove him into her arms, was it now? He is socially inept and has the personality of a stuffed pig. All this poppycock about reading the files while on the floor. Complete nonsense. I tried it myself. You try it, Ludwig. Spread some papers on the floor and see if you can remember anything on them in the time it takes to pick them up. Quite impossible to remember the information Hock alleges she did.'

'She has a very good memory, Herr Obersturmbannführer.'

'She's forgotten you.' Model laughed and slapped his knee, then laughed louder still. 'Oh come on, Ludwig. You have a wife who will soon bear you a child. Soon she will be in Paris. Cheer up. The Sorbonne and the delights of Madame Régnier should now be a distant memory for you.' His expression changed. 'Shouldn't it?'

'Yes, Herr Obersturmbannführer.'

'So when you took her to that grubby little hotel Obersturmführer, was it a trip down memory lane and nothing more?'

'Nothing happened. She got nothing from me, Herr Obersturmbannführer.'

'Other than the route into our building, our offices, our files,' Model snapped. 'Why else were you in her bed?'

'I didn't sleep with–'

'Shut up, you fool! Are you conceited enough to think she loves you when she does the same with Hock? So gather up that brain you suppose to have and use it. Let's get to Noiseau. She's behind those killings, I'm certain of it, which means the vixen has at last left her den.'

*

A military policeman approached the car as it pulled up outside the hotel. Hoffmann followed Model into the reception. Soldiers sprang to attention and the officer in charge of the military police approached Model and saluted him.

'I have questioned the old man, Herr Obersturmbannführer. We have to be careful with him. I think the shock of it has brought him closer to his maker.'

'So what? You're a policeman Hauptmann, not a bloody priest.'

The Captain of military police was taken aback by Model's retort and unfriendly manner. He gave his report. The old man knew nothing other than the sound of shooting. His daughter and son-in-law were out for the day... they normally run the hotel. His granddaughter was in the kitchen. One of the waitresses recognized the Régnier woman.'

'What did I tell you Hoffmann?' he said, rubbing his stomach. 'It never lets me down.' Pleased with himself, he turned to the Captain of military police with a smile. 'Leave the old man and waitress. I'll question them. Where are they now?'

'The old man is through here, Herr Obersturmbannführer. The waitress isn't in yet.'

'Well get her here. She's the main witness.'

Seeing two SS Sicherheitsdienst officers enter the room, the old man stiffened and struggled to get to his feet. 'Please Monsieur,' Model said, removing his greatcoat and throwing it over a chair, followed by his hat and gloves, 'sit, please sit. That business last night must have been an awful shock to you.'

Model's pleasant and friendly voice in the Frenchman's native language, brought a noticeable change in the man. He sat and looked up at Model, his strained face breaking into a weak smile. 'I'll help in any way I can.'

'Of course you will, Monsieur. I know it.'

'He should be shot along with his granddaughter, Herr Obersturmbannführer,' Hoffmann said in French, staring the old man in the eye.

It was the old routine. This terrified the old man and he gasped. 'We had nothing to do with this. I beg you to believe me. I never trusted that man. The German officers were regular customers. Good men and always very friendly,' he said crossing himself with his hand. 'Why should you shoot me for someone else's evil act?'

179

Hoffmann leant towards him. 'Someone has to pay for the lives of four German officers, so why not you, your daughter and son-in-law... your granddaughter?' Model glanced at Hoffmann as if to say, don't overdo it.

'No! Please, my granddaughter's innocent. She was in the kitchen. They're all innocent.'

'Come, come, Obersturmführer,' Model said, 'this poor fellow can't be blamed for the vile deeds of the Maquis. I'm sure we shall catch them. Shan't we, Monsieur?' Model's smile was no longer comforting to the old man.

'I don't know them, really I don't.'

Model still had a charming expression on his face; his bright eyes glowed with understanding and sympathy. 'I'm certain you don't.'

'He's lying, Herr Obersturmbannführer.'

The old man begged Model to believe him. 'Of course I believe you, Monsieur. Obersturmführer,' Model said sternly and still in French, 'you are not behaving in a way a German officer should. Please leave the room. I will not have you frighten an elderly, innocent man in this way.'

'But Herr Obersturmbannführer–'

'Leave the room!' Model bellowed.

Hoffmann left the room and raised his eyes at the military police officer outside. 'The games we play to put these scum at their ease,' he said. 'Do you have a cigarette, Herr Hauptmann?'

Back inside the restaurant, Model had taken a seat in a friendly position close to the old man who now looked up at the German officer with a pitiful smile. 'I really don't know who shot those officers, Herr Obersturmbannführer. I've never had trouble before–'

'There were two of them, I believe. Who did the shooting; the man, the woman or both?'

'The man.'

'You saw it.'

'No, it's what Isabelle told me. She saw it all.'

'Isabelle?'

'My waitress. I gave her the day off. I cannot open for business today. Anyway, she's in shock. It was a terrible thing for such a young girl to see.'

'Why don't we have some tea while we wait for her?'

'Yes, yes, anything, Herr Obersturmbannführer. You must come one evening, Herr Obersturmbannführer. My granddaughter is a wonderful cook; bring a guest, on me, of course.'

'How kind.' Model's smile was still full of charm. He patted the old man's clammy hand. 'The man who did the shooting, can you describe him?'

'He was scruffy, unshaven. Not the sort of fellow one normally has dining in my place.' The old man said struggling to raise himself from his chair.

'That description could fit half the French population. Anything more?'

'No Sir.'

'Go and organize the tea and tell the Obersturmführer to come in please, Monsieur.'

When Hoffmann entered the room, Model asked if he had checked the register. 'He's booked in as Monsieur Darel, a citizen living in Lille. There's no woman booked in with him.'

'Call the Gestapo in Lille. Check it out.'

The old man returned with a tray of tea which he had difficulty carrying. He eyed Hoffmann. Model took the tray from him. He even poured the tea while Hoffmann disappeared to make the telephone call to Lille. 'Try really hard to remember anything more about the gentleman, Monsieur.'

He shrugged. 'His eyes were cold. Shoot you as soon as to look at you that one. I asked for the money up front.'

'And why do you think he would shoot you as soon as to look at you?'

'Seen it in the eyes of men coming back from Verdun. There were those who looked terrified and those who looked hard. He was the second sort.'

'A military man?'

'Definitely. Seen it all before. That one can look death in the eye with a smile. What he was doing with such a lovely girl like her beats me,' he said, shaking his head. 'Young girls these days—'

'I thought you didn't see her.'

'The military policeman showed me her picture. Lovely looking girl.'

'Yes, yes, a lovely looking girl...' Model said, beginning to tire of the old man.

The old man caught Model's eye. 'I'm trying to help.'

Model strained another smile. 'Have you ever heard an Englishman speaking French?'

The old man nodded. 'Before the war, but this man wasn't English. His accent was French.'

Just then the waitress was shown into the room. Her eyes shone with the same terrible concern as the old man had shown when Model first arrived with Hoffmann. She received the same friendly smile, which disappeared when Model noticed Hoffman's eyes on the young girl's breasts. He threw Hoffmann a withering look then turned to the girl. 'Come in Isabelle, such a pretty name. Please, take a seat. There is nothing to worry about, really there isn't. I only want your memory. I know you had nothing to do with that unfortunate business last night. Now Isabelle, tell me exactly what happened.'

'After the shooting, you mean?'

'Start from the beginning.'

'From when he placed his order?'

'Why would I be interested in what he ordered?' Model said with irritation.

'I recognized her... from the poster.'

'Show me where they sat.'

'There Sir,' she said, pointing to the area away from the bloodstains and broken crockery.

Model noticed her finger shook and patted her other hand. 'Relax, Isabelle. You're not in trouble.'

'The man had his back to the wall facing the door and she had only him and the wall to look at. I thought that was rude. Any other man would let the lady sit where he sat.'

'Let's go and sit where they sat.'

From the chair where Panhanagan had sat, Model surveyed the room. Very clever, he thought. No one in the restaurant would have been able to get a good look at her yet her companion could see everything. 'You've been very helpful, Isabelle,' Model smiled, 'very helpful.' They moved back to the table where Hoffmann sat. 'Now tell me Isabelle, was there anything unusual about them?'

'What do you mean, Sir?'

Model puffed out his cheeks and shrugged. 'In their behaviour for instance.' Model saw the vacant but quite innocent look in the girl's eyes and he offered yet another charming smile. 'You must have seen many couples dining out. Do you think they were lovers or just friends, out for the night?' he said, glancing towards Hoffman, who shifted uneasily on his seat.

'Lovers Sir definitely, but what she was doing with a scruffy bugger like him, I'll never know. There's no accounting for taste, I suppose.' She flicked her hair and smiled at Hoffmann without realizing the agony she was causing him. 'She loved him. I could see it by the way she looked at him, you know... adoringly.'

'Adoringly,' Model said with a smile. 'What a wonderful way to express her feelings, Isabelle. I like that... adoringly, and she loved him. Did you hear that, Obersturmführer? How very romantic, don't you think?' Model leaned against the back of a chair and smiled. 'I suppose they even shared a room...'

'She wasn't booked in but yes, you could see by the state of the bed in his room they had been at it... before dinner.'

'Did you hear that, Obersturmführer? They had been at it before dinner.' Model turned to Isabelle, 'Did you catch anything they said at the table? Anything, however small or insignificant it may have seemed to you.'

'They always stopped talking when I went to their table, as if they had secrets to hide.'

'Secrets to hide,' Model puckered his lips and nodded. 'So what alerted you to the fact it may have been Madame Régnier?'

'When they first walked in the restaurant I offered them a decent table, but they ignored me and went for the worst table in the restaurant... tucked away in the corner. Anyway, although you could see she was good-looking, she tried to disguise it by wearing glasses and a wig, blonde, it didn't suit her. Her skin tone suggested her hair was dark, her eyebrows proved it.'

'This is excellent, Isabelle. How observant you are, eh Ludwig? How can you be so certain about this?'

'I'm training to be a beauty therapist and only do waitressing and some cleaning in my spare time to earn some money.'

'Anything else about Madame Régnier, Isabelle?'

'Yes. I could also see there was no prescription in the lenses of her glasses so why wear them? You just knew she was beautiful so why cover it up... unless−'

'Unless you have something to hide. What an intelligent girl you are, Isabelle.'

'I kept it to myself, because I wasn't sure it was her. I didn't want to make myself look a fool. The fellow she was with always looked up when someone came into the restaurant. I thought, he's either a nosy bugger or he's waiting for someone. The lady never turned round once.'

'This is very good, Isabelle. Did the man see you watching them?'

'He did a couple of times I know, but I smiled at him as if I fancied him, do you know what I mean?'

'No, but I'm sure Obersturmführer Hoffmann does. What happened then?'

'The four German officers arrived...'

'And you went over to them and spilled the beans.'

'Yes. They were regulars. One of them is really handsome. I liked him. So I said to him, "I think the woman sitting in the corner with her back to you is Madame Régnier the woman you're looking for." The woman got up and left the table, as if she had heard what I said. The handsome officer shouted out to her to stop. He and the other younger one took their guns out of the holsters and before you could blink an eye, the man over there,' she said pointing, 'just stood up and shot them, all four of them. I screamed. It was horrible.'

'Yes, it must have been quite upsetting. Try to remember what he looked like... height, weight, colour of hair, that sort of thing.'

Her eyes lowered. 'I only remember he was an untidy man; unshaven, scruffy hair, which was dark. He was ordinary really.'

'Well that's narrowed it down to several millions, but thank you Isabelle, you've been very helpful. You have a very bright girl here, Monsieur Raymond,' Model said to the old man who had been sitting listening, which brought a flush to the girl's cheeks because it contradicted everything the old man had always said about her. Model opened his briefcase and showed Isabelle a photograph. 'Is this the lady you saw?'

Isabelle nodded. Her eyelashes fluttered as she looked into Model's eyes for the first time. 'I've remembered something else, Sir. I overheard the lady say something about Spain.'

'Spain?' Model said, catching Hoffmann's eye.

'That's all I caught. They stopped talking when I appeared beside them, but it was definitely Spain.'

Chapter 25

Catherine and Panhanagan left Noiseau and made their way to Villecresnes, where they slept in a garden shed cuddled up to each other for warmth. Early in the morning, as a cock exercised its lungs in a garden close by, Panhanagan vigorously rubbed Catherine's hands, legs and thighs. She was still shivering when he returned from reconnoitring the area. They cycled a mile, which warmed them a little and found a café in a quiet street. They ordered coffee with cheese and tomato sandwiches. The café owner ignored them, his cigarette hung from the corner of his mouth while he read his book.

'Before today,' Catherine said, 'Model hadn't a clue where we were, other than a possibility of being holed up in Paris, because no one has come forward with information about me, so all the troops are still in the city. It won't take Model long to know we are connected to that shooting and the waitress will confirm it was me in the restaurant. Our location may suggest we're making a move to Spain, and the waitress, I hope, will confirm that too.'

'Why did you saySpain when she was so close?'

'It was a mistake, but then it didn't matter. Now it does. Model will soon have the whole area covered and the borders watched.'

'Let's move north then, get back across the Channel. I've done it before with Holloway.'

Catherine sighed and held Panhanagan's hand. 'Yes, we'll do that. I can't remain a blonde. The waitress has put paid to that too.'

'I should have shot the silly cow.'

'She's young, it's not her fault. Model will put it about that he is looking for a fair-haired woman travelling with a tramp.' She smiled and kissed his hand. 'A tramp I adore.'

'What will your mother and father say about that?'

She looked into his eyes. 'We ought to be going...'

*

Catherine's fingers stung with cold under her woollen gloves as they cycled through the Forêt Domaniale d'Armainvilliers, and through yet more woods to Villeneuve-Saint-Denis where they found a small *Les Routiers* in which to eat and stay the night. The old woman running the place, put the two bicycles in the shed and winked, saying she would never let on to the police or the Boche that she had a guest staying there. 'Why should they know my business?'

In their room, Catherine had a bath while Panhanagan shaved and washed his hair, then he jumped in behind her. 'Now then,' he said taking her breasts in his hands, 'let me teach you how to make love in a cramped bath...'

When they eventually went downstairs, encouraged by the smell of chicken stew, the old woman stroked Panhanagan's cheek with the back of her fingers and told him how handsome he was, winking at a smiling Catherine. She served them a vegetable broth and then they ate the chicken stew. In bed they curled up in each other's arms, made love again, then slept until six. The following morning, they made their way across the country roads, staying away from large towns by cycling around them and sleeping in barns at night. After two days, they reached la Boisselle, close to the small town of Albert on the Somme. It was a village that Catherine knew very well.

'We'll stay here for a few days with my godfather,'she said. 'We'll be safe with him. His house is isolated from the others.'

'They may be watching the house. I'll have a snoop around, then after a couple of hours we'll make a move.' When it was dark, they approached the small house. Catherine lightly tapped on the door at the back of the house where Jacko had his kitchen. He usually liked to sit in there during the winter to keep warm.

'Who is it?' a gruff voice said in French.

'Little Lady Catherine.'

There was silence while the information filtered through Jacko's aging head. 'Oh my gawd!'

'Shush Uncle Jacko, not so loud.'

The door opened and the two travellers were met by an old man with a toothless, grinning face and wide open arms. 'Oh my gawd, oh my bleeding gawd,' he said, squeezing Catherine to his body. Then he saw Panhanagan and grimaced. 'Who are you?'

'This is Panhanagan, Uncle Jacko. Let's go in before you alert the whole German army.'

Inside the house, Jacko turned to her and said, 'Jesus girl, what are you doing here? I thought you slipped out in 1940.'

'It's a long story and we're hungry. I've got some food. We'll talk over dinner.'

'I'll do it.' Panhanagan said. 'You chat to the old fellow.'

'Not so much of the old feller. It's Jacko,' he said to Panhanagan, who disappeared into the kitchen, closing the door behind him. 'That one's trouble; I can smell it. Does 'is Lordship or your mum know you're 'ere?'

'Of course they don't.' She kissed his stubbly cheek again. 'How are you really?'

'Feeling my age. Can't work anymore.'

'And the Germans?'

'They leave me alone. There's an officer who comes and we 'ave a bit of a chinwag. He's a nice bloke, not like those bleeding SS pigs, begging your pardon. Brings me grub, some booze and baccy, and 'e speaks bloody good English too. I like the feller.'

'How many soldiers are billeted in Albert?'

'About 'undred of them, close to the 'otel where I met you for the very first time with your mum. Do you remember that? A little darling you were. Is your mum all right? Still the beauty I remember 'er to be?'

'She hasn't changed.' Catherine smiled into Jacko's eyes and kissed him again. 'She and daddy really wished you had returned to England with us.'

Jacko shook his head. 'I've been 'ere too long. This is where I will 'ang up me boots.'

Panhanagan brought two mugs of tea and placed them on the table. He winked at Jacko and left the room closing the door behind him.

Jacko watched Catherine follow him out of the room with her eyes. 'How long's that been going on then?' he asked.

Catherine smiled then shrugged. 'I'm in love with him.'

'I can see that little Lady Catherine.' Jacko's eyes lifted to Catherine's and brightened. He touched her check with his old, wrinkled fingers. 'You're just like your mum; underneath that tough exterior...' He adjusted himself in his chair. 'I'm not going to ask what you're doing in France.'

'I'm not going to tell you.'

'This feller, when you get back to Blighty, any plans?'

Catherine nodded. 'I'm going to marry him and have three children.'

'Does 'e know that?'

'Not yet,' she replied, her smile growing with Jacko's.

Chapter 26

Model paced his office with his head bent in concentration. The room's acoustics sent the sound of his footsteps ringing in Hoffmann's ears, as he tapped an unlit cigarette on the gold cigarette case his wife had bought for him before he left for Paris. He looked out of his office window at some snowflakes dropping onto the Avenue Foch. He racked his brain for some clue of Catherine from her past, something that may help him discover where she might have run to. He lit his cigarette and glanced over towards a brooding Model. How different that gentle student of literature is now than she was when he had first met her, he thought. War changes people, he knew, but what a change? She was now a ruthless killer, a seducer and at the top of the Gestapo and the Sicherheitsdienst's wanted list; a very uncomfortable position to be in. He exhaled the cigarette smoke and shook his head. Then a memory of a photograph came to him, of Catherine and her mother posing with an English gardener who worked in the cemeteries from the Great War.

The telephone rang, shaking him from his thoughts. He watched Model replace the receiver without saying a word. Model shook his head when Hoffmann looked his way.

'Even though we've doubled the reward?' Hoffmann said.

'They haven't travelled on trains or public transport,' Model said, beginning to pace the room again. 'The spotter planes have seen nothing on the roads and both borders have doubled their patrols... nothing, they've disappeared. How could they just disappear like that?' Model looked thoughtful for a moment, then said, 'Have you come up with anything, Ludwig?'

'It's a hunch but I think they've gone north, Herr Obersturmbannführer.'

'Not Amiens again?'

'No, Herr Obersturmbannführer, but close. I was once in Amiens during a break in the semester and went to Catherine's home to see if she was there. She wasn't. I was invited in by her aunt, Madame Caron. We had tea together. There was a photograph of Catherine when she was very young, posing with her mother and an English gardener, a retired British soldier who looked after the

188

cemeteries from the last war. The gardener looked the same age as Catherine's mother. He had a large scar on his cheek, obviously a wound from the war. I never gave it any real thought until now. Madame Caron said it was a souvenir photograph, yet the gardener was holding Catherine and looked a little more than a man posing for a tourist, if you follow, Herr Obersturmbannführer, particularly as Catherine's mother had her arm locked through the gardener's arm.' Hoffmann lit another cigarette. 'It says on the birth certificate the Gestapo checked out that her father was unknown. Her mother was very beautiful, so perhaps she wouldn't own up to an indiscretion with a gardener, a bit like Lady Chatterley's lover–'

'Mellors was a gamekeeper.'

'But it would give her that English connection you talked about–'

'For God's sake, what an imagination you have,' Model laughed, 'an English connection yes, but a gardener indeed. She comes from better stock than that. What is your point?'

'The Somme district is good place to lose oneself, Herr Obersturmbannführer, and it's close to the Channel.'

After some thought Model nodded, 'I'll grab at anything at the moment.' He went to his seat and sat with a finger in his mouth caressing a front tooth while his mind raced. 'Clever, they took advantage of that business at Noiseau to let us think they were travelling to one of the borders and sent us in the wrong direction. Well it worked. It drew hundreds of troops away from the north.' Model pushed his chair back with one noisy movement and rose to his feet. 'With the possibility of an invasion this year all they have to do is sit it out until their troops land at Calais.' Model saw Hoffmann's features tighten. 'Really Ludwig, surely you don't think we're going to win this war?'

'But, then again, they just might not wait,' Hoffmann said without commenting on Model's question. He did not want to contemplate Germany losing the war. Unlike Model, with his cynicism towards Goebbels' speeches on ultimate victory, Hoffmann was loyal to the SS, to the Führer and the Fatherland.

Model nodded. 'You may be right; audacious is that girl's middle name. We must find her, otherwise those above will crap all over us and pull the chain. She has to be punished for what she's done and I shall allow you, Ludwig, to squeeze the trigger.'

They both walked across to the map of France. Hoffman pointed towards Albert, located between Amiens and Arras. 'Although Catherine was born in Amiens,' Hoffmann said, 'she once lived here in Albert, and here,' he said pointing to a small village named la Boisselle. 'One could certainly lose oneself around here. There are many villages and millions of hectares of farmland. She will also have friends—'

'Friends!' Model snorted. 'For the reward money we're offering, even her own mother would betray her. Get onto the garrison commander in Albert and tell him to round up any British gardeners who have not been interned, however old they may be, and lock them up. Then get onto the Gestapo and have them arrest everyone in that house in Amiens. You can go and question them.'

'Yes, Herr Obersturmbannführer.'

'And don't be soft on them Obersturmführer. I want answers.'

*

As Hoffmann's car approached Amiens, he instructed the driver to follow his route into the city. 'There is an address I need to check out before we make our way to Albert. Aim for the cathedral and then I will direct you.'

'Yes, Herr Obersturmführer.'

Hoffmann removed his weapon from the leather holster, then the magazine from the weapon to check it was loaded. He replaced the magazine with a click. Hoffmann saw his driver's eyes move to the rear view mirror. 'Don't worry Corporal, I'm not going to shoot you,' he grinned. 'You're quite safe, unless you take a wrong turn.' When he saw the expression in the corporal's eyes he laughed aloud. 'My God, Corporal. Have you never served at the front?'

'I was wounded at Stalingrad, Herr Obersturmführer. I was out of Russia and back in Germany before our army surrendered.'

'They did not surrender!' Hoffmann shouted. 'How dare you say such a thing? That cowardly swine Paulus surrendered, not the German army. The army would have fought on.' He saw the hairs on the neck of the corporal stand up, so he took a deep breath to calm himself and let it out slowly and silently though his nose. Hoffmann had lost many friends at Stalingrad.

'The cathedral is coming up, Herr Obersturmführer.'

Hoffmann knocked on the door of a house along Rue Flatters and waited. When the door opened, Hoffmann's eyes brightened.

190

'Excuse me Mademoiselle, is Monsieur or Madame Caron at home?'

The girl, who could have been anything between sixteen and eighteen, was very attractive. Her breasts caused the buttons to strain at the fastenings of her tight shirt. She glanced at the letters SD on the sleeve of Hoffmann's uniform. Like most French citizens she knew that the Sicherheitsdienst was the German intelligence service of the SS, with a reputation for brutality. Hoffmann found a little satisfaction in seeing a slight tremor of her chin. 'Please do not be alarmed Mademoiselle, I'm here simply to ask you a few questions.'

'What sort of questions, Monsieur?'

'We can talk on the doorstep if you wish Mademoiselle, or we can go inside and be more comfortable. As I said, you have nothing to worry about. I only want your help.'

Hoffmann thought he detected a flirtatious smile creep across the girl's lips as she stood back from the door and allowed him to pass. He removed his cap and stepped inside. 'Are you alone?' Hoffmann asked, as he looked round the room. He recognized nothing. He heard her say yes, as he looked out of the window and saw the great circular stained glass window of the cathedral a hundred yards away. That was something he did remember. He turned to face the girl, whose young, firm breasts were now exposed to his widening eyes. 'What are you doing?'

Her face became more seductive. As young as she was, she knew the effect her body had on a man. 'Isn't this what you've come for?'

Hoffmann looked into the young girl's pretty face and felt a stab of desire. 'Where are your parents?'

'You know. The Gestapo arrested my father and put him in Amiens prison.'

'And your mother?'

'She's away visiting her sister in Rouen,' she said, removing her shirt. 'My bedroom's through here.'

'What's your name?'

'Annette.' She pouted. 'My father is innocent. I keep telling the officer who comes here. He said he would help, but never does.'

'And what is the officer's name.'

'I've no idea. All I know is he comes here and tells me my father is well, and that he is personally looking into his case, then he fucks me and leaves.'

Ah, that old chestnut, Hoffmann thought. 'He's from the prison?'

'Yes. He's a fat pig and treats me as if I'm a whore. I hope you will treat me a little better, Monsieur.' Then her eyes softened and she reached for his arm and laid a hand gently on his sleeve. 'You could help me because you're in the Sicherheitsdienst. You are more important than the other man is.'

*

Hoffmann rolled off the girl breathing heavily. It had been a long time since he had had sex with a girl so young. 'How old are you, Annette?' he asked.

'Seventeen.'

Seventeen and she can screw like that, Hoffmann thought, and smiled to himself. If only the little minx lived in Paris. He glanced at his watch. His driver would have to wait some more, because when he was ready he would give this young beauty a second helping. 'Fetch me my cigarettes. They're in my jacket pocket.'

His eyes followed her movements as she walked across to his uniform jacket which hung over the chair. She turned with a smile on her face. 'Can I wear your jacket?'

'Give me the cigarettes first.'

She handed him his cigarette case and lighter and, as he lit a cigarette, she put his uniform jacket on. It hung to the bush between her legs; thick and hairy and still moist from the orgasm she had had. She then put on his cap and saluted him. He smiled at her laughing face. It's amazing how sex relaxes a woman, even a girl. Youth, he thought, so easily satisfied.

'Take it off now and let me see your lovely breasts.' Like a stripper, she slowly removed the jacket and turned so he could see her bottom; young, round and firm, still with the red marks where he had gripped her hard and squeezed them, as he thrust wildly into her. 'Do you have an ashtray?'

She went and fetched one. 'I'd rather you came back to see me than that other fellow. He always smells of alcohol and he's useless in bed. A girl likes it too you know, but *he* wouldn't understand that.' She handed him the ashtray and stretched out beside him. She

192

took him into her mouth and smiled up into his eyes. 'Do you like that?'

He did like that. Hoffmann stabbed the cigarette out and closed his eyes. When she finished, he glanced at his watch again and lit another cigarette. Like an obedient servant, she took the ashtray out, cleaned it, then returned and handed it back to him. It was a souvenir ashtray with a picture of a house and the words Mountfields House, printed in English.

'This is a pretty ashtray, Annette. Where did you get it?'

'It was in one of the cupboards when we moved in here. It's Wedgewood, that's why I kept it. I found a photograph too. I kept that as well. I like to see into other people's lives. That's English you know,' she said nodding towards the ashtray. 'Wedgewood is famous. I looked it up in a book. Madame Caron must have forgotten them. I'm not surprised... they left here in a hurry.'

Hoffmann sat up. 'Your name isn't Caron?'

'No, it's Bonamy. The Carons lived here before us.'

'May I see the photograph you have?'

'Yes,' she said excitedly. She jumped out of bed and went to her chest of drawers. 'It's in here somewhere. I kept it because she's lovely.' She returned to the bed and handed Hoffmann a photo of Catherine when she was not much older than Annette was now. She smiled. 'I bet she's even more beautiful now.'

He nodded. 'Yes, she is.' That is how he remembered her before she walked back into his life. That's how old she was when he took her back home and stripped her naked. He had no idea she was a virgin, all he knew was he had to have her; awake, drugged or even dead, it didn't matter. 'So you never met her, Annette?'

'No. My Dad did. He used to know Madam Caron, that's how we got the house when she suddenly decided to move. It's lovely round this part of Amiens.'

'What does your father do?'

'He's a lawyer.'

'And why is he in prison?'

Her bottom lip dropped and her eyelashes lowered. 'I don't know why,' she said softly. 'The Gestapo accused him of working for the Maquis. It's all lies.'

'I'll go to the prison and see what I can do.'

'Thank you.' She hugged and kissed him. 'Do you want to fuck me again?'

'You've quite an appetite, Annette.'

'I love sex, not with the other officer, but I do with you.'

'Where did Madame Caron move to after she left here?'

'I don't know. Dad probably will. Would you like a drink of something?'

'Yes, Annette. I'll have some water.'

'My Dad has lots of good wine.'

'Water will do.'

When she returned Hoffmann was pulling up his boots. He reached for his shirt as she offered him the water. 'Are you going? I thought we were going to do it again.'

'Another time, Annette,' he said. 'I must get to the prison and speak with your father.'

Her face lit up. 'Oh please help him, please. You'll see he's a good man and I'll always be grateful to you.'

'May I borrow that photograph? I'll return it to you when I next see you.'

She looked hesitant. 'Promise you'll come back.'

'Yes, of course,' he said, lowering his head. He sucked the nipple of her right breast, which grew in his mouth and his eyes rose to meet hers. 'Have you ever considered living in Paris?'

Chapter 27

The guard at the prison gate called his sergeant who appeared and saluted Hoffmann. 'I'm sorry, Herr Obersturmführer, we were not informed of a visit from the Sicherheitsdienst.'

'Since when do I have to make an appointment? I'm here to question the prisoner Bonamy.'

'May I ask why, Herr Obersturmführer?'

'No, you may not, Sergeant,' Hoffmann said. 'Take me to your commanding officer.'

The sergeant straightened his back, a movement well practiced after years of army service. 'Yes, mein Herr. One moment please.' After a telephone call, the sergeant said, 'Will you please follow me, Herr Obersturmführer?'

Hoffmann was shown into a room where he saw a major leaning back in his chair, with a glass of cognac on his desk. His lip curled. 'Under whose authority do you come barging into my prison without prior warning, Obersturmführer?'

'The authority of the Sicherheitsdienst, Herr Major. Please ring our headquarters in Paris. The number is here,' Hoffmann said, writing it on a piece of notepaper. 'You can speak to Obersturmbannführer Erich von Model.'

'Von Model!' the major laughed, banging the table with the flat of his hand. 'I thought he died of the pox. Does he still enjoy sticking it up young Obersturmführers, Obersturmführer?'

Considering how insulted he felt, Hoffmann remained calm, 'I would rather you not be so free with your tongue, Herr Major, otherwise you may find yourself facing the Russians instead of sitting on your fat arse in France.'

'Don't you speak to me like that, you pompous little prick. Who do you think you are?'

'For a start, the son-in-law of your Corps Commander. One call to headquarters, Herr Major and your orderly will be packing your bags.'

When the major saw the expression on Hoffmann's face he sniffed and smiled. 'Sit down Obersturmführer. Loosen your belt for a moment. Have a drink. Forget you are one of God's gifts from Paris and relax.'

'I'm here to interview a prisoner, not to idle my time away drinking, Herr Major.' Hoffmann met the scornful eyes across the desk. 'I wish to speak to Henri Bonamy. He has information vital to our investigations.'

The major suddenly ran a finger round the collar of his shirt. Hoffmann guessed it was he who was screwing young Annette Bonamy. 'What information does he have to interest you?'

'That's my business, Herr Major.'

'I don't think I like your tone, Obersturmführer. I am in command of this prison.' Specks of spittle burst from his lips as he shouted out the words. 'I'll not have any young cock from Paris coming here making demands. You'll go through the proper channels like anyone else.'

'If you like to do things by the book, Herr Major, then very well, I will too. I wish to make a formal complaint against one of your officers. Henri Bonamy has a very attractive young daughter. I have been speaking with her. She made an allegation against a German officer, someone from this prison she said; sexual favours in exchange for having her father released...' Hoffmann felt some satisfaction in watching the major squirm. 'Of course, you may feel you prefer to keep this matter in-house and investigate it yourself.'

'Err yes, perhaps it would be better that way,' the major said, his eyes rolling towards Hoffmann. 'Why get one of our own in trouble over a little French trollop?' He downed what cognac was left in the glass.

'Henri Bonamy, Herr Major...'

'I'll have someone take you to him, Obersturmführer. '

When the cell door opened, there were five men huddled together in it. Henri Bonamy's name was called out and the man stepped forward, looking nervously at the SS uniform before him and the diamond shaped SD badge on his left sleeve.

'There's an interview room over there, Herr Obersturmführer,' the guard said.

Hoffmann complained about the smell and demanded to be taken to an office away from the cells. Men began crossing themselves when Bonamy was being led along the path between the cells with Hoffmann following. Bonamy swallowed when the guard accompanying him pushed him onto a seat. Hoffmann nodded at the guard who left the room.

'They have made a terrible mistake Sir,' Bonamy said. 'I have no associations with the Maquis. I have never had any associations with them.'

'I've not come here about that. If you can help me with another matter then I will have you out of here today.'

Bonamy's eyes lit up. 'If I can help you Sir, of course I will.'

Hoffmann smiled. He always thought his smile showed him at his best; friendly, full of charm and as he was often told, it relaxed people. Hoffmann considered that he had the gift of allowing the movement of his mouth to reach his eyes, no matter how much he disliked the person before him. 'Do you know this young lady, Monsieur Bonamy?' Hoffmann said, laying the photograph of Catherine before him.

Henri Bonamy's eyes widened. He looked up into the charming smile with some relief. 'It's young Catherine, Madame Caron's goddaughter. Where did you get this picture, Sir?'

'I ask the questions Monsieur Bonamy and you answer them. That's how it works.'

'Yes, I'm sorry Sir.'

'So Madame Caron is not her aunt?'

'No. She's a close friend of Catherine's mother. Madame Caron helped bring her into this world when the doctor was delayed. She was actually born in the house in which I now live.'

'How did they get to know each other?'

'They were prisoners-of-war together in the last war. What's this about, Herr Obersturmführer?'

'I told you once Monsieur, I ask the questions. Please don't make me repeat myself. As I have said, if you give me the information I require you will be released.'

'Released, oh yes, I'll help you all I can. My wife is away. She has no idea I've been arrested and I have no idea what has become of my young daughter. She was out when the Gestapo came.'

Hoffmann felt sudden irritation. 'No harm will come to your daughter, Monsieur. Now, let us move on. I'm following a line of investigation and Catherine's name came up. I need to know more about her.'

'Well it can do no harm now, I suppose. I first met Catherine when she was seven... maybe eight years old. She was visiting Madame Caron with her mother. I'm the Caron's family lawyer and paid her a call. I don't normally do home−'

'Monsieur, would you please get to the point. I have to get to Albert.'

'Now that's a coincidence, because that is where the family used to live before—'

'As you say, you're a lawyer Monsieur, so don't speak in riddles. Which family are we talking about now? Madame Caron's family or Catherine's family?'

Bonamy could see the charm was beginning to fade, like the smile. He swallowed. 'I'm talking of Catherine's family, such a good-looking woman the Countess—'

'Countess?'

'Catherine's mother. Our little Catherine is an English aristocrat. She fooled everyone at the Sorbonne into thinking she was a simple French girl.' He let out a chuckle. 'I mean, she spoke French so well, with a French accent, nobody really doubted it.'

Hoffmann closed his eyes. How Model would crow. 'And Madame Caron, where is *she* now?' Hoffmann could feel his throat go dry. 'It's imperative that I find her.' Hoffmann looked Bonamy in the eye. 'She'll be safe. No harm will come to her. I just need to ask her some questions, as I am asking you.'

'She disappeared.'

'Disappeared!' What does that suppose to mean?'

Bonamy could now see the blood rise to Hoffmann's neck. 'The whole of the Caron family just... disappeared, really Sir. I tell you the whole truth.'

'And when did this disappearing act take place?'

'The last I saw of them was in September. It was when we agreed to rent the Caron home. I went over to sign the papers. I noticed luggage in one of the rooms as I passed and asked where they were going to move to. They said Biarritz, it's down on—'

'I know where Biarritz is. Do you take me for a fool?'

'No, Sir. I'm nervous. I want to help you.'

'Did Madame Caron suddenly decide to move, or was it a long-standing plan?'

'It was as if they made their mind up overnight. I had to put their furniture in a warehouse. There was a man with them. They said he was a friend. His French was good, but he had a slight accent.'

'English?'

'Yes.'

Hoffmann paced the floor again. Clever, MI6 guessed Madame Caron's presence would be used to threaten Catherine. British Intelligence certainly did their homework. 'Any other family friends?'

'The old English gardener. He's retired now, but he still lives in La Boisselle. It's a village–'

Hoffmann's eyes rose, which silenced Bonamy. 'If you give me one more geography lesson you'll rot in this place...'

'I'm sorry, Herr Obersturmführer.'

'Monsieur Bonamy, if Catherine were in France now, where would she feel most comfortable?' Bonamy shrugged, almost too frightened to open his mouth. 'Whoever leads us to her will be a million francs richer.'

Bonamy sat up. 'A million! What has she done to warrant such a high reward?'

'She's a dangerous spy, who has murdered several people. For as long as she is on the loose, hostages will be taken and shot.'

Bonamy swallowed. 'That would be a war crime, Herr Obersturmführer.'

Hoffmann struck Bonamy round the face with the back of his hand. 'Who do you think you are you little shit? You expect our soldiers to be murdered and for us to do nothing about it? We are perfectly in our rights to shoot you. You're cowards. All of you French are cowards, capitulating without a fight. Germans would defend the Fatherland to the death.' Hoffmann, who prided himself on his self-control, lost it. He walked away from the man, taking in deep breaths. 'Catherine,' he whispered, 'what are you doing to me?' Hoffmann glanced over towards Bonamy who kept his eyes lowered to the table. He can stay here, Hoffmann thought. He would tell Annette that there was nothing he could do for him and for her own safety, he would take her to Paris and care for her. She's a little beauty, eager and willing to please. 'Tell me about Albert... la Boisselle. How well do you know these places?'

When he had heard enough, Hoffmann left Bonamy to be taken back to his cell. He went and telephoned the office in Paris. There was no answer. Hoffmann decided that he would act on his own initiative and not let Model have the glory of finding Catherine or her accomplice, although the accomplice was nothing, a minion. A shot in the back of his head would save them the bother of sending him to a concentration camp.

Chapter 28

It was cold. The sky was clear and blue with no cloud. Only a low sun occupied the vastness above Panhanagan and Catherine, a solitary witness to the two minute figures cycling through the endless French country lanes, which seemed to swallow them up. Instead of Panhanagan following Catherine as he normally did when they were out, they cycled towards Thiepval side by side, as if they were tourists in a carefree holiday mood rather than the two most wanted people in France.

They had left Jacko's house and cut across the Bapaume Road and made their way towards Thiepval, towards the towering monument to the missing on the Somme. They stopped at a small cemetery. Catherine stood and looked down at her maternal grandfather and uncle's graves. 'I used to visit here with my mother. I couldn't be in the area and not come to pay my respects to my grandfather and uncle.' She took hold of Panhanagan's hand and squeezed it, as if for momentary comfort or strength. 'I didn't know them, but my mother was cut up about it for years. Poor Mummy, it always made her cry to stand here; looking, thinking...'

After fifteen minutes, they left the cemetery and cycled over to the great Thiepval Memorial. Although he had read about Lutyen's creation, Panhanagan had never seen it. Now he stood staring up at the columns of names carved in the stone.

'Jesus,' he said, 'those poor bastards.'

'There are over seventy-two thousand names up there; the missing of the Somme,' Catherine said softly. They were simply swallowed up in that filth, torn to shreds, not even enough of them to be buried and have a headstone that simply read, 'A soldier of the Great War'. My mother's first husband is one of them... they had only been married a week,' Catherine said, stopping below one of the piers and pointing upwards, 'there, see it, Lt R. Turner?' Catherine stood in silence for a moment, just staring up at the name. 'It's strange, but if he hadn't died, I wouldn't exist as I am. It's as if he died to give me life. Do you understand that?'

Panhanagan shrugged. 'If I die I'd want to be buried.'

She took his hand and kissed it. 'Don't say that. I had a cold shiver go straight through me when you said that.'

They heard the crunch of tyres on gravel and turned to see a car pull up. A German soldier got out and opened the door for an officer who climbed out with a younger officer following him. As the two officers walked towards them, Panhanagan put his hand in his pocket and gripped the handle of his PPK.

'Not here, Panhanagan; this place is sacred.'

The colonel smiled congenially and saluted Catherine in a gentlemanly fashion, his eyes flashing across them both. The younger officer ignored Panhanagan; his eyes were fixed firmly on Catherine. 'Excuse me, Madame, I must have a quick word with my lieutenant', the colonel said in French, then, he turned to the younger man and spoke in German. 'Don't stare at the young lady like that leutnant. Not only is it rude you are making her feel uncomfortable.'

'I'm sorry Herr Oberst... it's just that her face is familiar. I feel I've seen her somewhere before.'

The colonel turned to Catherine and reverted to French. 'Forgive the intrusion, Madame. I'm an architect when I am not a soldier. I have come to admire Lutyen's work.'

Catherine smiled and told him he spoke French well. By the sudden light in his eyes, he was flattered by her compliment. She still felt the young lieutenant's eyes on her and saw Panhanagan's eyes on him. Catherine spoke to the younger man. 'I feel we have met somewhere before, leutnant. Are you garrisoned in Amiens?' The lieutenant looked confused.

'He doesn't speak French, Madame,' the colonel said. 'Strangely he was saying he felt your face was familiar.' His smile dropped when he turned to his young companion. 'I told you not to stare leutnant, now her husband is giving you a very unsettling look so try to control yourself, there's a good lad.' He saluted Catherine again and said. 'I am on my way to Amiens and do not have much time to admire this monument so we must press on. It was a pleasure meeting you, Madame... Monsieur.'

'If you don't mind me saying so Herr Oberst, when you reach Amiens I should send your companion to a whorehouse. It might relax him a little.'

The colonel laughed and slapped his thigh, then repeated what Catherine had said to his young lieutenant as he led him away, blushing to the roots of his hair.

Panhanagan walked with Catherine to the entrance of the memorial garden and retrieved their bicycles. They left the site with Panhanagan following. 'What were those two talking about?'

'The lieutenant thought he recognized me but couldn't place me. Let's go and have a coffee.'

They stopped in the village of Authuille. From inside the café they watched a German motorcyclist and sidecar ride past, the passenger, sitting behind a machine gun, glanced towards the café as if thinking of stopping for some refreshment. The motorcycle rattled on and the village became quiet again.

'You look thoughtful,' Panhanagan said. He leaned across the table and, with a finger, removed a lock of hair from Catherine's eyes and tucked it behind her ear. He loved her shining dark hair and was glad she was no longer a blonde; it didn't suit her at all. She took his hand in an unconscious movement and kissed it, as another German military motorcycle and sidecar passed the café. Catherine frowned. 'They're obviously going to Albert, but why should they be travelling along this road?'

'Why don't you give that mind of yours a rest?'

'Surely they'd use the Bapaume Road directly into Albert. It's more direct and quicker. That's why we avoided it.'

'Perhaps he's lost.'

'Two of them, five minutes apart, I can't believe that's a coincidence. The Germans do things by the book. There has to be a reason for travelling on this road.'

As Catherine said it, a convoy of German military vehicles drove past. As each lorry passed, they could both see they were full of soldiers. 'Jesus,' Panhanagan said, looking uneasy, 'that's about two hundred men. Where did they spring from?'

'Has to be Arras and they do not want to be seen on the main road to Albert.'

Meanwhile, attracted by the unusual noise of several heavy vehicles passing, the café owner strolled up to the window. The Gauloises in the corner of his mouth was relit as he stared out into the road. 'They're also coming in from Amiens. They'll be looking for that woman.'

'What woman?' Catherine asked fumbling for her spectacles in her shoulder bag.

'My daughter was in Albert first thing this morning and said there were posters going up in the shop windows, at the station and on the public notice boards, of a young woman wanted by the Gestapo; God protect her.' He put a match to his cigarette again. 'They are offering to pay a million francs for information that will lead to her arrest.'

'A million!'

'That's what the poster says. They think she's in this area. It's also said the Germans will take hostages and have them shot in the market square if she's not handed over.'

Catherine's eyes found Panhanagan. She turned to the café owner with a look of diffidence in her smile. 'Oh well, I'm sure someone will be richer by a million before the end of the day. How much do we owe you?'

The Frenchman shrugged. 'Two coffees... on the house, Madame.' He glanced at Panhanagan. 'Where're you from?'

'Lille. We're making our way there now. Au revoir, Monsieur.'

The café owner nodded. 'Have a good journey,' and collected the cups and saucers.

'Do you think he knew?' Panhanagan asked Catherine as they mounted their bicycles.

'It was his daughter who saw the posters. They haven't reached here yet. I don't like this one bit, Panhanagan. Shooting hostages—'

'It's only a threat.'

'They are permitted to do so, by The Hague Convention, if their soldiers are murdered other than in combat. We've got to get back to Jacko. He'll be the first on their list.' They began to cycle quickly along the road that took them out of Authuille. 'They have somehow worked out our deception,' Catherine called across to Panhanagan. 'Model is cleverer than I thought.'

They cut down towards Ovillers-la-Boisselle and crossed the Bapaume Road to the village of la Boisselle and Jacko's home. He wasn't there.

'I'll go and see if he's in the Gordon Dump cemetery. Jacko often goes there and smokes his pipe.'

'I'll come with you.'

'No, I'll be all right. I'll cut across the field. It will be quicker.' She looked into Panhanagan's eyes and both of them knew what the other was thinking. Time was running out for them. They were beginning to be hemmed into a small pocket, as the BEF were at Dunkirk. Now Catherine also had Jacko to worry about.

Panhanagan watched her go. She sprinted away as she used to in Scotland. Back then she was an irritating toff, but now she was the most precious person in his life. He checked his weapon and looked around Jacko's house for more. Jacko had mentioned them the night before; weapons he had found while clearing out some of the deep trenches around la Boisselle. In the kitchen there was a bunch of keys hanging on a hook attached to the door. The second key fitted the cupboard door under the stairs and the lock turned with a clunk. Inside, under a blanket, were a Lewis machine gun and several drums of ammunition. There was also a short magazine Lee-Enfield with a telescopic sight.

'Oh yes, my little beauties,' Panhanagan whispered. 'Now Jacko, my old son, let me see if you were a proper soldier and kept them clean and oiled. He checked the Lee-Enfield and then the Lewis machine gun. Both were clean, oiled and in perfect working order. 'Jacko, you're a darling.'

*

'What's the hurry little Lady Catherine?' Jacko said and puffed on his pipe. 'What's up? You look as if you've lost a pound and found a penny.'

'The Germans have guessed we're in the area. When Panhanagan and I were in Authuille we saw a convoy of them making their way to Albert.'

'What, through Authuille...' he looked thoughtful for a moment sucked in more smoke. 'Probably lost. Anyway, they often stop at Albert for a break then go on to Amiens.'

'Not this time, Uncle Jacko. They're arriving from Amiens as well.'

Jacko's eyes betrayed his thoughts. 'Where's yer feller?'

'Knowing Panhanagan he's looking for those weapons you mentioncd last night.'

'They are still in good working order. Is he mad enough to take on Jerry?'

'Yes, he is. We've got to hide you. Is that trench still there or has it been filled in?'

'Cor blimey... you remember that? The general and I turned the old officer's quarters of that German trench into an underground den before you were born, when the Chinese fellers were clearing that part of the battlefield. Do you remember we stayed down there some nights? You didn't like it.'

204

'Well, it will be a godsend now.'

'This time of year it will be cold,' Jacko said, 'but at least Jerry shouldn't find us that deep below his feet.'

'Go there now. I'll get Panhanagan. There's no need to take Jerry on in a fight.'

The den was forty feet below ground, between the cemetery and the great mine crater, still untouched since it was blown on the first of July 1916. Jacko made his way there while Catherine rushed back for Panhanagan who was looking through the telescopic sight of the rifle.

'This will take a bloke out at a thousand yards.'

'We have a hiding place, there's no need for a fight. Jacko's already down there. Take what you can and let's get going. I'll bring some blankets.'

Panhanagan looked disappointed. He picked up the Lewis gun, a bag of ammunition canisters and the rifle with the telescopic sight, then followed her out of the house.

'I'll come back for the bicycles,' Catherine called to him. 'And we'll need some more supplies; water, what food there is left...'

When they reached the entrance to the trench, Panhanagan said, 'Stay with Jacko.'

Catherine watched him sprint like a hare across the field towards Jacko's house. He was in his element, she knew. When he returned, he descended the stairs, just as hundreds of German soldiers had done in the previous great struggle and joined the other two, who were now wrapped in blankets, their faces white in the glow of a candle. After an hour Panhanagan was restless.

'Well if you will both excuse me, I'm going to take a peek,' he said like a schoolboy out on an adventure, 'to see if Jerry has arrived.'

He was gone before Catherine could protest. Jacko chuckled. 'That one's trouble.'

Chapter **29**

Henri Bonamy had convinced Hoffmann that Catherine would, if anywhere, be holed up somewhere in the Albert area. There were many villages whose names were synonymous with the slaughter of 1916 and 1918, whose many military cemeteries were a permanent reminder of it. Bonamy said she would be safe in that area, because of the debt the local people felt they owed the British. Hoffmann wondered if their loyalty would hold over a huge reward. Already the posters were going up in the streets of Albert and attracting large groups of people jostling to read them.

Hoffmann telephoned Model, saying he was following some good leads and would keep him informed. It wasn't exactly true, but he knew Model wanted this business finished and there was nothing important to keep Hoffman in Paris. He omitted to tell Model about Catherine's aristocratic background; that information would only bring Model rushing to Albert, and Hoffmann did not want that. This was his show now, Hoffmann considered, and capturing Catherine would help his promotion prospects. Plus he had plans for her when he got her alone in a cell.

He had travelled down from Amiens with a company of Waffen SS troops and another company from Arras were expected to join up with him at Albert. 'Those troops will flush her out,' Model had said. 'Let me know the moment you've got her.'

*

When Hoffmann's convoy arrived in Albert, he reported to the Garrison Commander on the square in front of the Hotel de Ville. Local people watched with concern as the troops began to emerge from the vehicles and fill the square. Their anxiety heightened further when the convoy from Arras arrived an hour later.

'Herr Hauptmann,' Hoffmann said, saluting the garrison commander. 'I'm Obersturmführer Hoffmann. I presume you got the message from Paris.'

'I did, Obersturmführer. What's all this about?'

'You've seen the posters. We are convinced the Régnier woman is in this area. If she is then we will flush her out.'

Hoffmann met the garrison commander's eye. He saw a handsome man, the same age as he and impeccably presented in his

206

Wehrmacht uniform. His eyes fell to the Knight's Cross with oak leaves, swords and diamonds, drooped over the knot of the garrison commander's collar and then to the Iron Cross First Class pinned to his left breast pocket. It was every soldier's dream to wear such prestigious medals, yet it was odd, Hoffmann thought, to have such a highly decorated man in command of a small garrison in the backwaters of France.

'Why is there such a large reward for this young lady, Obersturmführer?'

'She's a very dangerous British spy; a threat to the Reich.'

'Good heavens, a threat to the Reich, indeed. I hope the British send more women to France with looks as good as hers.'

Hoffmann's lip curled. 'This is not a joking matter, Herr Hauptmann. This woman is a ruthless killer. She has killed several German soldiers and French civilians. More importantly, she murdered an irreplaceable agent of ours. A Frenchman commissioned into the British army's intelligence service. He gave us a great deal of valuable information before that bitch killed him. We need to question her and see what other information she may have taken from Sicherheitsdienst headquarters in Paris.' Hoffmann caught the smile that crept across Hauptmann Fries' mouth. 'May I ask what is so amusing, Herr Hauptmann?'

'You wish me to help the Sicherheitsdienst save face?'

'The Führer would expect you to do your duty. Have you arrested the Englishman Jacks?'

'No.'

'But you were requested to do so.'

'By whom?'

'Me, Herr Hauptmann. I contacted your office from Amiens.'

'Oh yes... I didn't consider it necessary.'

Hoffmann's face paled. 'You didn't consider it necessary?'

'You wish me to arrest an elderly man on the grounds that he is a threat to the Reich; a man with whom I have often shared conversations, a smoke and occasionally a drink. This threat to the Reich walks with a bent back and a cane, he lives alone minding his own business; a man who has spent his life caring for military cemeteries, whose only pleasure is to smoke his pipe and talk to the headstones of his fallen comrades from the last war. He may be English and regarded as our enemy Obersturmführer, but common sense must prevail here,' Fries said, looking directly into

Hoffmann's eyes. 'I am an officer of the Wehrmacht, not the SS. We treat people with a little more dignity and civility. Locking him up would be detrimental to his health and serve no purpose at all.'

Hoffmann grimaced. 'I still need to question him, Herr Hauptmann.'

'And so you shall Obersturmführer, in my presence. If he is at home we will do it there.'

'That suits me. I have no wish to harm an old man.'

'Let your men rest after their journey. If your pretty bird flies this way, then we know the nest in which she will attempt to roost. Someone will sing, I'm sure, particularly with the reward you're offering. Now, after we've had some coffee, you and I can go out to la Boisselle and speak to Herr Jacks.'

*

Four hundred troops and several vehicles now filled the square. The noise of it woke the town bringing people to their windows and onto the streets. Old women wrapped in shawls began to look at the posters on shop windows; in low whispers they discussed the huge sum of money offered just for giving information that would lead to an arrest.

'What does it matter if the Germans catch her? She's a British spy, a troublemaker, not one of us,' they said, unknowing that as a child the wanted woman lived amongst them.

Hoffmann drank his coffee and eyed the medal at Hauptmann Fries' throat, imagining it round his. 'What action brought you the Knight's Cross, Herr Hauptmann?'

Fries shook his head. 'The Führer enjoys presenting such awards, it doesn't matter to whom. It takes away the sting of losing so many men in a campaign. Mostly the recipient is undeserving; the real heroes are those who can no longer speak for themselves, Obersturmführer. It really isn't worth talking about.'

'You're very modest Herr Hauptmann, but you also have the Iron Cross First Class. That cannot be a mere coincidence with the Führer handing you an award ad hoc.'

'They decorate the uniform, nothing more.'

'For me, there was never really an opportunity to see action in the field, unfortunately. I was approached by the intelligence services while I was at the Sorbonne.'

'Then be grateful for it. Shall we go and speak with Herr Jacks, Obersturmführer?'

A third of the troops began a house-to-house search in the town while Hoffmann and Hauptmann Fries passed other troops making their way out of town towards the local villages, with orders to search every barn, house and field on their way. They were like beaters at a shoot, forcing birds into the air ready to be slaughtered by the guns waiting for them. The journey to la Boisselle was short, only three miles, and when the car turned into the village and past the war memorial it stopped outside Jacko's house. The soldier beside the driver jumped out, clutching his submachine gun in anticipation of violence. Only two small children could be seen. Hauptmann Fries told him to get back into the car. 'Do you want to frighten everyone with that thing?'

'Do you speak English, Herr Hauptmann?' Hoffmann asked.

'Yes I do, so no heavy tactics, Obersturmführer. I have a lot of respect for this old man.'

Hoffmann knocked twice, glanced at Fries and knocked again. 'He may be in the cemetery along the road,' Fries said. 'He often goes there.'

A small girl, holding the hand of her younger brother, approached them. They stopped by the car and looked at the German soldiers outside the house. 'Hello little ones,' Hoffmann said, crouching down to their level. 'Have you seen Monsieur Jacks?' The little boy stared at him in silence. He then looked up at Hauptmann Fries and smiled.

'Hello, Jean-Pierre, how's your mummy?' Fries asked. The boy produced another smile.

'What's your name, young lady?' Hoffmann asked Jean-Pierre's sister.

She rested her head on her shoulder and said, 'Rosette.'

'That's a pretty name. Now Rosette, have you seen the gentleman who lives here?'

She nodded. Hoffmann glanced up at Fries, then back at Rosette. Her brother began to suck his thumb. 'Have you seen him this morning?'

The girl nodded again, turning at the sound of her mother calling her. When the mother reached her children, Hoffmann stood. The mother's eyes caught the SS insignia on Hoffmann's collar. She gasped, clutching at her children.

'You see the affect you have on people, Obersturmführer?' Fries said in German then, reverting to French, he said to the mother, 'We're looking for Monsieur Jacks, Madame Tonier. He may be able to help us. Nothing serious, but do you know where he is?'

'You know Monsieur Jacks, Hauptmann Fries. He's probably talking to those grave-stones. He's barmy that one. He thinks those dead soldiers can hear him.'

'And do you think God can hear you when you speak to him, Madame Tonier?' Fries asked.

'That's different.'

Fries smiled and nodded. 'Yes, of course. Your priest tells you so.'

Madame Tonier stared at Hauptmann Fries. 'May I go?'

'Not just yet,' Hoffmann said. 'Has Monsieur Jacks had any visitors recently?'

She shook her head. 'I shouldn't think so. I've only ever known the Hauptmann to visit. He's a loner, that one. He's been here for twenty odd years and hardly passes the time of day with anyone. He only speaks to the dead.'

Hoffmann produced a smile. 'Maybe the dead are the only ones prepared to listen. Madame Tonier,' Fries said softly, 'it would be a great help to me if you would tell me about any visitors Monsieur Jacks may have had recently; for instance, a woman, very attractive, dark hair maybe blonde... early twenties. Her name is Catherine. I believe she lived here as a child.'

Madame Tonier did not trust this man. The Hauptmann was a gentleman; an officer of the Wehrmacht, whereas this man was in the SS, something quite different altogether. 'I haven't seen Catherine since the beginning of the war.' Her eyes found Fries. 'I can't help you, Hauptmann.'

Hauptmann Fries shrugged. 'Monsieur Jacks has done nothing wrong and is not in trouble, I assure you Madame.' Fries smiled at Madame Tonier. 'He will not be harmed, you have my word. It is Catherine and her accomplice the Obersturmführer wishes to arrest, not your neighbour. If he has been harbouring these two he does so innocently, out of patriotism, so to speak. It's something we all might do for a fellow countryman. He has no knowledge of their crimes.'

'But Catherine is not your fellow countryman, is she, Madame?' Hoffmann said quickly. Madame Tonier's eyes fell to the ground.

'Hauptmann Fries is right,' Hoffmann continued. 'I'm not interested in Monsieur Jacks, only Catherine. We're offering a million francs for any information that may lead to her capture.' His smile shone in the low sunlight.

'A million francs you say...'

'Yes, Madame. One million francs.'

She shrugged. 'That's a lot of money, but I can't help you. I'm sorry. As I say, I haven't seen Catherine for years.'

'Thank you, Madame Tonier.' Hauptmann Fries said. 'I don't think the Obersturmführer has any more questions.'

'Keep a lookout, Madame. Remember the million francs. It's for no more than giving us information that will lead to the arrest of Madame Régnier, as Catherine is now known,' Hoffmann said. 'One telephone call, we'll do the rest.'

Chapter 30

It was an hour since the convoy had passed through Authuille. Panhanagan calculated that it would have taken the Germans fifteen minutes to arrive at Albert. They would have to organise themselves before searching the area; the officer in command would need to give the troops a break to eat and drink before they began a search that may take all day. Looking at his watch, Panhanagan considered they would be leaving Albert about now. It wouldn't take long before they were on the outskirts of Albert, where they would begin to fan out across the countryside towards la Boisselle.

When he returned to the trench, Catherine was making some tea. 'The Germans certainly knew how to construct a trench,' he said to Jacko. 'And you and the general knew how to look after one.'

'Fritz's gaffs were always better than ours,' Jacko said. 'I've still got the original German plans for of the whole German trench system around here... what the Imperial War Graves Commission filled in and what was left untouched...'

As he spoke, Catherine and Panhanagan caught each other's eyes. 'No Panhanagan, it would be too risky,' Catherine quickly said.

'I've got to try.'

Jacko scratched his head. 'Try what?'

'Jacko, where do you keep these plans?'

'In a box with other things; letters from Catherine's mum and dad... photographs, that sort of thing.'

'It's a risk worth taking,' Panhanagan said. 'They'll be close, but I can still make it.'

'I don't like it,' Catherine said, taking his hand. 'They'll be looking for Jacko, not paperwork. I can't let you take that risk.'

'If Model is as smart as you say he is, and if he is in Albert, then he'll nose around the place. I certainly would and so would you.' Panhanagan watched Catherine run her hand through her hair, something she always did when she was under pressure to give a quick answer. 'You know I'm right, Catherine.'

'My head says yes, but my heart Panhanagan, my heart is beating too fast to say, go.' She threw her arms around him and kissed his lips. 'Darling, please be careful.'

Panhanagan smiled at her. She had never called him darling before. 'Catherine, don't follow me. I can look after myself. Jacko needs you here.'

Jacko's voice was controlled when he said, 'It's under the stairs Sergeant, in a blue box.'

They watched Panhanagan check the magazine in his PPK, as he always did before leaving anywhere. He winked at Jacko. 'Just keep your head down, Catherine,' he said, lifting the escape hatch, then he was gone.

'Christ, he's a cool character,' Jacko said taking Catherine's hand.

'I love you Panhanagan,' Catherine whispered. 'Just don't do anything stupid.'

Jacko squeezed her hand. 'Keep a grip on yourself, my lovely.'

*

Panhanagan crawled on his belly across frozen hard ground to the lip of the great mine which he used as cover. He surveyed the area with the telescopic sight from the rifle he had taken from Jacko's house. The land around was flat with an incline towards Albert, so he could see for miles. No wonder the British Army was slaughtered on the Somme, Panhanagan thought, it was totally without cover. He could see nothing moving. No sign of troops, no sign of any vehicles. He moved the telescopic sight towards the cemetery opposite the mine, about a hundred yards away, and saw movement. He focused on a black German Mercedes pulling up beside the cemetery wall; the driver and another soldier climbed from the front and opened the rear doors. Two officers alighted and made their way inside the cemetery. Panhanagan considered they had been round to Jacko's place, found he wasn't there and now looked for likely places he might be. If this was the case, he considered they wouldn't return to the house. He made his move.

Inside Jacko's home, Panhanagan went to the cupboard under the stairs and found the box that contained the plans. He tore them into shreds, placed the paper in a bucket and filled it with water, then concealed the other contents of the box behind other boxes at the back of the cupboard. As he was about to leave he heard a car pull up outside the house.

'Shit.' He reached for the silencer in his pocket. From behind the net curtain, he saw the two officers get out of the car. He recognized Hoffmann from Paris. The driver and the other soldier remained in the car. Panhanagan moved to the rear of the house when he heard the door open. Both the German officers were now in the house talking. Although he had kept the back door ajar, the wind had closed it.

'Shit!' he cursed, because he remembered how the rusty hinges made it creak when it moved. Panhanagan was trapped. His mind raced as he tried to work out a plan. He could kill both of them, then the two soldiers standing in the car and hide their bodies down one of the trench systems. The huge minus in this plan was the Germans would miss them and the search would be intensified; dogs, spotter planes, it wouldn't work. Panhanagan knew he was in trouble. He would have to sit it out and hope they both left the house without walking through to the back. Unfortunately, as he thought it, they appeared in the room. All three looked at each other as though they were each seeing a ghost and were lost for words. Hoffmann went for his pistol. His knees buckled and he fell to the ground. Fries didn't look down at him. He knew he would be dead.

'Do you speak English?' Panhanagan asked.

'Yes'.

Their eyes met. 'I have respect for that medal round your neck, Captain. You don't deserve to be shot in cold blood like that piece of SS shit, so I'm not going to kill you.' Panhanagan saw the look of confusion in Fries' eyes. 'If you promise to wait ten minutes and allow me to leave, you will remain unharmed. Do I have your word?'

'Is Herr Jacks safe?'

'Ah, so you're the officer who comes to visit old Jacko. Yes, he's safe and will be back in England very shortly.'

'And the girl?'

Panhanagan's eyes narrowed. 'I don't want to kill you Captain, so let's just say there is just me and old Jacko, no one else. Do you understand?'

'I do. What about him?' Fries said, nodding towards Hoffmann.

'I'll deal with him later if you keep those two goons outside away from here.'

'Go,' Fries said. 'You have my word.'

214

Panhanagan left through the squeaky back door and disappeared. Fries looked down at the staring eyes of Obersturmführer Hoffmann and removed a cigarette case from his pocket. It was gold and had an inscription on it, *my beloved Ludwig.* He removed a cigarette and lit it. Fries saw that his hand was shaking. He remained in the room at the back of the house and sat on an uncomfortable armchair drawing on his cigarette, his free hand fingering the Knight's Cross round his neck as if it were a lucky talisman. After another cigarette Fries left the house. The driver jumped from the car and opened the door at the rear of the vehicle. 'Albert...' Fries said, 'the Obersturmführer is remaining here.'

From the lip of the crater, Panhanagan watched the car move down the road in the direction of Albert. The officer had been as good as his word. In the distance Panhanagan saw the car stop close to pockets of soldiers moving towards la Boisselle. The officer got out and waved the men to approach him. There were about ten who gathered around him. The car then moved on towards Albert, with the soldiers following on foot. Panhanagan gasped. The Wehrmacht officer had deliberately stopped the troops from approaching the village and sent them back. Panhanagan watched the car approach another group and he did the same again.

'What the hell is he playing at?' Panhanagan whispered aloud. He struggled to work out a reason why he should do that. When he reached the trench, he followed his normal security precautions then entered. Catherine looked at him, but said nothing. Panhanagan saw uncertainty in her eyes. 'You frighten me, Panhanagan.'

'Did you find it, Sergeant?'

'I had to destroy the plans, Jacko. I couldn't take the risk of being caught with them on me.' Panhanagan went over to Catherine and asked her if there was anything wrong. She shook her head. He sat beside her and took her hand. It was cold.

'Any sign of troops?' Catherine asked, her eyes searching his face.

'The search is off. They've turned back towards Albert.'

Catherine looked confused, Jacko showed a different emotion. 'Jerry's gone, this calls for a winter warmer,' he said smiling, 'under that bunk my little Lady Catherine, I've got a bottle; helps take the chill out of the bones when I come down here sometimes. I reckon the sergeant could do with a tot after what he's just done.'

'He doesn't drink, Jacko.'

'A soldier who doesn't drink! I've never heard of such a thing.'

'Nothing to stop you having one,' Catherine said reaching under the bunk, feeling with her hand for the bottle; instead she pulled out a heavy suitcase. When she saw it she gasped. 'Uncle Jacko! Where did you get this?'

Jacko looked at it and shrugged. 'I'd forgotten about that.'

'Tell me.'

'Some posh English bird just knocked on my door one night and said, "Give this to Catherine if she comes this way, but hide it in a safe place," yea, that's about the gist of it, then calmly walks across to the field, jumps in some weird looking aircraft and buggers off, begging your pardon, me Lady.'

'When was this?'

Jacko shrugged. 'Just before Christmas.'

'What did she look like?'

This time Jacko grinned. 'She were a toff, nice looking girl though.'

'Susan,' Panhanagan said. 'How on earth would she know to come here?'

'I told her once this is where I would come if I was in trouble. Good old Susan, she remembered.' Catherine smiled. 'I could kiss her,' and blushed when she met Panhanagan's eyes. 'Metaphorically speaking.'

'What is it?' Jacko asked, looking at the suitcase.

'It's our salvation. Once we start to lose the light, I'll run the cable outside and send a message to London. Now that does deserve a drink,' Catherine said, continuing her search under the bed.

Chapter **31**

When Nora went off the air, Elizabeth Wyatt had made a bed up in the office. She had all the comforts of home, but it was boring and lonely. Sometimes she went for a walk late at night, passing the prostitutes around Shepherd's Market or avoiding amorous calls from drunken servicemen at Piccadilly Circus. She found the whole situation frustrating.

During the day she watched Greene pace his office looking beside himself with concern. He hung onto the fact that the last wireless message they received included two words saying, *'destroying wireless'*. That wasn't too serious. Her mission was over and the wireless set would be a burden to her, so destroying it was sensible to prevent it falling into enemy hands.

Then there was Panhanagan. Greene couldn't bring himself round to think that both had been taken, Panhanagan was too wily a bird to be caught in the nest. Greene hoped they were simply on the run and would eventually find the wireless set Susan had taken to France.

During this anxious period, Susan and Elizabeth spent a lot of time in the office together. Susan brought champagne into the office on Christmas day and cooked a meal on a small portable stove. On New Year's Eve she and Elizabeth toasted in 1944 and drank to Nora's health. During these hours together, Elizabeth spoke of Catherine, commenting that the occasional letter she received from her offered very little information about her life in Canada. They always seemed hurriedly typed and never written, which was not how Catherine used to correspond to her from France when she was at the Sorbonne. It was as if she was dictating them to a secretary; a duty to write before dashing off for some fun in the safety of North America, where there was no rationing, bombs or blackouts.

'No doubt she'll have lots to say when she returns, which could be any time,' Susan said. 'These cushy postings never last too long, they have to rotate them.'

She glanced at the expression on Elizabeth's face over the brim of her teacup. It was Susan who was writing Catherine's letters in reply to letters written by Elizabeth. 'At least she is writing. How is she anyway?'

Susan shrugged. 'I don't know. She'll never complain so you never get to the truth of how she really is.'

'Well, the good news is you have been promoted to sergeant, which is some compensation for the long hours of tedium.'

That brought a smile to Elizabeth's lips. It meant that when she returned to her unit she could live and dine in the sergeant's mess which was far more comfortable than the Nissen huts and canteens she had been used to so far in this war.

The following evening, Susan arrived at the office with some cake and a bottle of Champagne. 'We're celebrating my birthday. I was going to go out with a friend, but I thought of you all alone so here I am. What are you reading?'

'War & Peace. Like this war it seems to go on forever.'

'One of Catherine's recommendations?'

Elizabeth smiled. 'Yes. I was only thinking of her a moment ago. I hope she doesn't return with a Yank or a Canadian. That would break the hearts of many mothers of heirs to England's aristocratic homes.'

'I can't see that happening... from what you've told me about her.'

'Catherine's father once told me he found Aunt Bess by sheer chance and good fortune so he would never interfere in any of his children's choice of partner. I bet he would though. He adores Catherine and wouldn't want to see her with just *anyone*.'

'And Catherine's mother?'

Elizabeth gave a sharp snort. 'Aunt Bess would never stop Catherine doing anything she wanted to do. Those two are like peas in a pod.' As Elizabeth spoke, the wireless burst into life with Nora's call sign. For a moment the two women stared open-mouthed at each other, while their brains absorbed what they had just heard. Elizabeth grabbed her earphones and tapped out her response code, then decoded the message and thrust it into Elizabeth's hand: *Sorry for absence. Mongoose and I are safe. Thank you, Susan. You remembered. Send transport. End.* Elizabeth took the reply from Susan: *Not going to wait for a moon, will send transport now. Give me a grid reference. Stand by same time tomorrow. End.* Elizabeth put the message into code and sent it. When Nora's acknowledgement was received, the two women threw their arms around each other screaming like schoolgirls at the end of term.

'God!' Susan said, laughing. 'That trip to France was worth every second.'

'What trip to France?'

'Oh... the wireless set you checked out, remember, I took it out to France and Nora has just used it,' she said casually. 'Well Liz, she's not going to call back tonight, so let's finish this bottle and go out and celebrate my birthday.'

*

The telephone rang in Model's office, the sound of it sending him rushing to his desk. He was told that a signal had been picked up by a tracking station close to Amiens.

'Where exactly?' Model asked.

The voice on the other end said, 'We can't say exactly Herr Obersturmbannführer, but somewhere north-east of Amiens. Probably within a five mile radius of Albert.'

'That's where Obersturmführer Hoffmann is now. Have you heard from him?'

'Nothing, Herr Obersturmbannführer.'

'Send some wireless detection vans to the area and place them round Albert.' Model replaced the receiver and called out for Sergeant Adler, his new clerk who had replaced Corporal Hock. 'Has Oberstumführer Hoffmann called in?'

'Not since he requested troops to be sent to Albert, Herr Obersturmbannführer.'

'Well get hold of the Garrison Commander in Albert.' Model lit a cigarette and frowned. So Hoffmann was right, he thought. The pigeon had flown home.

Sergeant Adler poked his head round Model's door and said, 'Hauptmann Fries is on the line, Herr Obersturmbannführer.'

Model stubbed out his cigarette and picked up the receiver. 'Ah! Hauptmann Fries, von Model, SD, Paris. My assistant Obersturmführer Hoffmann seems to think he's on holiday. Do you know where he is?'

'I have no idea, Herr Obersturmbannführer.'

'Has he searched the area round Albert yet?'

'Yes, Herr Obersturmbannführer.'

'And?'

'Nothing to report, Herr Obersturmbannführer.'

Model expelled his breath. 'Hauptmann, I received a report only minutes ago that our wireless tracking station near Amiens picked up a signal in your area. I suspect it is the woman Régnier calling for an aircraft to get her and her accomplice out.'

'That's a huge amount of ground to cover, Herr Obersturmbannführer.'

'You've got men from your garrison and the four hundred I sent you from Amiens and Arras. That should be enough.'

'The troops from Arras have already returned, Herr Obersturmbannführer and those from Amiens are about to leave.'

'What! Who ordered this?'

'Obersturmführer Hoffmann –'

'What?'

'I complained that we have no facilities to garrison and feed four hundred extra troops, Herr Obersturmbannführer, so he called off the search.'

Model clenched his fists and ground his teeth. 'He took it upon himself to countermand my orders. Why didn't you stop him? You are senior in rank, Hauptmann Fries.'

'With respect Herr Obersturmbannführer, I am an officer of the Wehrmacht, not the SS.'

There was the sound of heavy breathing, then calmness returned to Model's voice. 'It is imperative this woman is caught before there is any chance of her escaping by Lysander.'

'I'm sure another signal will follow, Herr Obersturmbannführer.'

'I'm sending wireless detection vans and another unit of Waffen-SS with a senior officer, so you will be under his command.'

'I report to Oberst Müller. He is my commanding–'

'And what have the Wehrmacht done apart from impregnate local whores, Hauptmann? Nothing! I will clear it with Oberst Müller. Make yourself available for their arrival tomorrow and get Hoffmann to telephone me the moment he returns.' Model slammed the telephone down on its receiver. 'Bloody useless Wehrmacht.'

*

Panhanagan had been out reconnoitring the area and hadn't seen any troops all day. He guessed that it was probably Hoffmann who had initiated the search and Hauptmann Fries had called it off once

220

Hoffmann was dead. It still puzzled him why that officer was being so helpful. Granted he had not killed him, but Fries was still a professional soldier and he had a duty to the Reich. Maybe, as with many Germans, Panhanagan decided, Hauptmann Fries didn't like the SS. While he was out, Panhanagan took the opportunity to bury Hoffmann's body in Jacko's garden.

*

After a hot meal Jacko went to his room to sleep. A little later, when Catherine heard long, rasping snores coming from Jacko's room, she took hold of Panhanagan and kissed him. 'When we get back to England−'

'You'll be a lieutenant and I shall be a sergeant.'

Her lips tightened. 'What do you mean by that? And why do you keep looking at your watch?'

'And why are you in such a bad mood?'

'Her eyes lowered. 'I'm not and you avoided answering my question.'

'There's something I have to do. We'll have plenty of time to talk about England later.'

'I want to talk about it now.'

'When I get back.'

Catherine looked hard into Panhanagan's eyes. 'Where on earth are you going? It's as dark as soot outside. What could you possibly want to do out there?'

'I won't be long.'

Her hand went to his stubbly cheek and caressed it. 'Panhanagan, tell me. I'm frightened.'

'Just trust me. Stay with Jacko. I really won't be long.'

'You're being cagey. What are you up to?'

Panhanagan smiled, took her face in his hands and kissed her. 'I love you, Catherine. You really must trust me.'

A little light shone in her eyes. 'I love you too and I wish I didn't.'

'Why do you say that?'

'Because since falling in love with you I have become sick with worry for you; I much preferred disliking you.'

'Promise I shan't be long. Don't move from here.' Panhanagan kissed her again then left the house. He waited outside the front door until his eyes had adjusted to the darkness. The sky was cloudless, but there was some light from the stars, which winked in

221

the great dark dome. Like a cat in the night, he silently made his way to the Gordon Dump cemetery where Jacko always liked to sit and talk to the fallen. When he arrived, he waited and looked about him. He then made his way to the stone shelter house. A match suddenly struck and was put to a cigarette. 'There's no need for the gun. I am unarmed.'

'Hauptmann Fries.'

'So you got my message.'

'I could hardly miss it pinned to the corpse of your fellow countryman.'

'I needed to speak with you.' Fries drew on his cigarette and looked across at Panhanagan. 'Please, take a seat. We're quite alone.'

Panhanagan shone the red beam of his torch and could see Fries was not armed. He put his PPK into his pocket and sat beside him. 'Where's your car?'

'A hundred metres down the road. My orderly thinks I have a woman.'

'Can he be trusted?'

'Yes. I had the pleasure of saving his life during a very sticky moment at Stalingrad.'

Panhanagan refused the cigarette Fries offered. 'Is that where you were awarded...' He didn't say, the Knight's Cross, he just nodded towards it.

'Yes. They sent me here to rest. I was very glad of that as it turns out.'

'I don't blame you. I've heard the Russian winter is wicked.'

Fries nodded and smiled. 'We were really unprepared for that weather. The Russians are quite mad you know. Their generals don't care how many of their men they kill.'

'I saw you send those soldiers away from reaching La Boisselle, so you're obviously helping us. Why? And why are you here now, Hauptmann?'

'Two reasons. The first is to warn you... May I have the pleasure of knowing your name?'

'Panhanagan.'

'Are you army or military intelligence?'

'Army.'

Hauptmann Fries smiled. 'Good, a fellow soldier. Well Panhanagan, your wireless signal was picked up by one of our listening posts. The Waffen-SS arrive tomorrow. Do you know the name, von Model?'

'Yes, Sicherheitsdienst, Hoffmann's boss... based in Paris.'

'He seems to have worked out that your signal was for an aircraft to take you out of here. A Lysander he said. He has wireless direction vehicles on alert waiting for your next signal. When he has your location he will send in his thugs.'

Panhanagan began to nibble at the inside of his cheek. Fries had got it precisely right so he knew the man was telling the truth. 'Why are you telling me this? You could earn a big pat on the back for taking me...'

'No offence, but you hardly matter. They don't even know your name or what you look like. The *persona non grata* is Madame Régnier. She's the real prize.' Fries went inside his greatcoat and removed the poster of Catherine, copies of which were now going up all round Albert and the surrounding villages. 'Here's the wicked villain,' Fries said with a smile. 'She's worth a lot of money to some informer.'

'There's a point to this Hauptmann. So what's the second reason you're here?'

'My mother... late mother was a Jew. A son born of a Jewish mother makes him a Jew too. Although I am not a practicing Jew I would be deemed Jewish by the ethnic test and end up in a ghetto... or worse.' He smiled ironically. 'My Knight's Cross and Iron Cross wouldn't help me then. I have seen so many atrocities committed against Jews in Russia by the SS.' He lit another cigarette. 'My father could see which way the wind was blowing for Jews as early as 1925, so we packed our bags and went to England. My father had a sister living in Yorkshire. He secured a post teaching medicine at the University of Leeds. My mother, however, was offered the post of governess to a local aristocratic family outside Harrogate, because Elizabeth, the Lady Somerville could see the benefits of her children learning German. I think she was also sympathetic to my mother's plight; Lady Somerville is a very good person. My mother accepted the position and with it came a house in the grounds. Catherine and I grew up together. I am two years older than she and was almost like an older brother. Then my mother died of cancer when I was fifteen, so my father and I returned to Germany... after all, we are German and it was our home, all of my father's family lived there.'

'Is he a Jew?'

'No.'

'So you're Paul,' Panhanagan said, shaking his head. 'Catherine speaks fondly of you. You scratched some initials on a wall within the grounds of Mountfields. Where was that exactly?'

Paul smiled. 'In the hunting lodge across the lake. A heart with our initials. I'd like to see her.' Fries suddenly said. He saw the doubt in Panhanagan's eyes. 'Upon my honour, this is no trick.' He hesitated a little before he spoke again. 'You can trust me, Panhanagan.'

'Why didn't you tell this story to Jacko? He is close to the Somerville family.'

Fries shrugged. 'You can imagine the temptation to do so when I discovered he knew the family. But, in war, there are some things one keeps to oneself.'

'Open up your greatcoat. Let me see inside.'

'I came out without a weapon,' he said, unbuttoning the coat. 'I simply would like to say goodbye to a very dear friend.'

'All right,' Panhanagan said, 'but I will protect her, whatever the cost to you. I hope you understand that.'

Paul nodded and Panhanagan followed him across the field towards Jacko's house. He made Paul wait a minute, while he looked around to see if there was anyone else close by. Satisfied that there wasn't, Panhanagan whispered, 'Wait there. We don't want a bullet through your brain now, do we? Let me explain she has a visitor then come over when I give you the signal.'

When Panhanagan walked into the sitting room, Catherine jumped up. 'Where the hell have you been Panhanagan? I was worried sick.'

'Don't be alarmed, I've brought someone to see you.'

Her eyes widened. 'What! Who? Here... are you mad?'

'There's nothing to worry about. I promise. It was the reason I went out.' Catherine picked up her PKK and cocked it. 'Leave that. You won't need it. Now don't be alarmed,' he said, going to the door and raising an arm.

Catherine saw a German officer remove his hat as he stepped into the house. Panhanagan acted as a shield and when he moved aside so Catherine could see who it was, she stared for a moment.

'Paul?' At first her voice was uncertain, it had been ten years, but when he spoke her name she cried out his name again and threw her arms round his neck. She kissed him hard on his cold cheek. 'Paul... Paul, God, I hate seeing you in that uniform,' she said in German and they were young children again.

Panhanagan watched Paul embrace Catherine hard into his body. Although it was the action of a brother meeting his sister after a long separation, deep inside him Panhanagan felt unease seeing Catherine fit so easily into another man's arms. He left them and went into the kitchen to make some coffee.

'Paul... how... where... where did you two meet?'

'Let's just say we bumped into each other in this house. He shot the man with me. An Obersturmführer from the Sicherheitsdienst, sent down from Paris to look for you.'

'Hoffmann?'

'Yes, Obersturmführer Hoffmann. Do you know him?'

'Yes... so Panhanagan shot him.' She felt nothing for Hoffmann. 'That has saved me a job.'

'He spared me because of this.' His hand went to the Knight's Cross. He smiled. 'Panhanagan is a soldier's soldier. How's Herr Jacks?'

'So *you're* the officer who befriended him. He told me about you, but he didn't know your name.'

'I was visiting the cemetery along the road. Herr Jacks didn't see me standing behind him. At first, I thought he was chatting to himself then I realized he was talking to his fallen comrades. We got to know each other. He kept referring to the man he once worked with as 'his lordship' and when he showed me a picture of him and I discovered it was your father, I was overwhelmed, but kept the secret to myself.' Paul looked at his watch. 'I have to go.'

'Must you?'

'My lieutenant in Albert will be curious if I'm not back soon. Is Panhanagan your lover?'

'Yes Paul, he is.'

'He seems a decent chap. He will explain to you the danger you are all in. I will help where I can... somehow. If your people in England are on twenty-four hour standby then try them. At this hour my people will not be so alert. Then get out of here as quickly as possible and make your way towards Cambrai along the Route de Cambrai from Bapaume. Do you have a pencil and some paper?'

'Just tell me Paul. I'll remember it,' Catherine said.

'Right, it's easy enough. Approximately seven to eight kilometres before you reach Cambrai, there'll be a large forest to the left of you, take the second left, not Rue de Moeuvres, the next turning. That road runs along the edge of the forest. If you miss the turning don't worry, another two to three kilometres further along the road is the town of Fontaine Notre-Dame, turn back and the first turning right past the forest is your road.'

'How do you know this?' Catherine asked, impressed with the detail.

'I looked it up on the map before I left Albert. The forest will be perfect cover until your aircraft arrives and you will not be seen signalling it. It will also avoid having to fly over Bourlon or Fontaine Notre-Dame, so it should not be seen or heard. The Lysander can land close to the forest, there's plenty of cover for that too. You can take my car.' Paul said. 'Do you have a couple of bicycles in exchange?'

'Yes, you're welcome to them.'

'Well, goodbye Catherine.' He smiled. 'When we were children did you see our futures like this?' He shrugged. 'I am happy to say I have never had to face the British in combat. I should not like to have fought against the people who welcomed me to their country and gave my family a home.'

Catherine took hold of him again. She kissed his cheek then his lips. 'God go with you Paul. Come back to Mountfields. You will always be welcome there.'

When Paul left, Panhanagan followed him with the second bicycle then waited until he saw the two Germans cycle away from the car. Catherine set up her wireless and tried her call sign twice without response, little knowing her cousin was in a deep sleep because of an excess of alcohol she had consumed with Susan.

They packed the car with their belongings; the wireless, the rifle with telescopic sight and the Lewis machine gun with its ammunition and a can of petrol Jacko had stored away. They woke Jacko and then drove out of La Boisselle, with the spirits of the dead watching them leave.

Chapter **32**

Hauptmann Paul Fries answered the telephone and was greeted with a spluttering, angry voice. 'Hauptmann, where the hell is Obersturmführer Hoffmann?'

'Good morning, Herr Obersturmbannführer. I have no idea where he is. I am not responsible for him. He's not under my command.'

'Somebody must have seen him.'

'I have not seen him, Herr Obersturmbannführer.'

'This is becoming a farce. He is meant to be liaising with the Waffen-SS; instead, they are still sitting on their arses in Amiens.' There was silence for a moment then Model continued in a quieter and more determined voice. 'I'm coming down, Hauptmann Fries. I'm leaving Paris immediately for Amiens and I'll bring the Waffen-SS myself. When Hoffmann turns up, lock him up.'

As Model's car left Avenue Foch, a corporal ran out of the building waving at the car to stop, but instead, he watched it continue on its way and disappear. He returned to the office and threw the message on his sergeant's desk.

'What's that?' the sergeant asked.

'A message for Model. Another wireless signal has been picked up from the Arras area.'

'Don't worry about it. He'll deal with it when he gets to Amiens.'

'It could be important.'

'Corporal, listen to me, you and I have just arrived here on a nice easy posting after the misery of facing those Russian lunatics. This is Paris – wine, whores and no worries. What could be more important than that? Tonight, I thought we should go down to Pigalle and see some ooh la la.'

'I'm with you there, Sarge.'

*

Model regretted not taking the train. The roads were crowded with civilians pulling handcarts full of their worldly possessions, tired children crying and mothers close to exhaustion. Closer to Amiens sheep filled the road, which took an age to clear. Model sat in the back of the car with his head in his hands. That damned woman had caused him so many headaches, yet despite it all he admired her courage, instincts and self-preservation.

He arrived at the Waffen-SS barracks at midday as air raid sirens began to sound. A young officer met Model at the gate and saluted him. 'Welcome to Amiens, Obersturmbannführer von Model.'

Model didn't answer. He looked skywards and saw what he recognized to be Mosquito bombers flying in low, with Typhoon fighter cover above them. This was no ordinary raid, Model knew, not with specialist bombers such as the Mosquito. 'What target are they going for, Untersturmführer?'

'I can't think, Herr Obersturmbannführer. There is only the prison in that direction.'

As the young man spoke the first explosion sounded followed by black smoke rising to the sky; then another and another. 'For God's sake man, why are they bombing a prison?'

Model was silenced for a moment. The Maquis... there had to be some important people in there to risk a squadron of Mosquitoes in this operation. And why should they want them to escape? He wondered if this was connected to Nora... the imminent invasion.

'I have to go, Herr Obersturmbannführer,' said the young officer. 'I've been summoned by my commanding officer.'

The Waffen-SS troops Model was going to take to Albert were running around under orders to get into trucks and drive directly to the prison. They would be needed to round up escaping prisoners. Model stood in the middle of it all, watching the chaos and confusion. He began to laugh. He knew it was ridiculous. Everything possible was being placed in his way to prevent him getting to Albert with troops. He called his driver and instructed him to get out just in case heavy bombers followed to bomb the Waffen-SS barracks.

The raid was over before Model reached the Avenue de la Défense Passive that led out of Amiens. 'Where are you going?'

'This is the road to Albert, Herr Obersturmbannführer. We'll pass the prison very shortly.'

When they reached Amiens prison, on the outskirts of the city, Model could see the wall had been breached. Several prisoners were rushing to get through the gaping hole. Model watched. It wasn't his affair or his concern. He had a far bigger fish to catch.

'Slow down Kohl, and take a look. You'll read about the raid on Amiens prison one day, mark my words and you will be able to say to your grandchildren, "I saw the raid on Amiens Prison". They will laugh and not be interested in a word you say.'

As the car slowed, Model caught the eye of one of the men who had just scrambled over the rubble to freedom. When Henri Bonamy saw the SS officer looking at him, he gazed back in terror, but the SS officer only smiled at him as the car drove away. Five miles out of Albert, five Army vehicles passed them driving towards Amiens. Model shook his head. These were some of the troops he was counting on in place of the Waffen-SS, to help search for Madame Régnier and her companion. 'It's a conspiracy,' he whispered. That bitch had more lives than a cat. He was convinced of it.

*

Hauptmann Fries saluted Model when he arrived at his headquarters. 'We've heard about the raid, Herr Obersturmbannführer. You have to admire the audacity of the British.'

Model's eyes settled on the Knight's Cross with oak leaves and swords with diamonds. A bloody hero, he thought. That's all I need. 'Admire the British you say, Hauptmann? My thoughts are for our soldiers who died in that raid.'

'Of course Herr Obersturmbannführer, I meant no disrespect.'

'Has Hoffmann turned up?'

'No, Herr Obersturmbannführer, he... well, it's bad luck really; my orderly told me that Obersturmführer Hoffmann ordered him to drive to Amiens. When my orderly refused, Obersturmführer Hoffmann took my car and drove off in it... in the direction of Amiens. It was something to do with Madame Régnier.'

Model looked into Paul Fries' eyes as if he were searching his soul. 'Send for your orderly.'

When Corporal Siever arrived at Hauptmann Fries' office, he gave Model a smart salute and an exaggerated 'Hail Hitler', which brought a smile to Paul's lips. Sievers glanced towards Hauptmann Fries. They had known each other for three years and had served throughout the Russian campaign together, until they were both wounded and shipped back to Germany.

'I read through some notes Obersturmführer Hoffmann left in my office, Herr Obersturmbannführer. I have them here. I believe

Obersturmführer Hoffmann has gone back to the prison to interview a man by the name of Henri Bonamy.'

'You had no business looking through those notes, Corporal,' Model said at last. 'Hauptmann, put a call through to the prison.'

Within seconds the telephone rang. Paul picked it up, listened and replaced the receiver. 'All lines to Amiens prison have been severed, Herr Obersturmbannführer.'

Model shrugged. 'Hoffmann's an incompetent idiot. He had no right to be there, let alone question anyone without my authority. If he's been caught up in that mess then he has only himself to blame.'

Again, Paul and Sievers glanced at each other. Model looked up at Corporal Sievers and flicked his fingers at him. 'Thank you Corporal,' Paul said. 'You may go.'

'Have you had any reports of wireless traffic in the area this morning, Hauptmann?'

Paul shook his head. 'Do you think this woman you're looking for will come this way then? Surely Spain or Switzerland would have been a better bet.'

'No, this is where she is. I can smell her, she's out there somewhere.'

'She's a very attractive woman, Herr Obersturmbannführer,' Paul said, looking at a poster.

'God, what's up with you all? Let me tell you something about this woman Hauptmann, like a praying mantis she would eat you alive while you're screwing her. She spells death for anyone who gets close to her. I know her. If you did too you would understand what I'm talking about. It wouldn't surprise me if she has devoured that cock-happy Hoffmann,' Model sat on the edge of Paul's desk and finding it uncomfortable, found a chair. 'The British will do anything to get this woman out of France and quickly. She knows this area well and a Lysander can land just about anywhere. So far she has avoided capture, with the assistance of some gun-happy thug that none of us has ever seen, not one decent description of her accomplice. Do you have a cigarette, Hauptmann?'

'Take this, Herr Obersturmbannführer,' Paul said, handing Model Hoffmann's gold cigarette case. 'Obersturmführer Hoffmann left it here.'

'Thank you. I've always liked this case.' Model lit a cigarette and blew the smoke skywards then slipped the case into his pocket. 'Do you think we will win this war, Hauptmann?'

'No, Herr Obersturmbannführer, I don't.'

Model was silent for a moment. 'Goebbels would have you shot for saying that, but I agree. Soon there will be an invasion, then, it'll be curtains as the English say. I will tell you Hauptmann, the Russians and Americans will take our scientists after the war, to steal and to use German brains...'

'Do you really think that, Herr Obersturmbannführer?'

'Wouldn't you? The rest of us must make do.'

'And the Führer?'

'Do you see the Führer allowing anyone to take him alive?'

'Forgive me, Herr Obersturmbannführer, but I have never heard an SS man say such things.'

'My uniform betrays my convictions, Hauptmann. I am a German aristocrat; a true German. This woman we are chasing has got under my skin, but I admire her. I really do. She has courage, guile and intelligence...'

'A female Sir Percy Blakeney, Herr Obersturmbannführer.'

A smile spread across Model's face. 'You've read the story?'

'Of course. I once lived in England. What boy hasn't?'

'What were you doing in England?'

'My father taught medicine at the University of Leeds. Why do you think this woman is an aristocrat, Herr Obersturmbannführer?'

'One recognises one's own class,' Model said. 'When I was in England I stayed with so many aristocratic families. They're no different from us, you know. Were you ever invited on a shoot?'

'Yes, but not with the guns.'

'No, of course not,' Model chuckled. 'With the beaters, eh?'

'It supplemented my pocket money.'

'Pocket money... what a quaint expression...' Model stubbed out his cigarette and sighed. 'You can help me, Hauptmann. We'll seek her here and we'll seek her there together, eh?' Model laughed. 'I've got to get to her before that Lysander does. I've alerted the Luftwaffe–'

'With respect Herr Obersturmbannführer, surely that would be unwise if you want her alive.'

'Not to shoot the bloody thing down with her in it... before it gets to her.' Model suddenly showed displeasure when his eyes met Paul's. 'Where exactly have you searched, Hauptmann?'

'Bécourt, Aveluy and la Boisselle, the areas Obersturmführer Hoffmann suggested, Herr Obersturmbannführer. Although they are small villages, geographically it's a very large area. We just haven't the manpower.'

'Yes, I know,' Model conceded.

'Hoffmann called off the search. He said he was waiting for you.'

'He didn't contact me. If he has survived that raid, I'll have him transferred to the Russian Front. And the Englishman Jacks... has he been arrested?'

'No, Herr Obersturmbannführer. When Hoffmann and I went to his house, he was gone.'

'Gone... interesting. I wonder if he's gone with them and if so, why? What value is he to Nora or British Intelligence?'

'Nora?'

'Madame Régnier's codename. Didn't Hoffmann tell you anything?'

'Nothing, Herr Obersturmbannführer.'

'The man's a fool.'

Paul offered more tea, which Model accepted. 'Do you really think she's in this area?'

'Yes, somewhere... hiding like the vixen she is, waiting for dark.'

Paul turned to Model, who was glancing through a magazine. 'What happened to the Waffen-SS, Herr Obersturmbannführer? I thought they were arriving here with you.'

The smile that crept to Model's lips showed sardonic humour. 'A miracle happened, Hauptmann. The Royal Air Force knew our pack of hounds were about to leave for the chase, so they thought, tally-ho let's help the little vixen, let's go and spoil the hunt by bombing Amiens prison. Yesterday wasn't good enough and they couldn't wait until tomorrow, so it had to be today. Then, of course, you Hauptmann Fries send a convoy of urgently needed troops to Amiens. So we are now down to a handful of men.'

'I was under the impression they would be more usefully deployed in Amiens.'

'True, under normal circumstances it was a good move. But now... it's now pointless running around the country like headless chickens so we wait for the inevitable wireless traffic to begin, which it will. How's the moon?'

'There isn't one. Full moon was on the 10th Herr Obersturmbannführer, nine days ago.'

'Good, the pilot will have to use lights. This is beginning to look a little better.' Model stretched his arms wide and stifled a yawn. 'I'm hungry, Hauptmann. Are there any decent restaurants in this godforsaken pit of a place?'

'I know one I'm sure you will enjoy, Herr Obersturmbannführer.'

'Good. I'll buy you lunch and you can tell me how you became a hero of the Third Reich, Hauptmann Fries.'

'I'd rather discuss *The Scarlet Pimpernel*, Herr Obersturmbannführer.'

*

When they returned from lunch, Model went to the switchboard operator and asked if he had heard from any of the wireless listening stations in the area. The soldier sprang to attention and announced that he had only just taken over the duty. 'Hauptmann, send for the soldier who was on the previous duty shift.'

'Corporal,' Paul called out to his orderly, 'Get Sergeant Voigt up here.'

'Yes Herr Hauptmann, immediately.' Five minutes later the sergeant arrived.

'Where's Grenadier Liebermann, Sergeant?' Paul asked.

'Off duty, Herr Hauptmann. He went into town.'

'Was there any reported wireless traffic, Sergeant?' Model said impatiently.

'Yes, Herr Obersturmbannführer. They picked up a signal somewhere around the Arras area.'

Model rushed to the map on the wall and gasped. 'Couldn't they be more precise than that? It will be like trying to find a needle in the proverbial haystack. What time did you receive the message?'

'Ten hundred hours, Herr Obersturmbannführer.'

'What! Five hours ago.' Model threw his gaze towards Paul. 'What sort of circus are you running here, Hauptmann? Five valuable hours lost. I want an explanation and quickly.'

'I'll investigate it, Herr Obersturmbannführer.'

'There's no time for that. Bring me the soldier that took the message.'

The sergeant glanced at Paul and then at Model. 'I have no idea where he'll be, Herr Obersturmbannführer.'

Model squeezed his eyes closed. 'Don't you know the habits of the common German soldier, Sergeant? Just look in any whorehouse in town. If I didn't know better I'd think the Wehrmacht was in league with this woman.'

'I'll get to the bottom of it, Herr Obersturmbannführer,' Paul Fries said.

'Let's use what brains we have.' Model went back to the map and, with a pencil, he pointed to Arras. 'Arras here, Cambrai here. You have three straight roads that form a triangle, Arras to Cambrai, Cambrai to Bapaume and Bapaume to Arras. The signal came from within that triangle but closer to Arras than Cambrai, a triangle with numerous villages and hundreds of thousands of hectares in which to land a Lysander. Do you know this area?'

'No,' Paul lied.

'Don't you know anything, Hauptmann?'

'Munich, Herr Obersturmbannführer.'

'That's not helpful. Where would you land a Lysander?'

As both men poured over the map, the telephone rang. Paul answered it. 'It's for you, Herr Obersturmbannführer.'

Model almost snatched the telephone from Paul's hand. 'Model,' he said, then stood and listened, a smile creeping across his face. 'And when was this?'

Paul saw Model's eyes brighten. They glanced his way. Model nodded and replaced the receiver. 'Good news, Herr Obersturmbannführer.'

'She has made the mistake I knew she would,' Model said, returning to the map. 'Our mobile tracking vehicles in Arras have picked up a signal here, between Arras and the small town of Mercatel. I know that Lysanders use this area to pick up SOE agents.' As Model stared at the map, he did not see Paul suppress a smile. Paul knew Catherine was sending Model in the wrong direction. 'Surely London must know we'll be keeping an eye on all known landing areas, Herr Obersturmbannführer.'

'There's no moon to light the way for the pilot. He isn't going to take a chance in an area he doesn't know, so they have settled on a landing strip they do know and that, Hauptmann Fries, is their mistake.' Model gave a great self-satisfied sigh. 'I've also been promised one hundred Waffen-SS troops from Amiens this afternoon. Things are looking up, Hauptmann.'

'You have enough men here if it's just a case of waiting for an aircraft, Herr Obersturmbannführer.'

'I need to catch this woman, Hauptmann and I trust the Waffen-SS to do the job.' Model looked into Paul's face and with a contemptuous smile he added, 'Your men can man roadblocks around the area. You can at least manage that, I'm sure.'

'If that is a request I will consider it, Herr Obersturmbannführer. If it is an order, then I shall have to contact Oberst Müller.'

Model threw his arms into the air. 'I wouldn't want to throw a spanner into your little empire Hauptmann, so let me rephrase it... would you be good enough to use your men to erect roadblocks to assist me in the pursuit of an enemy of the Reich?'

'Certainly, Herr Obersturmbannführer. I'll organize it right away.'

'And scare her away? No Hauptmann, we'll wait until dark and surprise our little foxy aristocrat.'

Chapter **33**

The wireless signal picked up near Arras, and reported to Model, was sent by Panhanagan. He had travelled to the outskirts of Arras and deliberately sent a long message to London knowing the German listening stations would pick it up and pinpoint it to the west of the Arras area, thus sending troops there, leaving the real rendezvous free of trouble.

In a wood several miles away, close to Cambrai, Catherine waited anxiously waited for Panhanagan's return. They had found shelter in a cabin, used by schools during the long summer months. It was isolated and the perfect place for Catherine and Jacko to hide. When Panhanagan returned, he and Catherine went for a walk leaving Jacko smoking his pipe.

Catherine took Panhanagan's hand and squeezed it. 'Jacko doesn't want to leave, but they'll kill him if he stays, you know that, don't you?'

'I know. He has to take my place in the aircraft... you know that.'

Catherine couldn't argue with Panhanagan because she knew it was the only way to save Jacko from the Gestapo. 'We could put Jacko in the aircraft then you and I can make—'

'No. You're leaving with Jacko. Anyway, I've made a few plays to buy you time,' he said and explained that he was going to set up a defensive area should Model discover that he had been duped. 'It gives you a chance if they come this way. I can hold them for a few vital minutes. By the time I've slipped away from them you'll be gone.'

'You're mad. I can't allow that.' She took him in her arms. 'Panhanagan, please, we're so close to getting away with this. Don't risk anything now. Just leave us and make your way back to your unit. Go now.'

He kissed her tenderly on her forehead. 'It's vital you get away. Anyway, they may not have worked out our plan, so chin up, this time tomorrow you'll be back in England and I'll be with Holloway and Peters.'

'Holloway and Peters aren't in France. They were moved to Italy. My last transmission confirmed it. I didn't tell you because it didn't seem necessary.'

Panhanagan shrugged. 'So I'll rejoin the Maquis they were training.'

For the first time since they had known each other, Catherine felt a vulnerable young woman with fear and uncertainty in her heart. I'm going to lose you, she thought looking into his eyes. I foresee it as Anna Karenina foresaw her own death. She placed her head on his shoulder and closed her eyes.

*

Panhanagan finished the last of his defence and was now prepared for Model and his friends should he discover that he had been tricked. Model would be forced to drive down this narrow lane, with the forest on the left and a ploughed field to the right, towards Panhanagan's trap. There was no other way for vehicles to go. Panhanagan had manoeuvred Paul's car across the narrow lane that ran the length of the wood, he had punctured the tyres and filled the vehicle with wood. Jacko's can of petrol had been placed in the middle of the wood, so when a tracer bullet hit it, the can would explode and turn the car into a furnace. The barbed wire fence to the left of the car would not stop the troops climbing over it but his guess was they would take the easier route round the burning vehicle and through the gaps in the wood. That is where he would concentrate his machine gun fire. He had three drums and the sniper rifle, so a lot of damage could be done before he made his escape. Nothing, Panhanagan knew, would get near the vehicle, or be able to pass it, so the Germans could only pass on foot and into his machine gun fire. This would slow them down considerably, giving Catherine valuable time to escape. The burning car would also give light for the pilot.

He made his way back to Catherine and Jacko, at the other side of the wood where there was no road. From there she could signal the approaching aircraft unseen. Panhanagan looked around him. He felt there was nothing more he could do.

When he arrived at the cabin, Catherine walked towards him. She felt sick in her stomach with worry. 'Please go Panhanagan, leave now. We'll be all right. Just go.' She knew at worst Panhanagan would take on the Germans and be killed just to buy them minutes, and at best, even if she escaped and he survived, they were going to be separated until the end of the war, whenever that would be. There were now only three hours left to wait for the arrival of the Lysander.

Panhanagan watched Jacko make his way to a narrow road that ran though the wood. When he was out of sight Catherine took Panhanagan's face in her hands and kissed his lips. 'Jacko's gone for a walk. He said he would be away for an hour.' They made love on the bench and after, they held each other in silence. 'I'll never give myself to another man,' she whispered.

'And if the worst should happen?'

'I said I will never give myself to another man. Just make sure you come back to me.' Catherine was still wearing her coat; it was too cold to remove it. She buttoned up her blouse and put her knickers back on. 'Hopefully, the next time these come off will be for a bath in England.'

Jacko returned to the log cabin an hour later. He looked at the two young people before him and shook his head. 'I don't like you giving up your place, Sergeant. I don't want to go. Who'd have a chat with the lads if I'm not there? You get back with young Lady Catherine.'

Catherine reached for Jacko's hand which was cold. 'Uncle Jacko... the Gestapo will accuse you of harbouring spies and shoot you. Even Paul wouldn't be able to save you.'

'That was some coincidence... the Hauptmann and you as kids, eh? I always thought he was a gent.'

'I've had orders to stay, make a nuisance of myself,' Panhanagan said.

Jacko's red eyes found a smiling Panhanagan. He knew that wasn't true. 'I saw what you've done down the track. Good idea. That will hold them up.'

'Uncle Jacko, have you got all you need?'

Jacko nodded. He looked over at Panhanagan and said, 'I've 'ad my life. You've got yours ahead of you. Don't waste it 'ere son. Go back to Blighty and marry Catherine.'

Catherine and Panhanagan's eyes met. It was something they had never discussed. 'The Lady Catherine wouldn't want that, Jacko−'

Catherine gripped his hand and said, 'Yes I would,' and looked hard into Panhanagan's eyes for his reaction to her sudden outburst. Catherine quietly repeated her words. 'Yes, I would.'

She threw her arms round him and they held each other for a full minute without a word spoken. When she did speak, it was in a whisper. 'I've missed a second period.'

They untangled themselves, their eyes locked. Panhanagan handed her a small torch. Catherine thought his voice was irritatingly steady considering what she had just told him. 'You'll need that to signal the pilot. Look after Catherine, Jacko.' He pulled his SAS beret from his pocket and placed it on his head. 'Now they're going to face a soldier,' he said, 'not some wanker in the Maquis.'

'Panhanagan,' Catherine called out,' but he was gone, lost in the darkness; only the vapour from Catherine and Jacko's mouths filled the space he had occupied.

Chapter 34

Model left Albert with fifty Waffen-SS troops, which were all that could be spared from the chaos after the air raid on Amiens prison. He knew Catherine would show herself at the sound of an aircraft and Model didn't want to move too soon and send her into hiding again. Model poured over a map like a chess master working out his next move. 'Where is that aircraft going to land?' he whispered aloud. 'Where, where, where?'

Paul Fries grinned at Model's intense expression. He knew exactly where the aircraft would land and he intended to keep his men far away from the landing zone. 'Shall I set up roadblocks around the Abwehr's estimated location of the wireless signal, Herr Obersturmbannführer?'

Model switched his gaze to the area on the map and nodded. 'Yes, all right. And have fifty men ready to move at a moment's notice.'

Model studied the area again on the map, while his mind began to tick boxes. His experience of SOE activity suggested that they only flew a Lysander in during a full moon, a dangerous moon the Agents called it, because the enemy may suspect a landing. There was no moon that night and, although the sky was clear of cloud, it was very dark in the blackout, almost impossible for a pilot to recognize any landmarks. However, Model knew that from the air in the darkness, a flashing torch and a few burning cans of oil to light up a runway, could be seen from miles away. Model also knew the pilot would take chances and use lights to land. All his instincts told him that tonight was the night and closer to ten than midnight.

*

By seven o'clock the roadblocks were in place. Now several miles from Model, Paul Fries lit a cigarette and relaxed. He went to a local café with two of his subalterns and had a jolly supper and a couple of bottles of wine. His companions were surprised at the casual way their commanding officer was treating this, but neither complained. 'After all,' Paul said, finishing a plate of tomatoes in olive oil, garlic and basil leaves, 'this is an SS affair. They will take the credit so let them do the work.' His two companions laughed, agreed and toasted Hauptmann Fries who was a hero of the Reich.

Paul responded. 'Gentlemen, a toast... the Lady Catherine Somerville.'

'Herr Hauptmann,' said the younger lieutenant. 'Who is this woman?'

'The first woman I ever loved.'

The three men stood, hit each other's glasses and made the toast. After the coq au vin was eaten and the third bottle of wine was drunk, they began singing, *Soldaten sind immer Soldaten,* stamping their feet in time with the song.

*

Waffen-SS troops, under the command of Model, stood around their vehicles in the cold. He had taken a gamble and split his force, positioning half his troops at Moeuvres, where he could move north or south very quickly. The other half were at Bullecourt. With Hauptmann Fries waiting with another fifty men, he felt his board was covered. Now all he could do was sit and wait.

Model's troops smoked and chatted to each other, without fear of meeting much resistance if it came to a fight. At eight o'clock, sandwiches and coffee were distributed amongst the Waffen SS and at nine o'clock, orders were given to maintain silence and extinguish all cigarettes; a group of soldiers smoking would look like a cloud of fireflies to a pilot circling above.

Model felt his stomach begin to ache with anticipation. He had not been this excited for years. Everything was in place; all that was needed was the sound of a single engine aircraft and Madame Régnier was in the bag.

The soldiers kept their feet warm by wriggling their toes inside their boots; many squeezed their hands into fists. Clouds of vapour left their mouths, just as cigarette smoke had done earlier. It was so quiet; one could almost hear the dead from the last war turning in their graves to see what was happening - then close to ten o'clock, all heads lifted to the sky at the faint, but distinctive sound of an aircraft engine.

'Yes!' Model smiled. He had played the game to perfection. Men scrambled into vehicles waiting for Model's order to start the engines. Model strained his ears, but could not hear the aircraft. It was not circling any field close by and there was no glow from landing strip lights anywhere.

'It flew straight on, Herr Obersturmbannführer,' a fellow officer said. 'There.'

Model grabbed a map from his pocket and spread it out on his lap. The torch's beam found where they were positioned. He followed the course of the aircraft and banged the dashboard with his fist. 'Clever little bitch. She sent the signal from this area to fool us then doubled back on herself. They will be here,' he said pointing at the wood, 'using it as cover.'

The order was given, all engines clattered into life. Model's car was in the middle of the convoy, with three vehicles carrying twenty-five soldiers. He radioed the other half of his force to make it to a map reference he read out and to use all speed to get there. Hauptmann Fries' troops were utterly useless to him. They were too far away. 'Bloody hero,' he cursed, 'he may as well have stayed in Albert for all the use he is.' He drummed his fingers on his knees with his customary impatience. All he could see was the vehicle in front, with troops in the back checking their weapons. He looked at his watch. It had been three minutes since he had first heard the aircraft. They picked up speed and reached the north end of the woods.

*

Overhead there was a muffled sound of a single Bristol Mercury engine circling the fields. Catherine marvelled at the skill of the pilot to find his way to this field without moonlight. She guided him in by her torch when he was some miles away. When he was close, she received two flicks of light from the aircraft. Now Catherine signalled her call sign and she received another two flicks of light in return. She ran across the field and lit two of the landing lights while Jacko did the same to one in the centre of the field, where Catherine had placed him a hundred yards from where she was now. It didn't seem much from the ground, but from the air it allowed the pilot to drop the aircraft at the single light and aim between the other two lights at the bottom of the field.

Panhanagan also heard the aircraft engine choke and throttle back for a landing. In the distance he saw pinpricks of light that began to grow larger, moving in a single column down the narrow road alongside the wood heading right for his current position. He adjusted his beret, cocked the Lewis gun and picked up the rifle with its telescopic sight. The first round in it was a tracer. The marker he had to aim at was a white handkerchief that had belonged to Catherine. One shot into that and the whole place would light up.

The small convoy blindly headed towards Panhanagan's trap. A single shot was heard above the roar of military vehicle engines, followed by an explosion that lit up everything in the area. Another single shot killed the driver of the lead vehicle, which crashed into a telegraph pole and obstructed the road further. A sustained burst of fire from the Lewis gun, reduced the second vehicle to flames.

The Lysander pilot, making his run in to land, could now see everything clearly; he could even see his two passengers waiting by the edge of the field. Within a minute he was turning his aircraft ready to take off. Catherine followed Jacko up the aircraft's steps. When they were airborne, she looked down at the carnage Panhanagan was creating and could see tracer fire from both sides. A fierce fire-fight was taking place a hundred yards below her. She turned her head sharply to the port side, focussing on the light until it was just a flickering glow in the distance. Tears wet her eyes. She turned her head once more. There was only the fathomless darkness of the French countryside, and the uncertainly of seeing her lover again.

*

Panhanagan watched the Lysander disappear into the darkness beyond the woods. Although a few shots were fired at it, the aircraft had escaped unharmed. Now he could relax. He had used two of the three drums of ammunition. Two vehicles were on fire and he was beginning to receive more accurate incoming fire. Panhanagan emptied the last drum on troops moving into the woods. When the Lewis gun was out of ammunition he grabbed the rifle with its telescopic sight and ran to a new, pre-prepared position. He let the Waffen-SS know a sniper was now on the loose by dropping three men with shots to the head, which he knew would keep other heads down while he disappeared further into the forest.

*

The ambush had taken Model by complete surprise. It was swift and violent. Men were blinded by the light of the fire and the heat of it kept them at a distance. No one could see from which direction the gunfire was coming. Several men were killed, many took cover; it was chaos. The officer accompanying Model was dead. To augment his suffering further, Model saw the Lysander slip away into the distant darkness. When the firing stopped, he walked to the position Panhanagan had held, looked down at the discarded Lewis machine gun and bent to retrieve something left on it. It was a sand coloured beret. Wrapped in the beret was a folded poster of Madame Catherine Régnier. A note was scribbled on it. *Hoffmann is dead*. His identity discs and the address where he was buried, were included in the bundle.

Chapter 35

During her debriefing with Commodore Greene, Catherine looked over at the vacant desk once occupied by her cousin. Elizabeth had been sent away on leave, before being reassigned to Grendon Underwood with strict instructions, under the Official Secrets Act, not to speak about Nora or her mission.

'MI5 are delighted with the list of German agents, Catherine. A couple slipped through the net but they managed to catch most of them. Well done.' He looked into her eyes and smiled. 'I'd like you to stay on in intelligence?'

'I can't do that, Sir. I have my reasons. It's nothing to do with the service. If it's all right with you Sir, I'd like to take some leave.'

'Of course. Take a break, and if you should change your mind, you know where I am.'

'I'm having lunch with my father this afternoon−'

'Catherine,' Greene said, 'your father knows you were in France. He came to see me. He knows the military attaché in Canada and discovered you were not on his staff. He's no fool.'

'When did he come to see you?'

'You'd been gone three days. He was naturally very worried for his daughter, although he said he suspected you were in some form of intelligence agency. Your father is a well-respected, high-ranking officer, a personal friend of the King and Winston Churchill. Not a lot passes him. Between you and me, I think Winston whispered in his ear to speak with me. I told your father that you are a serving officer in the Secret Intelligence Service doing your duty as every serviceman and woman in the country is doing theirs. He looked me in the eye, nodded and asked me if there was anyone else more qualified I could have sent. I told him no. He smiled, shook my hand and left. Your father didn't want to know anything more. He's a professional soldier, Catherine. Wars cannot be fought without personal risk. He knows that. His last words to me before he left were that he was very proud of you.' Greene witnessed a slight tremor of her chin.

'He'll be thrilled to see Jacko,' she said. 'They are very fond of each other.'

'I was very impressed with your cousin, Catherine. I've put her up for a commission.'

Catherine smiled, but it was brief. 'Commodore, I'm frantically worried about Sergeant Panhanagan. As we flew out, he was in a terrific fire-fight and hopelessly outnumbered against several Waffen-SS. We got away because of him... only because of him.'

Greene saw this strong, young woman, fighting emotions and guessed Panhanagan and she had formed a close relationship, closer than military discipline allowed. He would have Panhanagan commissioned and backdated to the date of his departure to France. 'Don't give up hope, Catherine. These SAS types are mad as hatters, but very professional. He has probably joined up with the Maquis.'

Catherine forced a smile. 'He takes far too many risks,' she said softly. 'Commodore, I should like to recommend him for a gallantry award.'

Greene smiled. 'He deserves one. Just write out a report with your recommendations and I will put my signature to it. Address him as Lieutenant Panhanagan.'

'My father...?'

'No, me.'

'What made you send him?'

Suddenly Greene looked a little sheepish. 'Actually Catherine, it was your father's idea. He thought Sergeant... Lieutenant Panhanagan was the perfect fellow to watch your back.'

'My father didn't know him. He had never met him.'

'But your mother had.'

Catherine put her face into her hands and her shoulders began to shake.

*

Greene released Catherine from MI6 the following month. By June, when the invasion of Europe had begun, there was still no news regarding Panhanagan. Holloway and Peters, who were back in France organizing groups of resistance fighters, hadn't heard from him. On May 8th 1945, Catherine was at Mountfields when the news came through that the Germans had surrendered and therefore the war in Europe was over. Robins, the butler, entered Catherine's study where she was writing a letter. 'Excuse me Lady

Catherine, her Ladyship asks if you will join the family in the picture room. They are going to toast the end of the war in Europe.'

'Five minutes, Robins. How's your father?'

'In good health and enjoying his retirement, thank you Lady Catherine. You'll see him at the victory party her Ladyship is organizing.'

'Victory party! What about our troops fighting in the Pacific?'

'Er... yes, quite. I believe her Ladyship is referring specifically to Europe, Lady Catherine.'

When Catherine joined the others, she was offered a glass of Champagne and a toast was made by Lord James Somerville. After, Catherine spoke, 'To absent friends.' Her eyes met her father's. The family looked towards her sympathetically and repeated it. Catherine's mother went to her and slipped an arm round her daughter's shoulder. 'Don't give up hope, darling. He may be a prisoner-of-war. When I was reported missing—'

'You were reported dead, Mummy. Gran told me.'

'Yes, but I was discovered by the Red Cross in a German Military hospital weeks later. Poor Nana Somerville had to wait nine years to discover your father was still alive. She never gave up hope and neither must you.'

'That's no comfort, Mummy. You and Daddy were made prisoners-of-war. Panhanagan will be shot if he is caught. There will be no POW camp or even a hospital bed for him. I worry so much about him. It hurts not knowing.'

'Catherine, I know how you feel, really I do.'

'Mummy, I love him. I believe I have made that perfectly obvious to you both.'

'Yes, yes darling, you have.'

'So when that drippy Lord Shillington's son comes calling again, just tell him to bugger off. I'm sick of telling him myself.'

'Catherine darling... please don't use barrack-room language at home.' Lady Somerville said, glancing towards her husband. 'Neither of us would ever object to Panhanagan, you know that. He has proved himself to be a first-rate fellow. Your father has every admiration for him.'

'So he should.'

*

A few weeks later, Catherine was out when her uncle Sir Edward Wyatt telephoned. It was his brother-in-law who answered the call. 'James,' Edward said, 'this is a long shot' but the Yanks have a fellow in one of their hospitals. We're not certain at this stage whether he is Catherine's young man, but we're looking into it. The French have been to see him and say he's not one of theirs–'

'I'm not following you, Edward.'

'Before the fellow lost consciousness, he was muttering something in French, that's why they wanted to let the French have him, but another fellow who was picked up with him, says he's English. They fought together in the resistance.'

'Sounds promising.'

'The problem is he has no identification and the fellow picked up with him refers to him as Monsieur Mongoose. The Yanks think they are both raving mad and want shot of them. It's worth us investigating, wouldn't you say?'

'Where did they find him?'

'Dachau.'

'Oh Lord, is he in a bad state?'

'It's not good.'

'Where is he now?'

'Germany... in American hospital. They're concerned he may have typhoid.'

'They should bloody well know if he has. I'll get some of our people to take him off their hands and send him to one of ours. Thank you, Edward.'

*

There was only Catherine with her parents at the dinner table when the conversation Lord Somerville had had with his brother-in-law was repeated. When he mentioned Monsieur Mongoose, Catherine dropped her knife on her plate with a crash, which brought her parents' eyes upon her. 'That's Panhanagan,' Catherine said in a whisper. 'Mongoose is his call sign.'

Without another word, Lord Somerville rose from the table and went to the telephone in his study. When he returned to the dining room, the butler was putting cloches over half-eaten dinners. 'Her Ladyship has taken Lady Catherine to her room, my Lord,' Robins said.

*

James Somerville had arranged for the patient to be flown back to the United Kingdom and taken to the Royal Herbert Hospital in

Woolwich, the very hospital where he had first met Catherine's mother after he returned on a Red Cross ship in November 1918.

The call that the patient had arrived came through to the Somerville's London home in Belgrave Square, just as Catherine was having elevenses with her father. It was James Somerville who answered the telephone, conscious of Catherine's eyes watching for any emotion he may show. James glanced towards his daughter and nodded. 'It's him. An officer from his regiment has identified him.' Catherine put her face in her hands. Her father came and sat beside her and embraced her. She threw her arms around his neck and wept.

*

Looking through a hospital window, while chatting to a pretty nurse, a young lieutenant almost choked when he saw the three stars on the car as it pulled up in front of the building. He watched a sergeant dash from the driver's seat and open the rear door. A lieutenant general climbed out, followed by a beautiful young lady in civilian clothes. The general, walking slowly and awkwardly with a cane, made his way into the building. The young lieutenant rushed to the colonel's office and tapped on his door.

'Yes, what is it Harris?'

'Colonel, a general has just arrived at the hospital.'

'General!' he said, grabbing his service cap, 'who the bloody hell could that be?'

They hurried downstairs and met General Somerville in the hall, talking to a very nervous Sister. 'Good day, General,' the colonel said. 'I'm sorry Sir, I wasn't expecting you. I'm Donald, Colonel Donald.'

'Somerville,' the general said, noticing the eyes of the young lieutenant fixed on the ribbon of his Victoria Cross rather than his daughter, which was generally the case when the two of them were out together. 'This is my daughter, Lady Catherine, Colonel. I'd like to speak with you about a patient you admitted yesterday, Lieutenant Panhanagan.'

Back in his office, the colonel looked though the doctor's clinical examination records and nodded. 'His identity was confirmed by his Squadron Commander. I'm afraid he's in pretty bad shape–'

'One moment Colonel,' James Somerville said and then he turned to his daughter. 'Do you want to hear this, Catherine?'

'Every word and every detail.'

'I'm sorry, please continue, Colonel.'

The colonel's eyes met Catherine's briefly before he began. 'Frankly, I'm surprised Lieutenant Panhanagan is still alive. He was obviously a very fit man once, to have survived the beating he sustained.' He glanced at Catherine's burning, wet eyes again. 'I shan't elaborate on that. A witness statement, from a Frenchman who was with him, says Panhanagan was arrested by the Gestapo after being betrayed by a member of the French Resistance cell he was organizing. The medical report from the Americans says the scar tissue all over his body is evidence of torture. Both arms and legs have been broken, but they seem to have reset well enough so he shouldn't have problems with them, apart from rheumatoid arthritis when he is older, perhaps. He has suffered chronic malnutrition and he also has pneumonia. Lieutenant Panhanagan is now in a coma, which isn't a good sign–'

Catherine stood and left the office. Her father followed her out. Her hand was cold when he took it into his. 'I don't think it's such a good idea to go and see him just yet. Let's–'

'If he dies I want to be there to hold his hand.'

'You must be prepared for that.'

'I know Daddy, but I'll not desert him a second time.'

They walked into the Critical Care Unit together, Catherine reaching for her father's hand as she neared the bed. She caught her breath when she saw Panhanagan, rushed to his side then threw her arms across his body and began to weep. 'Christ Panhanagan, what have they done to you?'

James Somerville left the room and returned to the colonel outside. 'You might have warned her, Colonel.'

'I'm sorry, Sir. She appeared to be... If you would care for some tea General, I'll fill you in on the rest.'

*

Three weeks after Catherine's first visit, Panhanagan was still on the critical list. Every day she was by his side, waiting for the slightest movement of an eye, or to hear the latest news from his doctor.

'It's good that you talk to him. Also, hold his hand, stroke his brow,' the doctor said. 'It's amazing the affect it has when one is in a coma. Is he your fellow?'

'Yes.'

250

'Then kiss him. His lips, his cheek and his hands; just let your feelings pour out for him. That will make him want to wake up and hold you. Have faith. I've seen chaps in a similar condition pull through. There's only one slight problem that gives me concern, his lungs... got to get rid of that pneumonia,' the doctor left the room, the words, 'human contact,' like the sound from a ventriloquist's dummy, were heard behind the closing door.

From that day on, every time Catherine asked Panhanagan a question she requested that he squeezed her hand if he understood. He never did. During the fourth week, Catherine read a, *get-your-arse-out-of-bed, Panhanagan* card that had been sent to him from Holloway who was now back in England and planning to come with Peters, to visit him that week. Catherine managed to laugh at what Holloway had written.

'Holloway can be so funny, can't he darling?' Catherine said. She felt some pressure on her hand. It came as such a shock to her that she pulled her hand away, as if she had touched scolding water. Then she grabbed his hand again. 'If you just squeezed my hand, squeeze it again.' She felt pressure on her hand again. This time she raised it to her lips and called a nurse.

The next day Holloway arrived with Peters. Catherine was with the colonel when a nurse tapped on his door and announced their arrival. Catherine jumped up from her chair, threw her arms around Holloway and kissed his cheek. This was repeated with Peters, who looked extremely happy to have Catherine in his arms at last. The colonel was a little shocked at the lack of military protocol; an ex-officer and general's daughter indeed, embracing and kissing two senior NCOs.

'Colonel, may I have your permission for these gentlemen to spend a little time with Lieutenant Panhanagan? They're both from his unit.'

Peters and Holloway looked at each other and grinned. 'Lieutenant Panhanagan.'

Five minutes later the three of them sat around chatting for an hour about the times they had spent together, all the time including Panhanagan in the conversation while he slept. 'If only Susan was here,' Catherine said. 'What a strange reunion that would have made.'

'Sub Lieutenant Harcourt-Williams, do you mean?'

'It's Lieutenant Harcourt-Williams now,' Catherine said.

251

Holloway grinned. 'Tell me, Ma'am—'

'If you don't call me Catherine, James Holloway, I'll never speak to you again. That goes for you too, Ted. I'm a civilian now, so forget the Ma'am.'

'Catherine it is. Did you manage to put the skills you were taught into practice?'

'Yes, I did. I had some wonderful instructors,' she said, which brought a smile to their lips. 'Panhanagan was with me, watching my back.'

Both Peters and Holloway looked shocked as their eyes met. 'So that is where he disappeared to. He must be Mongoose and you Nora.'

'Yes, and you two are foxtrot.' The three of them laughed. Catherine raised a finger to her lips and whispered, 'Remember the Official Secrets Act.'

*

That night the three of them went out for a meal, with promises to keep in touch. A week after Holloway and Peters' visit, Catherine, who was staying in the officer's mess next door to the hospital, was woken by the mess sergeant. A senior doctor was on the line and asked her to come into the hospital. She rushed over not bothering to brush her hair or put on a decent dress. When she arrived at his ward, Panhanagan was sitting up in his bed looking groggy, but awake.

She went to him, 'Hello,' was all she could say.

'Catherine?' His voice was hardly audible. She put an ear to his mouth. He repeated what he had said, and added, 'Good to see you.'

'Don't speak. Just rest, I'll stay with you.' She took his hand in hers, and kissed it. The following day he was a lot brighter. She went into his ward and sat by his bed.

'Why aren't you in uniform?'

Catherine looked into his deep, dark eyes. 'The war is over, at least in Europe it is. I'm a civilian again. When you're feeling better and the doctors allow you to leave here, you're coming home with me... to Yorkshire. There's someone I'd like you to meet, Panhanagan,' she whispered, bending and kissing his lips. 'We have a son.'

Epilogue

Corporal Wilhelm Hock was killed during the British landings at Gold Beach, Normandy. When his personal effects were returned to his family, his mother found a picture of Catherine and a lock of her hair in his wallet.

Obersturmführer Ludwig Hoffmann's remains were removed from the garden of Jacko's old house and returned to Germany. The daughter he never knew now lives in Hamburg. His widow remarried and lived in Bonn until her death in 2001.

Obersturmbannführer Erich von Model learned that Nora was the Lady Catherine Somerville when he read of her marriage in *The Times*. 'Aristocratic beauty marries her man,' was written above a photograph of the happy couple. Model opened a bottle of Champagne and toasted her. On closer examination of Nora's husband, he recognized the man to be the fellow with a walking stick reading a book and leaning against a tree along Avenue Foch, the same man who had fought with such dogged tenacity at the woods outside Cambrai. It was a battle Model had lost. He cut out the picture and framed it. Model died of cancer in a Zurich clinic in 1971.

Hauptmann (later Major) Paul Fries was implicated in the attempted assassination of Adolf Hitler in July 1944 and was executed by firing squad in the courtyard of the Bendlerblock in Berlin, on July 20 1944. A framed picture of him in full German uniform hangs on the wall in the grand hall at Mountfields House in Yorkshire.

Rear Admiral Sir Charles Greene KBE was knighted in 1948. He retired from MI6 shortly after because of ill health. He died of a heart attack in 1953.

Susan Patricia Harcourt-Williams MBE, M.Sc, ran into Catherine and her three year old son Paul in Fortnum & Masons in 1947. They had tea together. They never met again. Susan rose to a senior rank in MI5. However, her career collapsed after she was exposed having an affair with a senior politician's daughter. It never reached the newspapers, but she was forced to resign. She left the service and taught mathematics in a girl's public school until her retirement. She died alone on the eve of the Millennium. She was 82.

Sergeant Edward Albert Peters MM, Croix de Guerre survived the war, but was killed in Malaya when his parachute failed to open. He is buried in the SAS cemetery in Hereford.

James Bernard Holloway DCM, Croix de Guerre left the army in 1953. He acquired a job as the residential caretaker at a public school in Yorkshire. He remained close friends with Catherine and Panhanagan until his death in 1979.

Frederick Alan Jacks DCM, MM returned to France to visit the cemeteries on the Somme with Lord James Somerville one last time in 1947. When he died in 1950 aged 74, the Lady Somerville and Catherine were at his bedside. He had requested that his remains be cremated and his ashes scattered in the Gordon Dump Military Cemetery in La Boisselle, Picardy, in Northern France. The family witnessed a gust of wind spread Jacko's ashes across the cemetery as if he was reaching out to all his old friends.

The Hon Elizabeth Hannah Fielding née Wyatt married her professor. She discovered her cousin Catherine was the field agent Nora when she attended a dinner in Paris in 1950. She was placed beside a woman writing a thesis about British female agents who operated in France. Elizabeth explained she was the agent Nora's wireless link during her mission in France and her greatest regret was she never got to meet her. When Elizabeth was given the agent's identity she left the table in a flood of tears. Two days later, both she and her husband were killed in a car accident close to Calais. She was aged 30. Nora, their three year old daughter survived. Catherine cared for Nora and adopted her the following year. Elizabeth and her husband are buried in the grounds of Mountfields House, Yorkshire.

Lt Gen James Henry Albert Somerville, the Earl of Kepwick, VC, CVO, MC & bar died of an embolism in 1963, aged 69. His widow wore something black every day until her own death in 1975. Lord James Somerville is buried in the grounds of Mountfields House, Yorkshire. His son Robert inherited the title and estate.

The Lady Elizabeth Patricia Somerville, Countess of Kepwick, MM, Croix de Guerre with Bronze Star, MA (Oxon) BA (Sorbonne) died in her sleep at Mountfields House in 1975, aged 78. Her last request was to be interred with her late husband James in the grounds of Mountfields House, Yorkshire.

Xavier Pierre Panhanagan MBE, MC, DCM, MM and bar, Croix de Guerre with gold star, Légion d'honneur, LL.B, left the army after he married Catherine in 1946. On Catherine's recommendation, he was awarded the Military Cross. He studied law and rose to be the senior partner in a large London firm. He died in 1987, aged 70 at the family home in Belgravia, London. Catherine, who was holding his hand at his bedside, watched him slip into sleep and die during the night. She climbed into bed with him and held him until she woke the next morning when he was taken from her. He is buried in the grounds of Mountfields House, Yorkshire.

The Lady Catherine, Mrs Panhanagan MBE, Croix de Guerre with gold star, Légion d'honneur, M.A. (Oxon) B.A. (Sorbonne). She devoted her life to her husband and four children, shunning the limelight when the full extent of her wartime exploits became known after the showing of a French television programme. In an interview, shortly after her husband's death, the only one she ever gave, she said, 'the part I played was very small compared to that of my husband.' Historians were quick to dispute that. In 1992, after the sudden death of Catherine's nephew, her late brother Robert's only child, Catherine's son Paul inherited the title and estate, becoming the 9th Earl Somerville. With Her Majesty's permission, Paul changed the title to Panhanagan-Somerville in 1993. Lady Catherine was last seen in public in 2004, at St Paul's church in Knightsbridge where she was a guest at a memorial service for members of the FANY who had died serving with SOE.

She pressed a small wooden cross with a single poppy attached to it into the earth. The name written on the cross was Madeleine. Catherine died in January 2009 aged 89. Like her mother before her, she requested to be interred with her late husband in the grounds of Mountfields House, Yorkshire.

(Madeleine) Nora Baker - Noor-un-nisa Inayat Khan GC, MBE, Croix de Guerre with Gold Star. Noor was murdered in Dachau. Her last word spoken before being shot, was *Liberté*. Of the three George Crosses awarded to female SOE agents, the light has shone on Odette Sansom and Violette Szabo. Noor, the least known of the three, will always be remembered as the agent who stayed in Paris to be the sole wireless link for other agents, when she could have left. She gave the Gestapo the run around until she was so tragically betrayed by a jealous woman.

Lightning Source UK Ltd.
Milton Keynes UK
09 February 2011

167228UK00001B/73/P